Weave for Me a Dream

An Historical Novel

By
Kathryn Lynn Davis

Copyright © 2017 by Kathryn Lynn Davis

The moral right of the author has been asserted.

www.duncurra.com

Cover Design: Earthly Charms

ISBN-10: 1-942623-63-1

ISBN-13: 978-1-942623-63-2

Produced in the USA

DEDICATION

To Susan Cusack and Lily Baldwin, whose friendship and faith inspires and uplifts me. They have traveled my own journey beside me, no matter where it led. Eventually they brought me to this miraculous moment when I finished this book I once thought lost.

And to my husband Michael, who continues to love, support and understand me, no matter how difficult a challenge that becomes. Thank you. I love you.

ACKNOWLEDGEMENTS

Of all the novels I have written, this one has taken the longest path with the most zigzags, dead-ends, endings and beginnings. I began it 27 years ago, and it has been the single biggest challenge of my career. I have finished it only because of the support, encouragement, honesty and enthusiasm of many of my friends and family. I want them all to know how much they mean to me. First, authors Cynthia Wright—who started me on the Indy journey several years ago—and SuzanTisdale. Because of their friendship, I reached this day, which I thought would never come. Next, those readers who have become friends over the years, particularly Jules Edenborough—who has read the manuscript and given me feedback more than once—Kim Feazell—my soul sister, and sometimes my reflection—Di Gorbette, Charlene Whitehouse, Donna Bayer Repsher, and Ann Alba.

I am grateful to my sister Anne and my dad Mickey, who read a very early version, and expressed to me their concerns as well as their praise, and Ann Reille, who roped in a reader completely outside my usual audience. His comments were invaluable. I even want to thank those who were less than thoughtful in their response. You all helped me understand, when the time was right and inspiration struck, exactly what I needed to do to make this into the book I'd always wanted it to be. I learned from all the reactions, even when they seemed merely hurtful. So I can only believe that everything evolved as it was meant to.

Finally, I want thank my one-time editor Linda Marrow, because it was she who first suggested I listen to Saylah's voice.

THE STORYTELLER

Amidst the soft dark movement of the water, among the green and swaying trees, Old Grandmother sat at her ancient loom.

With her gnarled and spotted hands she worked the shuttle, weaving wordless stories in the wind, weaving the water's light, through the fine-spun warp of the sturdy loom.

Her silver head bent to her task, she watched and listened, heard the voices of Time gone and Time to come, saw the faces of the children whose colored threads, interlaced and intertwined, were caught one by one in the ever-changing patterns that she wove into the living loom.

Her back was strong, if curved from years of toil, and this her great and final task, to echo weavers of another time, to create the fabric of lives lived, through the warp and woof of the enchanted loom.

She smiled, the old woman with the knowledge of the rhythm of the waters and the stars, and wept, and wove the stories that were lifted from the loom.

PART ONE

Chapter 1

Last night, I lay sleeping at the far edge of my dreams, and I knew that when I woke, the shape and color and music of my life would be forever changed.

"I can't get that line out of my head this morning." Illiann Ivy sat awkwardly on a delicate chair, her bare feet crossed on the fine brocade. "I had to read the page again, even though we both know it by heart." Her hazel eyes were pensive and she twined her fingers in her long dark hair. "I feel like Simone is speaking to me somehow."

Carefully, she set down a fragile leather-bound diary. Simone Ivy, her intriguing grandmother, had written it, but Illiann had known neither Simone nor Jamie Ivy—her grandfather. She looked at her mother expectantly.

"She is always speaking to us, don't you think," Saylah murmured, "through the faint ink on these pages from the past?" Her silver voice was alluring, just as it had been sixteen years ago when she married Illiann's father, Julian Ivy. Her expression was compelling; her green eyes shone with reminiscence and affection. She brushed the parchment gently, running her finger over the words as if to read the faded but elegant writing through touch rather than sight.

She sat cross-legged on the floor, because she was at ease there, but Illiann rose restlessly. The Oriental rug, once vibrant in shades of wine and pink, lilac and blue, was worn and smooth beneath the girl's feet. She touched the paraffin lamp, making the crystals suspended from the translucent globe shiver and clink together. When she was a child, her

Uncle Theron used to tell her he could feel Simone's presence in the tinkling of those crystals, stirred by an invisible breath of air, just as she thought she heard her grandmother's voice in the ethereal song now.

She moved around the ornate sitting room, tracing patterns on the wallpaper of blush-colored roses tangled with silver vines, contemplating the velvet loveseat, graceful rosewood tables and brocade chairs. The lace inner curtains filtered and patterned the light that shone through rose silk woven with silver thread. This room was very different from the rest of the large ranch house her grandfather had built years ago in the wilderness that was Vancouver Island.

She could not remember when she had last been in this place, which had called to her like a Siren's song when she was younger. Nor could she remember when she had last looked at the diary. She only knew that soon, too soon, she would say good-bye to both.

And to her mother. She glanced away as her chest tightened with a sense of loss far greater than she had felt when Theron left last year to study in France.

Saylah saw the fleeting expression on her daughter's face, and guessed what it meant. She caught her breath at an unexpected pain in her heart. In a week, Illiann and her brother Kit were going to boarding school in Victoria. Saylah, Julian and Sophia Ashton, a dear friend, had taught the children all they had to teach. It was time they learned about the world beyond their sheltered home.

Yet at fifteen, Illiann was no longer a child, Saylah realized with a shock as she watched her daughter's progress around the room. She had become a tall, lovely girl, who moved with her mother's ease and her father's energy. When she smiled, as she did now, openly—hiding nothing and promising everything—she was irresistible. And vulnerable. Saylah's heart fluttered with anxiety.

"I had to come today to see the diary again," Illiann said. "So I'd remember Simone in my dreams." She brushed the crystals until they danced together.

"Hush. They'll hear you."

Saylah and she and Theron were the only ones who knew about the diary. Long ago it had become a ritual among them, this piecing together of the exotic and beguiling Simone's life. They had kept the ritual secret, because they knew it would cause Saylah's husband pain. Simone had deserted Julian and his father when the boy was just nine.

Sometimes Saylah grew angry with the sad and enigmatic woman who had hurt Julian so deeply, but unlike her husband, she did not think Simone had disappeared on a whim. Too many pages in her diary were devoted to her love for her family, her fear for their safety – and her dread at the prospect of losing them. She seemed to be living suspended in clouds of fantasy, which she knew would soon disintegrate. Saylah understood that only too well.

"It's funny," Illiann whispered, "but I think I can guess how she felt. For her, it seems this ranch was just a dream."

And so it was – Jamie Ivy's dream of paradise that had turned out so differently than he planned.

"Sometimes I have felt the same," Saylah murmured. She was half Indian and had grown up among one of the last free Salish villages on Vancouver Island. She had never quite lost the cadence of their speech when she left her family and her People behind. Just as Simone Ivy had done.

Yet the Frenchwoman had left behind a precious gift. First Theron had discovered the small, ornate chest that held some keepsakes of Simone's. The questions about who she had been and why she had gone away had been a thread throughout his childhood, then Illiann's. As he learned French, he had taught it to Saylah and her daughter so they could read the diary together, discover its secrets and its wonders, and finally weave the thread into a gauzy cloth, which fluttered and undulated, obscuring like mist the enigma of a woman known only by the sweep of her delicate pen.

Saylah touched the parchment page tenderly. She had always felt a bond with this woman who had been exiled from her family. It had been eighteen years since Saylah herself had turned her back on the rituals and traditions of her childhood, yet the power of their enchantment had not diminished. With the thought came a distinct sense of Simone's presence. The scent of roses, which had faded over the years as the petals in the bottom of the chest turned to dust, was strong now, gripping.

"We never learned enough about who she was," Saylah murmured.

"Haven't you figured it out yet?" a new voice inquired.

Saylah and Illiann gasped, looked up in shock at Julian Ivy standing in the doorway. He had always been tall, his body muscular from years of heavy work in the sun, but now he seemed larger than before. His hazel eyes were unreadable, his brown hair falling unheeded over his forehead.

He glanced at the book on the faded rug. "My mother didn't *want* anyone to know her. It was all a game. 'How many secrets can I tell without giving myself away?' It was a game she never lost. Look around you. This room is still hers, and she hasn't set foot in it for twenty-five years."

Illiann had expected anger, but it was more like grief—or was it curiosity? She wished he had not found Saylah with Simone's most intimate gift in her hands. "Surely Jamie knew her well."

"I suspect my father knew her least of all." He left no room for questions, doubts or reassurance; Julian's odd combination of inquisitiveness and longing made his certainty absolute.

"How long have you been listening?" Saylah asked.

14

Kathryn Lynn Davis

Her husband smiled thinly. "For years."

Chapter 2

Rouen, France
Summer, 1894

Simone de Marchand drew back the sea-blue drapes and opened the leaded glass casements so the darkness, full of stars, caressed her. The breeze rising from the Seine caught her silver silk dressing gown and it billowed about her still-supple body.

The tall, square spire of the Cathedral of Rouen—stone enveloped in a lacery of stone—shone with an unearthly glow, as did the flying buttresses and spires of the other cathedrals. All else was swallowed and subsumed by the night, which would soon give way to dawn.

Her lover, the Duc de Montagne, sat in the ornate rosewood bed, watching. He was intrigued by Simone's pensive attitude, the faraway look he had glimpsed in her gray-green eyes as she rose. Her dark, unbound hair fell over her shoulders and the breeze lifted it across her cheek. She caught a scented strand in her fingertips and frowned at a streak of gray, turned silver by the soft, forgiving candlelight. She was silent for so long that he began to worry. "Did the night take you back again?" he asked at last.

"*Oui*, Claude," she murmured, her musical voice full of affection. With him there was no pretense, no lies of omission; he was one of the few who knew the truth about her. "But this time it was the dream, not the nightmare that carried me away." She focused on the delicate impression of the cathedral spire.

"You were back on Vancouver Island?"

Simone bowed her head. "Jamie." She breathed the name quietly, so the Duc would not hear. Tonight, before daylight came to burn away the dream, she craved the sound of that dear name, the texture of those fluid memories. With nimble fingers, she traced a phantom on the velvet draperies. It had been nearly twenty-five years since that phantom had been flesh and blood and joy and promise.

Yet even now she could see his face, and Julian's, on the night she had left them. Jamie, handsome and sensitive with his finely wrought aristocratic features, his curly light brown hair, his liquid brown eyes full of hurt, had held out his hand. She had been afraid to take it, afraid he would try to hold her back and shatter her fragile conviction. Tentatively, she had touched her fingertips to his, but Jamie had not gripped her tightly or clung or fought to hold her. He had gazed at her, eyes filmed with tears and resignation, and kissed her fingers gently, sadly, in farewell.

The simple gesture had destroyed her resolution as his anger or demands would not have done. She had almost fallen to her knees and begged him to forgive her, to let her stay. But Jamie, with his dreams and his fine sensibilities, would not have been able to bear the consequences. She had bitten her lip until she tasted blood, felt her own tears rise, and turned away to go to her son, to break his heart as she had broken her husband's—and her own.

Long brown hair tangled from sleep, Julian had blinked his hazel eyes repeatedly. He had gaped at her, bewildered, so vulnerable that she wanted to draw him close and hold him until the hurt and confusion went away. He had been a child, could not possibly have known that her pain was as great as his, that his refusal to kiss her good-bye had probed at the wound in her heart like the point of a well-honed knife.

That night, three men who had sought her for years had threatened her life and the lives of her family. For herself, she might not have minded quick death and a final end to the nightmare that had begun so long ago in France, but she dared not put her husband and son in danger. The men had given her no choice.

She tried to push the images away, surprised that they had come so strongly. She recalled clearly the lush island, the sound and smell of the sea, the scent of fir and cedar, and the mist that had transformed the light, softened and diffused it. She had wrapped that glow about her, drawn Jamie and Julian within a cloak of shimmering radiance, and together, they had created paradise.

She knew Jamie had died years earlier—the Duc had found out while checking on a branch of his family-owned company in Canada—but she wondered if her son still lived in the house Jamie had built for her, with huge windows that filled the rooms with the clear light she so loved? How happy she had been there, how warm and safe. But that had been long ago. Now Julian would be a grown man in his thirties. No doubt he had left home to find his own future. She leaned her cheek against the comfort of thick velvet. Jamie and his dreams had been her hope, Julian and his practical, loving mind her salvation.

The edges of her memory blurred, encircling the island in a haze of forgetfulness, like a curtain of mist drawn gently across a performance so moving, so beautiful that it broke her heart to see it.

"Je me rappelle," she murmured. "I will soon be fifty, Claude. That is very old."

De Montagne got up to join her at the window. "You are wrong, *ma belle* Simone. You are a 'woman of a certain age', ripe and rare, beautiful and wise. You will always be young."

"I began to grow old the instant I became Simone de Marchand."

The Duc brushed the white hair back from his forehead. "You need no longer bear his name. The Church annulled that marriage. Why do you insist on using it when it only causes you pain?"

"To remind him."

"To remind yourself, you mean." He frowned when she looked away. "Or is it to punish yourself?"

She did not answer, but pulled her gown closed, as if it might protect her from the truth.

The Duc took her shoulders and forced her to look at him. "You have paid for your sin, *mon amour*. It is time to forgive yourself. It's the only way to find peace."

"I do not think God will forgive me."

Claude despaired. Her usually lilting voice was flat and empty. "The *Bishop* will not forgive you. It was he who had you excommunicated. He is *not* God, but a man. And he is no fool. De Marchand is very powerful. The Bishop did what he had to do to save his own hide."

She nodded, and even that small gesture was alluring. She reached fluidly toward the cool night darkness, embracing all that lay unseen beneath her window.

Claude slipped his arms around her and toyed with her silver cross and long string of pearls, her only jewelry now. These had no color of their own, only the patina reflected from the light. They had belonged to her mother, and he knew they were precious to her.

"Even in this moment, you glow, *mon chére*. The candle flame caresses you like a lover, tinting you with silver and gold."

Simone smiled fondly. The Duc was not tall and his shoulders were not broad, but his eyes were kind, his face familiar, and the texture of his white hair soft beneath her fingers. It seemed he had always been there, solid and dependable. He alone had defended her on her enforced return to France. He had quickly become her friend, had taken care of her when her own strength failed. He knew her shadows, had lived within and without them.

Inexplicably, after her return from Vancouver Island, de Marchand had refused to release her from her marriage vows. Claude had threatened to tarnish his inflated image, which he held so dear. His weapon would have been the truth. The Duc had promised to make a fool of him unless he set Simone free. Eventually, de Marchand had acquiesced.

Since the day she left her husband's chateau forever, Claude had remained her unfaltering friend and protector, asking nothing of her but her company and conversation. They were comfortable with one another and, gradually that sense of solace had grown into desire. The French called her his courtesan, but the gossipers could not begin to comprehend the bond between them.

De Montagne's reputation was enhanced by the relationship. Everyone accepted that wealthy married men had mistresses. It was in a man's nature, so he was forgiven, though not always by his wife.

Claude had assured Simone that their relationship would not affect his marriage. "I will choose a woman of intelligence and understanding. These things are necessary to me, as is beauty and grace. She will be told you are my mistress before she becomes my wife, and if she cannot accept the truth, she will not become my wife at all. It is quite simple, really."

"You will never find such a paragon among women."

"Then that will be my fate." Claude spoke calmly, without taking his eyes from her face.

"You would risk so much for me?"

He gave her his answer without words.

Within the year, de Montagne married Patrice Fleury, a woman of wit, intelligence and understanding. Though she was not a true beauty, she had qualities the Duc valued more—a willingness to accept what she had no power to change, and a secret regard for the courage of Simone de Marchand.

Closing her eyes, Simone kissed the Duc's lips lightly. Because of him she was here, Rouen at her feet and velvet in her hands. She owed him her life, her comfort, her home, but he never demanded recompense. She gave to him freely and trusted him completely.

She cupped his face with tenderness. "Do I bring you pleasure, Claude? Are you happy?"

"You know I am, *cherie*. It is why I come to you." He lifted a strand of dark hair in his fingers.

Simone shivered at a sudden rush of fear that she might lose him. "But that is not why I *let* you come."

Claude sighed. "It does not matter why. You did not lure me against my will. You did not threaten me, unman me or coerce me." When she started to protest, he touched a finger to her lips. "It did not hurt that you were very beautiful, nor that you were bright and educated and experienced, that you had seen the world and found it lacking. It did not hurt that you seemed to want me as I wanted you, nor that you were enigmatic and unattainable, even when you lay in my arms. It did not matter why you needed me, only that you did. Perhaps the intrigues of which you are the heart lured me as well—the promise of excitement, danger, a kind of living I had not known before."

He paused, paced a little and spun to face her. "It is ironic, is it not, that now I come to find comfort and peace?"

Her gray-green eyes watchful, Simone smiled. "That is only because your children are growing so quickly, and the noise of their comings and goings is great. There will be no peace in your house for many years to come." She tried to hide her envy, but he knew her too well.

"You weep inside because you had to leave your only child. That is why you take children from impoverished homes and feed and clothe and train them. They worship you, you know. But that is not the same as hearing your son's voice calling up the stairs. You cannot stop mourning his loss, can you?"

Julian appeared in her mind before she could protect herself. *He was barely three years old, nightshirt crumpled in nervous hands. He had come to his parents' room in the middle of the night while a storm raged outside. 'You're prob'ly scared,' he'd lisped, though he was trembling. 'Came to hold your hands.' He'd climbed into bed, taken Jamie's hand, and hers, and smiled reassuringly with his gap-toothed grin. ''S'okay now. Don't have to be scared.' He'd snuggled down between them, warm and content. She and Jamie had fallen asleep to the soothing sound of his breathing.*

Simone's eyes burned. She swung from Julian to Claude. "No, I cannot stop."

"Things are different now than they were when you left the island." The Duc hesitated. He knew he was taking a risk, but he had sensed her restlessness, her unresolved yearning for the family she had given up. "I know you wish to go back, to explain, to see him once more."

"Of course I wish it, but I cannot make it happen. You know de Marchand will not let me go." She had tried repeatedly to escape from France a second time, but her former husband was vindictive enough to keep her in Rouen. He did not want to relinquish her fortune, though she had told him she had none to give. He had decreed that if he could not have his money, she would not have her freedom.

Claude had never understood de Marchand's motives in keeping Simone here. Especially now that he had a new wife. There seemed to be no end to the man's malice.

As the coming dawn caressed her face, Simone sighed. "I have not tried to escape for a long time now. I do not know if de Marchand's resolve is yet as strong."

"Do you still fear him?"

She was brought up short by the question. A few months ago, she would have said yes without hesitation. Now she was not so certain. What had happened to change her, and when? But that was not really the point. "I do not think so, but that does not free me. Besides, I wrote to Jamie and Julian for a very long time, and they never answered my letters. I do not think it is possible that my son wishes to see me again."

She was distracted by the shriek of a familiar voice in the street below. It was Mathilde, who had once been her nurse, and was now companion, cook and confidant. The sound reminded her that the day was rushing toward them.

She revolved toward the Duc, away from the city below, away from the ancient timbered houses and curving streets that led, inevitably, to the cathedrals. She turned from the window toward the marble-topped dressing table, the huge rosewood bed with its brocade canopy and silver gauze curtains. De Montagne's clothes were draped over matching Louis XIV chairs done in gray striped silk. The watered silk wallpaper, soft gray embossed with full-blown silver roses, made the room seem cool, like a drink of crystal water on a warm day. The tinkling of the chandelier was a lilting tune played by the vagaries of the wind.

"You should go. You should have gone long since. Patrice will be waiting." She used his wife's name deliberately, to remind them both that she was not simply an obligation or a figure without substance. "She, too, is a woman."

"Patrice has the children and the chateau and more friends than she can count." He trailed a finger down Simone's throat. "And most nights, *ma chére*, she has me."

"But those other nights can be very long."

As always, Claude was surprised at Simone's concern for his wife's feelings. He himself took great care to love Patrice in every way he could, to give her happiness and security. It was right that he should do so. But it was not Simone's burden.

The first light struck her hair and her billowing gown. Claude reached down to caress her throat, her shoulder, her breast, covered by filmy silk. Simone thought of other hands that had once held her, hands just as warm, but young and full of eagerness and magic.

The stone city fell away, until only the memory remained, of Jamie's fingers cupping her face, his smile as he drew her close, the wild beating of his heart.

Claude's sigh was full of regret. Simone was right. It was time to go home.

"I will come again soon," he whispered, brushing his lips across her forehead in a gesture so tender it brought tears to her eyes.

"Yes," she murmured. "I will be waiting." She embraced him, nestled against the warm, rhythmic beat of his heart, then released him and drew a deep breath, raising her head and straightening her shoulders gracefully, as she did all things. Drawing her gossamer robe closed, she settled her armor about her.

"I will not leave you, Simone. I have not stayed so long only to go away now. Remember that." He kissed her one last time and began to dress.

Drawn by the unexpected sound of a familiar voice outside, she leaned out the window to watch Mathilde perform an exaggerated mime in the street below.

A withered old woman grasped the servant's arm, drew her close and began to speak urgently in her ear.

Mathilde's expression was at first blank, then astonished. She appeared to forget she was holding a hen she had bought live at the market for dinner. She began to speak with animation, waving her arms up and down, holding the hen by its scrawny legs while it squawked so loudly that her own voice was lost. Feathers flew, landing in Mathilde's hair as the old woman backed away. She seemed to fear that at any moment, the infuriated bird would escape and attack.

Finally, the servant put the chicken behind her back and tried to pretend it was not still squawking, while the old woman babbled furiously.

"Ha!" Mathilde cried in triumph. "Told you so!" She forgot the hen, let it go, whirled and fell flat on the ground to catch it before it escaped entirely.

Kathryn Lynn Davis

"Mathilde!" Simone called down, "Please take more care. You will injure yourself irreparably someday."

Mathilde rose awkwardly and waved Simone's concern aside. "Madame!" she wheezed, stumbling toward the house. "Wait till I tell you what's happened!"

Chapter 3

For the third night in a row, Julian Ivy could not sleep. For the third night in a row, his mother's words ran through his head. *Last night I lay sleeping at the far edge of my dreams....* He thought he had freed himself years ago from the woman who had deserted him. But now, suddenly, he understood the feeling behind her words. Worse, he shared it.

He felt Simone was hovering beside him, watching. She had spoken so often of dreams, of a chimerical life easily destroyed by cold reality. Julian felt that he, too, was dreaming his life, yearning toward something precarious and out of reach, turning away from the familiar and safe. It was that knowledge, uncomfortable and vaguely disturbing, that had confused him when he found Saylah and Illiann so contented in that forbidden room.

In less than a week, he and his wife would take their children to Victoria and say goodbye to them. Not forever, of course, but none of their lives would be the same again.

In spite of himself, he felt a surge of exhilaration at the thought of the bustling seaport the family had visited last spring to choose a school for the children. With a grin, he remembered the bear of a man, Devon Fitzgerald, he had met on that trip. He thought of the print shop where Devon and his friends sprawled every afternoon, how easily Julian and his eleven-year-old son Kit had become part of the group.

He recalled vividly the feeling of those few rooms, filled with men and laughter and raucous voices—the sound of the presses clacking and whirring, the energy in the air, the sense of imminent change inherent in the political arguments among the men. He had thought of it far too often in the months since, remembering it with longing.

Devon had mentioned several times that he needed a partner, hoping to entice his new friend into staying in the city for at least part of the year. He had laughed boisterously when Julian declared he knew nothing about printing. *I've a feelin' you're a fast learner,* the Irishman had replied. Despite the ranch and his family's roots, which burrowed deep there, Julian had been tempted. He had thought, more than once, of taking Devon Fitzgerald up on his offer.

Saylah stirred and, feeling the first hint of dawn on her face, shook her hair out of her eyes to watch the sun rise, exploding out of the mist and streaking the sky with violent swathes of purple, fuschia and red. She laid her head on Julian's shoulder, wondering why he had sat for three nights, watching his reflection in the window fade with the sun's first rays.

Julian was only thirty-four, yet he felt old in the blaze of new light. His wife leaned against him, but still Simone's voice whispered in his ear.

I knew that when I woke, the shape and color and music of my life would be forever changed.

A shaft of too bright morning grazed Saylah's cheek, and she looked up, contemplating his expression curiously. "How can you watch such a lovely dawn and think only of the past?" She straightened. "Or are you thinking of the future?"

Welcoming the whisper of her breath against his throat, the feel of her smooth skin beneath his fingers, Julian hugged her tightly. He had never understood her ability to guess what he was thinking, but he'd come to expect it, even appreciate it when he himself was uncertain what he wanted to say.

"Both," he replied.

They sat in silence as the sky turned from scarlet to pink to lilac and the sun rose through trailing wisps of color and light. The stately fir and pine were silhouettes transformed into green fire by the light of the sun.

"Julian?" she murmured, wary of his reticence.

He turned to absorb the sight of her face. Over the years her delicate features, made distinctive by her Indian blood and the tenderness in her eyes, had given her beauty depth and character. "I was remembering Victoria in the clear, spring light."

Saylah nodded. "And perhaps the print shop and your friend Devon Fitzgerald?"

As always, Julian was startled by her insight. There was no point in trying to change the subject. "Yes, as a matter of fact. You know the ranch is my life, but the land is no longer an opponent, the worthy challenger it once was." With diligent and unyielding persistence, Julian had learned to subdue it. "I feel too safe here."

Saylah nodded. It was what she had expected. Her husband had been moody and unusually introspective since their return from the city. She had known for some time that his labor here had become too easy, a shadow of the crusade he used to wage daily.

Unexpectedly, he said, "I keep thinking about you and Ilya reading Simone's diary—using her to say good-bye. Or were you saying good-bye *through* her?"

Saylah was taken aback by the question, but she answered calmly. "If that was what we were doing, then it was appropriate."

Julian looked perplexed.

"I think," Saylah chose her words with care, "Simone is always saying goodbye."

"It's odd then that I feel she's holding me back." Surprised by his own confession, when the thought had not yet entered his head, Julian wondered what had made him say it.

"It is not she who holds you back, but the memory of your father. It is not her you wish to leave, but this place, which was your father's dream."

"Yes," he said softly. "I didn't know it until this moment, but you're right." He paused, pressing his face into the thick black hair at her neck. "I don't want to leave the ranch behind completely, just to find another challenge, an ambition of my own."

Saylah looked through the window at the brightening sky. "Yes," she said. "I have felt your restlessness and need."

"It doesn't frighten you?"

" A little." She brushed his cheek with her fingertips. "But you see, I too have been restless of late."

Julian felt a whisper of fear, but knew he must be patient.

Husband and wife rose as one and, opening the glass doors wide, stepped onto the balcony. They looked out over the sloping green hills to the forest, the rows of alder, oak and birch, the glittering promise of the river through the trees. A red-tailed hawk soared high in the sky, then floated on a gust of wind. Saylah and Julian loved this place—the dark, loamy earth, the shady groves of apple trees, the billowing fields of hops and oats. The sky, open above them, endless cerulean streaked with filmy white clouds.

Many years ago, Saylah had come here shrouded in mystery – always elusive, just beyond Julian's grasp. Over time, he had learned to understand her secrets, but the face she turned to him now was unreadable. "Tell me." He could wait no longer.

"I have been free here." She opened her arms to embrace the scene. "But there is so much more than this." Taking Julian's hand, she added, "This has been our paradise, and so it shall remain. The ranch is successful enough for the foreman to run it most of the time. We could perhaps live in Victoria part of the year, and come back for the summer and the harvest." Her green eyes were focused on a distant past, an unknowable future.

"You have been thinking of this, planning it for a long time." Julian was surprised.

"I saw the look in your eyes when we left Victoria. I knew this day would come."

Julian frowned. "You guessed *my* wishes, but is this what *you* want?"

For a long time she did not answer. She blinked in confusion and the color rose in her cheeks. She slipped her arms around his waist and felt the full force of their mutual yearning. Closing her eyes, she sang a wordless prayer to the spirits of her ancient past.

"I want to go back," she said.

Her husband felt a quiver of pure terror. "Back?" He thought of the Salish village where she had been born on a night of miracles. Those miracles had clung, made her a child of magic with the power to heal and see and dream. Because of her power, the Salish had called her their queen. Twice she had forsaken that life, and in the end, she had chosen him. He knew she had not forgotten her childhood; she lived so many of the Salish rituals, had taught them to the children to insure they were not forgotten. Always, he had been afraid that the lure of that past would call her away.

Sometimes he awoke at night, sweating, dreaming *her* dream, feeling *her* loss, *her* emptiness. His nightmare was that one day she would speak the words she had just uttered.

Saylah's skin was damp with a film of sweat.

"You're flushed." He reached out, as he had many times, to lift the hair off her neck, blowing gently on the exposed skin to cool it. She smiled at him with affection, and he felt some of the tension leave her.

Together, they contemplated the deer carved from the stump of the first tree Jamie Ivy had cut down on this land. Julian's father was buried beneath that tree.

"I feel I must go...to Victoria," Saylah murmured, "for you, yes, and for our children, but also for me. It calls to me. Or something calls, and I must find that voice and answer it. There are many stories to be discovered." When she was sixteen, she had begun to collect Salish legends. She had taught herself to write by copying down the stories from her village and those of the other Indian girls. At first, the task had been her consolation, her way of clinging to a life she had lost. Now, years later, it had become a sacred vow to preserve her People through their words and rituals. "That is what I mean about my restlessness."

Guardedly, Julian nodded that he understood, but he didn't. His wife had secrets in her eyes again, and voices in her dreams. He did not know exactly why, but he knew these things were dangerous to him. "So you think we should take the risk."

"I think we must."

Saylah smiled enigmatically, and Julian asked a silent question with the pressure of his hand on her back.

"I was just thinking of something Simone said in her diary." She stared at the carved deer and quoted softly,

"Somewhere in the darkness just before the sun rose through the trees,

I came to the rim of my dream,
and fell,
   and was
     awake."

Chapter 4

Victoria, British Columbia

Devon Fitzgerald woke from a sound, satisfied sleep. He was instantly alert, and aware of the sun streaming across the bed. It touched his hand, flung out from under the multi-colored quilt, highlighting the golden-red hairs, warming the sunburnt skin. He sat up into the wash of morning light and sprang from the bed. It was early, but he could not stay still. He felt a tremor of excitement as he drew corduroy trousers and a plaid shirt over his longjohns.

He lifted the cracked pitcher to fill the basin with cold water, then splashed his face several times, groaning at the chill and shaking the water out of his heavy beard. Several drops landed on his chest and snaked their way downward through curly red hair. Devon grinned. Why was he so full of energy this morning? he wondered. Usually he crawled out of bed, eyes slitted, mind fogged with half-remembered dreams. But today was different.

Part of his elation came from the knowledge that Julian Ivy had purchased a partnership in the print shop and would soon arrive in town. Julian had big plans. He was talking about reviving the newspapers that had once been printed in the shop, intended for the people too poor or too frightened to speak for themselves. Devon knew in his gut that Julian was a good man to have as an ally as well as a friend.

He contemplated his reflection in a discolored mirror, wiggling his thick red eyebrows comically. He pointed a finger at the strong, Irish face. "*You* discovered Julian Ivy, you clever divil," he congratulated himself jovially. "A leader of men if ever there was one. He just doesn't know it yet."

Frowning, Devon peered into his own turquoise eyes—Celtic eyes that might have reflected the spirit of an ancient past, if he had let them. Today he saw expectation, the sense of something sparking in the air, waiting to happen. He hurried down the hall toward the sitting room where several of his friends, down on their luck, had slept last night.

He stood in the doorway, shaking his head at the jumble of blankets, muddy boots, plaid shirts and disheveled hair. One man slept half-on, half-off the sofa, one sprawled in the chair, and two lay head to head on the floor. All were snoring noisily. "Come on, you bunch of ne'er-do-wells. 'Tis half past mornin' and ye're still lollin' about uselessly."

One man mumbled a response, but the others continued to snore. Devon kicked Davy O'Reilly gently in the shoulder. "Up! I say. There're things to be done!"

Davy sat up abruptly, eyes wide with fright, staring through the fringe of uneven dark hair that fell over his face. "What the divil—" he spluttered.

"Not the divil, lad, but Devon Fitzgerald."

His booming voice filled the room, and the other men opened their eyes.

"Must you sound so cheerful?" someone grumbled.

"Yes! for I've a feelin' about this day."

The men muttered unhappily. Their heads ached; the room seemed too crowded and stuffy; Devon's voice was jarringly loud and his red hair far too bright. They had stayed out late drinking, talking and arguing about everything from the words of an old Irish ballad to poverty to which barmaid was prettiest. Devon had invited them home to sleep it off, but 'it' had refused to go.

"Up, ye lazy sluggards. The sun is splendid this mornin'. Time to be movin'."

"Why should we get up?" a gangly boy demanded from the lumpy sofa that was half his length. "There won't be any work today." His tone was weary and dejected.

Devon shook his head at the sight of his friend's face, chapped and reddened by fire, his hands thick with calluses and scars from the tongs he wielded when he was lucky enough to get a few days' labor at the ironworks. But that was going to change soon; Devon intended to see to it himself.

"Work or not," he declared, "I'm expectin' trouble."

"You sound happy about it," Davy snapped peevishly. "You're just hopin' for a good long fight."

"Always is," another man interjected, unable to hide the touch of admiration in his voice. "He lives for it, ye know."

Devon laughed, undaunted by their insulting tone. They were right; he had a cause, an enemy with many times his power, a battle to fight and win. That was all in this world he needed to make him happy.

Chapter 5

"I can't sleep, Kit, can you?" Illiann whispered, tiptoeing into her brother's room.

Christopher Ivy stared, disconcerted by how silently she had come. One minute there had been nothing but the blank wall, the next, his sister stood, dark hair unbound, her face catching the faint glow of moonlight through the window. She looked uncannily like Saylah in that moment, though she had Julian's hazel eyes, not the clear green gaze which let their mother see so much.

Annoyed at his momentary alarm, Kit muttered, "I *was* asleep until you came in."

Illiann knew he hadn't slept all night. She had heard him toss and turn, get up, opening and closing books, groaning in frustration. The wall between their rooms could not possibly shut out the sound of Kit's impatience. Like her, he was thinking that tomorrow they would leave for Victoria.

Kit was ecstatic. At eleven years old, he had begun to feel bored on the ranch. Life here was slow and quiet compared to the living, breathing motion of Victoria. "It's the most exciting thing that's happened in my whole life," he crowed, brown eyes glittering. "Just imagine all the new friends we'll make, and the ships we'll watch come in from the sea."

Illiann was less enthusiastic. Like her mother, she loved the ranch, the forest and the boisterous flowing rivers of her childhood. She knew from her reading that there were other kinds of beauty, other wonders to discover. But she had just turned fifteen, and was changing so much inside that she was reluctant to give up her home and her past. "I've been thinking we should go to the woods tonight," she whispered. "The moon is full, and we won't be able to do it tomorrow."

Kit sat up, frustration and impatience forgotten. "*What* will we do?" he asked eagerly. He combed his light brown hair with his fingers, leaving it more disheveled than before.

Illiann thought of a photograph of her grandfather and smiled affectionately. Kit looked so much like Jamie Ivy. She knew her grandfather had been handsome and able to charm everyone he met. Kit had his own energetic charm. He refused to let shadows dim his optimistic view of the world. Kit was certain it was full of wonderful things just waiting for him to discover them all.

His sister reached out to ruffle his hair, but Kit ducked out of reach. He was too old for such caresses. "We could play the animal game," Illiann suggested. "You don't have to be afraid of the dark. Lord Byron will come with us."

At the sound of his name, the massive black German shepherd whined outside the door. She knew he was wagging his tail at the prospect of a midnight adventure.

"I'm never afraid," the boy declared. Playing games with his older sister was all right, but he had grown beyond fear, like his father, he thought proudly. He was out of bed in an instant, and did not bother to put on shoes; he and Illiann knew the woods well, had been walking them barefoot for years with their mother.

Kit disappeared into the hall, then poked his head back around the door. "Come on, Lily. I told you I'm not afraid."

"I know you're not," Illiann murmured, smiling fondly at her younger brother. When he was very little, he had not been able to say 'Illiann,' and so had called her Lily. Occasionally, he still did, and it always touched her. She followed him, scratching absently behind Lord Byron's ears as the dog rubbed up against her. It was true that Kit feared nothing. He had never learned how. That worried her a little.

The boy bolted ahead, Lord Byron thundering at his heels, before she could warn him to be careful. It would not have done any good anyway, as she knew only too well. Besides, tonight she herself was feeling reckless. She overtook Kit and ran ahead, laughing into the moonlight.

They did not need a lantern, but Illiann carried an unlit torch in case the clouds whispered in. They had come this way many times. At first, their parents had come with them, but as the children grew, Saylah sensed that they wanted these night visits to the woods to be an adventure, made sweeter by a sense of peril and secrecy. So she and Julian began to wander their own paths in the darkness, while the children followed theirs.

Lord Byron took the lead, glancing about, growling occasionally to warn off any threats. He seemed disappointed when nothing sprang at them from the underbrush.

Illiann followed her instincts, inhaling the scent of fir and cedar and moist air, ignoring the dangers beneath her feet. She preferred the forest at night; there were no people about, only animals and the voices of wind and water. Saylah had taught her how to listen with all her senses, so she could hear the waxwings and flickers rustling in the tops of the tall trees, the chattering of squirrels, beavers and raccoons in the dense undergrowth of fern and bracken and fallen pine needles. The rush and rhythm of the river merged with and accentuated these elusive sounds, transformed them into music. The rising chorus sang in Illiann's blood, and she wanted to dance with abandon.

"Lily! Wait!" Kit had fallen behind.

They came to the spot where they most often stopped, beside a wide pool with a swell of grass next to the river. Kit immediately began to leap across the glade, then paused, head raised, listening regally. "What am I? What am I?" he called while Illiann curled up on a flat rock, bare feet beneath her.

Kit was too old to move with the ease of childhood, too young to have developed the grace of a man. He could have been a black-tailed deer or a fox or an elk. But his sister knew he had chosen the cougar. He always chose a fearless hunter first. He hoped that by imitating the graceful but wily animal, he could absorb some of its power. Saylah had once told her son that Julian felt a special kinship with the golden cougar in its fluid strength and determination.

"You're a beaver."

Kit stopped on all fours to glare at his sister reproachfully. "You're not trying. It's no fun if you don't even try." He found a small hollow log and began to nudge it with his nose.

There was no longer any question. "All right, then, you're a cougar. Like Papa." She thought of her father, with his powerful tanned body, the grace and skill concentrated in each movement. Like the cougar, he was beautiful and strong, like the cougar, nearly invincible, Illiann thought with pride.

Kit sat up, folding his arms in disappointment, though *he* had challenged *her*. "You go," he said without enthusiasm. "Do your guardian."

Ever since the children were small, Saylah had taught them all she knew about the habits of the forest animals. She had made it a game where each person imitated an animal, and the others tried to guess which it was. Over the years, each had discovered a special affinity to a particular animal, which had become what Saylah called their spirit helper, their guardian.

Julian's was the cougar. Illiann's was of the water, which is why Kit had dared her to do it tonight. He did not believe she could succeed. But his sister had an idea.

She was excited, reckless in the knowledge that tomorrow they would leave the place she loved, whose secrets she treasured. She leapt to her feet. "I will," she said. "But you'll still have to guess." Quickly, she began to strip off her robe, then her night rail.

"You only have one guardian—what are you doing?" Kit demanded in outrage.

Illiann stood naked at the edge of the pond. "I'm doing what you asked." She was only slightly uncomfortable. She had become self-conscious as her breasts grew and her waist narrowed in the last few years, but she was determined not to let such thoughts destroy this night.

"You'll freeze. It's nearly winter." Kit glanced away, though he had seen her body many times. They often swam naked, so they could feel water and stones and currents against their skin. Saylah had taught them that as well. Julian had been the one most reluctant to remove his clothes, though in the end, even he had succumbed. But lately, things had begun to change for Kit, as they had for his sister.

"It's not even Autumn yet. Besides, I've done it before." Before the snow fell and after it melted, she and Saylah came down to the river every morning to bathe. Illiann had long since grown accustomed to the icy water. She raised her arms and dove in, shivering violently, then making her way to the edge of the pond where the water rushed over tumbled rocks. Lord Byron ran back and forth along the bank in agitation, churning up mud, bracken and ferns.

Instead of the dolphin, which was her spirit helper, Illiann decided she would do her mother's. She opened her arms and flapped them gracefully, raised her head higher and higher above the water, stretching her neck, arms spread, seeking with her feet the concealed boulder Kit had never discovered. Finally, she found it, and secure on the wide, flat rock, she appeared to stand on the rippled surface of the water.

Kit's mouth dropped open. The moonlight spilled through the trees, touching his sister's skin with silver, her long dark hair with radiance as water streamed over her shoulders. For the second time that night, she looked very much like her mother, like a spirit, something more than human.

She splashed her feet, making a churning in the water, then fell forward dramatically, undulated beneath the chilly surface, and found her way back to the rock, where she rose again, arms spread and neck stretched.

"That's not a dolphin, it's a loon. You're cheating." Kit was so stunned when she stood upon the water, that it took him longer than usual to recognize his mother's spirit helper. He was chagrined that Illiann had made such a dramatic gesture, when all he'd done was leap about. "I think *you're* loony."

"I'm not cheating, just making it difficult," she answered, laughing. "And you make it sound like loony is bad. If it's like Mama, it must be good." Illiann came out of the water, dripping and flushed with triumph and exhilaration. She used her gown to dry herself, then slipped on her robe.

Kit did not answer. He was staring at the silver-green grass he had crushed beneath his feet. It was true that he was not afraid of anything, and he loved his mother dearly, but sometimes she made him nervous. When Illiann seemed to stand on the water, she'd reminded him startlingly of Saylah's extraordinary power. Kit did not understand that power, or the spirits she sometimes spoke of. He didn't like things he couldn't understand.

His sister shivered in the late night breeze. She sensed Kit was disturbed by her dramatic little display, so she kept up the game to distract him. She knew he really wanted to do his own guardian, the red-tailed hawk. He pretended to soar free and unfettered, then swooped, wings spread, from a high stump. That returned him to a pleasant humor; he loved to remind himself and everyone else of the strength of his animal.

Only when Lord Byron sniffed at Illiann in concern did Kit notice how violently she was shivering. "I'm awfully tired," he said magnanimously. "I think we should go back."

Illiann leapt up and began to run to warm herself. Kit was beside her in an instant, and they raced toward the house, Lord Byron between them, thundering ahead, then racing back, barking with delight.

"Hush," Illiann said. "You'll wake everyone."

Lord Byron yipped and ran in a circle, wagging his tail furiously when the children reached the kitchen door.

They huddled together in front of the low-burning fire, the dog at their backs like a long dark cushion. Warming each other, they sat in silence, staring into the leaping flames.

"Lily," Kit whispered, "I might be just a little worried after all."

"So am I," his sister answered. "I'm afraid too."

Chapter 6

Edward Ashton turned restlessly in his sleep. The dream was pleasant in the beginning, as he strolled with his best friend Jamie Ivy around the ranch he had built and was bringing to prosperity. They laughed and spoke of their plans until a fine, thin breeze whispered in Edward's ear. Thinking he heard a familiar voice, he turned to look, but there was no one. And when he turned back to Jamie, he was gone—lifted by that wispy breeze and carried away into the sky. He tried to call out after his friend, but his voice would not come, and he woke making inarticulate sounds of regret.

For an instant, he lay still, tangled in the sheets, staring at the bulky objects in the room—the armoire, the hipbath, the Chinese trunk—trying to find something familiar, something he could hold on to. Then he saw it. The indistinct shape of his wife's hat tossed on the vanity.

"I'm here, Edward," Sophia Ashton murmured, resting her head on his shoulder. "What's wrong?"

Edward sighed. She was beside him: real and warm and tender. "Nothing" he said.

"You dreamed of Jamie again," she guessed, hurt by his refusal to respond. It was not the first time she had been awakened by the sounds he made when he tried to call out in a dream. She understood, because she had dreamed too. But not for a long while. Gently, she stroked her husband's damp sandy hair.

Without warning, the door crashed inward and a huge black shape hurled itself onto the bed. It was heavy and immovable, pressing Edward deep into the mattress. For a moment, he was confused, until he felt something wet slap his cheek. He opened his eyes to find himself staring into the face of a black German Shepard who regarded him soulfully.

"Brutus! Get off!"

The dog lay chest to chest with the man, feet planted solidly on the bed. Neither Edward's sharp command nor his attempt to push Brutus away seemed to have any effect. He turned to Sophia in silent appeal.

His wife tried to repress her smile, but didn't quite succeed. "He must have sensed you were having a nightmare, just as he used to with Paul. I can't help it if the dog misses his master." Their son Paul had recently left Vancouver Island for his fourth year studying law in Boston. "Besides, he's only trying to comfort you."

In spite of himself, Edward grinned. "Yes, but it *is* your fault Paul spoiled him and let him sleep on the bed. You never once objected."

Brutus, the third of that name, felt neglected and began to lick Sophia's face as well.

"Ah, but I've become wiser with age. Brutus, down!"

As the dog crawled awkwardly off the bed and slunk away to curl up in the corner, Sophia turned back to her husband. "Is something troubling you?"

Edward considered. "Not really." He looked away, his expression shuttered. He didn't want to think about the dream. Jamie Ivy had been his best friend for as long as he could remember. They'd come out to British Columbia together from Boston to build adjoining ranches and grow rich side by side.

Edward still missed Jamie; that ache would never ease. Especially when he'd lost the man's friendship years before his death. But he didn't want to think about that either.

"Are you sure?" Sophia made one last try.

"Positive." Edward was restless; he knew he would not close his eyes again that night. Without a word, he rose and tip-toed from the room, as if his wife were not wide awake and watching. He headed down to the first level, wove his way to a long-bolted door and stood indecisively, hand on the knob. Suddenly he whirled away, cursing. "Goddamnit. There's nothing there! Nothing at all."

He tried to believe it, but couldn't quite convince himself. Silently, crushing a sliver of memory, he crept out of the house. He was fairly certain Mary would be waiting. She very often was.

Lips taut and heart aching, Sophia turned on her side so her back was to the open door. It wasn't just that Edward was upset and she did not know why, nor that he had left her alone in their bed for the third time in a fortnight. It was that he had shut her out, become a stranger—the man she had always loved most in the world. But more than that, it was because she knew her husband was lying. Again.

Chapter 7

Patal stood in the doorway of his simple frame house and looked down at the beach below. Old Grandmother was sitting apart from the shadow of the bluff, the morning sunlight on her brown, wrinkled face, the skin so translucent that the veins were visible beneath. Her black eyes were focused on the loom before her as she set the warp threads, spacing them evenly with her gnarled hands. Beside her, on the sand tufted with wild grass, lay a piece of blanket she had removed from the loom before it was finished. She was singing the low pulse of a song that followed the motion of her deft fingers.

> "The shuttle, like the sea,
>   works slowly,
> Reshaping the land,
> The weave of the fabric—
> Foam upon sand,
> Color upon color,
> Water upon stone,
> Bone upon thread.
> The hushed and soothing rhythm—
> In my eyes, in my hands—
> All-powerful."

Patal scrambled down the path worn into the hillside by the passing of many feet. "You are weaving," he said to his grandmother. "You must have been dreaming again."

The old woman looked at her grandson with affection, narrowing her eyes to see into the shadows of the bluff that cradled him. His face was still blurred with the sweetness of his dreams, so his squared chin seemed softer, his hawk-nose straighter and his dark eyes glowed. His arms were muscled and powerful from swinging the ax, his back straight with the energy of his youth.

He spoke in Salish, and the deep, guttural sounds made Old Grandmother smile. When he called to her, she'd become aware of the crumbling sand, the damp grass, the pebbles pressing into her bare feet and calves. She crouched at the edge of the beach, with the murmur of water soft in her ears.

"Last night, for the third time, I dreamed of She Who Is Blessed," Old Grandmother said, obsidian eyes lucent with unspoken thoughts. She pointed with one weathered hand across the inlet toward Victoria. "She is there, and now I must go seek her."

"She Who Is Blessed disappeared years ago," Patal replied as he stepped into the sun and shook his dreams away. "Since then no one has seen her face or heard her voice."

"But soon I will hear it, as will you," Old Grandmother replied. "Always, my dreams have shown the truth." She brushed back the waist-length silver hair that she had not yet combed and braided. It rippled down her back, reflecting light like water.

"Perhaps She is not real. Perhaps the People imagined her. I think she is more likely legend than woman."

"You are wrong. She is, I think, too much a woman," Old Grandmother replied.

"Too much? I do not understand."

"It is not necessary that you understand all things, only that you believe." She bent attentively over the loom, concentrating on the patterns she was creating.

Patal was fascinated by her work. "How did you find thread so clear?"

Old Grandmother smiled to herself. "I soaked it for a long time in herbs and roots and pure water until it became resilient." She caressed the unusual threads. "Because of my dreams," she said obscurely.

"And what of She Who Is Blessed?" he asked.

"When I find her, I must bring her here, not just for her sake or for mine, but for the sake of the People." She was waiting, shadow-like, to reach for the hand of she who had once been called Tanu – queen and shaman.

"What if she does not wish to come?"

Old Grandmother looked out over the sweep of beach, the sand that gave way to polished stones, the stones to shells, the shells to gently lapping water. A great blue heron stood in the shallow water, still and regal, while terns and gulls searched the fine sand for their breakfast. She gestured toward the inlet, the ocean beyond, toward the cedar and fir behind them and the vast blue sky above. "She will come," the old woman said softly. "How can she resist?" She turned back to the strong, clear threads on the loom. "It is her fate, and my last obligation."

PART TWO

Chapter 8

Saylah closed the solid oak door of her new winter home, smiling at the thought. Not since she was a child had she moved from one place to another as the seasons changed. With sudden clarity, she remembered the thatched huts on the beach in which her people had lived in spring and summer. There they had fished and hunted and cured food for the long winter. Though she stood on a flagged stone path, she could almost feel the gritty sand beneath her feet and smell the tang of the sea in the air. Running her hand down one of the carved pillars that supported the porch roof, she felt instead the dark, weathered cedar of the longhouse where she had spent fall and winter year after year. Vividly, she could see inside the wide, deep building with its circle of fires and drums, the sleeping bench snug up against the smoke-stained walls. Carvings of bear and cougar held up the roof and dominated the center of the longhouse that smelled strongly of cedar and smoke. The animals had been the blessed and chosen protectors of her people, a reminder of the Salish's strength, an example of their skill as carvers. She was not simply remembering; she was there with all her senses and the beating of her heart.

A thrush burst into song from within a pale green drapery of willow. Startled, Saylah raised her head as the pure, clear notes ascended to the sky and were absorbed by a passing wisp of cloud. She stopped short when she reached the arbor covered with honeysuckle at the end of the front walk. In less than ten steps, a single thought had transported her back to the scents and textures of her childhood, to the lost homes she had known and loved and yearned for. Odd that it should have happened today, so unexpectedly and vibrantly. It had been a long time. She was grateful for the momentary gift which brought only good memories, untainted by the sorrow that had followed.

Following the curve of Crescent St., she turned on Humboldt and along James Bay toward downtown, compelled by an impulse she did not recognize, though most of her life such impulses had ruled and guided her. She took this walk often, but this morning she was more keenly aware of the scent of autumn in the slowly changing leaves of dogwood and broadleaf maple. She felt the strength and stability of the clapboard, stone and brick houses, their low front fences overgrown with honeysuckle. The once tidy gardens were wild with fallen leaves and petals and the damp autumn breeze which stirred them into disarray. The crisp air brought color to her cheeks, and she breathed deeply of the salt-wind off the harbor.

Downtown the stillness of early morning disappeared in the cacophony of hansom cabs, horses and wagons, electric tramcars and the nearby rumble of the railroad. People crowded the sidewalks, voices raised in laughter, anger and jovial conversation. The men were sporting everything from fine worsted suits to well-worn trousers held up by frayed suspenders over plaid felt shirts. Under their nut-brown, purple and black velvet and wool cloaks and mantelets, the women wore stylish gowns of green, yellow and violet, with leg-o-mutton sleeves, braided trim and jabots. They flitted about like birds, gored skirts flaring wide as wings about their ankles. With its bright yellow body, a redheaded tanager swooped among them and was lost in the swirl of puffed sleeves and flower-sprigged straw boaters. Saylah smiled at the colorful spectacle.

She moved through the throng, grasping the edges of her doeskin cape decorated with rows of scallops like fat, rounded feathers. For years she had collected flawed skins and stitched them together until there were enough for this hooded cape. To cover the flaws, she had used odds and ends of elkskin, cut them like scallops and sewed them on in rows. Finally, she had rubbed the cape with dogfish scales to keep it supple and waterproof. It was both comfortable and practical, but more important, it reminded her of home. This morning she kept it tightly closed, for the wind off the bay was chilly.

When she reached Cormorant, Saylah turned purposefully toward Potters Wharf. She enjoyed visiting the teeming docks where she often bought dinner for her family. She liked the sound and feel of the warped, damp boards beneath her feet as well as the sense of life, color and motion which was much different than in town. Here White, Salish and Chinese servants dressed plainly but practically, the colors of their wool and muslin trousers and shirts, skirts and blouses muted. The fishermen were always gaudy, in both their language and their clothing, and Saylah enjoyed being among them.

As she approached a pair of laughing fishermen, they fell silent, scowling. "It seems you had good fishing this morning. The salmon and sturgeon are particularly fat and healthy."

"Harrumph...." One of the men cleared his throat but didn't speak.

The other muttered, "Lucky is all."

Saylah gazed at them curiously, puzzled by their discomfort. "I think you must have skill as well as luck, or you would not have so many fine specimens." She paused, feeling the pulse of bewildered expectation racing through her, and couldn't help noticing the skyline across the harbor. She forced her attention back to the men. "Though it seems you are also lucky because you went out early. The day is beautiful now, but I think a storm will find us soon." She was trying to make them relax, but they remained rigid. She looked again toward the horizon. "Very soon indeed."

The day was perfectly calm and both men, along with some others on the crowded dock, stepped away from her. One fisherman nudged the other and whispered nervously, "Is that what they call *siwan*, that Indian magic?"

"Don't know and don't want to. Ain't no storm comin'. We're from the sea. We'd *know*!" the other said forcefully.

They were offended by her prediction, though it was based, not on magic or even intuition, but on the gathering number of dark clouds above the water. Unconsciously, she raised the hood of her cloak. "I did not mean to—" Before she could finish, the clouds unexpectedly released their burden of rain, drenching the entire wharf out of what—just a few moments past—had been a clear blue sky.

Everyone rushed to cover their heads, but most were too late. When Saylah tried to speak to the fishermen, they turned their backs, growling something about buying her fish elsewhere. She wanted to object, but suddenly she felt a hand on her arm and glanced down at a tiny Indian woman whose head did not reach Saylah's shoulder. Her face was a maze of wrinkles, her silver hair braided and tucked beneath the worn white shirtwaist she wore over a heavy wool skirt that was too long. Her eyes were dark and piercing; they captured and held Saylah's attention.

Without appearing to exert any pressure on her arm, the old woman led her to the end of the dock, away from the crowd. The rain pelted them, and they bent their heads against it.

"Forgive me for behaving like more than a stranger. I can only blame the spirits, who do not follow White men's rules. I am called Old Grandmother, and that shall be my last name." She spoke in Salish.

Drawing a deep breath, Saylah felt a leap of excitement that surprised her. She answered in the same language. "I am Saylah."

"You have had other names," Old Grandmother said, "and you will find still more."

Saylah grew still. "You sound very certain. Why is that?"

Leaning close, Old Grandmother murmured, "It is the same with all Salish." She smiled crookedly. "The White Strangers may have destroyed the rhythm of our days, taken our houses and our sacred land, but they cannot take our traditions. You, of all people know that, Saylah." She spoke the name cautiously, as if it were precious and must be treated with care. Clearing her throat, she added, "You must be confident to show your power before these strangers." The woman's gaze was intent, perceptive.

"That had nothing to do with power."

"That is what you think." Old Grandmother looked for a long time into Saylah's extraordinarily clear green eyes. "But you have real power; I know this."

Saylah frowned. She no longer spoke of such things. The skills the spirits had given her at birth had come from another life, another world. Thinking of it only made her sad. "*How* do you know?"

"Because I have seen many years and many sorrows. Because my uncle was Headman, my husband shaman, and some of his spirits linger to give me dreams of what has been and what will be. That is why I dare to tell you that to come here was courageous." She paused, rocked on the balls of her feet pensively and added, "But it was not altogether wise."

"I do not understand."

"Do you not?" She touched Saylah's elbow gently. "Have you not noticed that they do not know what to think of you? Because you treasure your heritage," she gestured toward her cape, pliable leather boots and thick hair falling in a single braid down her back, "because you do not try to follow their rules, you are a threat to their safe, settled lives. To hint at the power of magic as well—"

"I did no such thing. They assumed it was so."

"Exactly why you must take care. You are distinct among women, and the Whites do not welcome that kind of distinction. Whereas I – my People – seek it out." She stopped, eyes wide and alarmed, realizing she had spoken too quickly and too soon. "Forgive me. You do not know me, yet I lecture you as if you were a child. Perhaps there are a few things I still have to teach, but that is for later. Just now, I wonder if you will do me the honor of following me to a place where our men have gathered fresh fish and the air is not tinged with suspicion. There is no reason why you should trust me. Nevertheless, will you take the risk?"

Saylah could not turn away. She knew this meeting had not come about by chance; it was the beginning and objective of the undefined search that had begun in the moment when she slid effortlessly back into her childhood memories. Yet this strange woman who mesmerized with her eloquent gaze unsettled her. She nodded mutely.

The two women hurried away from the wharf and followed the northern curve of the harbor to a stand of firs that grew right down to the sea. Old Grandmother drew a canoe from among the reeds and grasses and slid it into the water. Only when Saylah took the oars by force did she allow the younger woman to row. She sat facing forward, away from the city, eyes fixed on the narrowest part of the inlet, and guided Saylah around the tapered slip of land to a low dock at the edge of the forest on the opposite shore. They secured the canoe to a barnacle covered piling and climbed the ladder to the uneven planks of the landing.

Using the gnarled walking stick she had taken from the bottom of the canoe – worn smooth by her hand and many years—Old Grandmother led the way into a wilderness of red alder, yew and hemlock trees among cedars and spruce. In the cool shadows where bracken and sword fern flourished, the fir needles silenced their footsteps. The wind sighed through the woven branches which rose and fell, creating speckled patterns that danced over the ground. There were splashes of bright color in the red-flowered currants and kinnikinnick vines, deer foot and thimbleberry. Such fanciful names for the fragile flowers running riot on the forest floor. The moist scent of dark earth, pungent fir and wild ginger filled the air. Saylah felt she could reach out and touch those sharp, familiar smells.

Now and then, a ray of sun pierced the living canopy overhead, touching the tangled foliage, separating and enhancing the myriad shades of green. The hush was absolute. It was as if Saylah were in a cathedral made, not of stone and glass, but of earth and light and sacred stillness. She took the beauty into herself, breathing the scented air as if it were water that quenched a long forgotten thirst.

She was astonished at the intensity of her recognition, the depth of welcome she felt in this forest—as if she were coming home. Julian owned many acres, and for all the years of their marriage, she had easily maintained her closeness to the earth, her worship of wind and water and the feel of soil beneath her feet. Her husband was proud of who she was and keenly aware that the woman he loved had been created and forged by her life with the Salish. Perhaps she had taken her freedom too much for granted. It had been many years since she had seen her People and lived as they lived. She did not know them anymore. The realization was a poignant sorrow.

The old woman seemed to understand. "There are few like you who have bound themselves to the eternal cycle of the Changer." She paused for a long time, looking out at the wind-rippled water that appeared ahead. "You see, I know your story." Her black eyes glowed. "I have been waiting for you, listening for the sound of your name in the wind. Today, at last, I heard it, so I came."

She touched Saylah's hand lightly. "You were chosen long ago. Or have you forgotten?"

"I am no longer the girl of whom you speak, nor have I been for many years. Perhaps I never was. When I failed the People, they turned away from me."

"They worshipped you. Always. Your power is in your spirit and your soul, and there it burns as bright as ever."

Hesitant to fall further into the past, Saylah stopped at the edge of the trees. "How can you be so certain?"

"I told you, I am a dreamer." She regarded Saylah intently. Her lips were parted, as if she meant to say something more, but she only shook her head. "I think you have had enough of talking. I have promised you fresh fish. Come."

They ducked beneath spreading branches of fir and cedar onto a small curved beach.

Saylah was vaguely aware of the canoes drawn up beneath the trees, and of the men who crouched in the shade. But she forgot them and Old Grandmother as the view overwhelmed her—the tranquil beauty that swept in an arc down the stone-scattered beach. The rain had stopped and the shapes of sinuous clouds seemed to be echoed in the limpid water of the inlet. It was shallow, emerald green and so clear that shells and rocks were visible, made sharper by the light upon the water. To her right, the shore curved into stands of fir, cedar and spruce which reached toward a narrow peninsula – lush, green and dripping with the recent rain.

There was no hint of buildings, factories or bustling docks. It was as if she had been transported to the wilderness where she had been born. With the spell of this lovely place upon her, she bent to remove her soft leather boots. Tossing them aside, she moved forward until the cold water swirled about her ankles. This was the refuge she had sought since her family moved to Victoria, but she had not known she was seeking it until now -- this isolated crescent with a view that stretched forever and a thousand sacred stones beneath her feet.

For that moment, when the sun came out from behind a cloud and struck the sea with a band of golden light, she gave herself up to the calm but searing beauty of this place.

Her heart slowed, and her breathing, and her thoughts fell away, leaving only sensation.

The voices in her blood sang with the beat of ancient drums.

She realized that whatever Old Grandmother had said about burdens and duty, in leading Saylah to this secluded arc of sand, the Salish woman had given her a gift of peace beyond reckoning.

Chapter 9

Simone slipped down the stairs wearing a velvet gown that fit her closely and flared out widely, swirling past her hips. It was a dark gray pattern stamped on lighter gray, and over it she wore a sleeveless silver caftan, which fell in graceful lines from her shoulders. Her dark hair was coiled about her head without ornament.

She went to the French doors and opened them to let in the morning air, turning when she heard a gasp.

Mathilde stood at the far end of the room, hands in the air in comic surprise, made more humorous by the look on her weathered face with its flat nose and shapeless lips. "Frightened me half to death," she cried. "Move more silently every day your feet walk." She shook her head and muttered under her breath, "Then again, best you be able to creep up on your enemies in silence, so they don't hear you come. Practicin' to pounce. What I'd be doin' if I were you." But she knew too well that Simone was not a woman who sought revenge. "A fool, that's what you are," Mathilde continued unremittingly. "But God blesses such fools, because their hearts're pure."

Simone did not bother to argue. Mathilde would not listen. She was too busy talking aloud to herself. She seemed unable to keep her thoughts inside. She was wearing her usual dress; she had only one pattern, made in wool for winter and cotton twill for spring and summer. It had a simple round neck, long, narrow sleeves, and a waist made invisible by Mathilde's own body, which was generous, with few curves. She had one gown in brown, one in black, one in deep purple, all colors which were out of style this season, but she did not care. "No sense puttin' peacock feathers on a cowbird."

Occasionally, as she did this morning, she wore a gingham apron over the dress, and the outfit was completed by a man's felt hat, with her lace veil poking out from underneath. She must have been to mass already. "I wish you would not go out before dawn," Simone said. "There is danger in the darkness, and I do not want you hurt." Mathilde, who had once been her nursemaid, was now her oldest friend.

The servant waved her concern away. "'S why I go about glowerin' and mutterin' so. Cutpurses are afraid of *me*." She chortled at her own cleverness. "Women alone must do what they can to keep their enemies away. Can't ignore those shadows lurking down the lanes. Turn and face 'em head on and shriek like a madwoman."

Mathilde removed hat and veil in one motion, leaving her short wiry gray hair standing on end. She dropped the hat on the brocade settee and shook her head vigorously with a sigh of relief. "Might try it sometime. Great deal of satisfaction in makin' the shadows run for a change."

Simone regarded her closely. She knew Mathilde was not referring to anonymous shadows on dark night streets. The servant often spoke in double meanings, hiding a warning or advice beneath apparently mindless chatter.

Mathilde was aware of Simone's attentive perusal, though her mistress' unlined face was placid. Funny how both women hid behind masks, the servant thought, though Mathilde less from pain than from necessity. She worked at making life bearable by making it amusing. She cherished her idiosyncrasies, used them to insure that she and Simone endured. They were survivors, both of them, unique in the nature and resilience of their strength. Mathilde got satisfaction from the knowledge.

She scratched her head, ran her fingers over her tufts of hair and snorted in disgust. "Good thing there're no mirrors in the house. The sight of this ugly face would probably frighten me into purgatory." She sniffed and straightened her rumpled apron. "I refuse to consider any other alternative."

In spite of herself, Simone laughed.

"Though why you have such an aversion to mirrors is beyond me. Not that you admit it. 'It is just that none I have seen are quite right,' you tell me. 'This one is too round, this one too square, this too large and this too small, this too old and this too new.' Lot of foolishness, if you ask me, which you don't," Mathilde grumbled under her breath.

"And you 50 years old and still the most beautiful woman in Rouen. Can't speak for the rest of France, but willin' to place a small wager. Gamblers, you and I, after all." She spoke to a Chinese vase, a fine lace doily, the elegant clock on the mantel, to the spot of mud she discovered on her worn but comfortable high-button boots. Anything that could not argue back.

Simone would not have done so anyway. She herself did not know what she was trying to escape each time she turned away from the image of her face.

"As a harridan, I can say these things with authority." Mathilde spoke solemnly to a wrinkled silk pillow on a graceful wingback chair. "I know about the cruelty of mirrors."

"I do not think you do," Simone replied. She had often envied the servant her ordinary looks and simple clothes.

Mathilde whirled. "Well, you've done your best to fight your looks. Always in gray. Makes people think you mourn the loss of That Awful Man." She could not hide her disdain.

"Not that I'd stay a minute longer if you started lookin' like the others. Garish, they are, with their great yellow and green sleeves looking like colored balloons about to lift them into the Seine. All bustle and fluster and no substance. Not to mention the necklaces and brooches and rings and aigrettes."

Simone suppressed a smile. "Indeed?"

"Yes, and now you ask, I did have something to say," she continued implacably. "Been fritterin' about since dawn, just waitin' to tell you." She strode across the Brussels carpet toward Simone. "Saw Marie Cecile this mornin'. Couldn't wait to tell me they found more of the DeM jewels hanging about the neck of the Virgin Mary last night. Sapphire necklace this time." She grinned, revealing the wide space between her front teeth, which were dark from chewing tobacco.

"You are wicked to gloat so," Simone admonished her. But she was smiling too, aware of how precious de Marchand's jewels were to him. He was a man who found his strength in the beauty and value of precious stones and beaten gold.

Simone glanced around at the delicate lace curtains— soft blue velvet on silver rods—the furniture, with its carved lion's heads and curved claw feet, softened by velvet and brocade in gray and pale blue. The crystal chandelier made the light dance along the dove gray watered silk walls. De Marchand would consider this room shabby and beneath his notice. "Why do you suppose he would do such a thing? It is most unlike him."

Mathilde sat abruptly in the closest chair, making the dainty legs and curved back seem ridiculous and precarious. "Marie Cecile's heard it's not him at all." Mathilde leaned forward, grinning. "Says she's heard of night-long tirades when he hears of each new discovery."

For months now, the jewels had been appearing, one piece at a time, on the holy statues in the Cathedral, left as anonymous offerings to the Church. Though the city of Rouen was expanding by the minute, it still had the atmosphere of a small town. Everyone knew everyone else and no one's business was truly secret. Many recognized the gems; they were distinctive pieces, finely wrought. Simone's mother had worn the jewelry with such grace and quiet beauty that the image had lingered long after she was gone.

Mathilde leaned closer. "Everyone's whisperin' it's that new young wife of his. Frail as she is, she daren't defy him openly. What a way to get revenge for her unhappiness with That Man! Giving his pretties to the Church. Can hardly march in and demand them back! Oh, it's so lovely." She hooted with laughter. "Imagine! Makin' him a saint and a fool all at once."

"You know quite well that Marie Cecile is a shameless gossip," Simone said primly to hide her smile. When Mathilde shrugged, grinning, Simone could not contain her laughter. "De Marchand? A saint?" she choked.

"Only wish I'd thought of it myself. What a time we'd have laughin' about it then."

The sound of the door chimes rippled through the room, and before Simone could move, Mathilde was up, muttering all the way to the double front doors downstairs.

She returned looking uncharacteristically grim.

Simone was on her feet at once. "What is it?" The old fear came back as instantly as an oil-soaked wick caught flame. Her poise vanished and she looked like an awkward child, uncertain whether to turn and run or freeze and pray she would not be seen.

Mathilde tugged on her gingham apron, refusing to meet her mistress' gaze. "Speaking of saints and fools, it seems one has come to call." She swallowed dryly.

"Henri de Marchand's waitin' below."

Chapter 10

The sound of the presses filled the air, along with the pungent odor of cleaner and ink and freshly printed paper. Julian Ivy paused to gaze around the pressroom of his shop with a smile. He watched the pile of flyers being turned out by the Fairhaven press with a sense of satisfaction. A rolling table stood nearby with two stacks of business cards and some forms for the hardware store a block away. He had just removed a set of catalogue galleys from the galley press.

Casey O'Connell peered over the cylinders of the press, copper eyebrows raised expectantly. "What're you thinkin' of *now*?"

Julian heard the thread of humor in Casey's voice and grinned in response. Since he'd come to Victoria, since the first day in the shop, long before he'd known anything about the machines or the process, he had begun to conjure up change, to create and to plan. "I've been thinking we should go to the banks and Government House and the department stores to solicit their printing business, now that we're getting proficient at this." He took a deep breath and added, "I'm also thinking about the cameras in the storage room. Kit's been using one, and is getting quite good very quickly, if I do take the liberty of praising his skill myself. The other camera is for making a photograph *of* a photograph in order to print pictures right along with the text. Now that we're starting our own newspaper, I think we should include photographs."

Julian was flushed with a pleasurable sense of anticipation, a feeling that had become familiar to him in the past month. He loved this place, though it was always chaotic, filled with fine powder, splattered ink and flying bits of paper. It looked rough and unfinished; that was what he liked about it. The shop itself was part of a narrow, paved alley shared with a shoemaker, a cigar factory and a book bindery. People passed at all hours of the day, their voices echoing between the tall brick buildings and dust rising under their feet.

The street was alive, vigorous and ripe for growth. Each day he had choices, decisions and responsibilities -- so much to do. Julian felt he belonged here, that at the age of 34, he had begun to find his place in the modern world. He had been good at ranching, because he liked to work hard, but he hadn't chosen that life. His father had chosen it for him. Now he spent most days trying to understand the different presses, the intricacies of setting type and composition and design, the weights and textures of different kinds of paper. Oddly, he was not frustrated, but exhilarated by all he did not know. He would learn in time.

"Ah!" Casey said. "And here I was believin' you were dreamin' of that mysterious lady." He pointed to a framed yellowed image sitting on the desk in the composition department, which comprised the single small office in the shop.

For a moment, Julian didn't know what he meant. Then he realized Saylah had placed an old daguerreotype of his mother and father's wedding portrait there. If she had done it five years ago, or even last year, he would have been irritated, but today he was not. Instead he felt…he tilted his head, rubbing his jaw as he tried to name the feeling. But he could not quite do it. He paused for a moment as his thoughts turned inward.

Casey cleared his throat, perplexed by Julian's expression. "You've gone right off to sleep in front of me eyes, lad. You *must* be dreamin'. Not that you'd let it slow down your work. Devon was right about you." Casey had not known Devon in Ireland, but they had met soon after their individual arrivals in Victoria, and their common background had drawn them together.

Casey was happy to work in the shop while Devon went around collecting crusades, besides writing and helping out with the machinery. Since Julian had joined them, Casey—who was neither an idealist nor a planner, felt the possibility of success in the charged air.

"I wonder how we can build up enough support to give the *Colonist* a run for its money," Julian said unexpectedly. He'd been thinking about how to compete with the foremost newspaper in Victoria for a while, and he wasn't going to let anything distract him.

"There, see what I mean? All I'm needin' is enough in me pocket for a pint and a warm bed and time to do as I please. I'm not burstin' with ambition like you."

"You must be thinking of Devon," Julian said.

"You're wrong there. 'Tis somethin' besides ambition that drives *him*. He's a puzzle, is our Devon. But 'tis part of his charm after all."

"It does make one want to be the first to make the puzzle into a whole picture," Julian mused. He had spent a good deal of time trying to do just that. "Where *is* our wee red-headed lad this morning, anyway?"

"Probably plasterin' the city with those flyers of his. 'Tis his particular battle this month."

Julian grimaced at the glaring flyer tacked to the wall.

MEN, WOMEN AND CHILDREN!

COME OUT OF THE SHADOWS AND GATHER TOGETHER!

STEP OUT FROM UNDER THE TYRANT'S HAND!

TOGETHER WE'LL DEMAND PROTECTION FOR YOUR HEALTH, YOUR WAGES, YOUR SECURITY!

JOIN THE ARMY OF PROTEST!

"I'll give him one thing – he's absolutely unafraid, if not altogether wise. He does seem to enjoy the prospect of turmoil."

"With that silver tongue of his, I'd be thinkin' he could hypnotize the light posts into following him."

Julian nodded thoughtfully. "Yes, but people are more difficult. He's so big and broad and his hair and eyes blaze like flame. The workers would no doubt run if they saw Devon Fitzgerald coming, for fear of getting burned."

"Did I here me name spoken with disrespect?" Devon boomed as he slammed the front door behind him, making the shop bell ring wildly. He carried a handful of creased and grimy broadsides.

"Hit every light pole in town with those, have you? And every blank wall? Any takers?" Casey inquired with a hint of irony.

"Not just yet. They need time to think." Devon squared his broad shoulders and smiled winningly.

"You mean to *feel*, don't you?" Julian inquired. "Once you get their rage sparked, they'll go after what they want with the same enthusiasm you do. *If* you manage to reach them."

"Have faith, me boyo. Don't you know I'm irresistible?" He grinned. "The workers'll come 'round."

"Have you ever thought that perhaps you might be over zealous? That there might be a more effective approach?" Julian was a great one for reasoning things through.

Devon shook his head emphatically. "Thinkin' is a waste of time. Act! That's what I say. Act with vigor and passion and rage, and all the other angry men will follow."

In spite of himself, Julian felt the Irishman's spell begin to draw him in, and that was dangerous but exciting. "Once you have your angry army lined up in the street, what will you do with them?" he demanded.

Devon was taken aback. "Start a revolution!" It was as much a question as it was an exclamation. "And in the meantime, I want Robert Barrett to know I won't be goin' away. I'll be round and about, makin' his rest uneasy!" His tone was benign, but he slapped the papers onto the table and pounded them with his fist.

Julian and Casey exchanged glances. Sometimes the devil seemed to creep inside the jocular young man and make him mercurial and dangerous, though whether to himself or to others, they weren't quite certain. "What is it you really want?" Julian was both curious and concerned.

"I want that man to burn in hell." Devon's eyes smoldered until he realized what he had revealed. He spoke carefully, calmly when he added, "I want to befriend and defend the workers at the ironworks." He breathed deeply until his natural smile came back.

Glancing out the window, Julian noticed a boy of about sixteen bringing his bicycle to an abrupt halt in front of the print shop. He pointed meaningfully. "Seems to me the workers don't want your help, if that young man is any indication. He's shaking his fist and his face is quite red. I'd say he's angry at *you* not Barrett."

Devon peered out the dusty window, heaving a great sigh when he recognized the boy as one of Davy's friends from the factory. He stared more intently. "'Tis no' just his fist he's wavin'. He's carryin' a monster of a rock in that hand, and I'm thinkin' 'tis no' for show."

At that precise moment the boy leaned back as far as he could, took careful aim, and hurled the rock toward the plate glass window.

Chapter 11

"We have now completed our lesson on the history of Victoria and Vancouver Island," Miss Reynolds—headmistress of Miss Chadwick's School for Girls—said with satisfaction and relief. History was not her favorite subject. One had to be so careful, after all, about what one said and didn't say. "For the rest of the day we will study deportment."

She folded her hands gracefully before her to demonstrate. She was wearing a gray cashmere gown with epaulets, braid and silver buttons that made it resemble a military uniform. The tapered waist did nothing for her too thin figure, and the gored skirt was so wide at the bottom that it folded in upon itself again and again.

Resolutely, Illiann Ivy looked around the irreproachably clean room with its whitewashed walls and unmarred oak desks. Along the sides at precise intervals were coat hooks, each holding a straw boater and blue wool cape: *"We do **not** wear hats inside; it is unforgivably gauche!"* Miss Reynolds had warned on the first day. Illiann did not mind; she hated hats.

The desks were arranged in five orderly rows of six, each occupied by a fifteen- to eighteen-year-old girl. Each wore her hair in either a neat braid around her head or a tidy bun. Each was dressed in a pin-tucked white shirtwaist and blue serge skirt with two rows of plain white trim around the hem. Each sat with her hands crossed demurely on her desk, eyes on Miss Reynolds, feet delicately crossed at the ankles. No one looked the slightest bit inclined to object to the teacher's bald announcement. Illiann did not know if the other girls were afraid or bored or perhaps they simply didn't care, but *she* did.

With a tiny sigh she raised her hand and stood quietly beside her desk until the teacher noticed her. "Yes, Miss Ivy? What is it now?" Miss Reynolds could not quite keep the annoyance and apprehension out of her tone.

"I am wondering when we will study the Salish Indians." Illiann glanced around the room at several dark-haired girls with the slightest olive cast to their skin. There were blondes as well, and two red-heads, but Illiann suspected many of the young ladies in this class had Native blood somewhere in their past. "They played such a vital role in the city's history." She did not raise her voice and her expression was wide-eyed and innocent.

Behind her she heard a gasp, quickly suppressed, and what she could have sworn was an exclamation of admiration. Perhaps it was Laura Hart, who tried to hide it, but appeared to enjoy Illiann's challenges to the rigid rules at Miss Chadwick's.

Flustered, Miss Reynolds began to flutter her hands, check her hair, pace in a tiny circle. She took a long, deep breath to steady herself. She had been doing that frequently since Illiann Ivy began to attend classes. The teacher wished she could ignore the girl, but she could not. There was something peculiarly compelling about her presence. Miss Reynolds knew the other girls felt it, though they pretended not to listen to her impertinent questions.

"As I said, we have completed our study of the history of the Island. Some aspects of the past are best forgotten. We are quite cultured here in Victoria. We do not consider the uncivilized behavior of the natives. It is not our concern."

The other girls stirred, some to gaze at Illiann in tight-lipped disapproval, some to sit more rigidly upright, staring forward with determination, as if afraid to meet her eyes, some casting quick, curious glances her way.

Laura Hart smiled ever so slightly before reassuming her proper pose. No one spoke up to agree with Illiann, but that wasn't surprising. The other girls were terrified of making the headmistress angry with questions she did not wish to answer. They seemed to feel safe among the misconceptions and omissions that kept their world predictable. "I just thought that since our second governor, James Douglas, and many leading citizens like John Todd were married to Indian women, and their children were half Salish, it might make the subject of interest to us." Illian was careful not to express her frustration.

The girl simply refused to relent, and Miss Reynolds could find nothing to object to in her mild tone and downcast eyes. That was what drove the headmistress daft. Illiann never did anything improper, but she asked probing, disquieting questions on nearly every subject. Miss Reynolds rarely had the answers. "The wives and daughters of our great leaders rejected their pasts. They became English in everything but blood. Therefore, you are mistaken," the woman snapped. "Again. It was a very improper question indeed. Not at all ladylike."

Illiann bit her lip to hold back a smile. If she could not learn what she wanted to know, at least she was certain her continuous queries disturbed the unruffled surface of this too calm classroom. "I see," she murmured as she slipped back into her seat, hands folded and ankles crossed.

That's precisely the problem, Miss Reynolds thought in indignation. She was very much afraid that Illiann *did* see something the teacher could not. And that something threatened to disrupt her safe and predictable world.

Chapter 12

"I'm here! Where are you, Devon? I've brought the new photographs I made today," Christopher Ivy shouted from the sidewalk, touching with reverence the special pocket in his satchel which held the exposed glass plates. A box camera was carefully wrapped in layers of flannel inside his leather school bag. Yesterday Julian had allowed his son to take it home for the first time, and Kit had been careful to keep it safe.

He was so excited by the thought of his new photographs and the ones he had left with Devon yesterday, that he did not immediately notice the broken plate glass window. He propelled himself through the door of the print shop just after Devon collapsed, clutching his head where the rock had hit, hurling him backward in a shower of splintered glass. Kit froze, forgetting his satchel as it slid from his shoulder and onto the floor.

Julian rushed toward him, but the boy did not notice. He stared in shock at the tall muscular Irishman he so admired covered in blood and moaning quietly. The part of his face that was visible was pallid and twisted in pain.

"What—? Who?" Kit sputtered, turning toward his father, bewildered.

Too late, Julian tried to block his son's view. "The sky's blue this afternoon. The rain has been and gone. I heard some boys getting up a game of stickball in the street. Don't you want to join them?" His voice shook as he tried vainly to get the boy away.

Kit did not move, did not even shake his head. He gawked at the man lying on the floor, the window in fragments around him. He felt queasy and thought he might be ill right then and there. A moment ago he had been happy, practically grown up. But he didn't feel grown up anymore.

It was not that he'd never seen blood before. He hunted, had seen animals killed for food, had helped skin them and divide the organs and preserve the hides. He had also watched Saylah heal injured animals, but not once had he witnessed the death of an animal for sport or cruelty or pleasure. He had seen Geordie MacKinnon bruised and bleeding when his horse threw him and kicked him in the ribs, but that had been an accident. The rock lying beside Devon and the gaping hole where the window had been told their own story. He simply couldn't understand it. "I…saw…a boy outside…on a…bicycle. His…hand was…in the air. Did he…do…this on purpose?"

"I'm thinkin' they'd no intention of hittin' our Devon," Casey managed. "He just happened to be standin' in front of the window, laddie."

Coughing and wincing, Devon rasped, "'Tis just my Irish luck."

"More likely your obstinacy." Julian was in shock. The broken glass had cut his friend in a hundred places; there were shards caught in his chest, throat and arms. The blood was flowing sluggishly but constantly from the wound on his head. "We'll have to get a doctor."

Casey looked up. "I'll no' be trustin' doctors. Nor does he. Fools all, who've not a clue what they're doin'. Right, me boyo?"

When there was no response, Julian muttered, "He's unconscious. Besides, my wife isn't a fool, and she knows very well what she's doing. I'm sending Kit for her."

"Your wife?" Casey frowned in confusion. "A doctor?"

"She's a healer," Julian explained patiently. "She learned from the Salish when she was a child, and later she studied with Dr. Helmcken here in Victoria."

Nodding, Casey rubbed his throbbing temples. He was afraid for his friend. He had always thought something like this might happen. Devon loved stirring up trouble too much. He only hoped Saylah Ivy could help.

Julian took out his handkerchief and pressed it to Devon's worst wound. "Can you start up the kerosene stove in the back?" He turned to his son. "Listen, Kit, this is important. You need to go as fast as you can, quietly, without telling anybody, and get your mother. Tell her to bring her boiled herbs, some bandages, disinfectant, blankets." He knew exactly what his wife needed after watching her work for so many years. "Can you remember all that?" Kit's vacant eyes concerned him.

For a moment more, the boy stood immobile, then he blinked, shook his head, and without a word, plunged toward the door.

Julian stared after him for a moment, appalled by the look of dread on Kit's pale and beautiful face.

Chapter 13

"Edward!" Mary Clarke cried out. "You mustn't ever go away!" She held Edward Ashton tightly, weeping at the pleasure he had given her, at the warmth of his body, the faint scent of fir and mist-laden air that mingled with the smell of his sweat. Her tears fell on his skin, and she traced them with a fingertip. "You have to leave your wife soon," she murmured, running her hand over the light curly hair on his chest. "I want you to make me feel like this all the time." The pale yellow lamplight blurred the outline of his face, softening the sculpted features.

Edward stiffened. When he did not answer, Mary looked up, suddenly fearful. He was staring out the window in order to avoid looking at her. She knew this with a certainty that chilled her. "You're the only one who makes me feel strong, who makes my fear go," she murmured desperately. She was a schoolteacher at a small local schoolhouse. All her life, she had known nothing but words and books, the smell of dust and chalk, the voices of children not her own. Her walnut-colored hair was always braided and coiled at the nape of her neck, except when she lay with Edward. Only then did her pale blue eyes sparkle and the color creep into her cheeks.

She was not the kind of woman to meet a man like this, to come to his bed without marriage, without promises, without hope. But she had not been able to resist Edward's charm, his strong body, sandy hair and gold-flecked eyes. In those eyes, when he held her, she saw all the promises she did not hear and all the hope she needed.

Edward turned. "I don't have the power to change things for you." He could not even change himself; he had always known that. Slowly, Mary's face came into focus through the haze of his distress. Edward started, surprised to find her there. He was horrified by the entreaty in her eyes and the grip of her hand on his naked arm. Only then did he fully realize what she had said.

"I could never leave Sophia," he declared.

His tone was very flat, very final. Mary sat up, drawing the linen sheet over her body, partly to hide her shame, partly to hide her trembling. "Why not?"

"Because I love her too much." He added silently, 'I *need* her too much.' "I thought you knew that from the beginning."

"How could I?" Mary asked, astonished. "You're here with me."

Edward opened his mouth, but no words came. There was no answer he could give her. He did not understand this need to prove again and again what he could never prove, because he did not know what it was. Did he want to show he was desirable? Powerful? Successful? Why, when all those things were so unquestionably true?

"Why *are* you here?" Mary asked softly. The chill had begun to settle in her chest when she saw his distant expression.

He was surprised into an honest answer. "Because something drives me from inside and won't let me rest. A need so deep I can't begin to understand it. And you never will."

Chapter 14

"Mama! Wait for me, Mama!"

Illiann had to call out twice before her voice penetrated Saylah's dazed thoughts. She was on the way home with fresh fish wrapped in cedar bark in her woven bag. Pausing at the sound of the commanding voice, she turned to find her daughter running to catch up with her. "Are you finished with school already?" For the first time, Saylah wondered how long she had been lost on that tiny crescent of paradise.

Illiann removed her straw boater so the cloud-drifted sun could touch her face. She was barefoot, her high-button boots and scratchy wool stockings stuffed into her book bag. Her braid had come loose, but she did not try to repair the damage. Despite the things weighing on her mind, she was immediately aware of Saylah's distracted smile. "Where have you been?" she asked, consumed by curiosity.

"With the Indians," her mother replied, placing an affectionate hand on Illiann's shoulder.

The girl could not help but respond to Saylah's smile; she could feel her mother's contentment in the lightness of her touch. Her pulse beat more quickly. "Were they your relatives?" She had always wanted to know more about the people among whom her mother had spent her childhood. There were things Saylah did not realize Ilya knew about her mother's past, but that was the girl's secret, and she would not reveal it until she sensed the time was right. She smiled at the thought while waiting breathlessly for the answer to her current question.

"All Salish are related in some distant manner. But no, these are not *my* People."

"Then how did you find them? And why haven't you looked before?"

"You are full of questions, are you not?"

"That's what the teachers tell me at school. I'm afraid I'm too curious about things they'd rather not discuss. Today I asked when we would study the Salish, and Miss Reynolds got flustered and told me they don't think about the Natives."

Saylah smiled at her daughter's obstinate expression. "Well then, perhaps *you* will have to teach *them*."

"I couldn't...." Illiann trailed off when she noticed the sparkle in her mother's eye. Like Saylah and Julian, she could not resist a challenge. "Maybe I *can* teach them something."

You will teach them a great deal more than you realize, and certainly more than they want to know, Saylah thought.

"You didn't tell me how you found the Indians today."

"Ah, yes. It was quite extraordinary. A woman named Old Grandmother came looking for me." Saylah shook her head to remind herself that this morning had been real, that the encounter with her past had actually happened.

Illiann leaned forward, face animated and eyes bright. "Why?"

"I am not exactly certain."

Illiann was confused; her mother could see it in her eyes. Saylah hesitated, but only for a moment. "I think it is because of what I was when I lived among the People."

"What *were* you? Papa said you would tell me when you were ready." Illiann waited, eager and half afraid. She had begun to think her mother would never be willing to share her secrets. Yet the girl wanted so badly to know. Over the years, she had grasped the fragments Saylah offered and cradled them like precious pieces of colored glass. She stored each one away, hoping someday she would have enough to make a multi-colored picture of her mother's past.

Saylah counted her breaths and the pattern of her heartbeats. Illiann was right; it was time. "The People called me a Dreamer, a Healer, a Dancer. I was a part of the celebrations and the prayers and feasts. I was raised to be Shaman, and for a brief time, so I was." Her voice was low and full of things unspoken.

"Shaman." Illiann whispered reverently. She had often sensed her mother's inner strength and intuition—a kind of power the girl felt in no other.

"It was a very long time ago." Yet the memories were vivid in her eyes. For years now, as Saylah gathered the oral legends and stories like flecks of gold from the fine silt of a riverbank, the buried voices in her blood had begun to sing again. She heard those voices like the dawn song of the birds, felt them like a rush of water about her ankles. Once she copied the words onto paper, she held the voices in her hands, felt the impalpable lure of the magic, and the part of her past she most loved. Sometimes it frightened her – the power of those ancient voices to ignite a primitive stir of emotion.

Illiann sensed her mother's shifting mood, the longing in the turn of her head and the curve of her throat. "You still miss them, the People of the village where you grew up."

"I have tried to keep them by me in small ways." Saylah caressed the edge of her doeskin cape. "And Old Grandmother has the power, the knowledge and the will to take me back, to remind me of all that was sacred and precious, and still is, in my dreams."

"It's good that she helps you remember." The girl wished she had something as compelling to recall.

"Yes, but when I was young there was too much sorrow I could not ease. In the end, you see, my comfort came, not in forgetting, but in learning to remember from a distance. Today those memories are very close." She barely noticed as they turned onto Crescent Street.

"I wish I could meet them. May I?" Illiann could not hide her enthusiasm. She fell into her mother's eyes, into the memories they shielded and the yearning they revealed.

Neither mother nor daughter moved for a long moment. An invisible spun glass web held them together, captive in its finely woven strands.

Into the heart of that stillness came the sound of pounding footsteps. A moment later, Kit appeared, panting, and grasped his mother's cloak.

All the way home, he had repeated over and over the list of things he was to tell Saylah to bring. "Bandages, herbs, disinfectant, blankets. Bandages, herbs, disinfectant, blankets." He had used the words like a chant to protect him from the memory of Devon's bloody face. He did not want to let his father down. He had spoken the list aloud repeatedly—bandages, herbs, disinfectant, blankets— focusing on the harmless words until they drowned all others. He had to get it right. He mustn't forget a single thing.

Bandages, herbs, disinfectants, blankets.

His mother turned, watching with that hushed calm that meant he had her complete attention. Bandages, herbs, disinfectants, blankets. "Mama!" Kit cried hoarsely, "I need you!"

Chapter 15

Simone closed her eyes, said a silent prayer to the Virgin Mary, and drew her cloak of refinement around her. "Send de Marchand away."

Mathilde shook her head. "Tried. Won't go." She stared at the marble tiles and mumbled under her breath, "Face as dark as midnight, too. No sense of the ridiculous, that man. No sense at all."

"Then perhaps you'd best ask him up." The words, spoken quietly, belied Simone's anxiety.

"He means trouble. Can wager your fortune on that. As if you had one to wager." Mumbling imprecations, the servant shuffled down the stairs and returned a moment later with de Marchand behind her.

"Here he is," Mathilde said flatly. She refused to announce him as if he were an important guest. "Don't owe him courtesy," she told the subdued painting on the wall, so de Marchand could not hear. "Be rude to say what we really owe him."

"Mademoiselle." De Marchand nodded curtly at Simone. He had never addressed her as Madame, as if, by refusing to use her title, he could make their brief marriage go away completely. He also did not call her by name, though his reasons for that were more obscure. He glanced at Mathilde, waiting for her to leave the room.

With a snort, she planted herself firmly on a chair in the corner, arms crossed over her shapeless bosom.

Disgusted, barely controlling his rage, de Marchand turned back to Simone. "Have you not done enough to me? Have I not paid enough for one mistake?" he demanded without preamble.

He wore a well-made blond wig that emphasized his age, rather than masking it. His coffee-colored eyes were dim, his jowls heavy, and his lips thin and rigid with anger. His violet silk cravat was well tied, but clashed with his multi-colored waistcoat and brown morning coat. He looked all of his sixty-five years and more. An indecipherable emotion simmered beneath his fury, alarming her with its intensity. She could not begin to guess what he was feeling; he had always been a perilous puzzle to her.

"I do not know what you mean, *monsieur*. I have never asked for anything from you except my freedom. And that you will not give me."

Face averted, de Marchand paced recklessly, barely avoiding a vase of fresh flowers on a marble pedestal. "Is that it, then? Are you trying to pay me back by giving away what I most value?" He turned and caught his heel on the rug. "Why must you punish me like this?"

Mathilde was muttering to cover her wicked smile. "Whine and complain in *my* house, will you? All this to-do about some sparklin' glass."

Simone was as perplexed as she was angry. "Are you speaking of the jewels in the cathedral? Do you think I am responsible?" He did not have to answer; surely nothing but an attack on his precious fortune would have brought him here so precipitously. "I have no wish to punish you." As she said the words, she realized they were true. His rage was not threatening, because there was no courage behind it. Even when he did threaten, she knew he would not act. She knew too much.

But not about the jewels. She hadn't the faintest idea where they were, though it was impossible to convince him of that. She had tried again and again, but he would not listen. She had told him that when she left, she had taken nothing, wanted nothing to remind her of their disastrous marriage.

She looked at his ashen face, where the blood came and went in a splotchy rush, at his liver-spotted hands, the lump in his throat each time he swallowed convulsively. She could never like him, but at that moment, she pitied him. She had tried to hate him, to blame him, to make him the uncaring villain who had ruined her life, and for years she had been successful. But she could not do it anymore. She did not want to gloat; she wanted to weep, and she hated that. She had prayed for a stone heart to keep the tears away, but her heart had remained flesh and blood.

She revolved gracefully and moved toward the window, her skirts whispering about her ankles. "I do not wish you ill."

When de Marchand found his voice, his anger had turned to supplication. "Then why do you humiliate me by using my name? And worse, humiliate my wife, who bears it honestly? The people of Rouen think of you first when they hear of Madame de Marchand." His voice broke, revealing a hint of the repressed emotion she had noticed earlier.

Mathilde supposed he did not see the irony in what he said, but she chortled with suppressed laughter. "See!" she told her left boot in a whisper. "A blind old fool, an arrogant fool who never thinks of anyone's pain except his own."

De Marchand saw by the line of Simone's back and the proud tilt of her head that she was stronger than he. The knowledge chilled him even as it fueled his outrage. "Can you not see that all I have left is my family and the glorious history of my ancestors? Don't take that from me too."

Whirling, Simone stared at him in astonishment. *His* ancestors? Had he made himself believe the jewels had been passed down for centuries through his family? That they had not been her mother's treasure, and would still be, had her father not forced her to marry him? "What you have lost, you lost through your own choice, not mine. I only wanted you to lose a wife."

For the first time, he seemed to hear her, and to understand. "Then why did you take so much more, Simone?"

She was shocked by sound of her name on his lips and the anguish with which he spoke it. "I took nothing but pain. You know that."

"So you will not stop this persecution?"

Mathilde rolled her eyes dramatically. "Who's persecuting whom, I'd like to know?" she huffed under her breath.

"I cannot stop what I have not begun," Simone said simply.

De Marchand sighed. As the air left him, his body seemed to fold inward on itself. He had been a fool to come. "Well," he said. And that was all. He knew anything else would have been dangerously unwise.

Simone could not bring herself to offer him her hand, but she took a deep breath and did what she had never found the strength to do before. "I bid you good afternoon, Henri. I bid you good-bye."

He froze for an instant, hand outstretched and lips parted, but no sound escaped him. Then he spun on his heel and was gone. She heard the door slam behind him; the reverberation echoed up and down the stairs for several moments. Then all was silent.

"Well rid of that one," Mathilde declared firmly. "Must've gone soft in the head, accusin' you like that. Jewels don't even belong to him."

Simone was only half-listening. What had she seen flaring for a moment in his eyes? It had certainly been more profound than anger or petty greed. "I am sorry, I did not hear—"

"He's got more than a lot of nerve claiming the fortune belonged to his family. Ridiculous." Mathilde brushed her palms together as if making short shrift of the idea.

"Yes," Simone murmured in distraction, turning instinctively toward a concentration of vivid colors against the far wall. As if mesmerized, she approached a small shrine – the only altar she had touched since the haven of the Catholic Church had been denied her.

One day Mathilde had dragged home a garishly painted statue of the Virgin Mary. "No one wanted it. Thought it couldn't hurt to give her a nice warm home. Needs it, don't you think? Doin' her a kindness, really."

Mathilde had turned her head this way and that, like an artist evaluating his work. "Clothes and hair are very ugly, but still the Madonna. Always pray directly to Her. A mother, after all, and more understanding. Jesus, our Savior's kind, but he's a man, like his Father. Easier to talk to a woman."

"I do not talk to any of them. The Bishop of Ouen has proclaimed that they are not to listen to my prayers." Yet Simone was drawn to the unattractive statue, drawn irresistibly to the memories of her childhood, when she had found comfort in the rituals of the Church. She had tried to turn her back on those memories, as the Church had turned its back on her, but the habits were too deeply engrained.

The next day, Mathilde had brought a small table for the statue, and then made a lace cloth to cover the marred top and spindly legs. She had also dug out discolored silver candleholders and a small mottled bowl for fresh flowers. These she had cleaned until they shone, and placed them on the lace circle with the Madonna. Nearby, she arranged a tray with many candles, enough for each of her mistress's prayers.

At first Simone had come only in the middle of the night. She had knelt and made the sign of the cross, but there were no prayers left inside. Little by little, the words had come back when she ran her fingers over her mother's pearls as she would over a rosary. Now the tray was covered in layer upon layer of melted wax, layer upon layer of supplications whispered into a darkness touched by tiny bursts of flame.

She had brought a plain footstool on which to kneel, and wept the morning she found a beautiful old rosary curled at the Madonna's feet.

Now Simone picked up the rosary, running her fingers lightly over the beads. She knelt, head bowed, to whisper her repentance for her sins and ask for compassion from a gaudy, discarded statue with a wooden face – unsmiling and impenetrable.

She could not recreate the past, she reminded herself. Too much had happened in the years since she left Vancouver Island. "I believe I have forgiven de Marchand, Lady Mother. Perhaps now you can find it in your heart to forgive me."

Chapter 16

Saylah collected everything she needed and bundled it into a hansom cab, where her children were already waiting. No one spoke as they hurtled toward the print shop.

"Devon Fitzgerald is hurt!" Kit had cried, inarticulate with panic when he first came upon his sister and mother. "Papa said to come!" He had tugged on Saylah's hand like a young child and his eyes were wild with fear.

By the time the carriage drew to a halt, the wildness had gone. Kit's hands were no longer shaking, but he was quite pale. He lifted the blankets from the back of the carriage, and Saylah carried her healing bag, containers of herbs and a small block of ice.

When Julian opened the door, he was shaking with relief. "Thank God! I didn't know what else to do." He kissed Saylah's forehead, just to feel her soft skin beneath his lips for an instant. He needed that reassurance.

Saylah touched his cheek. "Do not worry. We will do what must be done." She followed her husband to the back room, lit by two oil lamps, where Devon was stretched out on a cot Casey had found stashed behind the machinery.

The Irishman lay unmoving, his greatcoat for a blanket, a crumpled jacket for a pillow. Julian had ripped a piece of his long johns free and wrapped it inexpertly around Devon's head. The pourous wool was saturated with blood, the man's face lacerated, bruised and swollen.

Saylah paused for a fraction of a second, then moved forward briskly. "I will need hot water," she said, "cloths soaked in disinfectant, and the help of a strong man."

Julian and Kit went to see to the water and cloths, while Casey removed his coat. There were still splinters of glass in many of the cuts on Devon's face, and a huge lump crusted with blood on his forehead. She was disconcerted to discover a similar wound on the back of his head, which must have struck the floor when he fell. He was half-conscious, and kept struggling to get up, but each time, he fell back with gasps of pain and surprise. Saylah murmured softly, trying to calm him as she cleaned the cuts, removed the glass and washed the blood away.

Finally, Devon stopped thrashing about.

"Can you drink some tea to ease the pain?" she asked, holding a mug of steaming lady fern to his lips, cupping his chin until he swallowed. "I will need to sew up the cut on your forehead." She spoke normally, as she did to Julian, hoping to soothe Devon with the pretense that all was as it should be. She did not like two of the wounds on his face, which sliced through to the bone, or that his head was injured both front and back. She was afraid he might have a concussion. She nodded to Illiann, who knelt on the other side of the cot.

With her daughter's help, Saylah bathed Devon's wounds in disinfectant and bruised cottonwood leaves steeped in water, then used a poultice of skunk cabbage leaves to dull the pain. While Julian held a lamp nearby, she sewed shut one wound with cat sinew and Illiann did the other. Both were very deft, very gentle.

When they had done all they could, when they had cut away Devon's filthy shirt, removed all the fragments of glass they could find, bathed his arms and chest and wrapped his forehead, Saylah directed Casey and Julian to wrap him in several warm blankets. Devon lay still, eyes closed, hands inert at his sides.

"Will you sit and talk to him, Casey? Your Irish voice might ease him." Saylah spoke softly; she did not want to alarm her patient. "Try to keep him still. I think the blows to his head may be dangerous. If he slips into sleep, he might slip away."

Casey nodded, but could not think what to talk about.

"Tell him tales from your childhood," Saylah suggested. "Tell him things you thought wonderful and magical and your voice will reach him."

When she rose to go, Devon grasped her hand to keep her from leaving. "Sure, an' you're an angel from heaven, right enough." It was the first time he had spoken.

Smoothing back the hair from his forehead, she murmured, "I am only Saylah, and I must prepare the cab to carry you to our house."

"No! Me own rooms are good enough."

"I do not think so. Someone must watch you through the night to make certain you stay awake."

Moving into the front office, Saylah leaned heavily on Julian's desk, tense and exhausted. She tried to calm herself by breathing deeply, but her chest was tight and her hands shook on the cluttered desktop. To regain her composure, she concentrated on the papers scattered before her. The first thing she noticed was the daguerreotype of Jamie and Simone Ivy on their wedding day. In spite of her distress, she smiled.

Julian had come up behind her and noticed she was looking at the photograph. He did not quite know what to feel about her tender smile, but it was not the anger he expected. Heart pounding, he slipped his arms around her waist and drew her close.

Before he could speak, or even decide what to say, Kit stumbled into the room. "Will Devon be all right?"

Saylah and Julian turned, startled. Both had forgotten the injured man for a moment. "I hope all will be well," Saylah said as firmly as she could manage. "It is most important that he allow himself to rest and heal."

Julian shook his head. "That, my dear, could be a problem. Devon Fitzgerald only knows one way to live, and that's too passionately and too perilously."

But he wondered as he said it if he was also thinking of his mother.

Chapter 17

Sophia lay rigid, listening, as she had so often, to the sound of her husband's uneasy dream, alert to the moment when he woke and tried to call out, making inarticulate sounds instead.

He had slept soundly all night and then, well before dawn, the distressing dream had crept into his mind. As he had so often since the Ivys moved to Victoria, he waited until he caught his breath, then got up. With a silence born of practice, he dressed in the dark, slipping from the room without waking his wife.

Or so he thought.

Brutus began to whine as Edward descended the stairs, then struggled with a door below—she could hear the lock creak in protest. It was odd about the dog, Sophia thought, but in the last few days, the animal had seemed to sense his master's agitation. At the sound of the door swinging shut, she winced.

What was it that frightened Edward in his simple, lonely dream? What shape did his demons take, and why? She had asked him; she had asked herself; she had asked God, but received no answer.

Brutus sat at the foot of the bed, whimpering. She closed her eyes and the sound stopped, but the dog rubbed his huge black head back and forth against her feet, unwilling to go away.

The dog's distress mirrored Sophia's. For months she had tried to talk to Edward, to comfort him, though his silent anguish ate away at her until it nearly overshadowed her sympathy and compassion. She could not help him when she did not know what was wrong, when he closed her out as if she were a stranger.

"I hate you for that," she said to the papered walls.

She was shocked by the bitter words. How could she hate him for being in pain? But that was not why. It was because he had allowed this distance to widen between them. His nightmares were the only things he would not let her share. Was he protecting her from something? Had he committed a sin so unspeakable that he could not confess it, suffered some loss that he could not forget? The unanswered questions had begun to torment her imagination.

Brutus tilted his massive head, watching her intently.

Sophia rose, slipped into a rose-colored wrapper and marched down the stairs in determination. The door to the storage room had long been closed and locked; no one had entered it in years. But now the bolt hung loose and a footprint in the dust from inside told her, though she had already guessed, that she would find her husband on the other side of that door.

She picked up the lamp burning low on the hallway bureau, pressed the stiff latch and descended the shadowy stairs into the basement.

Edward was huddled over a trunk, cobwebs in his hair, several trunks open behind him. At the sound of Sophia picking her way across the crowded floor, billows of dust rising around her ankles, her husband rose, his face registering frustration, determination and confusion. He was covered in dust from head to toe and his hands were grimy. "What do you mean, sneaking up on me like that! Sticking your nose into my business!

He blinked, wondering where the words had come from. He'd just told Mary how he felt about Sophia, and he'd spoken the truth. Yet he was unreasonably irritated by his wife's appearance in the basement. "It's dirty down here," he forced himself to speak softly, affectionately. "I don't want you touched by this filth."

"It's all right," she reassured him, "it will all wash clean." She took a brief, fortifying breath. "Whatever are you looking for, my dear?"

The problem was, he didn't really know. He just knew it was imperative that he find it. "That's not something you need to worry about. Now go away and leave me to it. Go." He flapped his arms as if she were a stray chicken he could shoo away. "Go!"

"Edward, please let me help you. I want to. I'm perfectly willing…"

"I don't care. I just want you to go."

So she turned on her heel and left.

Chapter 18

The Ivys returned with Devon to Crescent Street. The two-story yellow house with its mansard roof and long front porch—supported by pillars covered with miniature climbing roses—was not large compared to the ranch, but the garden was bursting with flowers and fruit trees, and the pale orange trim and dormer windows gave it great charm. Saylah, Julian, Kit and Illiann half-dragged half-carried Devon through the arched front door to the parlor and onto the sofa. The sun struck the wide French doors and stained-glass windows, transforming walls and floor into canvases of ever-changing shape and hue.

Even through his pain-drenched haze, Devon noticed the colors and light; they called to him, but he shut his eyes against them.

Saylah worked in the kitchen, making broth and herb infusions for her patient, as well as dinner for her family, while Kit brought armfuls of pillows and blankets that Julian used to make his friend as comfortable as possible.

Devon's legs hung over the end of the sofa, but Illiann and her father managed to rest his ankles on rolled blankets. He remained silent until everyone stood back for the first time. He could barely make out their pinched faces and drooping shoulders. For a moment he could not remember who they were. He nearly slept as they ate hurriedly in the dining room, but Illiann leapt up and talked him awake.

When the family had eaten, Saylah fed Devon some broth and tea and told him not to let himself drift off. "You may have a concussion, and it is dangerous to risk sleep."

He moaned as she treated his head wound again and placed ice wrapped in a linen towel on his forehead and at the base of his neck.

"Try to behave," Julian warned, before he and his wife went off to bed.

Normally Illiann would have been at work in her room, doing her homework on her new Merritt typewriter. At least that was what she told everyone. They needn't know precisely what she was doing. But this evening she had volunteered to stay up all night to make sure the red-haired giant was as comfortable as he could be, and to keep him awake. She was drawn to him in a way she did not wish to examine. Besides, the responsibility made her feel grown up; she knew her mother trusted her to do what she promised. Kit sat beside her for a long time, playing shadow games on the wall with unsteady hands. He was afraid to leave his friend alone, even under his sister's care.

Devon was not helping things. He complained about every position, about a headache, about his sore back and his exhaustion. "I really can no' be stayin' up like this. My whole body just wants rest. Mayhap your mother is wrong. I'd feel a deal better if I could get some sleep."

Finally, in exasperation, Illiann said, "I have a teacher I think you should meet. I've a feeling you two would get along quite well.

"Why?" Devon asked. "Is she pretty?"

Illiann smiled. He was being purposely obtuse. "I wasn't thinking of her looks, just that she's stubborn and thick-headed."

Devon tried to glower, but it made his head ache. He noticed Illiann was attempting to hide her smile, but she couldn't disguise the spark of amusement and challenge in her eyes. "You don't understand the weight I'm carryin'— the reason for my affliction—or you'd be a mite kinder, I'm thinkin'."

She did not respond, but Kit leaned forward eagerly. "Tell us!"

"'Tis unwaverin' I am in my mission to rid the ironworks of the unscrupulous men who run it and make the people suffer. I've been after tellin' the workers how I feel, and the way to change their lot, but they're no' listenin' yet."

Kit stared, open-mouthed. "You mean that boy did this to you just for *talking*?"

"You've a deal to learn yet, Christopher Ivy." Devon's eyes were level with Kit's; even swollen and slitted, the Celtic light singed the boy with its heat. "Talkin', when 'tis done with energy, faith and fury, has more power than any weapon on earth. Guns or knives or cannons can no' match a man with a deep, sweet voice and a cause to believe in."

"No, but a boy on a bicycle can do more than a little damage," Illiann interjected, breaking the tension and Devon's Irish spell.

"Maybe he didn't understand that I'm tryin' to help. But he will in time. They all will." He spoke with more vehemence than was wise, wincing at the various pains in his body.

Illiann sat back on her heels. Devon was enjoying his quick temper; she could see it on his battered face. An old Scottish proverb came to her like a whisper of caution. 'He must needs run, whom the devil drives.' Handsome as he was, and full of fire, this man was dangerous and might well burn any who touched him.

Aware of Kit's distress, Devon tried to divert the boy. "I'd no' mind seein' some of your photographs, lad. To keep me from dyin' of boredom." He gave Illiann a sidelong glance.

Kit looked suspicious. "*You* developed and printed them. You know what they look like." Folding his arms across his chest, the boy sat and glared.

"Oh, but Kit, *I* haven't seen them! I've wanted to for ever so long," his sister said. "I thought you were keeping them a secret."

"I was." His accusatory glare deepened.

"Have pity on an old man, boyo. I'm needin' a little entertainment to distract me from my achin' bones." Devon grimaced, rolled his eyes and moaned.

Grudgingly, the boy rose and went upstairs to get the portfolio his father had given him to hold his photographs. He kept it hidden in his room.

Returning to the parlor, he plopped down on the floor, opened the leather portfolio and handed over half a dozen prints. Devon examined each one critically and at length before making a comment. "Dramatic lightin'," he said about a photograph of an alley full of barefoot children covered in dirt. He said of another that portrayed a father and son walking beside a tall iron fence, "Quite a moment you've captured. 'Tis packed wi' mood and feelin' and shadow. You've a flare for makin' portraits, young Kit. That you have."

Devon passed the photographs to Illiann, who was charmed and impressed by her brother's talent. The pictures told her more clearly than anything before that Kit was growing up. "Why have you been hiding these? They're beautiful." She was amazed and moved by the images spread before her.

Kit brightened. "You mean it?"

"I don't lie. You know that. Nor, I suspect, does Mr. Fitzgerald."

"'Twould be a waste of breath, that. And don't be callin' me Mister Fitzgerald. I'm no' a mister at all: just Devon. Now, Kit, I'm thinkin' 'tis time you start workin' with me in the darkroom, and mayhap learn to develop the plates and print on your own."

The boy was ecstatic; the skin of his face—much lighter than his sister's--glowed. "Can I? I'd work hard." He tried and failed to hide a huge yawn.

"We'll be talkin' about it when I'm better. But for now, 'tis off to bed wi' ye." Devon glanced at Illiann for confirmation.

She nodded. Kit gathered his photographs and went upstairs without protest. Illiann followed, leaving her patient for a moment to change into a wrapper. Afterwards, she settled on the floor beside the sofa to brush out her waist-length hair.

Never one to miss an opportunity, Devon watched her closely. She looked quite different in the muslin wrapper with loosely gathered sleeves and lace along the curved neckline. The pale fabric accented her slightly burnished skin and thick dark hair, which shone as she stroked it with the brush and ran her long graceful fingers through the gleaming strands. He had thought she was all angles and sharp edges, but he had been wrong. Illiann Ivy had the soft allure of a girl who did not yet realize she had become a woman.

Too soon she put away the brush and turned her attention to his wounds. With Saylah's healing bag at hand, she treated Devon with herbs and oils, and then replaced the bandages. She seemed to know without being told that the pain had come back, for she made a new pot of ladyfern tea and propped his head on her lap so he could swallow it. Devon had begun to feel woozy and almost, he could make himself believe an angel had taken Illiann's place.

She massaged him skillfully behind the ears and at the base of his neck; his eyes closed of their own accord. Illiann leaned over and took his hands, rubbing until the blood started flowing again. "You can't go to sleep, Devon Fitzgerald. You know you can't. I'll have to tell you stories."

He hadn't the strength to object.

Illiann got a few pillows and arranged them on the floor to make a seat, leaning one against the sofa, so she could see Devon's eyes. She began to tell him the stories she had learned at Saylah's knee—the haunting rhythmic legends of a time of spirits and miracles.

After awhile she realized the cadence was putting him to sleep, so she sang several native songs, and one Irish jig she had learned from a friend on the ranch.

"Please," he croaked, "something from here."

"But don't you want a story from your homeland? It's filled with magic too."

He muttered something derogatory about magic. "I live in the real world, and that's here and now."

Illiann was astonished by his flat, resolute tone. "I treasure my heritage. It's part of who I am, who my mother is. I'm always causing myself problems by trying to learn more about the Salish."

"There! You see! Clingin' to the past only brings trouble. I've left mine behind, where it belongs!"

All at once, Illiann thought she understood. "Is that why you're so dogged? Because of something that happened in your past?"

She had touched a nerve and he didn't like it. "'Tis my nature to be this way. It's nothin' to do with long ago. I don't believe in holdin' onto to it like 'tis sacred, is all. What's happened, happened. What's gone is gone. Today is all you've got to make things right, or mayhap better." In spite of his unshakable faith in the present, he sounded just a bit discouraged, and not because of his injuries.

Illiann was moved in spite of herself. The more he objected, the more convinced she became that he was lying, perhaps even to himself. "Are you talking about the iron works?"

"Aye. The workers are kept for overly long hours, unprotected and underpaid. They're bein' abused by the very men I mentioned before. Powerful men, wealthy men and owners of such places tend to be aye greedy and dishonest. They rise to the top, tho' I can't be tellin' you why."

He was in pain, his gaze cloudy, and she'd fuelled the anger that never seemed to leave him. "Is that true?"

"Aye, lass, I fear so. How is't you don't know that, living here in Victoria as you do?"

"We've only been here for a couple of months." Her cheeks were nevertheless flushed with embarrassment. "You know that, Devon Fitzgerald."

"Aye, well…" was all he replied.

"Is Papa going to join you on this crusade?" she pressed.

Devon glanced at her with his celtic blue eyes. Was there an edge of incredulity in her voice? He decided to ignore it. "He will indeed, of that I'm certain."

Illiann believed him, but his fervor frightened her. "If you somehow manage to defeat these wealthy unscrupulous men, what will you do then with your passion and your anger? You'll have no one to fight with anymore."

He opened his mouth to answer, then realized there was nothing to say. He had not revealed anything, really, yet this girl—who was barely more than a child, who couldn't possibly understand what he had experienced and how it had forged his future and his fury—had seen, in only an hour or two, straight through to his naked soul.

Chapter 19

Julian and Saylah stood on the balcony off their bedroom, elbows on the railing, gazing over the sloping rooftops of Victoria to the softly undulating water of the bay. For a few moments, it shimmered, gold on stippled blue, radiant with the setting sun. Alone for the first time since dawn, husband and wife had leaned together, not speaking, seduced by the distant luster.

They listened to each other's breathing as they fell under the spell of the cool autumn night. The stillness between them was resonant with things unspoken.

After a long while, Saylah turned to consider her husband's hazel eyes in the settling darkness, his brown hair, brushed back from his face and curling unfashionably below the collar of his shirt. He looked tired, she thought. Tired and troubled. She wanted to ask what was wrong, but the instant she parted her lips, he drew her heavy braid over her shoulder and began to unweave it, strand by strand.

Julian buried his face fleetingly in the scented luster of her thick, dark hair, then let it fall down her back until it settled below her waist, stark black against the soft white of her dressing gown, which fell straight to the floor from the gathers at her shoulders. The wide sleeves billowed as a breeze rippled past.

He almost forgot his disquiet in the filmy half-light that caressed his wife's face. He smiled and she took his ink-stained hands, pressing them palm to palm as she kissed the joined tips of his fingers. "Tell me what is troubling you."

He stood unmoving while the cool night air settled on his skin like mist. "I'm worried about Kit. You should have seen his face when he came racing into the shop this afternoon."

"He is fearless, is he not? Just as your father once was."

"Until he saw Devon on the floor amid the broken glass. He found fear in that moment, though he wasn't looking for it." Pensively, Julian conjured the image of his ailing father, beautiful with the unearthly glow Jamie Ivy had not been able to disguise completely, even at the end, when he had lost his faith. Julian did not ever want to see that expression on Kit's face, watch the light flicker out in his son's bright eyes or the hope turn slowly to defeat. He had not been able to protect his father from disillusionment, but he would protect his son, he vowed in silence.

Kissing her husband lightly on the forehead, where his determination showed in the furrows of his brow, Saylah murmured, "You cannot shield our children from all harm. If you did, you would also protect them from the chance to find joy and adventure and triumph and love. Would you take those things from Illiann and Kit along with the danger?"

Julian opened his eyes, which he had not realized were closed, unclenched his hands and turned from memory to the image of his wife's compelling face. She had guessed what he was thinking, but that did not surprise him, especially because she shared his concern.

"I know. I just want them to be strong and unafraid."

"You mean indestructible."

Julian grinned at his own foolishness. "Yes. I'm afraid I'm a dreamer like my father after all."

"You always have been," she said with affection. "You cannot help yourself. Nor can I." She noticed for the first time a kind of tension in his body that had nothing to do with anxiety. "There is something else?"

"More dreaming, I'm afraid." Julian ran his fingers through his hair and tried to explain. "I realize Devon is mad as a hatter, that he's stubborn and unwise and too full of ideals. He goes about trying to prove what he believes in the wrong way, but he believes so fervently, so passionately."

"You envy him?"

"Perhaps a little. But I also have ideals and goals, and, like him, I want to change things. Only I'm sure there's a better way to go about it. Obviously his broadsides and rabblerousing have been a disaster. After what happened today, I've been thinking maybe we can use *The Voice*. More gently, more slowly, so people don't realize they're beginning to think differently. Devon's young and rash, but I have had a great deal of experience with being patient. Perhaps too much."

Saylah nodded. "So you have." She liked the breathless way he spoke, the exhilaration in his voice. "With Devon's youth and your wisdom and imagination, I know you can make a difference. I always knew it, from the first time you told me about the print shop." She paused, eyes sparkling. "You know, I think *The Voice* might be a good way to teach Kit about the world and keep him close at the same time."

"As long as he does not neglect his schoolwork."

There was little likelihood of that. Kit always did his schoolwork with little effort. It came to him naturally, as so many things did. Julian thought sometimes that perhaps too much came easily to Kit. He had never learned to fight for what he wanted, never learned what it meant to lose. He kept the thought to himself, though he suspected his wife had sensed it from his expression. "He's at the shop every afternoon anyway. And he loves taking photographs, especially portraits of children and people in the street. He's rather good at it, actually. I was telling Casey earlier that I want to use photography to change the look of the paper. Kit could be part of it." He was making plans faster than he could put them into words. Only when the murmur of his daughter's voice, singing a Salish song, rose from the open window below did he stop still. Julian frowned. "Illiann."

"Yes, Illiann." Saylah grew serious. "She too is growing up."

"Our daughter is fierce and resilient, like you. I don't doubt she will make her own way in the world."

"She will—eventually. She is open enough and resolute enough. But I think just now, she is struggling with her past and the prospect of becoming a woman, though I do not think she has recognized it yet." Saylah told him about her conversation with Illiann on the way home, about the girl's frustration and desire. "She wants everyone to understand what it is to be Salish, because she herself wants to understand. She knows they can't explain it to her, but she keeps asking nonetheless."

"You can tell her." Julian was perplexed by the strain in his wife's voice.

Saylah blinked, sighed and locked her hands behind his back. "I suppose I am wary of sharing my knowledge with Illiann, of examining it myself. But today something happened, and it changed me somehow. I met an old Indian woman at the wharf." Saylah described the strange meeting, Old Grandmother with her mystical knowledge, the hidden inlet and the walk through a tangled forest leading to the moment on the beach when sand and stone and water had seduced her.

Julian felt the same sharp fear he had when Saylah first mentioned being restless, when she'd said she needed to seek out new stories. Her face was transformed as she spoke: her cheeks glowed and her eyes shifted to opaque green, except for the flicker of fire in their depths. He wanted to forbid her to see the old woman again, but of course he could not. Saylah had obeyed nothing all her life except the expectations of her People and the urgings of her soul. Yet he could not bear to lose her, and the Salish were the only force strong enough to pull her away.

Wisely, he did not speak of his fear; it would not be fair to her. She had followed him here because of his dream, and he would not try to stop her from following her own. Besides, in spite of himself, he could not help but respond to her animation—the anticipation that touched her with youth, vitality and hope.

Struggling to speak around the lump in his throat, he drew her close and murmured, "It will be exciting to see what the future holds for us."

Saylah met his gaze earnestly. "Even if it holds the past?"

"Even then."

Chapter 20

Simone awoke to the sound of thunder, the brilliance of lightning, the violence of rain that lashed the windows. She hurried out of bed and cracked open the leaded glass. Despite the heavy clouds that layered the sky, there was a faint thread of light along the horizon.

The door opened, and a young girl stuck her head in. "Madame?" she said tentatively.

Simone's attention was on the turbulence in the air, and she did not hear. The cathedral bells rang out, softer than thunder, yet clearer and more poignant to her sensitive ears.

"Madame?" the girl repeated.

Simone turned, startled, as a wash of rain swept over her. "Claire! You should be asleep." Behind her, lightning transformed the watery sky into quicksilver. "As for me, because there is a storm, and because it is just past dawn, I will go out. There will be no one to see."

"I know. That is why I have come." Sometimes, when she thought it was safe, Simone went to the Cathedral to pray in one of the darkened alcoves. "I guessed you might, and I did not want you to go without some tea and a little food." The girl nodded toward the silver tray she was balancing precariously. "Marcel made tiny cakes, and I found a pear."

Claire was worried. She had just turned fourteen and, in her newfound maturity, she was beginning to understand how complicated Simone's life was. "Mathilde always says you don't eat enough, that you don't take care of yourself."

Simone was touched by the children's gesture. "Claire, *ma petiite*, I did not bring you and Marcel here so you might wait on me."

"But you have done so much already. The Duc has taught us to ride; Mathilde is instructing us in cooking, and

Marcel is so happy with his painting master. We *wanted* to do this, to thank you." In her enthusiasm, she stumbled; the china teapot teetered and fell, spilling amber liquid across the priceless rug.

Claire was horrified, but Simone shook her head gently.

"It does not matter. These things can be replaced." She smiled. "I am grateful you are so thoughtful." She knelt to retrieve the teapot and broken lid."But I want you to have fun, not always to worry and struggle. I want to care for you, not have you care for me."

She delighted in seeing their faces, once grim and drawn, brighten with expectation. Besides, they were a kind of atonement for her sins.

The thunder rumbled and she rose. "I must go."

While she put on a simple gray damask gown, Claire found her shimmering silver rain cloak. Hair still tumbled around her shoulders, Simone took one tiny cake and the pear, and then flung her cloak about her.

"May God be with you," Claire murmured.

Simone smiled softly. "Perhaps today He will be."

Chapter 21

In her dream, Saylah stood naked in water that swirled gently about her waist. She stared at the sky while the stars drifted down until they floated on the surface of the pond and she touched them with her outstretched hands. Far away, carried on the wind, she heard a name, a distant sound that curled among the treetops, too high for her to reach. She listened, enthralled, while the stars played over the dark rippled water, but she could not hear the name, only its echo and its promise. She needed the sound and texture of that word to add to the soothing motion of water and stars. For with that name came peace. *Come to me. Come easy. Come.* It taunted her, enticed her, and in the end, left her unsatisfied.

She awoke reaching upward with both hands to capture a sound and a feeling she could not grasp. The dream had not come for a long time. Not since she had chosen to marry Julian sixteen years ago. Before she made that choice, it had haunted her, since the night she left her village and her People. Odd that it should return to her now.

You have had other names, and you will find still more.

Saylah raised her head, certain she had heard a voice and not a memory. But she and Julian were alone in the room. Julian still slept; she listened with relief to the sound of his breath, the sighs of his dreams. It came to her then that the voice was Old Grandmother's. The woman had touched Saylah through her dream. She could feel the plea curl in the air like smoke, like mist that spiraled up from the sea to wind itself into the tops of the tall trees—ethereal and infinitely fragile.

Instinctively, Saylah reached for the stones that formed a half-circle on the low table beside the bed. She picked them up one by one, rubbed their familiar, smooth surfaces. These had become her sacred objects, cold to her touch, because she had not held them in so long.

She picked up the loon her daughter had made for her and cupped it in her palms. The voice still lingered, drifted about her shoulders, calling, tugging gently at her heart, her Salish soul. So quietly that it was little more than a breath released, she sang a Salish prayer.

Julian did not stir, though Saylah's silver voice slipped into his dreams, and he smiled, unconscious.

The voice like smoke came closer, echoed softly in her ear. She could no longer ignore its call. She must go see Old Grandmother again; the frantic rhythm of her heartbeat told her it was time.

The voice fell silent.

Chapter 22

When Sophia knew her husband was out helping to round up the straying cattle before the weather turned bitterly cold, she picked up an oil lamp and headed for the basement. The bolt was locked once again, but this time she had the key—the extra that hung with the others in the small cupboard she had set up years before in case there was some kind of emergency and the extras were needed. That had been so long ago that Edward must have forgotten.

"He seems to have forgotten a lot of things," she whispered to herself, breathing deeply to suppress the sudden ache in her chest. Balancing the lamp with care, she placed the key in the lock and turned it, expecting resistance—but there was none. Edward must have oiled the bolt. Shivering at the realization, and not at all certain why, she opened the latch and climbed downward, searching for some clue to her husband's secret demons.

Lamp held high, she stopped still at the bottom of the worn stone steps, mouth open in astonishment. While the basement was as chilly and damp as always, someone—it had to be Edward—had put everything away, closed all the chests, then swept the floor and dusted the trunks. It was not like him at all. It came to her then that she could not pick out the chest he had been rifling through the day before.

She recognized their son Paul's possessions in trunks in one corner—everything they'd kept from when he was a baby. But other than those, she had no idea where anything was. Had Edward moved the chests and trunks intentionally, so she would be lost in her own basement?

And if so, why? "Why, Edward? What are you hiding?" Sophia felt ill.

Just then she noticed a discarded bookcase with a cracked shelf standing halfway across the room. It was empty except for a pile of papers near the bottom. Her heartbeat increased until she could hear the blood pounding in her ears. Stumbling forward, she knelt, reached out to touch what she now saw was the post, then withdrew her hand. Another secret hidden away?

Sophia sat unmoving until her knees began to ache and her feet to go numb. She surprised herself by ignoring her green velvet gown and sitting flat on the floor. With one hand, she swept the post into her lap, regarding it warily. The chill in the room cloaked her like ice. "Don't be ridiculous, Sophia," she said in an effort to break the unnatural stillness. "It's merely five innocuous letters, tossed here by accident, no doubt."

But she did not quite believe it. As she shuffled through the pile, her pulse returned to normal. *Innocuous, just as I suspected.* Then she came to last one, from Saylah and Julian, catching Edward and Sophia up on what was happening in Victoria and ending with an invitation for the Ashtons to come visit.

Sophia began to pick invisible lint from her skirt. There was nothing urgent in that letter, nothing dangerous, nor anything to cause fear. Yet here the post lay in the basement. She noticed the date was over a week ago. So this too Edward had hidden from her. She knew it as certainly as she felt the damp seeping into her bones.

She could no longer stay pent up in the house. Determined to find some relief, she headed for the stables.

She took her heavy velvet cloak and flung it over her green muslin gown, pulled on riding boots and set out toward the barn.

Brutus bounded at her side, hurrying ahead, then rushing back, excited by the prospect of a good run. Sophia saddled her mare with skill and fury. Despite the heavy morning fog, she was not troubled by the blank white wilderness before her, but only by Edward's secrets.

Enveloped by stillness, she mounted the mare. Holding the reins in tense fingers, she crossed her arms and held her loneliness close to her chest, protecting it like a frightened animal she sought to soothe. But the hurt and confusion did not go.

Sophia had never been shut out like this before. It was clear her husband did not want her here, and she needed to be away.

Perhaps Edward could conquer his demons alone.

Chapter 23

It was a week after Devon's accident when Saylah put on her deerskin cape, collected her healing bag, and made her way down to the wharves. She did not know how she would get across the harbor, but was certain there were Salish with canoes along the shore, bringing their fish or their baskets or weaving to sell. Perhaps she could pay one to take her to the neglected dock.

To her surprise, when she arrived at the spot where Old Grandmother had hidden her boat the first time they met, Saylah found a small canoe placed carefully among the tall ferns and reeds. Bending down to examine it, she discovered a worn strip of leather holding four tiny carvings—Wolf, white crested Owl, Raven and Thunderbird. Though she had not seen the figures for many years, she knew them keenly and at once.

Her breath caught and she had to struggle for air as an intense awareness of the past overwhelmed her like a wave whipped to fury by a fierce winter storm. She forced herself to touch the figures cautiously and then to grasp them in her fist. These four animals were the spirits who bestowed on a child the strength and authority of the Revered Ancestors, the Dreamer, the Dancer and the Healer. These four had converged on the hut in which Saylah had been born. They had given her the gifts of skill, influence, power and the promise of her future —and that of her People. These four had decided the shape and texture of her life; they had prophesied her name; they had blessed her and cursed her from the moment of her birth.

Now, over thirty years later, Old Grandmother had returned those spirits to her, and, in tying them to the canoe, had issued an invitation. Or was it a command?

The frantic fluttering of tiny wings distracted Saylah. She looked up into the shadowy places among the firs to find a flicker hovering, its vivid yellow body a bright contrast to the deep green branches. Suspended above her, the bird seemed to wait, then, suddenly, to fly towards the water and back. She followed it with her eyes.

Toward the end of the summer when she had been transformed into a woman, just such a flicker had come to her in a waking dream. It had led and she had followed, to a prophecy she had not understood until that autumn, when she had become an exile from her family and her home.

The flicker came so close that she could look into its eyes through the blur of wings. Before she could reach out to touch it, the bird flew toward the shore, back to her, and again toward the shore.

She knew then, as she had known that long-ago summer at the end of her childhood, that she must follow. She could not resist the call of the spirits and the diminutive bird, waiting for her in the lacey spray of a wave upon the rocky shore.

Chapter 24

Simone crept silently down the stairs and out into the street, where she lifted her face to the sky and dropped the hood of her cloak so the rain could touch her. She drank it in like wine for a long moment.

"Holy Mother, Mary and Joseph! Came upon me like a ghost!" Mathilde clutched her chest dramatically. "Heart's stopped beatin' from the fright."

Simone was relieved to see her friend's masculine hat with the lace mantilla flapping underneath. Her face was indistinct in the rain, her shapeless dress more shapeless than before, the color blurred to gray. "No matter how early I rise, you have always been out before me."

Mathilde shrugged. "Why not, I'd like to know? Cathedral's quiet early, before the whole town goes to say their prayers. Much good it will do them," she added under her breath, addressing a ripple in the overflowing gutter. "Not enough prayers in all the world to make their black souls white again. Dirty your fingers just touchin' their coattails. Though there *are* those who try to buy their way to Heaven." Her black eyes glittered with satisfaction.

"Take de M, for instance." She glared up at the sky, as if berating the heavy clouds. "Marie Cecile dragged me to church in the dark and showed me a string of rubies in Saint Catherine's hand. Poor Henri—losin' so many of his family jewels. 'S why can't get that young wife with child." Mathilde grinned wickedly. "No doubt on her knees with prayers of thanks for it."

She tilted her head like a curious bird. "Think that's her plan? To drain his manhood *and* his treasury? Must remember to give her more credit. The merchants certainly won't." Mathilde threw back her head to laugh at her own joke, and her hat fell off and tumbled into the gutter. She cried out and chased it, arms flapping, mantilla clinging by a thread to her gray tufts of hair. "Don't wait for me," she shouted over her shoulder. "Catch the damned thing if it knocks me flat. Know where to find me by my handkerchief, left to flap out the window in the wind."

Simone watched helplessly as Mathilde's boxy figure retreated, stumbling on the uneven cobblestones. She tilted one way and then another, like a barge on a bilious sea. Finally, she pounced toward the sidewalk, but Simone could no longer hear, and could not tell if her cry was one of triumph or distress. Whichever it was, she reminded herself, Mathilde would survive. As she said herself, proudly and often, *Too old, stubborn, loud and ugly for God to waste his time on. More important things on his mind. Can't be bothered with the likes of me.*

Smiling with affection, Simone went on her way, following cobbled streets that twisted toward the Seine. Ancient timbered buildings crowded the narrow streets, punctuated by gothic churches with flying buttresses of stone. It might have been intimidating if it was not so familiar.

Head bent, she quickened her pace and nearly collided with Madame Arnaud, who was collecting barrels of rainwater.

"Ah, Madame de Marchand. I have prayed for you this week. I have made many novenas for your soul. My Marcel and Claire are so happy now that you have taken them into your home." The woman put a callused hand on Simone's sleeve. "You have given them hope, Madame. All the blessed nuns and priests, all the sainted ladies in France could not do that for my son. That is how I know your heart is pure, that they are mistaken who speak ill of you."

The depth of the other woman's conviction startled Simone. Not so long ago, she had seen Marcel running wild, had recognized the intelligence and misery in his eyes. She had called the boy and his sister to her and, gradually, his despair had begun to fade, his hope to be born. But that did not make up for her own weakness. "I have sinned," she said. "They do not lie who say so."

"We've all sinned, come to that, but not all have learned kindness and generosity. Not all have learned to see the pain of others and ease it. Marcel and Claire are not the first you have given a future where none was possible before. Do not tell me of your sins. I am listening to other voices."

With that, Madame Arnaud swept her wool cape closed and went inside her husband's butcher shop.

Touched and bemused, Simone headed for the cathedral. A few minutes later, she arrived, pausing before the ornate wooden doors.

How often had she stood like this, tracing the carving, the cracks and warps and indentations of many hands through many centuries? She pressed her soft white cheek against the wood. As she reached for the iron handle, the church bells began to ring, and an old woman appeared from inside the church.

She stopped to glance suspiciously at Simone. "You should not be here," she said sharply. "You are forbidden."

Thunder exploded and the stone church trembled. *You are forbidden to grieve on a day so beautiful,* Jamie had once told her. When he realized she was longing for the comforts of her religion, he had held her and kissed her until she smiled. Later that week, she had come in with an armful of wild roses to find a priest eating heartily at the kitchen table. He had turned, put out his hand and murmured, 'My child, your husband tells me you have missed the Church, and that you wish to make confession. So I have come.' Over Father Bouchard's head, Simone had met her husband's gaze, her eyes filled with tears of gratitude.

She had not meant to confess, but her fear and guilt had been too powerful to resist. She had told the good father everything, and in the end, he had forced her awake, out of the dream of her happiness, and Jamie's and Julian's.

As the old woman slipped away, Simone realized the doors were too heavy after all. She could not make herself go inside. She began to walk, head bent against the rain. Despite her resolution, when she passed the graveyard, she stopped to stare at the gray carved stones. Her mother was buried here, under a shady tree, but her father's body lay elsewhere. He was buried at the crossroads outside the city. He, too, had been cast out by the Church in the end.

Simone had never gone to the lonely crossroads. She was not strong enough for that.

On impulse, she turned and turned again until she stood beside the Cathedral of Ouen. The clouds were violent and threatening, but the sun broke though briefly, lighting the church with an ethereal glow.

Once, she had been seduced by that glow; it had given her hope in the midst of confusion and apprehension. The cathedral rose in front of her as it had that day so many years ago, full of the faithful, her friends, her father's family, the de Marchands, and Henri de Marchand himself.

Simone had hovered outside the great doors, dressed in white silk and lace, her dead mother's pearls wound into her dark hair, covered by a veil so fine it seemed woven of light. She had looked up at her father pleadingly. "Why, Papa? Why now? Why have you not spoken to me in so long?" He had told her of the engagement, then left for Paris to see to her dowry, to make certain nothing went awry in this binding of two old and revered families. Why then had Simone felt so certain he was running away?

Alphonse Destranges did not meet his daughter's eyes. He was remote and chilly. "Because you are no longer a child," he said impatiently. "Because now you look like a woman, like your mother when I met her."

Simone did not understand. Her father had told her the same thing over and over, but he would not explain. So there they stood, her white hand on his arm, while 30-year-old Henri de Marchand waited.

They swept into the cathedral and the organ music swelled to carry them down the virgin white carpet toward the altar. The bride did not notice the scattered flower petals. All she knew was that her father's arm was rigid beneath her hand, that his face was pallid and set in unfamiliar lines.

Suddenly, the sun broke free of the clouds, shimmering through stained glass windows that rose from the ground to the high vaulted ceiling. The congregation gasped as the tinted light fell across Simone's flowing gown and veil.

Streams of blue and red and gold enveloped the bride as she approached her groom. The cathedral glowed from end to end when Alphonse Destranges gave his daughter's hand into de Marchand's. They turned, bathed in dancing colors, to be married.

Simone felt her father watching with eyes so full of regret and sadness that it broke her heart; it was no longer whole to give to the man who stood beside her. The priest spoke the ancient Latin words binding the two as man and wife, and de Marchand grinned down at his bride gloatingly, until she trembled.

Yet Simone was certain God was there in that breathtakingly beautiful light, that glow too lovely to be real. She looked to the sky, made into leaded fragments by the fine stained glass, and prayed with all her passion and fear and hope. "Let him be good to me. Let my terror be of my own imagining. Let me be happy in this life I have not chosen."

She had put all her faith in that brilliant hued light, but it had been an illusion that disappeared with the passage of the sun. The truth had been far worse than her fears. No matter how often her father had told her she looked like a woman, she was still a child and could not have imagined the horror awaiting her.

The colored light, the sacred vows, the Church itself had betrayed her.

It was her birthday on the afternoon of her sunlit rainbow wedding. She had just turned fifteen.

Late, very late that night, she fled France for what she thought was forever.

Three months later, she met and married Jamie Ivy.

Chapter 25

A man was waiting when Saylah pushed her boat into the reeds and climbed the shaky ladder to the dock where she had first landed on this wild peninsula.

"You are Saylah, are you not?" he asked. "I am Patal, the grandson of Old Grandmother. She has sent me to meet you."

He was tall, his black hair worn in a single short braid, his muscled arms and callused hands revealing that he worked hard to provide for himself and his grandmother. "I am glad you came. I am not certain I could find my way through the forest on my own."

Patal smiled. "If you could not, then you are not the woman my grandmother is expecting. She says you can make miracles."

"She exaggerates."

"Does she?" He raised a quizzical eyebrow. Without another word, he started away. Saylah tucked up her skirts and followed him into the lush, verdant stillness of the trees. When they came out onto a wide swath of land, she paused to take in her surroundings.

The reservation was a small village poised between the dense forest full of life and noise and motion, and the peaceful waters of the bay. There were twenty frame houses grouped around the ruins of the decaying Longhouse. Part of the cedar walls remained, though they were crumbling under the onslaught of salal and lichens that had crept from among the trees. Four giant carvings marked the corners of the building which had once housed the entire village. Though the paint was faded and the edges dulled with time, the features of Whale and Eagle, Frog and a human figure were still visible.

Saylah recognized Old Grandmother's house long before they reached it by the totem that stood in front—a woman crouching, sturdy yet graceful, who held the faces of her people in the circle of her arms. Her long braids twined with her fingers to reinforce her grasp. The doorway was a large oval in the totem. Old Grandmother stood in the traditional entrance, smiling when she saw that Saylah wore the figures of her spirit guides on a thong around her neck.

When the old woman beckoned, Patal melted away and Saylah stepped into the two-room house with its clean white walls and a thick rug on the scrubbed pine floor. There were fir boughs above the door and on the table, so the rooms smelled of the forest touched by the tang of an ocean wind.

Old Grandmother stood back, allowing the younger woman to look around, knowing she would be drawn inexorably to the two large cedar chests.

Saylah knelt before them, running her fingers over images of Raven, Whale and Deer, carved and stained with red and black.

"Do not hesitate," Old Grandmother said. "Open them."

Saylah smiled and lifted the first lid.

The air was hushed and cool, and the fragrance of cedar rose around her. She touched with reverence the finely woven blankets and robes, shawls and rugs that filled the chest. Some were heavy and soft, to cradle the wearer and keep out the chill of winter, some filmy as the fragile webs of spiders in the sun.

"These are beautiful," she cried, overwhelmed by the workmanship and time each piece had taken.

"I hold them here until the day comes when a stranger reaches out, as you do, to caress the woven strands."

Saylah looked doubtful.

"You must have faith, *ladaila*, as I do. But why do we linger inside? It is warm and the beach is inviting. Come."

They made their way down a sloping path to a cove where a loom and a long wooden box lay sheltered by the bluff. The two women sat cross-legged and barefoot on the sand.

Saylah listened, taking the sound and cadence of the waves into herself. She gazed with contentment at the beach bathed in sunlight and felt the healing power of that light upon her skin, let it sink into her pores and warm her from inside.

"It is my favorite place," Old Grandmother announced.

They sat in companionable silence, eating a stew of mussels, scallops and clams from cedar bowls. When they had finished, the silence lingered. As Saylah put her bowl aside, she looked up to find Old Grandmother watching and waiting.

"There is something you want from me, is there not?"

"Yes. We need your silver voice. My dreams have told me it is time to give my stories into someone else's keeping, and I trust them only to you, who lives in both worlds."

Saylah was speechless.

"You think it is a blessing, this passing of traditions, but it can also become a duty, and then, too quickly, a burden. Only because you are one of the People can you understand how necessary it is."

"A long time ago, I chose to be of the People no longer." In the beginning, she had cherished those in her village, believing in them wholly—until they destroyed her faith. She had loved them and resented them, blamed them, raged at their ghosts, and finally, forgiven them and set them free. She had returned to the place of her birth only once after she met Julian, and then from nearby and in a dream, to make certain she would not regret the choice she was about to make. Never again had she approached their beaches or forest, their Longhouse or sacred streams.

"You can change your dress, your speech, your language and your customs, but you cannot change the flow of your blood. You were born of the People; you cannot alter that fact, ever," Old Grandmother admonished her. "You can try to forget, try not to dream or remember, but you will not succeed. Your soul is Salish, and your spirit. You know that, Tanu, and have always known it."

The old woman had used the name Tanu, the Salish word for Queen. No one had called her Queen for many years, and the sound was unbearably sweet. Once it had tasted like poison, but no longer. Perhaps, after all, during the secure and happy years of her marriage, she had outgrown the ache of memory.

"We can speak our stories and pass them thus to our children, and our children to their children. But there are few written symbols for the words we speak, as there are for the words of the White man. Because of that, our history is fleeting, dependent on the voices that pass it from one to another."

The old woman touched Saylah's hand. "I ask you to give them a significance that cannot be forgotten or washed away as the People grow silent, one by one. Give them words written in ink, so they can *see* our voices long after we speak no more. Write out our legends and our history, and in that written silence, make us immortal."

Chapter 26

Edward Ashton could not find his hat. Time and again, he stopped to scratch his sandy head in confusion. He knew he'd had it when he left the house. But then, he'd had Sophia when he left the house, or at least, he thought he had, and now he'd lost her too. His greatcoat lay in the front hall, forgotten, and the evening was chilly. He had lost his waistcoat and wandered about in his shirtsleeves, befuddled. The only thing he could find was a bottle of whiskey, which he brought repeatedly to his chapped lips. He held tightly to the tall neck, afraid if he weren't careful, he would lose this comfort too.

He staggered, slipped and sat down abruptly among damp clumps of bracken, then wondered how he'd gotten there. He lifted the bottle suspiciously, but it was still cold and solid in his hand. He stared through the amber liquid, watching it slosh from side to side, transforming the woods from a murky underwater kingdom to a vivid tangle of branches and greenery.

"Shhophiiia!" he shouted in a voice so slurred it did not sound like his own. Edward glanced over his shoulder to see if someone else was calling his wife, but he saw only a huge red cedar, its branches rustling with the invisible movement of birds and squirrels and a gentle wind.

"Where are you, Sophia? You forgot to come home." The words sounded hollow, and he wanted to weep, but couldn't remember why.

He heard footsteps and his heart pounded with gratitude. Sophia was coming at last. He felt vaguely uneasy, like he'd done something wrong to make his wife angry, but he pushed the thought away resolutely.

The footsteps stopped and he saw a pair of button top boots and the hem of a lilac skirt heavy with dew. He looked up, grinning, into Mary Clarke's face. Edward narrowed his eyes. Did she take him for a fool? Pretending to be Sophia like that. Did she think he wouldn't know the difference?

"Edward! What in God's name are you doing out here?" Her astonishment was tempered with simmering anger and a humiliation so deep that she did not recognize it herself. She had not seen Edward Ashton since the morning when he'd told her the truth, and for that she prayed in gratitude and supplication every day.

Mary rubbed her arms, shivering. She wanted more than anything to walk away, to turn her back on the man who had hurt her so much that even now, the pain swept through her like an icy wind. Yet she stood firm, regarding him through pale blue eyes, trapped by the sight of his drunken vulnerability. The dapper and charming Edward Ashton sat in a clump of bracken, a whiskey bottle clutched in one hand, wearing a wrinkled linen shirt and trousers that would soon be ruined, if they weren't already. His hair was dirty and unkempt, and he had not shaved for several days.

With difficulty, Mary found her voice. "You don't look well, and it's chilly tonight." She could not force herself to speak his name, as if they were comfortable acquaintances or even friends. That would have been too much of a lie.

When Edward blinked at her, uncomprehending, she said sharply, "You're shivering. Do you want me to take you home?"

His eyes were bleary and unfocused until a flash of cunning lit them from within. He raised his hand and shook his finger at Mary. "*You* took my hat, didn't you? And my waistcoat and jacket! You've hidden them in the woods so I'm forced to play hide and seek with you. Well, it won't work. I'm waiting for Sophia."

Mary knew Sophia was gone. Everyone knew. Sighing, she struggled to put her fury aside. Whatever he had done, she couldn't leave him here like this. Tears flooded her eyes, and she was shocked to realize they were tears of pity.

She grasped Edward's accusing finger and held on until she had his attention. "Come with me. You need some coffee and a bath."

Edward tried unsuccessfully to regain the use of his captured finger, but Mary held it too tightly. "I'm not leaving until you return my hat!" he declared. "Where have you hidden it? You'd best just tell me straight away, or I'll have to force it out of you."

Mary felt an unsympathetic desire to laugh. "Might those be the things you're looking for?" She pointed to a tall sapling, covered with a neatly hung jacket, waistcoat, and, perched jauntily on a jutting branch, a fine beaver top hat.

Edward squinted in that direction. "Thought that was one of the McKinnon boys spying on me again," he muttered. "So that's your game, is it, Mary Clarke? Trying to frighten me back under the covers. And me a grown, intelligent man."

Mary shook her head. "Grown you may be, but that's as far as I'm willing to go at the moment. Come, Edward. You'll make yourself ill if you stay out here."

Edward tottered to his feet. "Never been ill a day in my life. You'd do well to remember that." After only two abortive efforts, he managed to cross his arms and huff, "I'm not going anywhere without my hat."

For a moment, Mary thought he might actually stick his tongue out at her, but he settled for a threatening glare that was more of a pout than anything else. She removed the garments from the sapling and handed them to Edward, who stared at them blankly.

"What am I supposed to do with these?" he demanded, completely flummoxed. Did she expect him to dress in the woods? Had she lost her mind? "Better be kind to her, just in case," he muttered under his breath. "Never know what lunatics might do."

"Stick them in your hat for all I care," Mary said, exasperated. He was worse off than she'd thought. "I'm taking you home, and that's all there is to it."

Edward swayed alarmingly. "Going visiting? Have to wear my hat. Only proper, don't you know. Can't be rude to the host." He reached up clumsily to put the hat on his head, where it rested askew on his disheveled hair. "Now," he said, straightening his shoulders and nearly toppling backward into the bracken. "S'all right now."

"Yes, it's all right." Mary was torn between laughter and tears as she took Edward's arm firmly and led him toward her small two-room cottage.

Apparently satisfied by her assurances, Edward went docilely enough. He waited while she opened the door, allowed her to guide him to the wingback chair by the fire, where he sat scratching his three-day growth of beard, unaware that his wet trousers made a spot on the flowered chintz. He was fascinated by the flames, and sat motionless, staring, moving only to adjust the angle of his hat at regular intervals.

When Mary handed him a mug of coffee, he took a sip, then gasped and glowered. "This isn't whiskey. Where's my whiskey? You've probably hidden it in my hat."

Mary opened her mouth, closed it, opened it again. "Actually, that's precisely what I did. And you won't find it tonight. Drink your coffee while I heat some water for your bath."

Edward rose up, flushed with wrath. Mary pushed him down into the chair with her index finger, as startled as he by her easy success. "I'm being very nice to you," she pointed out calmly, "and you certainly don't deserve my kindness. So at least be quiet and don't fight me anymore. I don't expect gratitude. Miracles are in short supply of late."

Still looking puzzled, Edward did as she asked while she moved him into the kitchen next to a basin of warm water. She washed his hair and combed it out, then shaved him gently, afraid and hopeful that, at any moment, he might stand up to object and make her cut his throat by mistake.

But Edward had run out of energy. He slumped forward, turning when she asked, holding a warm towel under his chin.

Mary looked into his eyes and saw the gold flecks had nearly disappeared. His eyes were bloodshot and surrounded by dark circles. His skin was slightly gray; no doubt he had not slept for days. Without thinking, she ran her hand through his damp, sandy hair. He looked up at her pleadingly. She did not know what he was asking for, but she realized with alarm that she was enjoying this.

For once, it was not she who needed *him* to make her feel worthwhile, nor did he want her body to assuage his own distress. Edward needed her to take care of him tonight. She had never hoped for that.

"I'm tired," he whispered as she dumped the water into the metal sink. He looked desperate, cold and alone.

Mary drew him up and guided him to the bedroom. While he stood silent, she removed his wet trousers. She went out to hang them near the fire, and removed her own clothes in the crackling warmth. When she returned to the bedroom in her chemise, Edward was sitting on the bed, looking lost.

Brow furrowed, he watched her unpin her hair, then untwist the braid and shake her head. He was wearing his hat again. She got into bed beside him, removed the top hat and hung it on the bedpost. Edward touched her shoulder tentatively.

"Sophia's gone."

Mary felt no lingering spark of anger, and that astonished her. She had lived off her fury since that morning at the Ivy ranch, fed on it as if it were meat, and all she had to sustain her. Now, quite suddenly, it was gone. She drew Edward's head down beside hers on the pillow and whispered against his parted lips, "Only for a little while. She'll be back before you know it, waiting in the hall with your top hat brushed and gleaming in her hand."

Edward smiled and collapsed into sleep.

Chapter 27

Illiann approached Miss. Chadwick's School for Young Ladies with anticipation and determination. In a way, she had made her choice for today's assignment because of Devon and his passionate aversion to the past. *I don't believe in holdin' on to it like 'tis sacred. What's happened happened. What's gone is gone.* The more he argued it was best to forget, the more she remembered. Her mother had started her thinking that way when she said; *Perhaps* **you** *will have to teach* **them**. Devon had only encouraged her. *Today's all we've got to make things right.* He didn't realize that simple statement had made the decision for her. Today she would risk a great deal to show her reverence for the Salish culture.

She could hardly wait.

Early this morning, she had made certain her plain white shirtwaist was clean and ironed, her blue wool skirt unwrinkled. She had braided her hair and wound it irreproachably about her head, had even shined her black button boots. She had smiled through all these tedious chores, eager, for once, to be on her way.

When she reached the inner gate at the school, Miss Reynolds was on duty.

At the sight of her, the teacher narrowed her eyes and pursed her lips, emphasizing the pallor of her parchment face, her dull gray hair pulled tight into a bun. "I've told you more than once, Illiann, that we prefer you be early so we can organize the young ladies."

Illiann had always wondered how one 'organzied' a group of girls headed for the same innocuous classroom, the same uncluttered desks, and the same dry, unrevealing lessons. It was all part of the puzzle that was Miss

Chadwick's. But she held her tongue and looked up with wide innocent eyes. "I'm so sorry. I'll try very hard not to come on time again."

Miss Reynolds glowered. Illiann Ivy was a troublemaker. Today she carried a bulky leather bag over her shoulder. Miss Reynolds stared at it pointedly but did not ask what was inside. It was far too early for a battle. In the teacher's opinion, the girl was too clever for her own good. "Well, see that you do, or rather, don't." Illiann had confused her again.

"Yes, ma'am. Or no ma'am. Of course."

Illian was being polite and obedient. Miss Reynolds was suspicious. Feeling distinctly uneasy, the teacher turned to lead the way into the three-story brick building shaded by spreading oaks.

Illiann followed, swinging her leather bag. When Miss Reynolds disappeared inside, she grinned and pulled the door closed behind her.

~ * ~

The rumor spread quickly through the school. Laura Hart had noticed Illiann's bag, her flushed cheeks and secret smile. She was up to something, no doubt about it. Even the girls who disliked Illiann had learned to recognize when she would do something exciting to shatter the boredom at school. Laura Hart was waiting, as were the others, because Illiann was more secretive than usual, and her eyes had an intriguing gleam.

By late afternoon, Laura guessed Illiann would reveal her surprise during deportment class. Today each pupil was to perform a dance of her own devising.

"Don't think of the traditional steps," the instructor, Miss Worthy, had told them, round face beaming. "Be creative. You are to show us something about yourself in this little dance. Three minutes each. Don't forget. I want you to surprise me."

"But she doesn't," Laura Hart had sighed. "Not really." She was fairly certain Illiann meant to surprise Miss Worthy regardless. Laura encouraged everyone to hurry into their sports outfits so they wouldn't miss a moment, and she started a whispered rumor at the back of the younger class. It spread rapidly through the room, making the girls wriggle in their chairs with expectation.

Those in the upper class assembled as usual on the floor of the large, echoing room used as a gym. Each wore a blue striped pinafore with long, gathered sleeves. The wide skirt ended halfway down the calves to reveal matching striped bloomers and high button shoes of soft white leather. Each girl's hair was caught up under a matching striped cap.

Illiann secretly shook her head over these outfits intended for 'physical activity.' She claimed they were more cumbersome than regular gowns.

Laura had hoped the other girl would defy convention and wear what she liked, but there she sat primly on the floor, ankles crossed and hands in her lap, her hair covered properly by her cap. Still, she did have the leather bag with her. Laura motioned the other girls forward, her heart beating with excitement.

She had unlatched the back door of the gym, and as the first few girls did their dances, the girls from the younger class began to creep in, crowding behind a tangled pile of nets and equipment. They peered out, wide-eyed, to see what would happen next.

Illiann was vaguely aware of the commotion, but she was thinking of her dance and nothing could distract her. She watched, chewing her lip to keep from smiling, as each girl rose to perform.

Some had brought crowns of flowers to put in their hair, others single roses to clasp in pale hands. One or two had brought tasteful scarves, which they trailed behind them in small waves of pastel. The young woman at the piano danced her fingers over the keys, according to the chosen pace of each student's dance. The girls tripped delicately in small circles, swayed ever so slightly, turned gracefully, but circumspectly, this way and that.

Illiann was perplexed; each dance looked the same to her. She shivered. For the first time all day, she became nervous.

"Miss Ivy," Miss Worthy called. "It's your turn now."

She rose slowly, concentrating on keeping her hands steady as she opened the leather bag. She turned her back on her classmates, who saw only that she lifted one foot, then the other, and tied a leather thong around her waist.

"What music?" the pianist called.

"I will make my own." She turned, and everyone gasped. At her waist, she wore a primitive drum made of red wood with an animal skin stretched over the top. On her ankles and wrists, she wore deer hoof rattles. At the last moment, she removed her cap and let her hair tumble to her waist.

The silence in the room was so profound that anxiety made her freeze. *You must do what you think is right*, her mother's voice whispered inside her head. *Perhaps* you *will have to teach* them. Then she saw the expression on Laura Hart's face, the glow of anticipation in her eyes. Illiann took a deep breath and began to spin.

She beat out a rhythm on the drum, which mingled with the sound of deer hoof rattles, creating a soft pulse that filled the silence. She swayed, eyes closed, then leapt high, turned, and increased the rhythm of her drum. She pretended to circle a fire, to bow before it, then leap across, punctuating each movement with the beat of the drum.

The other girls were captives to the pulse of her music, bewitched by the sinuous movement of her body, which was evident, despite her bulky clothes. Whether they were shocked into immobility or dazed and enchanted by her grace, no one could look away. The younger girls stopped giggling to stare, transfixed.

Finally, Illiann used her fingertips to increase the rhythm on her drum until it ceased being a pulse and became an imperative. She began to spin in smaller and smaller circles, until her hair spread around her like finely feathered wings, her skirt stood straight out from her body, and the drumbeat became frenzied and wild. For that moment, as she spun, she was lost in her own rhythm, her own desire. She was free.

When she stopped, her hair continued to swing, enfolding her. She was drenched with perspiration that made her clothes cling to her.

Miss Worthy found her breath at last. She rose, swallowed several times, and cried, "I have never, in all my life, seen anything more appallingly unladylike."

Laura Hart could not help herself. She burst into laughter and enthusiastic, inexcusable, unladylike applause.

Chapter 28

During his first day back at the shop, Devon seemed distracted as he worked on the printing press, which had broken down twice in the last month. He was so relieved to be off his lumpy sofa and out of his gloomy house, that even the challenge of mechanical repairs exhilarated him.

"It's been dull without you here. Though I've been making plans." Julian greeted his friend cheerfully. "I think I know how to help you in your crusade for the working men of Victoria, and in spite of your reticence on the subject, I'm beginning to understand your motives. Illiann said she tried to get you to explain the night of your head injury. I was eager to hear what she discovered."

Devon froze, wracking his brain to remember what he had revealed. Of one thing he was certain. In a haze of pain, anger and exhaustion, he had revealed too much. "What was she after sayin'?" he asked warily.

Julian shrugged. "She said you don't like to talk about your past, which didn't really surprise me. It just amazes me that any one man can talk as much and as passionately as you do without revealing his own secrets." He waited to see if the Irishman would answer, but he appeared to be focusing intently on the gears he was oiling. Julian smiled to himself.

"In any case, I believe in your cause, if not always your approach, and I've been thinking about using *The Voice* to spread our message. We can write a series of stories about real people, real families and the challenges and difficulties they face every day. We change the names so they're safe from reprisal by the owners."

Devon looked uncertain. "Sounds a bit tame, I'm thinkin'."

"But think how many people we could reach with those stories. We'd be stirring up feelings they might have buried or forgotten, by showing them characters they know and understand, because they have the same problems."

His friend was dubious. "I'd no' be seein' how it'll bring change. 'Tis just a story."

Julian shook his head. "It's the truth, and that's different. To make something happen, to make people transform themselves, you must be wise and kind and careful. First, you have to catch their interest and then show them that you care about their plight. You have to get them angry enough to open their eyes, but not angry enough to abandon common sense. That's what our stories will do. Second, you have to help them rediscover their faith. Third, give them hope by giving them a purpose and a goal they can attain—give them a plan, and thus, a future. Fourth, you must fan the embers of their confidence and courage, and when you've done all these things, only then can progress begin."

In that moment, Devon remembered exactly why he had wanted Julian Ivy as a partner; beneath his caution was ambition, and beneath his composure, passion. He had no more wish to remain silent and obscure than Devon did.

He knew then for certain that together they would set Victoria back on its heels.

Chapter 29

Kit let the door to the gymnasium slam shut and whistled for the dog. Although the teachers did not approve, Lord Byron always followed his master to school. The huge black shepherd usually curled up beneath an overgrown bush just inside the gate to wait for the end of the day. "Are they afraid of him, do you think?" Kit asked a classmate.

"Maybe. Or maybe they're just jealous because he's so loyal."

Kit had to admit, he liked the feeling of having Lord Byron waiting for him, prancing with delight and ready to run. "There, boy. Good dog. Let's go for an adventure, shall we?"

Since Devon had been injured, the boy had been feeling a sense of expectation and a coiled energy that made him restless. Today he wanted to relieve the tension in his chest. "Let's go exploring."

Lord Byron's head bobbed up and down as he loped along beside Kit, and the boy took it for a nod of agreement. "I want to go toward Beacon Hill. It's sort of wild and dangerous, Papa said. That doesn't scare me, though. I like it, and I bet you will too. We're going to take some photographs." He carried the bulky camera in a cushioned deerskin pouch his mother had made specially for it. It bounced softly against his back as he went along.

He began to run, chasing the dog through the fallen leaves, kicking up a multi-colored trail that settled back to earth with a whisper. Lord Byron was in his glory; it had been a long time since he'd run so freely.

"You miss the ranch, don't you boy? Sometimes I do too, but only a little. I like living in Victoria just as much. There's a surprise or a mystery everywhere I turn." Seeing a piece of rope tangled in the leaves, he whirled it over his head and sent it sailing. "Go get it!" he shouted.

Lord Byron obliged, barking at a passing squirrel and veering momentarily off course to chase it.

Smiling, Kit followed, running in and out of the pine and cedar trees, passing through the shade of aspens and maples. The fragrance of the pine needles was pleasant and pungent, the earth soft with recent rain, but dry enough for him to avoid the patches of mud.

When they were deep into the woods, he began to look around for a place to set up the camera. "What about in a tree?" he called to the dog. "You wouldn't like that much, I guess. You'd have to stay on the ground." Still, Kit continued to peer up into the thick branches, hand above his eyes to block out the sun.

Lord Byron tilted his head, looking upward with his master until he suddenly froze, then began to thump his tail and nudge Kit with his wet nose. He moved toward a particular yew tree. Kit followed his lead, as he had learned to do while they traveled the borders of the ranch and the nearby forest back home. Lord Byron had never let him down.

Kit saw a movement above and paused, narrowing his eyes as if it would help him see. The thick needles undulated, revealing a fragment of blue that did not begin to match the sky. "Hey! Who's there?"

A tousled blond head appeared among the leaves. "What do you want?" the boy asked aggressively.

Kit was unimpressed. "Don't mind us," he replied. "We're just out for a stroll, Lord Byron and I."

"Lord Byron?" In his surprise, the other boy forgot to look menacing.

Kit threw up his hands. "I can't help it. My sister named him. She was reading some mad English poet at the time."

"Oh." The boy in the tree seemed to realize he'd lost his advantage. "UUhhmm, you shouldn't be here. They don't like small boys and dogs."

"'They' who? And I'm not so small. I'm bigger than you."

"You are not. Besides, I was here first." He stuck out his chin in an effort to look defiant.

"You think that means you're the only one allowed? Because I don't think it does. Not unless you're at home. Even then, your family gets to be there." Kit could be just as defiant. He folded his arms across his chest in a silent challenge.

"Well, my second home is here, and I like it better than the other."

"What do you mean? Do you live in the forest?"

"Sort of. At least I'd like to. Up in the tree. I found a fort up here and I fixed it up so I can come whenever I want to get away."

Kit forgot his feigned belligerence. "Really? Can I see it?"

The boy, who was mostly visible now, crossed his own arms. "I don't even know you." It was an accusation.

"I'm Kit Ivy. There, now you know me." He pondered for a moment. "I know! I'll let you look through the lens of my camera. I'll bet you could see a lot from up there."

Lord Byron had been jumping back and forth between the trunk of the tree and the place where his master stood. Now he stopped and woofed softly up at the other boy. The rope still hung out of his mouth, and he looked rather humorous with his eyes rolled back in his head and his fur dotted with crushed leaves.

"Can I play fetch with Lord Byron too?"

"Sure." Kit was feeling magnanimous. And very curious.

The boy mulled this over for a long moment, then seemed to make up his mind. He liked the look of Kit Ivy. "Okay. Come on up. There's a kind of ladder on the other side. By the way, my name's Will."

Kit nodded and followed Will's directions, locating the pieces of pine nailed to the tree at regular intervals and beginning to inch his way up. His pulse quickened. This was an even better adventure than he'd hoped for.

When he reached a rough platform, he stood slowly, not trusting the buckled wood. Besides, he was busy trying not to stare. Will was extraordinary-looking. His body was slight, his hair thick, curly and golden. His eyes were arresting—tawny topaz in color, their gaze piercing. His sun-browned cheeks contrasted sharply with his pale white neck, and a hectic flush came and went beneath his skin. He was wearing a deep green double-breasted wool jacket that ended at his waist; the matching trousers were full and gathered below the knee over gaiters that covered his legs and were caught beneath his brown leather shoes like stirrups. He had tossed a darker green cap onto the platform, along with a pair of gloves.

He noted Kit's curious glance and explained, "For cycling. My bicycle's down there." He pointed to the overgrown bushes that nearly concealed his shiny black cycle.

Kit was delighted. "I've wanted a bicycle for ever so long. You're lucky."

Will snorted indelicately. "Think so? Then why do I come here so often to get as far away from home as possible?"

Brow furrowed, Kit answered, "I don't know. How could I? I just met you and you're being very secretive."

"I am, aren't I?" Inhaling deeply, Will puffed out his chest with mock pride. "Well, if you really let me look through your camera, and maybe even take a photograph, then I'll teach you to ride the bicycle. We'll be friends after that, and I can reveal the truth." He lowered his voice to barely above a whisper. "But you have to swear you won't tell. Not anyone, not ever."

"I swear," Kit said passionately.

Will looked as though he very much wanted to believe it. But was it worth the risk?

Chapter 30

Laura Hart saw Illiann in the school courtyard, bulky bag hanging loosely from her shoulder. "I can't believe what you did back there." She indicated the makeshift gymnasium, unable to hide her admiration. "You must be really brave."

Illiann frowned, considering. "I don't think so. It was probably more selfish than anything. It was just easier to be myself than to pretend to be a stranger."

"Well, I couldn't have done it. And I can't imagine why you would think it was selfish, just because it was easy for you." Laura regarded her intently. "Do you mind if I walk with you?"

"I'd like that." No one from Miss Chadwick's had ever sought Illiann out before, none had chosen to walk with her, though they usually arrived at the school in twos and threes, giggling and whispering together. The sight of those intimate groups of girls had only increased her sense of isolation. The mist that swirled through the willow trees and fell in drifts over her skin was more familiar, like the musical trill of the orange-crowned warblers in the branches overhead.

With a smile that made her cornflower blue eyes sparkle, Laura swung into step beside her. "I wish I could be more like you. I wish I wasn't afraid to act from my heart."

Illiann remembered her enthusiastic applause. "I don't think you're afraid of anything. You ask as many questions as I do."

"It's not the same." Laura ducked her head when two well-dressed women passed. She seemed suddenly ill at ease. "I'm a coward at heart."

"Will others think ill of you if you walk with me? Is that what you mean?"

Laura was miserable, torn between her admiration for Illiann and her lifelong habit of pretending to do exactly as she had been instructed. There was peril in the stubborn expression on Illiann's bronzed face, the glow in her hazel eyes. That's what kept Laura from turning away. "To hell with it. I don't care."

Both girls were shocked by her choice of language, and they stared at one another for a long moment in uncomfortable silence until, as one, they began to laugh.

"Friends?" Laura asked, extending her hand.

Illiann grasped it enthusiastically. "Friends."

Chapter 31

Simone's blue taffeta silk gown swirled about her ankles. Her silver silk slippers made no sound on the Persian carpet. She crossed the drawing room, oppressed, all at once, by the tasteful lace curtains, the dove gray walls, the pale and paler shades of blue. The room was lovely, quietly expensive and lifeless.

Instinctively, she turned to the homemade shrine at the far end of the room, seeking the brilliant colors of the abandoned statue of the Virgin Mary.

She froze and her skirts settled around her. During the night, someone had made a miracle. Gone were the garish orange and blue robes, the green cloth that had covered the Virgin's bright yellow hair. Gone were the roughly carved features and fat round face; they had been replaced with lovely, well-defined cheekbones and fine lips caught in a secret smile. The black eyes had been painted gray with a hint of green, giving them a soft expressiveness, the yellow hair painted lustrous black. The robes were gossamer silver, like woven moonlight. The halo, once the same vivid yellow as the hair, was also silver; it glittered with crushed abalone, and three tiny pearls caught and held the candlelight.

Marcel and Claire erupted from the kitchen with Mathilde at their heels, just as Simone sank to her knees, her fingertips brushing the hem of the Virgin's robe.

"Do you like it?" Claire cried, breathless with excitement. "Marcel did most of the work, but I mixed the paints and found the lace, and Mathilde and I found the pearls."

Marcel murmured quietly, "I only thought—"

"He *thought*," Mathilde interrupted loudly, "you'd grown weary lookin' at all that awful color. How a person could find a moment's peace with splotches of orange and blue and green dancing before her eyes is beyond me," she told the settee firmly, while glowering at her mistress.

"It is beautiful," Simone's throat was unaccountably dry and she blinked rapidly, reaching out to draw the children close.

Mathilde grunted. "'Bout time these ragamuffins did something useful." She spoke with affection to the ornate plaster coving on the ceiling, while reaching down to pull up the brown wool stocking that was rolling down her leg at an alarming rate.

Simone smiled gratefully. Mathilde had given her time to collect her thoughts. "You are brilliant, Marcel," she said sincerely. "Soon you will be selling paintings to French noblemen for more than this townhouse is worth."

"Not," Mathilde pointed out to the swaying chandelier, "that they'll realize what they're getting. Wouldn't recognize a treasure if you dropped it on their toes."

Marcel flushed with pleasure. "It is only a little statue. Every time I passed, my head ached from the terrible hues. I had no choice, you see." He spread his hands in a charming gesture of surrender.

"I see." Simone turned to Claire. "And where, pray tell, did you find such tiny pearls for the crown?"

Claire released her breath in a rush. "Mathilde let me look through an old box of bits and pieces. There were some beautiful things, though not as beautiful as the diamond earrings that I saw in the cathedral."

"True," Mathilde announced, shaking her head so her tufts of hair quivered. "Another gift from de M's coffers was discovered only yesterday. Marie Cecile says the whole city is mystified."

Simone considered her old friend closely. "I believe you are becoming obsessed."

"Small matters bring the most joy, especially to That Man's cost. Claire, Marcel, to your books." She changed the subject without taking a breath.

Simone kissed the children on the forehead. "Thank you," she said. "I do not think anyone has ever given me such a wonderful surprise."

"We wanted you to like it so much," Claire confided.

"Then leave her to enjoy it in peace," Mathilde grunted.

As they left the room, Simone turned back to the Virgin Mary in her new robes and paint. For the first time, she noticed the hands, which had once been cracked and broken. Now they were patched and glued and painted—healed—and a tiny carved rose had been placed in each palm.

Mama! Look what I made for you!

The words were so clear, the voice so real that she turned, expecting to see Julian holding out his hand to her. But he was not there; the pale blue perfection of the room remained static.

What was it her son had brought as a gift for her birthday on Vancouver Island? He had carved it himself, from the wood of the maples that grew in abundance. The statue of the Virgin in front of her now was perfect in every detail; Julian's carving had been rough and imperfectly formed. Why should the one bring back the image of the other?

Oblivious of her silk skirt, Simone sat cross-legged on the floor, as she and Julian used to sit when they picnicked by the river. It had been on such an outing that her son had given her that precious carving. She could see his face glow with pride and trepidation as he laid it in her hands.

"Unwrap it now," he'd said. "I want you to be happy."

He had been so young and so sincere.

Later, when they lay sated with food and fine chocolate and the surprises she had produced from inside the picnic basket, the boy had become restless. "What is it that troubles you, *ma petit Jules*?"

"I have work to do, and it's late."

She recalled too well how she'd grieved for the awareness she saw already in his hazel eyes. "Today, for my sake, you will not think of that. Today is for fun, for being a child." He had stayed for a while, laughing with her, listening while she sang silly songs. She had given him a taste of her sherry, saying, "This will be our secret, *non*? You must not tell your father." Jamie would not have cared, but it was a game she and Julian played, making secrets of the little moments they shared.

So many secrets.

So many lies.

She was remembering so much that she should have forgotten, had struggled to forget. Why had it come to her now, so clearly that she wanted to reach out and brush the untidy hair from her son's forehead?

She ached because she could see, hear, smell that day so vividly, but could not recall Julian's handmade gift. She had taken it with her when she left, along with the plain gold wedding band Jamie had slipped on her finger the day they were married, and a rose from her favorite wild bush. She had kept those things in a small rosewood chest for years.

She had left Jamie and Julian a chest as well, left part of herself behind, so they would not forget her. What had she hidden away in that chest? She no longer knew.

Running her fingers through her hair, she pulled the pins loose as Jamie rose before her. *You are cold, my love. Come, let me warm you.* She had whispered in reply, *I can never be cold again, cherie. You brought me back to the heat and the light.*

Simone covered her ears to shut out the images. Long ago she had stopped allowing their faces into her mind, the sound of their voices, the feel of their hands. She had sworn to forget, so the yearning would stop.

And this was her punishment; she could not remember.

She wanted to pray, needed to murmur the familiar Latin phrases that offered grace. She turned back to the silver Madonna, to the unfamiliar image of herself. It had been so long since she had seen the reflection of her face that she did not recognize it. That, too, she had forgotten.

Chapter 32

Illiann had returned from school, taken off her boots and stockings and curled her bare feet beneath her in the cherrywood rocker. She was reading from the post, which included a letter from her Uncle Theron. Julian leaned on the mantel and Saylah was perched on the settee. The oval beveled mirror on the back wall reflected the French doors opposite, and the stained glass windows added ephemeral color; the fitful afternoon light spilled in, filtered by dark drifting clouds, making enigmatic patterns on the polished wood floor. The walls were lined with bookcases packed tightly with volumes of every size and color. The Ivy's were smiling at Theron's acute sense of humor when the Chinese servant, Sung-li, appeared in the doorway.

"Someone has come," she announced in slightly accented English. "Mrs. Edward Ashton."

She had barely finished when Sophia appeared. "I'm sorry. I should have written. I only decided at the last minute, you see."

Saylah and Julian were perplexed by the look on Sophia's face.

"Illiann, why don't you help Sung-li prepare dinner?"

"Of course, Mama." With a sidelong glance at their unexpected guest, Illiann followed the servant from the room. Something was wrong, but she knew she would have to wait to find out what.

"You're always welcome here. You know that," Julian said.

"We have missed you, my friend." Rising, Saylah went to welcome Sophia with a firm hug. "Where's Edward?"

"I told him to stay at home," Sophia said breezily, in the light tone they had come to know well. "He's dragging about morosely, so I said he didn't deserve to come. He implored me to stay with much drama and devotion—Brutus whining in agreement—but I told him I needed a vacation, so I wouldn't be swayed." Her velvet hood fell away from her face. She shook out her hair, smiling, to assure them she had not changed.

Sophia's cheeks were bright with color from the rising wind outside, Saylah guessed, but she also seemed a bit distracted. She carried her soft leather gloves, and her hands were tan from the sun.

"In fact, I decided I'd planned everything too carefully all my life. It's time to be spontaneous, to take a chance."

Nodding, Julian put aside his questions. "Well then, of course you will stay with us."

When he reached out to hug her, Sophia kissed him briefly on the cheek, then turned toward Saylah, whose eyes she did not meet. Saylah was far too observant; Sophia was afraid she would lose her composure. Only half aware of what she was doing, she sank into a chair, her cloak collapsing at her feet. "I would love to stay. But, you see, I'm not sure how long I'll be in Victoria."

"What is wrong, my friend?" Saylah asked. She could no longer contain her curiosity. "What made you leave?"

"I believe my husband needed to be alone. He is troubled, but cannot speak about it." Sophia thought, but did not say that she too needed some time to herself. Only now that she was able to breathe without effort did she realize she had long been without air.

The fire began to penetrate her heavy clothing at last. The clouds were dark and the wind cold. The sky had forgotten its season and slipped forward into winter.

"You know you can trust us." Saylah knelt before her, black hair falling loose around her, and took Sophia's hands.

She met Saylah's eyes for the first time."I know. I realize now I will be fine—in time. I felt so suffocated by the pain Edward feels that I cannot heal. He won't even let me try."

Chapter 33

The crystal chandelier cast a mellow light over the Harts' dinner table, making the Crown Derby china, the silver and crystal gleam. Agatha Hart, in a black gown of glace silk, sat at one end of the huge table, her sable hair curled and pinned up with a feathered aigrette of jet beads. She smiled at her husband, but not too widely. He had put aside his beaver top hat, but still wore his morning coat and brocade waistcoat. His fair hair glistened in the soft light, and his smile, for once, was relaxed.

"Laura," Arthur Hart said mildly, turning his blue gaze upon his only child, "did anything exciting happen at school today?"

Laura nearly choked on her clear soup. "How could you possibly know already?" As soon as the words were out of her mouth, she knew she'd made a mistake. She felt the color rise in her cheeks and her spoon clattered against the side of her bowl.

"Know what?" her father asked, just as Agatha cried, "Oh dear! It's something dreadful. I just know it is."

Arthur gave his wife a quelling glance. He could see that Laura regretted her outburst; he could practically hear her mind churning as she sought some calming half-truth. That only made him more curious. "I was just using a turn of phrase, but now I think you'd better explain."

His daughter adjusted the already perfect neckline of her lilac velvet gown. She glanced furtively at her mother, who sat back in her chair, drinking her wine and looking disapproving. She tried to think of a way out, but knew she was being a coward. "We did our interpretive dances in Deportment."

There was a rebellious glint in her gaze that gave her father pause.

"And? We are most eager to hear more, aren't we, Agatha?"

Agatha stopped with her crystal glass halfway to her mouth, too startled, for a moment, to think of an answer. "I'd rather not, thank you, dear. I'd much rather listen to the crickets. Harmless little creatures. They never cause one a moment's worry." Knowing how Arthur preferred a gentle, well-modulated voice to a harsh one, she used her eyes to convey her displeasure to Laura.

"I rather think they put one to sleep," her husband replied. "And it is not yet time to retire. But you were saying, Laura, about the dances?"

"Just one dance in particular, really. Illiann Ivy's." Now that she'd started, she couldn't seem to stop. "She's part Salish, you see, so she did an Indian dance. Miss Worthy was quite distressed. The whole school was watching, so everyone saw her drum and deer hoof rattles. Illiann spun so fast it made me dizzy, and she was positively drenched in perspiration."

"Young ladies should never perspire in public," Agatha intoned piously. "How awful for you to have to watch such an appalling breach of etiquette.

"I'll wager you were thoroughly shocked! Any decent young lady would be." Agatha glared at her daughter. "You'd best be wary, Laura Constance, or you'll find yourself frowned upon by Society." She always pronounced the word with a capital 'S'.

Laura felt a deplorable desire to giggle. She glanced helplessly at her father.

Unconsciously, Arthur Hart tugged at his sideburns. He preferred to keep the peace in his home, since he got very little at the ironworks where he was a partner and manager. "Is it, then, safe to say that your day was anything but dull?"

"Actually it was quite exciting," Laura said before she could stop herself.

Glowering, Agatha turned to her husband. "Really, Arthur. I'm quite surprised at you. Dullness is a good thing, decorous and conservative."

"Well, my dear, I'm sure you are correct, even if I'm inclined to take another view. You always know best about these social niceties. We must all remember to follow your excellent example."

Laura suppressed a grin at the glint of humor in his eyes. "I liked the dance. It made me think. Illiann is the only interesting girl at Miss Chadwick's."

"Have you gone mad?" Agatha cried. "You will make us social pariahs, that's what, and I shan't be responsible for the outcome."

Arthur met his wife's gaze steadily. "We shall certainly *not* hold you responsible, if that eases your mind."

For some reason it did not reassure her in the slightest.

Laura smiled into her soup.

Chapter 34

The chandelier made of deer antlers cast quivering light over the Ivys' dinner table, with its beige linen cloth—embroidered only along the base. The silverware had come from Jamie Ivy's second wife Flora, and though scrupulously clean, it showed its age and the love with which it had been handled. Saylah and Flora had discovered the water glasses outside the glassworks, ready to be thrown away because the rims were uneven. Both women had been enchanted by the curved rims and had taken the whole lot (60) home with them. The ones on the table, and a few in the cupboard, were the last that remained. The old china plates did not match one another.

"I can't believe you still have my favorite plate," Sophia cried in delight, clutching it as if she could see her image in the rose-covered china.

Saylah smiled quietly. "We knew you would be coming to visit sooner or later, so we brought yours and Edward's right along with us." Every one of her family and friends had a plate of their own—completely different from the others. Saylah made sure of it. Some, like Kit, pretended not to care, until he couldn't find his. Then all hell broke loose until it was safely back on the table.

Saylah just wanted everyone to feel at home.

"And the glasses," Sophia paused, tracing rings around the top of hers. "Do you know, I didn't really approve of them in the beginning. But seeing them again makes me smile. Come to think of it, they always make me smile."

Kit and Devon snorted in disgust, but Illiann and Saylah exchanged a warm glance with Sophia

Watching her family with fondness and care, Saylah become aware of Devon's restlessness. She had invited him because she wanted to make certain he ate properly as he healed. She also saw that Kit was about to burst from keeping something inside. She touched Julian's leg, but he had already noticed.

"So what did you do after school today, Kit?"

The boy let out a huge breath of relief and began to regale them all with the details of meeting Will, though he did not disclose the secret location of the tree house.

"What's his surname?" Julian asked.

Kit blinked at his father. "I don't know. He didn't ever tell me." Now that he thought about it, he'd felt that his new friend didn't really want Kit to know who he was.

Devon listened and watched with interest. Illiann, Kit, Saylah and Julian all tried to talk at once, then subsided all at once. They took deep breaths and tried again when there was a pause they might fill. Their guest, Sophia Ashton, was more subdued, though she seemed to be absorbing the energy and excitement of the others. Devon interrupted when Kit stopped to take a breath. He cleared his throat and everyone turned toward him expectantly.

Disconcerted by the sudden stillness, he paused, then, as he always did, found his voice again. "Mrs. Ivy—"

She interrupted him. "Saylah."

"Well then, Saylah, I wanted to be tellin' ye about a friend o' mine, Davy O'Reilly. He hurt his hand something awful on a piece of heated iron. I was after tellin' him you might take a look. He can't afford a doctor, unable to work as he is. It's a big family and 'tis difficult for them. The bosses don't help."

"How awful!" Illiann exclaimed. In that moment, she felt guilty for the ease of her own life. "I'll go with you, Mama. Is there anything more we can do, do you think?"

"I'd like to come too." Sophia spoke up for the first time. "I'm sure I can be helpful." Her cheeks were pink with color, her eyes bright with interest.

Julian raised his head. Perhaps this was the opportunity he had been waiting for. "I think there's something *I* can do, Dev. Remember I mentioned those stories in *The Voice*? What if we did one about the O'Reilly's?" He turned to his son. "I think you could help, too, Kit."

"How?" The boy was skeptical.

"I'd like to include some photographs with the story. But, and this is the difficult part, we don't want anyone to be recognizable."

"Mayhap you could get them with their faces turned away or something," Devon suggested. He was astonished by everyone's willingness to become involved. He was used to either rage or apathy, not hope and practicality.

"Why?" Kit asked, full of confusion. Then, quite suddenly, it cleared. He turned to Devon. "If someone guessed who they were, would they be in danger, like you are, from flying rocks?"

Saylah, Devon and Julian exchanged a glance that posed a silent but weighty question.

Finally, Julian turned back to his son. "We think they might be."

Kit went pale, but tried to hide his discomfort. He remembered all too vividly the night his father and mother had brought the wounded Devon home. *You mean that boy did this to you just for* **talking**? he had asked in bewilderment. And Devon had answered, *Talkin', when 'tis done with energy, faith and fury, has more power than any weapon on earth.* "Devon," he said, "do you think *photographs* 'can match a man with a deep, sweet voice and a cause to believe in'?"

Kit was throwing his own words back at him, and it took Devon by surprise. He had not realized the boy was paying such close attention. For the first time in his life, he wondered if he shouldn't be more careful about what he said.

"They can be, nearly." He did not know if that would frighten Kit off. He should have known better.

Kit squared his shoulders and sat up straight. "Then I'll just have to be extra careful, won't I?"

"Yes," Saylah agreed, though she wanted to say much more. "Please take care, whatever you do."

"We'll talk more about it later," Julian said.

Silence had fallen for a few moments. All this time, Saylah had been aware of her daughter, who was obviously fascinated by the conversation. But there was a flicker in her eyes, an unnatural pallor that came and went in her face. "Ilya,"—the affectionate nickname her friends and family called her—"my dear, are you becoming ill?"

Surprised by the soft sound of her mother's voice, Illiann dropped her fork, which knocked over her glass, spilling what little water was left.

The girl had been caught up in the exchange between Kit and Devon. She was proud of her brother and his sharp memory, and proud of his courage. She could tell her mother and father were, too. Maybe she could make them proud of her as well. "I'm not ill at all. It's just…today at school we had to do a dance that expressed something special about each of us. So I took my drum and rattles and did a Salish celebration dance." She raised her chin defensively, though no one spoke a word of criticism. Even if they had, she knew she would not change anything.

Saylah felt a flame of pride and fear combined. That Illiann had done this on her own initiative, without asking permission, without believing permission was needed, made Saylah glow. Her daughter was no coward; that was clear. And Saylah had encouraged her without realizing it by challenging Illiann to show the whites what the Salish believed in. For an instant, she closed her eyes and allowed herself to see the image of the girl whirling, drum in hand, hair in a wild whirl around her head.

Saylah smiled. She couldn't help it. Then she opened her eyes and looked into Julian's. They were full of pride and wariness in equal parts. They clasped hands beneath the table. Both knew Illiann was following her instincts as Saylah had taught her to do. They just weren't certain that, in this case, it was wise. As one, they turned to consider their daughter thoughtfully, brows furrowed.

"You must have felt it was necessary, Ilya. I know you don't usually act heedlessly. What was so important to you?" he asked quietly.

It was the last thing his daughter had expected. "I don't know, exactly. I just know I had to do it. I *had* to."

"Something inside would not be silent until you set it free?" Saylah asked. She, of all people, understood that kind of yearning.

Illiann let out a sigh of relief. "Exactly."

Silent for a moment, Saylah looked from one person she loved to another. "It is not always sensible to follow these impulses, but that has never stopped me or your father."

Devon blinked at Illiann, turquoise eyes clouded and hands clenched. He did not realize how tense he was until Sophia's voice shook him awake.

"Good for you!"

"Sure an' the teachers must've been apoplectic, and the other girls horrified." Devon sounded a little envious.

An image flashed through Illiann's mind of Laura Hart applauding, and a few other girls joining in. Even some of the younger girls had come out of hiding and clapped tentatively. She had expected derision or icy stares, not approbation. As she placed the drum in her over-sized schoolbag, Laura Hart had whispered, *Thank you*.

Saylah contemplated her daughter, trying to understand. "You were very brave to do such a thing, but perhaps not altogether practical."

"Practical!" Devon hooted. "That's after bein' an understatement if ever I heard one."

"It's no more impractical than you getting everyone riled up, and then standing in front of a plate glass window," Illiann declared. The swelling on his temple had not gone down completely, and the black stitches stood out against the mottled red background.

She started to say more, but Saylah rescued her. "Perhaps we're all a little mad. Each one of us in our own peculiar way. Don't you think?"

No one responded to her oddly candid insight. No one had the first idea how.

Chapter 35

"Careful! There are two of us on here!" Will bent his head into the wind, concentrating on steering his bicycle as it headed down a path near Beacon Hill.

Kit was perched awkwardly behind his new friend, holding on for dear life.

"Watch out!" Will cried. "Bump ahead. Sent you sprawling more than once."

"Who are you talking to?"

Color crept up his friend's neck, and the bicycle wobbled precariously. Kit tightened his grip, praying to the spirits of his mother's ancestors for a quick and painless death.

"Myself." Will shrugged. "Lots of times the house is so quiet I talk to myself to make a racket."

"No one else is there?" The house on Crescent Drive was always noisy and bustling, but Will's house sounded cold and empty.

"The servants are forbidden to make noise. They tiptoe around because they're afraid of my stepfather, even though he's hardly ever there. He works all the time. He thinks it's important to be rich so people respect you. That's okay with me, 'cause it's better than having him around."

Kit could not imagine such a thing.

"My mother goes to luncheons and boating and bathing, and I don't know where else. She's very busy. I guess she's already important, 'cause my stepfather said once she was quite wealthy. That's why she has to go to all those places, to 'keep the family's head up in society,' my stepfather says. But sometimes I miss her." A trace of loneliness was woven through his words.

"I'm sorry." Kit didn't know what else to say.

"They don't talk much anyway. My stepfather says words are dangerous."

Devon had said the same thing. And he had several stitches on his forehead to prove it.

Surprisingly, Will kept the cycle upright until they coasted to the bottom of the hill. Releasing the breath he'd been holding, Kit let go, clutching the seat just long enough to propel himself backward over the wheel. Flinging his arms up to keep his balance, Kit swayed in the middle of the path, waiting for his head to clear and the dust to settle.

Will overreacted when the weight was lifted from behind him and the cycle veered into the ferns at the side of the unpaved road. Laughing, he leaped off, running the last few feet as the wheels came to a stop.

"What d'you think? Isn't it great?"

Running his fingers through his curly sable-colored hair, leaving it more disheveled than before, Kit nodded. His heart was still beating too fast and his cheeks stung from the sharp wind on the downhill ride. "It's a little scary, but I don't mind." The prick of fear had added spice to his first time on a cycle.

"Ready to try it alone?" Will was flushed and his unusual amber eyes sparkled with excitement. The sun shown through the leaves of maples, spruce and oak, making his hair glimmer like gold. He wore a biking costume of dark blue cashmere, the trousers fastened below the knee, the tailored jacket over a light blue sweater. His ribbed stockings were extra strong and his boots somehow managed to look shiny despite the dust that covered them. He had taken off his blue yachting cap to wave it about vigorously.

Kit guessed that the outfit was expensive, just as he guessed the Hawthorne bicycle had been costly. The black enamel finish looked as though it had been hand-rubbed and polished, and the shiny metal parts were nickel-plated. It had both a bell and a lamp on the handlebars, and a small tool bag for oiling the gears and patching the tires.

"Come on," Will said. "Let's go to the bottom of the hill, where it's flatter. Aren't you glad we left Lord Byron at home? He would've been running in circles around us, and we all could have ended up in a heap on the ground." Will seemed to find the idea amusing. "But he can come next time. He's fun."

Fun was very important to Will.

Kit practiced balancing on the awkward seat, while steering and pedaling at the same time. When he finally managed to go several yards without pitching head first over the handlebars, he let out a whoop of joy. Riding a horse had been exciting, but he'd gotten too used to it. This was a new challenge, a new sensation. He loved the wind in his face and the rotating of the petals and the bumps as the ground threw up its obstacles one after another. He loved the feeling that he could control the cycle, making it wobble by shifting his balance, and then settling it back on the path. He could veer off course or point it directly where he wanted to go.

"See?" Will panted, coming up beside him. "Now no one can stop you. You can do anything." His tone was resolute, his expression grim.

For some reason, Kit wondered if Will was talking to himself again.

Chapter 36

"Hello?" Pausing on the threshold, Illiann waited for a reply, but heard none. At her mother's request, she had stopped by Devon's house after school. She had come more than once since he had been injured. Today she was supposed to take the stitches out of the wound on his forehead and rub it with salve so it would heal cleanly. "Are you here?"

Silence.

Warily, she stepped inside. "Devon Fitzgerald?" When he still did not respond, she shifted the healing bag on her shoulder and moved down the hall. She paused in the parlor, shocked by the dim dustiness of the room without Devon in it. When he was there, his size and dramatic coloring seemed to expand, dwarfing the minimal furniture, giving color and life to what she now saw was a shabby room. It smelled musty and the drapes were worn, their color indeterminate. The oil heater in the corner was rusty and the sofa and armchair mismatched.

Nose wrinkled in distaste, she continued into the kitchen and stopped short. A bottle of milk sat on the table with a half-eaten bowl of oatmeal. There were crumbs everywhere, and a mouse nibbled a moldy slice of bread in complete unconcern. Illiann shuddered. The wood-burning stove appeared to be coated in hardened layers whose origins she did not wish to imagine. There were dishes piled precariously beneath the pump, and when she pulled back the curtains, they shredded in her hands.

Illiann sneezed at the billows of dust and hurried from the room. As she passed, she glimpsed Devon's bedroom through the open door. The covers were rumpled and his longjohns tossed over the footboard, along with several days' worth of clothes. The brass bedstead was corroded and sagging. There was another room with books, a table and a wooden chair, all thickly coated with dust. Devon obviously didn't spend much time there.

Finally, she stopped at a closed door, puzzled, staring at the sparkling crystal knob. All the others were discolored metal. Every other door was open.

That intrigued her. "There's no reason on earth to open that door, except to feed your curiosity," she told herself firmly. She paused with her hand on the knob, but in the end, she could not still the whisper that urged her on. She opened the door and went inside.

Unlike the other dim rooms, this one had tall windows on two sides. There were no heavy curtains, no layers of dust, so the afternoon light streamed in when the clouds parted from time to time. The walls were painted white and the windows large and clean. At one end stood an easel and a scrubbed pine table covered with tubes of paint, brushes and a palette that might itself have been an image of some brightly splashed motion frozen in multi-hued layers of thick paint. Against the wall were stacks of canvases, most painted in oil.

Illiann stared, stunned by the light and color. It might have been another world, a lost paradise, so bright was it, so alluring and full of treasure.

She could not resist. With a quick glance over her shoulder, she knelt to examine one canvas after another. There were paintings of fields and mountains, moors and streams done in vibrant washes of color. There were no real outlines, no boundaries between sea and sky, river and fern-covered bank. One seemed to blend into the other, yet each held its own vivid impression. Illiann felt she could walk through the meadow, and smell the heady scent of the wildflowers. She imagined the icy water of the river rushing past as the wind caressed the tousled trees.

She touched the tubes of paint, sniffed them, admiring the texture and odor of the vibrant hues. She found one last canvas hidden in a corner and turned toward the wall. She turned it eagerly and felt a strange tightening in her chest.

Devon sat on an old-fashioned brass bed, the kind passed down through many generations, with a feather mattress and a handmade quilt with lacy edges. His red hair looked bright against the muted colors of the background, and he had not yet grown a beard. He looked very young and vulnerable with his smooth cheeks and bent head. He had buried his face in his hands; his entire body spoke of despair.

A cheval glass stood near the head of the bed. Where Devon's reflection should have been was the figure of a slight, auburn-haired girl in a linsey-woolsey gown, head in her hands, tears running over her concealing fingers. Illiann stroked the image reverently.

Devon's hair did not cover the back of his neck, and it stood out, white and exposed. He seemed defenseless, completely without guile or anger. Illiann didn't like it. His innocence frightened her much more than his rage.

She turned the painting back to the wall, bewildered by so much emotion.

All at once, the door was flung open and Devon stood on the threshold, face flushed with anger. "What the divil are *you* doin' here?"

She motioned toward the landscapes. "These are of Ireland, aren't they? They're of a place you love; every stroke of the brush tells me that. What, in God's name, are *you* doing in Victoria?"

Devon was so unnerved by her perception that he told her the truth—a gift he had given to no one else for a long time. "Because you can't live in Paradise forever."

She was knocked off balance by a rush of pain. "I know you can't," she said, trying to blink away the unexpected memory of the ranch along with her tears.

The sight of those tears struck Devon below the heart. For a moment, he tried to see the paintings through her eyes, because his own had been tight closed for years.

Illiann struggled for control. "I didn't know you were an artist."

Devon admired her determination, even though it irritated him. "I stopped paintin' long ago. I just could no' bring myself to toss it all away."

Illiann regarded him skeptically. In the whole house, only this room was kept clean. The empty canvas stood ready, the charcoal to sketch the outline, the tubes of paint laid out beside the palette. A whole room, ready and waiting, just for a memory? This was not a room for storage of discarded and forgotten things.

"'Tis why I keep this locked," Devon said, as if he read her thoughts and chose to deny them. "So I don't have to remember."

The sun blazed through the window behind him, making his anger brilliant with its white glow. Illiann felt the power and the weakness so strongly that she closed her eyes against it. "I only came to ease your wound."

"Did you? It was almost healed until you opened it just now and made it bleed."

For the first time in two years, Devon could not stop his pain from showing in his eyes—bright, sharp and glittering—before Illiann turned away and freed him.

Chapter 37

"Shhhhh!" Will held his finger to his lips, but in spite of the admonishment, Lord Byron gave a short sharp bark. "We have to be quiet," he told the dog sternly. "No one can know what we're doing.

A few feet away, Kit was setting up his Rochester folding camera, attaching it to the tripod with great care. "Don't be silly. We're just taking some photographs. We're not on a secret mission or anything." In spite of himself, he lowered his voice, grinning when he realized what he'd done. Will was hard to resist when he got an idea into his head.

"But you said it was dangerous. Your father even admitted it." He crept closer and Lord Byron moved stealthily at his side, glancing from right to left as if on the lookout for evildoers. "Besides, if it's not, why did Davy have to argue forever to get these people to let us onto the street with a camera?"

Kit peered through the viewfinder, lining up the wall of the crumbling house with the dark alley full of trash. Only the foot and hand of a little boy were visible in the frame. He had to be careful; Davy had promised no one would be recognizable. "Because they don't want their pictures in the newspaper."

"Why not?"

"They don't want anyone to know who they are." So far, he had gotten a photograph of one man in silhouette, a young girl with her face turned away, a group of people with their backs turned. The clouds overhead helped by whisking shadows to and fro, revealing, then concealing features and expressions. It was Devon's friend Davy O'Reilly's neighborhood, and he was determined that Julian get the photographs he needed.

"Why not?" Will repeated. "Because they're afraid, that's why!"

Kit stood up, the shutter release in his hand. "I guess so."

"Because it's dangerous!" Will crowed in triumph, dragging Kit's thoughts away from shadow and light. "Why else have we been sneaking around all morning? And why is Devon Fitzgerald watching us?"

Kit heaved a sigh of surrender. Will wasn't going to let this go. "Just in case someone tries to hurt us. But they won't." Glancing over his shoulder, he watched the tall Irishman lurking—there was no other word for it—at the end of the block. "Anyway, it doesn't matter now. We're finished." He was glad, because despite his apparent unconcern, he was nervous. The air on the long block of rundown houses and shabby people was eerily static, as if everyone were tiptoeing about, voices hushed. A chill of foreboding ran up his spine.

"So, who's Devon protecting us from? His friends?"

Partly in exasperation, and partly because of his own trepidation, Kit sputtered, "No! From Robert Barrett. Devon says he doesn't want this story to be written."

Will blinked once, twice. "The man who owns the ironworks?"

"Yes."

"He's awful powerful, isn't he? My mother says he's got a mean temper when he's been crossed. She hears about it at all those luncheons. You sure you want him mad at you?"

"Not at me. My father's publishing the story." Kit collapsed the bellows of the camera and put it gingerly back into the satchel, along with the glass plates.

Will glanced around covertly and for the first time, really noticed the people in shabby, colorless clothes, the houses in ill-repair, the leafless skeletons of trees, the street full of holes and without a sidewalk. "Your father doesn't like people who do this to other people. Make them live like this. Does he?"

"No, and Devon doesn't either."

Will pondered this for a moment, his expression changing every second as if the wind were shaping him a new face with each new flurry of air. "Neither do I."

It was almost, but not quite, a question. "So?" Kit wasn't certain what he was asking, but he knew his friend's answer was important.

Recognizing Kit's discomfort, Will decided to stop tormenting him. "Ah, don't worry. It'll be okay. I know it will."

But of course, he didn't.

Neither, it turned out, did Devon Fitzgerald.

Chapter 38

It was still early when the door chimes rang through the house on Crescent Drive. Saylah was working in the garden, pulling weeds and thinning the rows of carrots, cabbage, peas and rhubarb.

Sung-li—the sixteen-year-old Chinese girl who came in several times a week—was working in the kitchen. Before she could wipe her floury hands on her apron, the chimes sounded imperiously a second time. "I come!" she called.

She hurried to the front door and opened it.

"I am Miss Reynolds from Miss Chadwick's School for Young Ladies," the woman on the porch said primly. "I have come to speak to Mrs. Ivy."

"Yes, miss," the girl said quietly. "Please wait in sitting room." She indicated the half-open door and disappeared.

Saylah came in, wiping her hands on a smock that had recently covered her dove gray gown, her long braid hanging loose down her back. She was a stark contrast to Miss Reynolds, who wore a severely tailored tweed jacket and matching skirt, a shirtwaist with a starched front and a striped vest and narrow tie. The outfit was as close to a man's suit as a woman could get, and her gray hair, drawn rigidly into a bun, as well as her nondescript eyes, only emphasized the austerity.

Saylah's heart sank. She guessed this would not be a pleasant interview. "Sung-li will bring us some tea if she's feeling kindly this morning." She tossed the bundled up smock onto the settee and sat gracefully in the cherrywood rocker. "I suppose you have come about Ilya."

Miss Reynolds pretended to misunderstand. "Ilya?" She put a finger to her lips, brow furrowed. "Surely you're referring to Illiann." She paused, her frown deepening. "Yes, I'm afraid I have."

Saylah waited. It was something she had learned to do with great composure.

"I can see that I must get directly to the point," the principal sniffed. "Yesterday the girls were to create a dance, a tasteful little performance." She glared. "Your daughter's was not tasteful. It was, in fact, *quite* unladylike. The entire school is in an uproar."

"Was it one of the rules that the dance should be ladylike? I thought the girls were to express a part of themselves, to use the dance to say what words could not. It seems to me that is precisely what Ilya did."

"There are always unspoken rules of behavior." Miss Reynolds spoke stiffly. "Illiann doesn't seem to recognize them. Rather, she seems intent on breaking them and, in point of fact, on emphasizing her Indian blood. We at Miss Chadwick's find that most distressing."

"My daughter does not choose to deny her heritage." Saylah spoke calmly, suppressing her sudden anger. "Why should that distress you? It is part of who she is, who I am."

"Yes, well, precisely my point. And I'm sure I speak for the entire school board when I say that we would be a great deal better pleased if we felt Illiann was willing to make an effort to change, to try to fit in."

Saylah ran graceful brown fingers over the interwoven strands of her braid. "You wish for my daughter to become like you?"

Miss Reynolds cleared her throat uncomfortably. "All we ask is that she learn the unspoken rules, that she stop making so much of her differences from the other girls. She is forcing us to see her as separate and alone, instead of as one of us."

"My daughter is by no means alone. She has her family, her friends, her ancestors inside and beside her." With her unsettling green eyes, Saylah pinioned Miss

Reynolds in her chair. "The Salish tell a story of a squirrel who tried to take another's face, his possessions, his character—to change himself into someone he was not. That squirrel's soul was not reborn like the souls of his ancestors; instead, it turned dry and brittle and was carried away like dust in the wind."

She leaned forward, hands pressed together in a gesture of prayer. "Our souls are bound to the earth and to our traditions. To forget these things, to lose the knowledge of earth and sky and waters, is to betray our senses, our heritage, all that is sacred. I will ask Illiann what she is willing to do to get an education in this city, but I will not force her. I am sorry, Miss Reynolds, but I do not wish for my daughter's soul to turn to dust."

Chapter 39

"There's the last line set," Julian announced, displaying the galley that held the type and the half tones of Kit's photographs he had stripped in. "Will you proof it for me, Casey? Then we only have to make the plate and we're ready to print."

"Be delighted." Casey grinned, whisking the galley away to the galley press, singing an old Irish song as he went.

Julian sat back with a sigh of contentment. He had insisted on setting the story himself. The photographs were far more powerful than he had dared hope, though the half tones weren't as sharp as the originals. Somehow, the blurred edges only added to the moodiness of the shots. He was proud of Kit and his artistic eye.

He put his feet on the desk and pretended to smoke a huge cigar.

Devon grinned and picked up a cup, handing it to Julian with a flourish. "Drink up! 'Tis only water, me lad, but 'twill be whisky later."

Julian nodded in agreement. The first edition of *The Voice* was brief, but he suspected it would not be ignored. Casey and Devon had worked up a few other stories about groups in Victoria who had also been neglected, and Casey had sold a couple of ads to the shoemaker and the building painter with whom Julian shared the alley.

Casey executed a little jig as he waved a piece of inked proof paper and dropped it on Julian's desk. Devon swooped down to scoop it up before Julian could touch it.

"You need a cold eye to proofread, and don't be tellin' me any different." He wiggled his thick eyebrows in an attempt to look severe. When he had finished reading, he declared enthusiastically, "'Tis a good head you have on your shoulders, Julian Ivy. This should open some eyes, I'll wager, and start the war in earnest."

"I'm not looking for a war," Julian said. "For the moment, it's a cause, and our weapons are words."

Devon threw back his head and laughed. "What difference does it make what you call it? So long as you're ready to fight?" He could barely contain his excitement. "By God, 'tis time and long past time. Ready or no', they'll have to listen now."

Chapter 40

"What did she say?" Illiann asked, settling herself across from her mother when Miss Reynolds had gone.

Saylah regarded her daughter, hair unbound, bare feet curled beneath her, flowered muslin gown rumpled and stained from working in the garden. She sprawled in the chair where Miss Reynolds had sat rigidly, skin sickly white and unnaturally red by turns. Illiann's face and arms were golden from the sun and the quarter of Salish blood in her veins.

"I told your teacher a story, but I do not think she heard me. I suspect she learned to listen to different voices." Hands curled around the polished arms of the rocking chair, Saylah watched a mote of dust dance in an emerald ray of sunlight. "Tell me, my daughter, why, exactly, did you do that dance?"

"I wanted to remind myself—and them—of who I am, and to show them I'm not afraid."

Saylah understood the yearning all too well. Her daughter was barely fifteen, and yet she had begun to be a woman. But Illiann did not know what being a woman meant.

The girl leaned forward so her hair fell over her shoulder in a thick black wave. "I'm not even sure what I'm feeling anymore. Before, everything was simple, but now it's all different, and I'm confused. But I can always find comfort in going back to your memory of the beauty and rhythm of your life before. That I can understand."

Saylah stared down at her hands. "I fear I did not tell you enough about my life with the Salish. It was not, I think, what you imagine. You see," she told her daughter gently, "you cannot hold on to something you have never known, except through my memories. You have memories of your own to make."

Illiann leapt up. "That's just it. I want to make memories. I want *something* so much it burns inside me, but I don't know what it is."

Disconcerted by her daughter's passion and frustration, Saylah whispered, "You want a dream to follow."

"Yes. A dream like yours." Illiann sat at her mother's feet.

"It is difficult for you to know my dreams, when even I do not." Saylah smiled and touched her daughter's tangled hair. "To the Salish, a dream is a warning or a promise—a gift from the spirits. For the Whites, it is an image in their heart; they either flee from it or seek to make it real." She was intensely aware of the weight of her daughter's head on her knee, the scent of honeysuckle in her hair. "To the People, dreams are a responsibility. You must be strong to seek them and learn to understand them. You must train yourself to hear the pure, unsullied voices of the spirits, untainted by your own whispering voices."

Saylah's eyes were softly clouded, her smile dreamy and distant. She began to unbraid her hair, and her fingers moved dreamily, gracefully through the blue-black strands. "My village once had a dream of what I should be, and for many years, I walked their dream and thought it was my own. They needed to believe in something beyond what was tangible, because reality was change, and change was frightening to them."

"I don't understand. You said you were a shaman."

Saylah looked at her daughter's face, at the softly rounded chin, the high cheekbones and curved dark brows, the eyes full doubt and wonder and curiosity. "So I was. That is why the People set me apart. They wanted me to be— more. They made me believe I could and should be more."

"What do you mean?"

Saylah pictured the words in her mind and sorted through them like bright beads. "They wanted me to have the power to revive their past and rekindle their dying faith."

"No one is that strong," the girl cried.

Saylah smiled sadly. "I learned that in time, and it cost me much pain." She stared at her hands for a long time in silence. "Because of the role I accepted, I was not allowed mistakes or shows of weakness or tears. When I was a girl of 15, I would never have dared to ignore the rules and do the dance, as you did."

Illiann's gaze was full of compassion.

"I did not tell you this so you would grieve for me. It is only that I do not wish for *you* to be constrained by what others think and expect. I am proud of you for the risk you took, grateful that you have learned to listen to your heart.

"But you must also remember this; the dream I walked among the Salish was strong. I could not fulfill it, nor could I destroy it. So I left to find a dream of my own."

Illiann smiled. "You found Papa."

"Yes." Saylah paused. "I have tried to show you glimpses of another world, so you would know there was more than one way to live your life, more than one path to follow. I have tried to show you that you have a choice."

"You've shown me much more than that," the girl murmured. "The courage it takes to let go of one vision, and the grace it takes to build another. I will not forget, my mother. I swear."

Chapter 41

Determined to keep busy in the days after her arrival at the Ivy house, Sophia offered to take the lunches Saylah had made to the shop for Julian and the others. The sky was heavy with burgeoning rain clouds, the crisp air full of moisture, and by the time she reached the bustling alley where the print shop was, the wind off the sea had split the dark rain clouds, put color into her cheeks and cleared some of the fog from her head.

The moment she stepped into the shop, she was enveloped in the clatter of the presses, the sound of voices raised in cheerful argument, the warm air full of smells she could not identify. She was caught up at once in the energy of the place. Somehow, as she sat reading her newspaper every morning in her elegant dining room with flocked wallpaper and Wedgwood china, she had never imagined where it came from. She had never imagined this.

Sophia set down the basket of food and insisted that Julian show her everything -- the composition room where the type was stored and set and the pages laid out, the stockroom and bindery, the hand press for posters, the proofing press. But he loved most the two Fairhaven cylinder presses. Both were in use, turning out the newspapers that were piling up on the delivery table.

"We can't eat yet," Julian had told her. "Once they're all printed, we still have to sort and fold them."

"Then I'll help," Sophia said firmly, removing her soft leather gloves and velvet cloak to reveal a cashmere gown edged with delicate French lace.

The men laughed, but Sophia searched the storeroom until she found a fairly clean apron, which she tied around her waist three times. She took the well-worn sleeve protectors Julian offered and slid them up her arms. Then she set to work with a fervor and skill that astounded Casey and Devon, but did not surprise Julian at all.

All four of them helped stack the first copies of *The Voice* against the back wall in the composition room, then stood back, smiling in satisfaction. Everyone agreed they could not spend another minute in the close, airless pressroom, scattered with misprinted pages and shreds of paper. They locked the door carefully, took the basket of food and went to eat it under the shade of the maples in a nearby park.

When they returned to the shop less than an hour later, Julian reached out to unlock the door, but it swung inward at his touch. He and Sophia glanced at each other in surprise. "I remember locking it. Don't I?"

"You most certainly do." Sophia was immediately suspicious of that soundless swinging door.

Devon moved abruptly, pushing his way inside. The others followed more slowly.

"What is that smell?" Sophia began to cough and had to cover her nose with the lilac-scented handkerchief she fished out of her reticule.

The four of them made their way to the composition room, where the newspapers lay, just as they had left them, stacked against the wall. Only one thing had changed.

A pile of newsprint had been doused in kerosene. The can for the little stove stood empty nearby. The smell was bad enough; it permeated hair and clothing and made the already stuffy rooms unbearable.

But on top of the papers, in plain view, lay a box of matches. One had been struck, then left with its black charred tip beside the box.

"They were goin' to burn the place down," Devon shouted.

"I don't think they were," Sophia said unsteadily. She pointed to the wall above the papers, where someone had scrawled, 'Beware the lies.'

The men stood rigid while kerosene fumes rose around them, until Sophia finally said what the others were afraid to acknowledge. "The whole shop could have burned."

"And the rest of the alley would have gone with it," Julian muttered.

Lightheaded from the kerosene, transfixed by the sight of the sodden papers and dark, blurred rivulets of ink, Devon and Casey remained silent.

"It was a warning, a threat." Sophia busied herself with sweeping up the matches and returning them to the shelf. "The question is, are we going to listen?"

Julian nodded grimly. He was so angry that his voice shook when he replied, "Indeed we are, but it will only make us more determined. I am not a fool, but neither am I a coward. Let's go back to press."

Chapter 42

The carriage rocked gently from side to side, lulling the Duc de Montagne into a waking dream. He was dancing with his wife Patrice, but when they turned and turned again, he held Simone in his arms. Then it was Patrice, then Simone, whirling and whirling across the marble floor, faster and faster, until he could not catch his breath. The music swelled, filling his ears, his head, and his chest, which felt as though it might burst. He gasped and came back to the present with a jolt.

"Your Grace, are you well? You're very pale." His manservant Peter worried. He knew the Duc thought he had been successful at hiding his frequent pain and discomfort over the past few weeks, but Peter was not blind.

"I am fine," Claude rasped. "It is just that I have not had much energy of late." He told himself that if he dismissed the symptoms, they would disappear.

"I think your grace knows this is different," Peter insisted. He was profoundly alarmed at the grayish cast to the Duc's skin and his struggle to draw each breath. "We must get you to a doctor."

A heavy weight settled on Claude's chest, pressing against the bones that seemed to shatter and pierce him with hot shards of pain. Suddenly, he was frightened. He couldn't remember the last time he had been afraid. Perhaps when he was a child. Life had always been too tranquil for him; everything he needed -- money, children, friends, connections, a title, three chateaus, his wife -- had come easily, without worry or ache.

Only Simone had been a struggle before he won her, and afterwards, as he tried to fight the demons that plagued her. Through her eyes, he had seen what fear and regret, if left for too long, could do to a person. Now, for the first time in all the years he'd known her, he understood exactly how it felt. He was overwhelmed with uncertainty and dread. The pain was too great. He could not bear it. He wanted to weep, but even in that moment of helplessness, he could not surrender his dignity so easily.

"Your grace, please," Peter insisted. "You need attention."

Claude realized his arms were crossed over his chest and his fingers curled and frozen. He glanced out the window at the blurred landscape. "Patrice," he murmured, "tell… not…worry. You… safe." He turned to his manservant. "Take…to Simone," he managed to whisper. "Must…see her." The effort of speaking exhausted him. "Please, tell her…I am coming." He slumped against the carriage wall, head resting among the folds of the brocade curtains.

Peter saw there was no point in arguing; he knew the Duc too well. Hands shaking, he grasped his master's cane and knocked on the roof twice, sharply. The hatch opened to reveal the driver's curious face.

"Let me out, and take him on to Madame de Marchand's. I will walk there and warn her. It is urgent that you take great care. You understand?"

The driver had never seen Peter so flustered. "*Oui*. As you say."

Before the hatch closed, Peter had opened the door and vaulted into the street.

"*Merde*," the driver muttered at the sight of the Duc's ashen face. He shivered, though the sun shone and the air was warm. "I feel a storm coming, and I fear it is very fierce and very dreadful."

Chapter 43

Sophia began to open cupboards and peer inside.

"Don't worry. I learned how to clean up kerosene on the ranch," she said in a no-nonsense voice that contrasted with her frilly gown. She wrapped the filthy apron around herself again and bustled about, striking off on her fingers what they should do. "We need to get these out of here." She pointed to the ruined papers. "Is there somewhere fairly safe we can take them?"

"The painter next door keeps an open wagon parked down the alley," Devon volunteered. "I'll go see if we can use it."

Following Sophia's instructions, Julian and Casey began to help with the clean-up.

Soon Julian's brown hair was coated in newsprint and kerosene and some foul solution Sophia had found in the cupboard that they used to scrub the walls and floor.

"We have to hurry and get this done if you're going to reprint today," Sophia said. Her face was flushed with heat, her auburn hair sticking to the sweat on her skin, her hands nearly black and her cheeks streaked with dirt. She was glad for the hard, exhausting work. Out of her pain and confusion, she had created a whirlwind of efficiency, determination and pure obstinacy.

"The plates, the galleys of type—" Julian said in alarm.

"They're intact. I checked," Casey assured him. "Mrs. Ashton's right, I'm thinkin'. They were only after frightenin' us."

Julian crouched beside the pile of kerosene-soaked rags, cotton shirt clinging to his back and chest. Rivulets of dark sweat ran down his face and stained the fabric further.

He thought about the warning on the wall; he did not have to think about the threat of fire and destruction. That he could smell in the air. But Casey was right; they could have destroyed the plates, the presses, spilled out the ink, unbound the galley of type, making a mess that would have taken days to clean up. But they hadn't. Why not? What did they really want from him? He looked from Casey to Sophia, who watched him expectantly. "Reprinting will mean an awful lot of extra work for everybody."

"We're waiting," Sophia murmured. "Tell us what to do."

"I'll be stayin' as long as it takes," Casey agreed.

Painstakingly, the three began to repeat the long process they had already been through once that day. They did not listen to the voice of wisdom and prudence, which might have told them to wait, to think this through, to clear their heads: or to the voice of fear, which might tell them to flee.

Chapter 44

Simone froze when the doorbell chimed. She had been feeling restless all day, plagued by a sense of vague foreboding, which was given voice by the sound of the bell. She headed for the door, but before she reached it, the Duc's manservant, Peter, bounded up the stairs, pausing at the top to gasp for breath. "His Grace is ill," he managed. "His driver is bringing him here. He sent me ahead to warn you."

As she tried to take it in, Simone realized how very ill Claude must be to have frightened Peter so. He had been tired a great deal of late, and several times she had caught him breathing hard for no reason. His color had not been good either. She had asked him about these things, but he had waved her off. "You cannot bring him here," she cried. "You must take him home."

"But, Madame, he intends to see you, no matter what you say."

"How far away is the carriage?"

"I think…four blocks."

"Then *I* will go to *him*. Mathilde!"

The woman was there in an instant, holding out a cloak. "Wear mine. Pull the hood far over so no one sees your face. Won't suspect you'd be wearin' black tattered wool."

"Bless you for your foresight."

Peter began to breathe normally at last. "We must hurry. We must go."

"Yes. I am coming."

Mathilde squeezed her mistress' hand in reassurance. Wordlessly, Simone flung the cloak around her and followed Peter down to the street. Her pulse throbbed in her throat and she was breathless by the time he took her elbow gently and guided her toward the Duc's carriage.

Simone swallowed dryly when he pulled the door open and she saw Claude huddled in the far corner. His skin was puffy and pale and his gray eyes glittered unnaturally. He was breathing heavily and clutching his chest with curled fingers. She threw back the hood of Mathilde's cloak, and when he saw her face, some of the color returned to his cheeks.

Simone perched gingerly on the seat beside him. "Claude, you must go home. Your wife will be waiting. And the children."

Gradually, a gleam of determination crept into the Duc's eyes. "It is an hour at least to the chateau. I will not make it that far."

"Do not be silly. You have plenty of time. Years, probably."

"Simone, *mi amour*, we have never lied to one another. Let us not start now. Instead, let us take the moments we have left and say what must be said." His face was contorted with pain and he fought to regain control of his ailing body. Sweat ran down his face in rivulets, and his skin was both parchment white and flushed at the same time.

Simone squeezed his hands, to let him know she was listening, and that she could not bear to let him go. "We have said a great deal to one another over the years. One more thing will not matter."

"It matters, *cherie*. It matters a great deal." He raised their locked hands to his lips.

His gaze was ineffably sad, and she ached because she could not take the sadness away.

"I beg you, do not grieve for me. Look instead toward the future, as you have not allowed yourself to do before. I would be more honored by your renewal than by your sorrow."

"I will try." She shivered when he pressed his cool lips against her knotted fingers. The chill went through her cloak, through her cashmere gown to her bare skin, and pierced that fragile barrier to her heart. She held tighter, trying to force her warmth into his sluggish blood. Simone's eyes burned with dry tears. "I promise to try."

Claude smiled, and his face was transformed by regret and a tenderness so fine and fragile that, for a moment, it eclipsed his illness and the gray cast of his skin. Simone bit her lips to keep her tears from overflowing. For his sake, she must keep her composure. She tried to take a breath, but it would not come.

"I want you to find peace, *cherie*, but you will not find it here. I do not think you will find it at all, until you go back to the son you left behind. I have often been jealous of his hold on your heart. I should have encouraged you long since to return to Vancouver Island in order to finish what you began. But I was too selfish, too afraid you would not return."

"De Marchand holds me here, not you."

He shook his head. "You are a prisoner only of your own imagination. It is time to break those chains." He was breathing shallowly, but forced himself to go on. "You must go back, I think, before you can go forward. All I know for certain is, you will never be happy, and the nightmares will not end, until you see your son face to face and hear him speak your name."

"Claude, please." She did not know what she was asking for, only that it was urgent and necessary.

She lay her head on his shoulder, and he was unbearably touched by her vulnerability. "Listen to me now. For love of you, I deprived you of what I knew you needed most in the world. For love of you, I not only release you but also beg you to go. If not for Julian or yourself, then do it for me, in expiation of my sin in keeping you too long beside me."

Simone looked up, eyes filmed in tears. She could only nod; the pain in her chest had taken her voice.

The Duc took off his signet ring, holding it out to her on his trembling palm. "I want you to have it."

"No! I cannot."

"I do not make this gift recklessly. Do not reject it or you will break my heart."

She did not want to argue; his eyes were feverishly bright and he began to cough spasmodically. Cupping his face in her palms, she murmured, "All right, then. I will do as you wish." She took the ring and brushed his lips with hers. "I will live without you, Claude, but it will not be the same." She did not know how to say goodbye. She never had. "*Je taime, mon ami. Je me rapelle.*"

"*Oui. Je taime.*"

For a few minutes, they sat, his head on her shoulder, his breathing ragged in her ear. Then he began to choke, and she held him tight, trying to massage the spasms away, until his body went slack. In that moment, he seemed lighter, as if a weight had been lifted from his heart. It was called pain. She knew because it had taken root inside her the instant it freed him. She closed his eyes with the barest touch and settled him in the corner, as if his head had fallen naturally against the seat, and he had slipped away in his sleep.

Simone opened her palm and stared at the signet, touched beyond words that he wanted her to have it. Then, with great care, she slipped the sapphire and diamond ring back onto his finger. She knew Patrice would notice if it were missing.

Taking a deep breath, Simone put Mathilde's cloak about her shoulders and cracked the door open. "Peter," she whispered.

He appeared instantly; he had been waiting. "Is it…is he?"

"Yes. The Duc is at rest. You must have the driver take him home at once. And Peter," she touched his arm. "Swear you will not tell Patrice he asked to see me."

"But, Madame, the carriage was nearer to you. He would never have reached the chateau in that state. Should he have missed you both?" Peter had just begun to realize that perhaps the Duc's notorious mistress was guided more by her heart than by greed or pride.

"Just do this, please. Swear on his signet ring. The driver too."

All at once he was grateful to have something he could do for her. He barely touched the ring and murmured, "I swear."

He called the driver off his perch, and he also swore. "It is easy to explain. We say to his wife, 'Once we knew he was ill, we hurried back to Madame de Montagne as quickly as we could. But, alas, it was too late. His Grace is at peace now. For that, perhaps Madame can find it in her heart to forgive us. *Non*?"

He did not wait for a reply, but climbed up to his seat and held the reins in his hands, waiting. Simone and Peter exchanged places. "Thank you," she said quietly. "Bless you. Take care of him as you have always done, with devotion and kindness."

Peter admired her in that moment. He could not mistake the affection and sorrow in the last glance she gave the sleeping Duc. Simone could have caused a lot of heartache for her rival—the wife who had everything the mistress must desire—but she had chosen not to do so.

"I will." Tears welled in his eyes. "He was a good man. I will miss him."

Simone nodded, unable to speak. With great resolve, she closed the door and watched the carriage drive away.

She would never forget the weight of Claude's ring in her hand. She would never forget that he had died in her arms. She would never forget the look in his eyes as he told her why he had kept her beside him.

Those things were beyond price and beyond pain. The carriage disappeared from view and loneliness engulfed her as she stood alone in the empty road, waiting, yet knowing no one would come to rescue her again.

She had realized something beyond her grief in the past few dreadful minutes: it was time and long past time that she learn to fight her own battles. That knowledge had seized her heart as she kissed her lover one last time and let him slip away.

Chapter 45

Devon sought reassurance in the raucous laughter, the shouting and boisterous singing at the Irish pub down near the harbor.

"Ho! Devon, me lad," someone called, "heard you've been gettin' into trouble again, crusadin' against the wealthy and wicked."

Devon sighed. He had been selling copies of *The Voice* on the street corners of Victoria for hours, shouting about hope and a new beginning for the workers, when he began to realize how many faces were turned toward him expectantly. They had been eager and angry and had offered up their empty hands to be filled with purpose and direction. They believed he could change their world, because he had told them so.

He, Devon Fitzgerald, had been struck dumb by their faith, and the realization that he had no answers to give. "The wealthy and wicked have locked up their wine cellars for the night," Devon shouted, forcing a smile, "and I've no' a dollar to me name. How am I to talk with a throat so parched that even saltwater would soothe it?"

There was general laughter, a hat was passed and three beers set on the counter where Devon leaned one muscular freckled arm. He grinned, picked up a mug and downed a beer in a single swallow, wiping the foam from his beard with a flourish. He drank the other two while his friends looked on, shouting encouragement.

The barmaid passed, and Devon caught her around the waist.

"Sweet Eileen," he said, in a wistful lilt, "have a heart and be kind to a countryman whose dreams would be forgotten if no' for the thought of your dear face."

Eileen leaned away, held captive by his arms around her waist. "You've a silver tongue for sure, Devon Fitzgerald, but I'll not give you my heart to break."

Devon raised one red eyebrow. "Perhaps you have something else to offer?"

Eileen ignored the suggestive mirth that erupted and slipped out of Devon's arms. "Neither will I sit home and wait while you shout your anger to the world, and me alone, waitin' for a knock on the door and the police to tell me they've killed you at last." She leaned close. "I'm a bit tipsy, and you know what they say: 'Drunkenness and anger speak the truth.' You came to Victoria to die, and don't be thinkin' I don't know it." Pulling him down by the hair of his beard, she kissed him on the mouth and turned away.

The laughter rose like a wave in a storm, and suddenly Devon was drowning. He crossed the bar without a word, followed by groans of disappointment. "Where's the speech you promised?" A young man staggered and tried to block Devon's way. "You're not nearly drunk enough, laddie. 'Tis a shame to go home still sober." Mugs were pounded on the table in time to the rising chant, but Devon did not hear.

All he heard was Eileen's whisper: *You came here to die.* And woven into the sound, Illiann's urgent question. *Why are* you *here?* The words followed him down alleys and up hills until he found his front door and pulled it open impatiently.

He stood in the entryway, listening to the unnatural silence. The stillness weighed on him. Usually he brought men home who had nowhere else to go. Usually they were drunk, as he was. He realized he needed the noise and laughter, the complaints and arguments and quick flaring tempers that as quickly flickered out. He needed voices to fill the stillness—the one thing he could not fight. Because with quiet came memory.

Lying down, he slept fitfully and dreamed of Ireland, of Deirdre waiting on the steps carved from the earth on the side of the mountain. But when he reached for her, she wasn't there, and the earth crumbled beneath him, and he fell and fell and fell.

He awakened with this head throbbing and his anger churning once again. He could not seem to silence it; it flowed through his blood and his breath and his dreams like the smell of bitter almonds lingered on the air.

Though he tried to shut them out, he could not stop the vivid colors that flashed in his mind as he paced the hallway up and down. The images had been creeping up on him lately, especially in his sleep, nudging him awake with a prickling like the skin when a limb falls asleep – unbearable and a profound relief both at once. The colors lingered, teasing him with a longing to find a brush in his hand and a blank canvas before him.

He struggled against the desire to take those hues and make them into something bright and meaningful. He did not seek that kind of blissful torture again. If he succumbed to the temptation, it would consume him, body and soul.

In the end, he was not strong enough to fight it anymore. He made his way to the white room where moonlight came through the windows, but it was not enough. He lit the lamps and the chandelier, suspended over nothing, until the room blazed.

Illiann's voice filled the brightness; it had not faded in the hours of his absence. *These are paintings of a place you loved. Why, in God's name, are you* here? He could no longer turn away from the question, from the memories as vivid as the paints on these abandoned canvasses.

I didn't know you were a painter, she had said. He could see her sitting cross-legged on the floor in the middle of the room. Unerringly, he crossed to the painting turned toward the wall. He bent down and saw the prints on the fine dust of the frame and knew Illiann had touched it, turned it, examined it, and thereby looked directly into the heart of his despair. She knew nothing about him, yet she knew everything, more than any of the men he called his friends.

He waited for the outrage, but it did not come. Instead, he was drawn to the brushes, an empty canvas and tubes of paint. He remembered the smell of that paint, remembered the exhilaration, the pure untarnished pleasure of creation, and the pain. Always it came back to the pain. And Deirdre.

He thought of Illiann doing her Indian dance in a roomful of proper young ladies. She had been turning backward to something lost, hanging on too tight to something not there anymore. Her mother's past. But she had not been afraid—not of failing, of embarrassment, of her own loss of face. She had performed that dance for herself and no one else. So no one else mattered.

Devon realized he was running the dry brush over the canvas in sweeping arcs.

He was unaware that he had replaced the brush and picked up a charcoal pencil, unaware that he had begun to sketch bold, dark lines and strikingly shaded planes. He told himself he was not aware; he had become accustomed to such lies, such self-delusion. He had known since he entered the room that he would paint again, known long before the first stroke what he would create. It grew now beneath his fingers, though his eyes were closed, and the brightness of too much light burned painfully, hypnotically against his lids.

Chapter 46

Julian turned, half awake, the sound of rain thrashing against the glass, his heartbeat thrumming in his ears. It was not yet dawn, but he could not sleep; his mind whirled with thoughts he could not shape into logic or coherence.

He reached for Saylah. Even in her sleep, she came to him easily, curving against his body, her head on his shoulder. With a touch so light it was only a promise, he traced the curves of her high cheekbones, the graceful arch of her brows, her lips, parted as if to put her dream into whispered words.

Earlier that evening, he had drawn his wife into the sitting room, lit only by the light from the golden-red fire, to explain what had happened at the print shop.

"No one was hurt?"

"Not this time." Julian frowned. "Do you think I'm making a mistake?"

"No. To run away because of someone else's cowardice would defeat you." She could smell the kerosene on his clothes, feel the gritty dirt that dusted his body from head to toe. The odors, the grime, the dampness of his sweat-soaked shirt were the marks of a long, tense day. "What is it that troubles you?"

"I have dealt all my life with threats to my future, to my heart, my faith, to the land that was our livelihood. But I never before faced a threat to my safety."

Julian could not stay still; he went to stare out the window at the maples and oaks arched over the cobbled street. He took his hands from his pockets and rolled up his sleeves. "Today I remembered how my father spent his whole life dreaming of a world full of kindness and possibilities and a beauty so pure it broke your heart to see it. " He felt Saylah come up behind him, but he did not turn. "I remembered how, when he saw how cruel the world could be, he turned inside himself and gave up. "

To Saylah, the memory tasted bittersweet. "He was not strong enough to bear more ugliness and pain."

"He wasn't strong enough to try to make it better." Julian paused and took a deep breath. "I told him I had no magic in me, no vision, just a strong back and willing hands. I said he was the one with the passion. All I had was obstinacy and physical strength. He looked at me so oddly, as if he were seeing me for the first time. I think he knew then what I've only begun to learn. I always had that passion inside. He said I was the strong one, and he the weak. But I don't think I believed him. Not until today."

Saylah could hear Jamie's gentle voice saying those words, could remember vividly his face, pallid with sorrow yet lucid with dreams. Julian had inherited his father's charm, his intensity of vision, but not his frailty or his blindness. "Jamie was right," she murmured. "I think you are stronger than even you know."

Turning, her husband drew her close. She smelled of fir and fresh air and he kissed her, breathing in her breath like a rare, healing balm.

Now, hours later, she lay in his arms, so still, so peaceful, that her calm enfolded him, and his thoughts ceased their spinning. Once he had been frightened by this power of hers, this utter stillness, which allowed her to observe and absorb, yet shut out the world around her. He had felt threatened and excluded by her self-contained silence, but now she drew him into the tranquility. He rested his cheek on the top of her head and sighed.

~ * ~

In her dream, Saylah stood on a crescent of beach, breathing in the tang of salt air, the scent of fir and spruce, the rhythm of the softly lapping water. A sense of serenity settled around her as the distant sound of her name rose on the wind.

The wind became warm and caressing, like a gentle hand, and she slipped from sleep into waking. Julian was watching her, his fist wound in her hair. His own hair was disheveled, his hazel eyes misty with sleep. His arm tightened around her as she traced his lips with her fingertip.

Desire rose within him, tangled with a vague disquiet. "I love you," he whispered.

"Yes." She kissed him, opening her lips to his, running her hands down his body, still scarred from the heavy work begun in his childhood. Still warm and familiar and exciting.

Julian pressed against her, felt her nipples brush his chest. He kissed her deeply and when she rose to take a breath, she bit his lips playfully, tasting each spot with her tongue.

Julian touched the tip of her nose with his and both shivered at the frisson of heat that raced over their skin. The rain on the window was a symphony of sound; they absorbed the music into their own rhythm, until their breath and heartbeats echoed the fury of the storm that coated but did not penetrate the glass.

She cried out when he drew away, but he whispered, "Wait." He rose to retrieve the cedar comb from the bureau. Then he sat cross-legged on the bed, and Saylah lay with her head in his lap. Julian spread her waist-length hair across the bed and began to comb it, catching each small snarl between his fingers, working the strands free one at a time, tenderly.

Saylah sighed with pleasure. Long ago, when she was too weak to lift her hand, he had begun to comb her hair this way. Now it had become a ritual between them when one or the other needed comfort.

Julian lifted her hair in both hands and buried his face in the fir-scented strands. Then he leaned down to kiss her.

It was enough, that momentary cessation of worry. It was what they sought, what they surrendered to each other, what they made of nothing more than their two bodies and their faith in one another. It was exultation, exhilaration, wonder, and as these things faded, it became peace.

Chapter 47

"Come on," Laura called to Illiann. "Hurry up."

School had been let out for the day, and the girls were on the way to Laura's house. Suddenly, she was impatient, and tried to urge her friend forward. "I can't wait to show you my room." Her cornflower blue eyes sparkled, and she could not contain her excitement.

Illiann was fascinated by the wealthy neighborhood along Dallas Road, on the bluff above the Straits of San Juan, and she refused to move faster. Besides, they were headed directly into the wind off the turbulent sea below.

The huge houses were set far back from the street and the drives swept into grand curves. The collection of graceful porticos, marble columns, stone turrets and wooden gables made the homes seem heavily bound to the earth, yet the structures reached toward the sky in fantasy re-creations of another time and place. Illiann was blinking, trying to take it in, when Laura grasped her arm and pulled her up a pebbled drive.

Before she had time to catch her breath, she found herself crossing the marble foyer and climbing the graceful stairway at the Hart home. Laura did not give her time to look around, but took her directly to a room on the second floor.

It was done in ashes-of-roses and burgundy, and the wine silk drapes had been pulled back to reveal delicate lace under-curtains. The canopied bed was covered by a fluffy duvet patterned in intertwined roses. The walls were ivory, and from the domes of the lamps hung fragile crystals that swayed and tinkled as Laura moved around.

She flung open the wardrobe, leaning so far forward that she nearly disappeared into the layers of silk, velvet, brocade and silk. "Ah! My first ball gown. Papa said I'm too young, but Mother insisted. She said I have to know how to dress and walk and twirl like a lady so I may appear In Society." The words were muffled as Laura wrestled with the fabrics foaming around her as if they would suck her in. "Here!"

Flushed in triumph, she held up a pale orange gown. The sleeves belled up above the shoulders and puffed out hugely, emphasizing the heart-shaped neckline. The dress appeared to be made of silk, though it was difficult to tell under the layers of cascading lace—at the neckline, over the sleeves, the bodice, the waist, the full skirt. There was lace trim and lace edging and masses of lace gathered and swept up on one side, where it was secured with a cluster of peach-colored roses. As if that were not enough, there were wide rust-colored ribbons draped, strung, woven and tied in huge bows.

Illiann was caught off-guard. "Oh," was all she could manage.

"Isn't it dreadful?" Laura grinned when Illiann's mouth fell open. "Oh, dear. Did you think I *liked* it? No, no. My mother had it made for me. She said it had infinite 'style.' I told Papa later it had so much style it was drowning in it. She really expects me to wear it." Laura tossed the dress on the bed and plunged back into the wardrobe.

"Look what I've found. It's too small for me, but you should try it on." The shimmering aquamarine gown was made of stamped silk and brocade.

Illiann hesitated, but Laura paid no attention.

"Come. I'll help you hook it."

To please her friend, Illiann removed her uniform, allowing Laura to slip the gown over her head. She loved the caress of the silk on her skin; she had never felt anything like it before. The slightly curved neckline ended in small cap sleeves, and from the waist fell individual bands of brocade edged with silk embroidery. They were fastened a foot above the hem, which just touched the floor.

Laura unbraided her friend's hair and caught it on top of her head in a loose chignon. She found a small turquoise aigrette and fixed it into the dark tresses. Rummaging through her jewel box, she found a delicate emerald necklace and draped it around Illiann's neck. Then she stood back, hands clasped before her. "The color changes everything— your skin, your eyes, your hair. It's remarkable. Look!"

Illiann was astonished when she saw the image in the mirror. The fitted aquamarine gown revealed a figure she did not know she possessed. The waist was cinched in tight and curved to a v in front, and the bodice clung to her natural curves to emphasize the swell of her breasts. Until that moment, she had not realized how much her body had changed in the past year. Who was that elegant girl with the long sun-browned neck and slender arms?

"Do you like it?" Laura asked eagerly.

"I didn't think I'd like wearing a gown like this, but I was wrong. It's lovely."

"*You* are," Laura said.

"I can't believe it."

"You will," Laura told her. "Just give yourself time."

Illiann held her breath. She was just beginning to recognize how enlightening it was to be Laura Hart's friend. She suspected she would learn a great deal in the days and weeks to come. All at once she couldn't wait.

Chapter 48

"'Tis a wonderful marnin', don't you think?" Casey called to Julian and Sophia as they walked through the door. "And us with not a single copy of *The Voice* remainin', and people talkin' about your paper on every other street corner. We'll be needin' to print some more first thing. Isn't it grand?"

"So it is." With a broad grin, Julian pounded the other man on the back. Neither spoke of the previous day's adventure.

Sophia left them to congratulate each other, located a fresh pair of sleeve protectors and a clean white apron, and set out to make herself useful. While Julian and Casey saw to the presses, she surveyed the three small rooms. In the cobwebbed corner of a dark cupboard she found the account books. She pulled them out, coughing at the dust and wood shavings that wafted out to settle on her auburn hair and her shirtwaist, which was now more beige than white.

"I'm going to work on these for awhile," she announced. "They've been sadly neglected, but I might be able to put them in order."

Julian watched in compassion as she carried the books into the composition room that was also his office, stacked them on the desk and set to work. No one would have blamed her if she had stayed in the house, trying to work out her hurt and confusion, but she had chosen otherwise. He admired her strength of purpose, and was grateful for her help.

"She's a proud woman, is Mrs. Ashton," Casey observed, "and stronger than she can understand."

"How do you know?" Julian asked.

"I've eyes in me head. Or maybe it's me fey Celtic heart whisperin' in my ear."

Julian raised his eyebrows, eyeing Casey's his broad-shouldered frame, callused hands and square, weathered face. He did not look like a man with a fey Celtic heart.

"Enough o' this nonsense. 'Tis time we were getting' to work."

"Indeed." Julian replenished paper and ink while Casey tinkered with the main press. Both men worked enthusiastically, whistling as they moved about.

Fifteen minutes had passed when the door opened and a man cleared his throat to get their attention. "Mr. Julian Ivy?" the stranger asked, glancing from one to the other. He was tall and fairly attractive for a man of his age, with pleasant features and fine blond hair that had begun to turn silver.

"I am he." Julian moved forward, instinctively straightening his shoulders and drawing himself up to his full height. His hands were stained with grease and the rag in his hands filthy, as was his linen shirt, which had been freshly boiled and dazzlingly white when he left home less than an hour earlier. There was a smudge that crept from his cheek into his dark hair, which was unkempt. He did not bother to smooth it back.

"Sorry to call in without an appointment, but I wanted to meet you, Mr. Ivy. I'm Arthur Hart." Mr. Hart was already impressed. The younger man exuded confidence, energy and resolve, which Hart admired, in part because he had never possessed them. "I'm the manager at the ironworks."

Unseen behind one of the presses, Casey dropped his wrench; it clanged loudly on the floor and spun there for a moment.

Julian paid no attention. "A pleasure, Mr. Hart. Can I help you in some way?"

Hart rested his gold-tipped ebony cane on the floor. He had hoped to delay a little longer. "Yes, well, it's about this story in your paper."

Julian waited.

"My partner, Mr. Barrett, and I want you to realize that it's frightfully easy, in cases like this, for people to overreact. You get them upset and frustrated, and you don't know what they might do." His voice was firm, but he looked away more than once, revealing his insecurity. It was as if he were speaking from memory. "So distasteful and dangerous."

Julian's hazel eyes were opaque. *"I don't know. We're just telling the story as it happened. Seems those workers were already upset. As it happens, we're planning a series on the poor and disadvantaged. I happen to think people should know what's happening in this city. They should hear the truth and be able to judge for themselves."*

Hart shook his head in resignation. "You probably also think Truth is always good and pure. It can be ruthless as well."

Julian felt sorry for him. His clothes alone marked him as privileged and wealthy, yet he looked, in that moment, like a man bereft.

"We'll be careful," Julian assured him. "I assure you, I am not a fool."

"No, indeed." The other man considered, and then, for the first time, voiced his own thoughts instead of his partner's. "If I'm not mistaken, that's precisely what Mr. Barrett fears the most." He nearly smiled, but caught himself in time. "This series of yours. I'm officially against it; that's just the way it is. But I was thinking that, in the end, it might prove to be most interesting."

Chapter 49

The sound of bone against wood woke Saylah from a light sleep. She had come to the little curved beach today because the air was crisp, the sun high and the sky uncluttered blue. She had barely settled herself on a blanket before the waves lulled her into forgetfulness. Now she glanced up curiously to find Old Grandmother poised beside her, loom on the sand tufted with pale green grass.

The old woman was tidying her long gray hair with a carved wooden comb. She closed her eyes in pleasure as she drew the comb through the flowing strands. After each stroke, she took the loose strands from the comb and smoothed them in her lap.

"Why do you do that?" Saylah asked.

"Hand me the wooden box and I will show you."

Saylah picked up the box, which was so light she thought it must be empty. Reverently, Old Grandmother opened the lid to reveal a thick swathe of hair coiled upon itself again and again, bound by a supple leather thong. "You see, I am saving it. My hair will perhaps be useful one day." She smiled at Saylah's surprise. "There are things even you do not know, *Ladaila*. Someday I will tell you, when the spirits whisper that it is time."

For the first time, Saylah noticed the fabric on the loom. She had never seen thread spun so fine and clear. She touched it cautiously, afraid the threads would break in her hands, but they held firm. "This work is very beautiful. What are you making?"

"You have your secrets and I have mine. This, too, you will understand in time."

"You are very mysterious today," Saylah said.

The old woman nodded, running her finger along one of the most vivid threads, which appeared throughout the fabric in uneven designs. "Someday, this strand will be unbroken, and its path so compelling that it will draw to it all other strands until they flow together like a river to the sea. Only then will the design be set and the fabric at last complete."

Saylah gazed at the loom, brow furrowed. "I do not understand."

"If you do not now, my daughter, the day will come when you do. It is not, after all, such a difficult puzzle to solve. You need only open your eyes and your heart."

Surprised by the sudden lump in her throat, Saylah found her eyes were damp.

Old Grandmother touched her hand. "Do not worry yourself, Tanu. Lie back and listen to the sea, and let it wash away your troubling thoughts. You will know when it is time."

Leaning back on her elbows, Saylah drank in the ocean air and listened to its pulse and knew, in the very center of her heart, that she had heard the truth.

Chapter 50

"Christopher Ivy, please come. I want to talk to you." Sung-li spoke in a low-pitched whisper and motioned him toward the kitchen.

Shrugging, the boy went. He was curious, and as incapable of ignoring his curiosity as he was of succumbing to fear.

Set out on the kitchen table was a glass of milk, a piece of chicken and a slice of pound cake. "You're trying to bribe me." His tone was accusing, but his gaze kept wandering covetously toward the cake. Sung-li was an excellent cook.

"No! I only make it nice for you. You are hungry always, is this not so?"

"I'm a little hungry," he admitted. Sung-li watched him consume the snack so quickly she was certain he would be ill. He pushed the plate away and rested his elbows on the table.

"Christopher Ivy." She always addressed the family by their full names. "My honored grandfather asks if you will do for Chinese what you do for the other workers."

Kit was disappointed. "It's only a story in a newspaper. It didn't change the world or anything."

Sung-li shook her head. "You do not know. The people talk; they feel much; they tell others. They—" She tried to find the word she was seeking. "They come together. New friends, new…un-i-son. It good for all. You see that?"

"Not really." She was so serious, as if she held the future of her people on her shoulders. Kit sat up straighter. He knew the feeling. It had plagued him since he learned from Will that someone had threatened his father. Kit and Ilya were not supposed to know, but his friend had told them people in the city were talking about the kerosene and the warning on the wall above the newspapers. According to Will, the print shop, along with the entire alley, had very nearly been burned to the ground. He felt sick and helpless at the thought.

"You should ask my father. He's the one who decides what to print."

Sung-li knelt beside the table, hands clasped under her chin. "I…wish you to ask. He will listen to you."

Her confidence in him shone in her black almond eyes, and a lump formed in his throat. How could he say no when he could not even speak?

Chapter 51

Sophia, my dearest,

I wanted to write you immediately upon your departure, but I knew—somehow, in spite of my witless behavior in the past months—it would be better to wait. Better to dry all the self-pity and whisky from my system, and speak to you in a rational tone. Better to allow you time to enjoy the freedom you are no doubt enjoying as the Ivys' guest.

Do not accuse me of sarcasm, for such is not the case. I understand, I believe, why you left, and begrudge you neither your departure nor one moment of your time away from me. I will endeavor to explain what I think you wish to know, though, to be honest, I do not fully understand it myself. I had thought to protect you from the darkness of my thoughts, but I now realize that was a foolish mistake: one I should never have made in all but the most recent years of our marriage.

You are stronger of heart than I, and of will, which has, in large part, caused me to thrive ever since the moment I met you. I have forced myself to imagine how I would feel should you turn your back on me in a time of distress, and refuse, categorically, to discuss either the reason for your distress or the possible remedies for them. It would break my heart, as I, apparently, have broken yours.

No matter how blind I am to your feelings, or how foolishly I behave, you must never ever doubt the depths of my love, admiration, and profound respect for you. That I have made you doubt it—for indeed I fear I have—has left me doubly broken-hearted. For the truth is, and always has been, that I cannot live without you. If you do not believe me, perhaps you might ask Saylah, for she knows our hearts better than we ourselves, I think.

So, to get directly to the point. I have examined my fear and my nightmares, though I was more than hesitant to do so before. But you were right, my darling, as always. I could not outrun these things, so my best chance was to turn and face them. They are one and the same—the terror and dark dreams—and they come from the past, as perhaps you guessed.

The past is haunting me.

I am telling the truth when I say I do not know exactly why—or what—it is about long ago which troubles me so. But I do know it has to do with Jamie and Simone (all so very, very long ago). I wrack my brains looking for the answer, but find only a strange hollow darkness. It appears to be empty: of memories, emotions, everything. Except sometimes it shimmers like black water in the winter, letting me know that something is there, waiting for me to discover it.

All I ask of you is that you be willing to take a chance: to postpone any decision about our marriage long enough to give me time to force that hollow darkness into the light. I do not want to know what it is—that frightens me most of all—but you are right; I will never find peace of my own or peace in your arms until I do.

Ever Yours,

Edward

Chapter 52

Night had fallen and the factory was chilly and deserted when Robert Barrett motioned his partner into the abandoned office just off the factory floor. A single oil lamp barely nudged at the shadows that clung to the walls and ceiling, making the room more eerie than if it were in total darkness. Arthur Hart suppressed a shiver of apprehension.

"What are we going to do about Julian Ivy and his gang?" The top of the desk, crowded with files, reports and stray pieces of iron, was covered in a fine film of black dust that Barrett disturbed when he brushed his hand across the surface in frustration.

His hair had gone gray when he was young, but it was thick and full. It should have softened his harsh features, but he was always scowling. Hart could not understand it. The man was one of the richest in Victoria; he had power over thousands; his wife was a famous beauty, Diana Blanshard. Her first husband had been a distant cousin, also named Blanshard, and she had not looked at another man until she met Robert.

"I hardly think they're a gang," Hart said. "Ivy is a gentleman."

"I don't want to hear you sing his praises. He's dangerous. Haven't you noticed the workers muttering and glaring at anyone who rides in a proper carriage? They're unhappy, and that man made them so."

Arthur Hart scratched his head. He hadn't been praising Julian Ivy. He was quite certain he had only been stating the obvious. Wasn't it important to know one's enemies in order to defeat them? The problem was, though he would never admit it to his partner, Arthur was not certain Julian *was* their enemy. Besides, Ivy had not made the workers unhappy; if anyone was responsible for their misery, it was Barrett himself.

For a long time, Arthur had been turning a blind eye to the way his partner treated the employees. It made him ill to think about their wretched lives, but he no longer had the power to help them. He felt ridiculous and ineffectual, so he tried to deny what he knew to be true. "You don't care if the workers are unhappy. You've said it often enough. So they mutter a bit. They won't do anything about it. They're too frightened," he said bleakly.

"Of course they'll do more, with a rabble-rouser like Devon Fitzgerald goading them on." Barrett spat the name, not in disdain, but in rage. "I've seen him watching, spying like some skulking criminal. God knows what he'll do next. He's determined to break us, and I suspect he's capable of anything. We have to stop him." His eyes glittered sharp as ice in the murky room. "He and Ivy together are a curse I don't intend to live with any longer. So, I ask you again, what are we going to do about them?"

"Surely you're exaggerating. What if we tried to befriend them?"

Barrett shook his head in disgust. "You just don't understand people. Never have. That's why you need me. If you want to control them, you first make them grateful to you, then force them to depend on you, then ensure that they fear you—the deeper the better. After that you've got them in your power. But that's beside the point.

"Devon Fitzgerald won't be befriended, nor will he give up. He's too driven. He doesn't care about the workers. He's out to get *m...us*." Huffing and puffing, Barrett turned red. He swept his hand across the desk, sending papers flying and staining his fingers with grime.

Arthur was stunned. "Why are you so sure?"

Barrett struggled to pull himself together. "I don't know. I just am."

You're lying, Hart thought. *You* do *know*.

"Look, Mr. Ivy and his newspaper are giving the workers false courage and false hope. You came from here." He waved his hand to indicate the cramped, dirty room. "You should know that."

Hart clenched his fists. He endured a lot from his partner, but he found it more and more difficult to stand by quietly and be demeaned. "You're overreacting."

"I'm warning you, if you don't do something about this, I will." Barrett paused, finger to his lips, as if a thought had struck him. "Ivy couldn't publish any more rubbish if the shop closed down. The best way to cripple your enemies is by putting their money under siege. We have to make certain he loses all his customers. And don't ask me how, Hart. Even you can figure that out. You should start at once."

Still his partner hesitated.

"Wake up, man! You're in as much danger as I am. The workers hate you too, you know. In case you haven't grasped my point, remember this. I'll do anything to protect my fortune and family. Anything! Do you understand?"

Hart was very much afraid that he did.

Chapter 53

On the morning of the Duc's funeral, Simone rose early and made herself ready. She was not going to attend— that would have been cruel and an insult to his family—but she intended to be nearby. Wearing Mathilde's black dress and mantilla to disguise herself, she slipped out, silent as a wraith, and made her way to the graveyard. She found a secluded spot beneath the oak tree where her mother was buried and settled there, where she could hear the voices of the choir rising from inside the cathedral, touching with warmth the chill winter air. She knew the low branches of the tree hid her from view, and her dark gown and mantilla made her blend into the background, which was just as she wanted it. Wrapping her arms about her body, she tried to warm her hands.

And waited.

At last the funeral procession came out, carrying the ornate coffin covered with flowers. Where did they get so many in the dead of winter? she wondered. There were hundreds of mourners; it looked like the whole town had come, including de Marchand and his frail new wife. She saw Claude's widow and his children gathered close in their grief.

Simone watched the pallbearers release the coffin, watched Patrice bend her black-veiled head. But she stood straight, and from the outside, appeared strong. It was why Claude had married her, that strength, that ability to accept what was irrevocable. Simone ached with compassion for the widow.

Simone could not cry. She had forgotten how, had made herself forget. What had once been a release and a relief was now a danger. One unbearable pain acknowledged would bring back all the others. She watched in a daze as the service was read and the mourners dispersed, each returning to their warm houses where their families waited.

Gradually, gray clouds engulfed the watery sun, and Simone rose at last. On an impulse, she headed toward the empty cathedral. The clouds had dimmed the light; it would not fall through the colored windows, staining her pale white skin.

She began to walk resolutely. She must pray for Claude, though she was forbidden.

This time, she did not linger on the threshold, did not give herself the chance to turn away. Claude deserved her prayers. He deserved much more, but she had nothing else to give.

Chapter 54

Kit used a pair of cloth gloves to slide a newly developed glass plate into a tray of water. The image on the negative was clear, except for the blurry part where Will had moved too suddenly. He was standing with one foot up on the pedal of his bicycle, grinning with pride. Behind him, the lake glimmered in the afternoon sun.

The black curtains rustled and Julian appeared, wrinkling his nose at the odor that permeated the tiny, airless room. "I don't know how you bear it, Kit. Those chemicals are dreadful."

Kit shrugged. "It's worth it when I finally print the image." He bit his lip, trying to put into words how he felt. "It's like I took it out of the air and saved it so we'll never lose it. You know?"

"I understand. Perhaps that's why your photographs are so powerful."

"Do you really think so?" Kit tried to hide his eagerness for praise, but failed miserably.

"Absolutely." Julian ruffled the boy's untidy brown hair. "Everything you do, you do well."

The boy flushed with pleasure. His father's certainty reminded him of Sung-li's confidence that Kit could accomplish what she could not. "There's something I want to say."

Julian picked up the resolve in his son's tone. "This sounds serious. Perhaps we'd better adjourn to my private office."

The private office was the broom closet in the storage room, but Kit was glad to escape there after the malodorous gloom of the darkroom. "You said you're going to do more stories like the first one. What are these stories going to do, exactly?"

Julian was taken aback. "They're meant to illustrate peoples' strengths and their problems and to draw attention to the need for change."

"But after that what will you do? To *make* things change, I mean?"

Crossing his arms, Julian leaned against a ragged mop, looking thoughtful. "We're just…we're planning to… get men in power to pay attention to a population they've ignored until now. We're also going to go in and relieve some of their distress. Your mother and Ilya have volunteered to help heal those who can't afford doctors, and we're organizing groups to improve their houses and get them more efficient and less dangerous stoves and plumbing. We'll assist these people however we can. We want to give them hope, because a lot of people in Victoria have no idea what that is."

Pursing his lips, Kit nodded solemnly. "Okay."

"Why?" Julian asked, consumed by curiosity at his son's sudden interest.

Kit was trying hard to understand how such plans could possibly make anyone angry enough to threaten to burn down the shop. He did not want his father to guess what he was thinking. "I just wondered…these other stories…might one of them be about Chinatown? I guess there're a lot of poor people there."

Watching his son's expressive face, Julian considered. "Is that *your* question, or someone else's?"

Kit examined the worn toe of his right shoe. "Sort of someone else's. Sung-li. She asked me to ask you." He looked up, brown eyes shining. "She needs your help too, Papa. I guess they all do. Are you going to help them?"

Julian rested his hands on the boy's shoulders. "I don't know if I have that kind of power, Kit. But we're going to try. I promise you that." He had made the same promise to

Devon, but not until he looked into his son's expectant gaze did he realize exactly what he was saying. The kerosene soaked newspapers and Andrew Hart's visit, as well as the high sales of *The Voice* told him two things. This idea had grown beyond his personal desire to make a difference; it had become an imperative, and therefore perilous.

Chapter 55

Saylah dreamed she had become the loon, floating on a midnight pond. She huddled, camouflaged by sibilant reeds. Beside her a baby loon pressed close, heart beating frantically. Both pulses raced with fear because determined hunters prowled the darkness. Danger hovered, real and palpable. The air seemed to pant with tainted breath, like the beat of a distant, threatening drum.

The two loons waited among the reeds, motionless, black as night—and that was their protection.

Until the moon appeared from behind a cloud, making a silver path upon the water. It betrayed them by revealing the shape of their bodies in the shimmering light. Soon the hunters would notice; there was nowhere left to hide.

The stars began to weep in empathy; their tears fell on the sleek black feathers and clung. Where each one struck blazed a speck of burning light. And with the tears that turned to light, the loons became invisible in the moon-dappled flow.

Still, Saylah knew they were not yet safe. The pulse of her blood mingled with the ominous pulse of the midnight drums, filling the sky with an insistent rhythm—a distinct and escalating warning without words.

Chapter 56

Sophia sat, pen in hand, staring at the blank white paper in front of her. It was not yet dawn, but she was restless, and she found herself back at the heavy oak desk for the third time in as many days. The lamplight was dim, yet too bright for her weary eyes. She was tired of listening to her own breathing and the sound of her own heartbeat.

She glanced at the iron bedstead with brass knobs finished in white enamel covered with a serviceable blue down quilt; nearby stood the washstand and oak bureau, both simple, useful and handsome. A Wilton rug in shades of gold covered the scrubbed pine floor, and a sturdy wardrobe stood against the other wall.

Sophia sighed. She missed her ivory inlaid Chinese lacquered desk with its crystal inkpot, the blue silk wallpaper, brocade chairs and velvet settee, the royal blue velvet drapes and thick Brussels carpet in the drawing room at home. She missed the paintings on the walls, the sense of space and freedom, the knowledge that the house was hers, that she was not a guest there.

On the desk beneath her hand lay his letter—so precise, so thought-out, so tender. Confused still, but trying, at last, to understand.

She had not answered yet, had found much to occupy her since—working at the shop, buying new clothes, learning to ride a bicycle so she was not hobbled. She had been running frantically without moving; she was hovering in limbo, committed to her work here, yet still holding tight to her marriage and her past.

The walls creaked, complaining of the moisture always heavy in the air. The wind sighed beyond the window like a disembodied human voice.

It reminded her of the voice of Edward's nightmares.

She felt strangely detached from her tumbling thoughts, as if she were sorting out the problems of a stranger. It was easier that way.

She ran the dry pen over the page in meaningless loops and curls, and her hand shook as she imagined words and sentences. Not, by any means, the sentences she had long intended to write.

"Help me," she said to no one. Then realized she was stronger than that. She did not need help. She had come to doubt herself, and she must never do that again.

She was strong enough for anything. She closed her eyes and dipped the pen in the inkpot.

Forcing her hand to remain to remain steady, she formed the greeting slowly, resolutely.

Dear Edward,

She stared at the two words, but they blurred and faded into one another.

Doggedly, she dipped the pen again and began to write.

Chapter 57

Simone slipped into the breathless stillness of the cathedral. The light was dim and cool and strangely welcoming. She knelt, lighting several candles, and said novenas for the Duc's soul. The thick wool of Mathilde's shapeless gown was little protection from the cold stone floor.

As a hush fell around her, she listened to her own breath, her whispered prayers, the guttering of the candles. She felt the chill of the ancient stone, smelled polish on the walnut pews, the melting candle wax, with its hot, moist scent, the incense that made her light-headed.

The light shifted outside and the stained glass began to glow, illuminating with soft color the statues she so loved. She saw a glimmer of brilliant green out of the corner of her eye and turned. It did not belong in this hushed dimness. She held her breath, peering at the statue of a saint between the alcoves. He held one hand outstretched, and in it lay an emerald necklace, vivid against the painted stone.

Her heart began to pound. She knew that necklace—the large tear-shaped pendant surrounded by diamonds, the emeralds set in gold that were linked for the chain. She stood in the aisle, uncertain what to do. *You should go*, she told herself, but something about that costly piece of jewelry held her immobile. Why?

Simone stared, transfixed, until, in a white-hot flash, she remembered the last time she had seen it. She grasped the edge of a pew to keep from falling.

It had been a lifetime ago—two lifetimes, or perhaps three—the night of her first wedding.

She felt again the muffled sound of her footfalls on the carpeted stairs, the rasp of her breath, which seemed awfully loud in the stillness of the sleeping house. The clothes she had donned so hurriedly chafed against her skin. She was only grateful her maid had thought to take out an extra petticoat, chemise and gown. She absolutely could *not* have put the wedding dress over her head again. She grabbed the balustrade as nausea rose in her throat. She struggled hard to control it; she didn't have time to be sick.

Her heart nearly stopped when she reached the bottom of the stairs and saw a dark figure hiding in an alcove. She would not escape after all.

"Hush!" the figure warned. "It's me, child."

Simone was so relieved, she collapsed, shivering, into Mathilde's outstretched arms. "I…must…go," she sobbed without tears. The woman had been her nurse from childhood, and was the only friend left in the ruins of her world.

"Yes. Get away from Rouen, away from France," the servant whispered urgently. She held up a silk bag, open to reveal a mound of glittering gems. "Take these."

Simone shrank away. "Those are de Marchand's." She would not call him her husband. The words were a blasphemy. "I cannot touch them."

"Belonged to your mother. Yours now."

"They became de Marchand's the instant we were married." Simone's gray-green eyes were wide with desperation. "I have my mother's pearls, her crucifix, her kingfisher pin. That is all I will take from this house."

"Don't be a fool. Can starve on your pride, you know."

Simone had refused.

Rolling her eyes in a silent plea to the heavens, Mathilde had gone off to bundle up some of Simone's clothes, along with her rosary and Bible. Then the servant had taken her down to the Seine and a boat on its way to Marseilles, where the girl would find a ship heading for

England. Mathilde had known the Captain; he had found a couple who would chaperone.

The servant had started to turn away, but Simone clutched at her, hugging her tightly. "Thank you. I cannot bear that I will never see you again." There was a lump in her throat and her eyes ached, but she did not weep as Mathilde took off her heavy cloak and put it around the girl's shoulders. "Forgot a warm cloak in our rush to get away. Hurry now. Go with God, *ma petit*, with God and all the angels."

Her face was streaked with tears. "Are you sure you will not take even this?" From her voluminous pocket she retrieved an emerald pendant. It dangled from her fingers, magnificent even in the dim light of the moon.

Just as it dangled now from the fingers of a stone saint.

The emeralds sparkled, bringing Simone sharply back to the present. What had Mathilde said a few weeks back when she'd come in with a chicken under her arm?

Marie Cecile couldn't wait to tell me they found more of the de Marchand jewels hanging about the neck of the Virgin Mary last night.

Simone had been worried, because Mathilde had gone out so early.

Everyone's whisperin' it's that new young wife of his. What a way to get revenge for her unhappiness with That Man! Making him a saint and a fool all at once. Mathilde had unabashedly enjoyed the thought of de Marchand's plight. Only wish I'd thought of it myself. Ooh! What a time we'd have laughing about it then.

Simone had actually smiled, though she knew it was wicked. It was hard to resist the servant's zeal.

Then, one morning before dawn on a stormy day, Simone had met the woman in the street. Mathilde had been crowing with delight.

Marie Cecile showed me a string of rubies in Saint Catherine's hand. Poor Henri—losing so many of his family jewels. No wonder he can't get that young wife with child. Think that's her plan? To drain his manhood and his treasury?

Until this moment, it had never occurred to Simone to wonder how de Marchand's wife could be responsible for the offerings when her husband was still insisting Simone had stolen the gems. He was neither that clever nor that imprudent. She remembered with painful clarity the day he had shown up at her door uninvited. *He means trouble*, Mathilde had warned. *You can wager your fortune on that. As if you had one to wager*. Then de Marchand had come crashing in, raging at Simone's imagined betrayal.

Have you not done enough to me? Have I not paid enough for one mistake? He had not bothered to hide his contempt. *I do not know what you mean*, she had replied. *I have never asked for anything from you, except my freedom. And that you will not give me*. He had not believed her. Now she thought she understood why.

What if Mathilde had had the jewels all along?

Deeply shaken, Simone subsided onto a bench. She could not begin to sort out the thoughts whirling through her head, making her dizzy so the candle flames spun in glittering rings before her eyes. The implications were staggering. Soon she would have to go home and face them. But not just yet.

Simone covered her ears to stop the voices of the past from consuming her. Again.

Chapter 58

Devon hovered in the shadows, out of reach. Illiann held her breath as he raised a brush and began to circle her slowly, his arm a bridge between them, the brush, like a fingertip, touching her with paint. Gently at first, and then wildly, he drenched her in color from head to toe, then turned away, back to the circle of blank canvasses around them. Determined to force him to look at her, unwilling to be ignored, Ilya began to spin, streaking the expanses of white with azure and verdant green and sunlight yellow, with gold and orange and rust—the colors of flame—then burnt sienna, sable and scarlet, burgundy, and, at her feet, violet and a hint of blue.

The designs were unrestrained, brilliant and compelling, and in spite of himself, Devon stared in wonder. Unable to resist, he turned at last to Illiann, but she was spinning so fast that she could not stop.

She was consumed by a fear like ice, that when she ceased turning, when the last drop of paint disappeared from her body, so would her spirit, captured only in the patterns her passing had made on the ring of canvas. But neither could she continue in her narrow, whirling path, because she could not catch her breath; she was suffocating.

At last, reluctantly, she tried to slow her progress, to grow still and quiet and acquiescent, though not to Devon. Never to him.

She awoke, gasping, to the frenzied cadence of the Indian drums.

Confused and frightened, she crouched in bed, while outside clouds massed, turning gray, then ominous black.

Chapter 59

"Papa! It's nearly dawn. Have you been sitting here all night?" Laura Hart did not need an answer. She could tell from her father's tangled silver-blond hair and bleary reddened eyes that he had not slept. He had opened his waistcoat and untied his cravat, leaving his shirt partially undone. He slumped in his chair before the dying fire, an empty brandy glass dangling from his fingers.

Laura took it from him, setting it gently on the end table. "Something's bothering you."

Arthur Hart roused himself just enough to answer. "Work, you know. Unrest and dissatisfaction, low production, bickering. Nothing new there."

"I don't believe you. The last time you sat in the study all night, you were afraid the Works would close down."

Hart was startled fully awake. "You don't know about that. I never told you." He felt sick, imagining how disturbing that knowledge would have been to a sensitive girl like Laura.

"No, but Mama did. She thought we might lose everything. I guess she couldn't keep it inside."

He flexed his numb fingers repeatedly. "Laura, I never intended to drag you into that. You needn't ever be anxious about money or the future. That's our job."

"I know, but I love you, Papa. I can't help worrying when I see you like this. Please tell me what's wrong."

Laura was far too perceptive, Arthur thought. She looked defenseless in her soft blue wrapper, her hair tousled from sleep and her cheeks bleached of color. He had to tell her something or she'd make herself ill, and he couldn't have that. "Barrett's on the rampage again. You know how he is."

Laura was skeptical. "Does this have anything to do with Mr. Ivy and his newspapers?"

How did she know these things? "Sit down, my dear." He motioned toward the settee, but she gathered up her wrapper and settled on the Persian rug at his feet.

"What is it?"

He laid a hand on her curly hair. "I can't sleep because I've been thinking about the men at the ironworks." His stomach churned. "I wonder…do you think they hate me?"

Laura would not have been more surprised if he struck her. "Of course they don't. You've helped them lots of times. I used to go with Mother when she visited with food and medicine. She didn't much enjoy it, but she went. The families I met always spoke kindly of you. I think they were grateful." She was pleased when her father spoke to her like this, as though he cared what she thought, as though she could help ease his anxiety.

Arthur leaned down to meet her eyes. "That was a long time ago."

Brow furrowed, she considered. "I suppose it was. Before Mr. Barrett came, anyway." Her clear blue eyes were troubled. "That's what you mean, isn't it? That it's different now?"

Her father nodded. "He told me I was coddling them, and I didn't disagree. I didn't fight for what I believed. Not like *you* did for Illiann Ivy. Not like Julian Ivy did for my workers."

"Mr. Barrett doesn't like Ilya's father, does he?"

"It's safe to say my partner is annoyed by anyone's opinion but his own. That makes Mr. Ivy dangerous, because he's not afraid to say what he thinks."

"Do you wish Mr. Ivy would stop?"

"A bit," he agreed unwillingly. "But I wish even more that he wouldn't. No matter how much Barrett raged, Arthur did not want *The Voice* to fall silent.

Chapter 60

Saylah awakened in Julian's arms. With a sigh of relief, she rested her head on his crumpled nightshirt.

He tried to stroke her hair, but his fingers caught in the tangles. She had not slept peacefully, tossing and turning with the tumult of her dream.

As he murmured her name again and again, her trembling subsided and the violence and the tempo of the dream began to fade. When she was certain she could speak calmly, whispered, "I must go back to the Salish."

Julian had known this was coming since the day his wife first met Old Grandmother, but that did not make it hurt any less. "I don't want you to go," he said, "because I'm selfish; because, with all the men who talk to me hour after hour, I'm lonely for your company. Because I miss you."

Saylah smiled and cupped her husband's face in her hands. "I have missed you too, but we knew it would be like this, at least for awhile. I am only glad you have Sophia, or you would never get home at night."

She put her arms around his neck, aware of the scent of his body, wrapped in sleep, the touch of his skin under her cheek, the brown hair that curled over his chest. She found his heartbeat with her palm and listened, eased by the rhythmic pulse.

Julian closed his eyes at her caress.

"I must go," she said again.

"I understand. I won't stop you. You know I won't."

Saylah raised her head and smiled. "Yes, I do." She began to kiss him, but the door flew open abruptly.

Illiann stood on the threshold, disheveled and anxious.

"What is it?" her parents said in unison.

"I keep hearing a drumbeat. It's keeping me awake."

Saylah was taken aback. Had Illiann really stepped into her mother's dream? "It woke me as well."

"What does it mean?" The girl was obviously shaken.

"I will go to the People. I feel I am needed."

"Let me go with you!"

"No." Saylah's answer was clear and final, made more dramatic by Julian's echo.

"But you promised to teach me. Maybe I can help."

"Not in the storm."

"The storm must have been in your dream, Mama. Listen. The air outside is still."

Saylah glanced at the window and realized her daughter was right. She was chilled by a sense of foreboding

"Papa? Please!"

"Your mother is right. She has already answered your question. Go back to bed now."

"Go now," Saylah murmured. "Try to sleep."

Fighting a wave of anger—they had dismissed her like a misbehaving child, had not even listened to her warning—Illiann turned to away. The drumbeat followed, imperative and undiminished.

Chapter 61

The gloomy morning had slipped into a grim afternoon of threatening clouds, when Agatha Hart heard the door chimes sound. She was in the drawing room, pretending to write a letter, but her thoughts were too scattered and the words would not come. Arthur was up to something; she was sure of it. She knew him well enough to mistrust both the deep furrow between his brows and the bounce in his step when he left that morning.

A servant appeared in the doorway. "Who is it, Alice?"

"A Mr. Smith has come to call. I didn't think you would want me to let him in. He's waiting on the porch." She pressed her lips together in disapproval. "He insisted on speaking to you personally."

Agatha's mouth went dry. "Thank you. I'll go this way." By slipping out through the French doors in the drawing room, she managed to reach the porch without being noticed by the neighbors.

She saw Mr. Smith before he saw her. He had called once before. He worked for Robert Barrett and had come to encourage Agatha to make her husband accept Barrett's offer for the ironworks. She should have been appalled by his brazen approach, but she had been more concerned about her family's well-being.

"Mrs. Hart." The broad-shouldered, lumbering man nodded brusquely but did not bother to remove his felt hat.

Agatha knew from experience he did not waste time with pleasantries. "What is it?"

"Mr. Barrett said to stop by and ask if you know what your husband's up to?"

She could see that he did not expect her to know. He had not come to ask, but to reveal. Agatha was insulted, but the threat implied by his size and his harsh, gravelly voice kept her from speaking out. She shook her head.

Mr. Smith nodded smugly. "Mr. Hart's been worryin' Mr. Barrett. Doesn't see the threat from Ivy and his thugs. Wants to bargain with the workers."

Agatha rubbed her temples with her forefingers. Arthur had always been impractical and quixotic; it had almost ruined them when he first took over the works. He was weak, and one of them had to be strong, especially now. It would have to be her.

"Mr. Barrett wants you to talk to Mr. Hart like last time. Remind 'im you like your life and want to keep it." He raised dark eyebrows in a silent but eloquent warning.

She could not believe the impertinent underling was trying to bully her. She drew herself up, cheeks flushed with anger. "I'll thank you to tell Mr. Barrett I will speak to Arthur for my own reasons. Tell him, as well, that I do not like being threatened and, in future, if he has any messages for me, he should deliver them himself."

"Only lookin' out for your interests. I'll tell 'im you don't want 'im to anymore."

If possible, she stood straighter still. "I am perfectly capable of looking after myself."

"Then why'd you agree to see me?"

"My motives are not your concern, just as yours are not mine. The important thing, Mr. Smith, is that we know we are working toward the same end: the preservation and financial success of the ironworks. Can we agree on that?"

"Guess so." Smith did not believe in wondering and worrying, only in doing.

"Excellent." Agatha's voice was clipped and precise. She was back in control.

Chapter 62

The wind whistled and moaned through the gray-blue waves that crashed against the shore as Lord Byron attacked the rocky beach. The air was frigid and heavy with moisture that turned it a strange shade of milky white. Kit and Will followed the dog, scanning the grainy sand for interesting rocks and shells. They were planning to build a new wall at the tree house and decorate it with shapes and shards thrown into their hands by the sea.

"I might give this one to my mother," Kit said, holding up a speckled green pebble with a vivid yellow pattern splashed across it. "She collects stones."

"What for?" Will was playing his usual game of glancing over his shoulder every few minutes, pretending someone was watching. Just now he was poised on the balls of his feet as if ready to flee. He also kept a sharp eye on Lord Byron, who barked and cavorted a short way down the strand.

Kit sighed at his friend's theatrics. At least Will was never dull. "She says the special ones have magic." He dug the toe of his boot into the sand. "But that's just my mother. She's like that." The dog distracted him from his embarrassment, thrusting a stick into his hand and nudging his leg eagerly. "You want to chase it?" he asked. "Go on, then." He threw it as hard as he could, end over end. Lord Byron chased it joyfully, wagging his tail and barking out his pleasure.

"Hey! I saw someone over the ridge there. I think he's watching us."

Kit turned to see where his friend was pointing, but Will grabbed his arm. "Don't look! He'll know we've seen him."

"*I* haven't seen him, and anyway, if we glare right back, it might scare him away."

"I'm not kidding this time. I saw someone. I might have seen him before. He's following us, Kit!"

The urgency in his voice, along with the high color in his cheeks, told their own story. Kit turned when he heard Lord Byron thundering toward them, but the dog froze in mid-bark, staring at the embankment. He flattened his ears against his head and his fur stood up in a line down his back. He growled deep and low in his throat. Kit felt a chill that had nothing to do with the ocean wind.

Will moved closer. "What should we do?" His voice was lost in the hiss and thunder of the waves.

"Who is it, boy?" he asked as though he expected an answer. "Go see." He pointed at the clumped bracken and ferns on top of the rise.

Lord Byron disappeared over the embankment, barked and growled ferociously, then reappeared, looking dejected. The dog did not join them on the beach; he seemed to be waiting for *them* to join *him*.

"Come on," Kit whispered. "Whoever it was must be gone." He sounded brave, but inside, he was quaking. The only other time he had seen his dog react like that had been when a cougar endangered Ilya back at the ranch.

Will followed slowly, rubbing his arms through his jacket.

Warily, the boys approached the rise where the dog was, and peered over the tangle of greenery, but saw nothing until they stood directly above the road. There were imprints of two large boots in the fine mixture of sand and dirt, despite an obvious attempt to smooth them over.

"Oh dear," Will muttered. "Oh dear, oh dear."

"Oh *dear*?" Kit demanded. "Is that all you can say?

Will couldn't help it. He grinned. "Should we chase him?"

"You saw him. Is he big?"

"Pretty tall and pretty strong. He didn't have any hair though."

As if that made him less threatening. Kit sighed and motioned the dog to his side. When Lord Byron pressed close to his leg, he buried his hand in the dog's thick fur. It was something to hold on to. "Then maybe we shouldn't chase him."

"But there're two of us and only one of him." Now that the man was gone, Will had regained his spirit of adventure.

Kit despaired. "That's just dumb. What do you think, Lord Byron?"

The dog ran toward the road, turning back to see if the boys had followed. He seemed to agree with Will.

Swallowing his dread, Kit nodded to his friend. "Let's go."

Lord Byron raced ahead, nose to the ground, turned back, and then raced ahead again. He paused at the base of the yew with the tree house in its upper branches. Jumping up frantically, Lord Byron clawed the steps nailed to the trunk.

Kit and Will looked at each other. "Do you think he's up there?"

"I don't think so. Lord Byron's hair isn't standing on end and he isn't growling, but the man must have been here or the dog wouldn't act like that. Let's go see."

The boys climbed hand over hand, step over step, holding their collective breath while Lord Byron admonished them from the ground.

Finally, they stood on the platform and glanced around cautiously, until they noticed the heavy tarp Kit used to protect the camera from small animals and wet weather. It was slightly askew.

He cried out, diving for the floor so quickly that it shuddered beneath his weight. He threw off the covering and knelt down, peering at the folded box with the round lens protruding. Barely breathing, he removed the lens cap and stared backwards into the lens. "Will, come look. It's scratched. It wasn't before; I just used it today."

Solemnly, his friend joined him. "Don't the plates look funny, too?"

Kit lifted the three plate holders and shook them slightly. They clinked with the sound of broken glass, as if someone had hit the pile straight across the middle.

"Jesus God!" Will cried. "He was here. Right here. How did he know where we were? How did he know about the camera?"

"And why? *Why*?" Kit drew his knees up to his body, locking his arms tight around them.

"It was my stepfather." Will's voice was barely audible. "I know it."

Kit gaped at him blankly. "I don't understand."

"He doesn't trust me. He doesn't even like me."

"But that's no reason to follow you. Anyway, isn't he working right now?"

Will's eyes turned wintry gray. "He wouldn't do it himself. He'd hire somebody. That's why he can do anything he wants."

The defeat in his tone sent a chill through Kit. He was confused and terribly frightened. "Who *is* your stepfather?"

Will was saved from answering when Lord Byron began to bark raucously.

The dog bolted, chasing a horse that emerged from a copse of spruce a little way down the road. The ground was muddy, and it churned up around him, weighting his paws with thick, dark ooze, but that did not stop him. He followed the horse tenaciously, snarling when he got close.

The rider reached down to pick something up, then tossed it as hard as he could toward the dog. The animal yelped and fell back in the mud.

"Hey!" Kit jumped to his feet and shouted after the man he couldn't see well enough to identify. "Hey! You can't throw rocks at my dog. Come back here!"

The rider didn't pause, but quickly disappeared from view.

Kit scrambled down the tree and went to Lord Byron, who was limping. The boy reached for the injured leg and examined it gently. "I think it's only bruised, not broken. I'll have Mama look at it at home." He buried his head in the dog's sleek fur, seeking comfort from the familiar sensation. All at once, he remembered how Will had teased him about being in peril as he made the photographs for his father's article. He had dismissed his friend's concern, but could not do so any longer.

"We have to do something, find out who he is."

"If I'd had my horse, I could've gone after him. He wouldn't have gotten far." Will was giddy with relief, now that they were out of immediate danger.

Lightning flashed overhead and thunder followed, so loud that it shook the treetops. The distant waves crashed violently against the rocky shore and rain began to pelt them. Lord Byron tried to hide under his master's arm. This time, Kit and Will moved as one, ducking their heads and running blindly, seeking cover.

Chapter 63

The clouds hung low and dark in the sky, though the rain had stopped for the time being, as Illiann alighted from the streetcar. She did not want to go home, because Saylah would not be there, and inside the house, with the storm brewing outside, Illiann would not be able to escape the premonition of danger that still haunted her.

Half angry and half frightened, she had found herself drawn to Devon's house. She sensed that she should fear him more than the rhythm of the drums, but this fear was somehow alluring, and she could not resist. Despite the warning voice in her head, she had come, drawn by the intensity of her dream.

"I must be mad to come here," she said aloud, just to hear the sound of a human voice. Illiann was ambivalent, yet her will pushed her forward, would not let her retreat, as it had not let her retreat from the dance she knew would cause havoc at Miss Chadwick's.

She had not seen Devon in a while, and had thought she did not miss him. Until this morning, when she shrank from the mesmerizing rhythm of the drums and knew he would understand. Now the image of Devon and his clean white room was with her, vivid and compelling. Despite the voice in her head that warned of danger, she had come, drawn by that arresting memory.

She almost turned away at the doorstep, but seemingly of its own accord, her hand rapped loudly, and she heard the echo fade in the silence beyond. The curtains were closed, but that did not convince her. She was vacillating about trying the knob when it began to rain again.

Before she could talk herself out of it, she opened the door and stepped inside. She paused to listen for a long time, cold fingers wrapped around the dented knob. She heard nothing but a dusty hush, and deep inside her body, a heartbeat that was not her own.

She turned unerringly toward the door with the crystal knob, stopping when she saw that it was cracked open. Cautiously, she crept forward until she could see inside.

She held her breath when she saw Devon move through a beam of light that pierced the clouds and the glistening windows. He was wearing a smeared, filthy smock, holding a paintbrush and pacing back and forth, deep in thought. She suspected he had not heard her knock, and was certain that if he had, he would not have answered.

His concentration was intense, his turquoise eyes alight with pleasure, his mobile features transformed. His curly beard was streaked with paint, his red hair dirty, but his skin glowed, and he smiled, exultantly.

Illiann tilted her head so she could see the canvas he was working on. He had given that vast whiteness life and color. She drew in her breath and her throat went dry.

The image was of a girl/woman with long black hair flying, blended so the ends appeared to mingle with the rain-dark clouds. Her long graceful legs were spread in a leap, and the grass was strewn with tulips and poppies, gathered under her as if ready to burst into flame. Her skirt swirled around her, a rust-colored blur, and her hands were outstretched to catch the rain. Her face was raised, glowing with ecstasy.

It was Illiann's face, and this her dance. She knew now what had brought her here. She went very still, watching in rapt silence.

Devon paused to rub his forehead, leaving a streak of orange behind. Suddenly Illiann was terrified he would look up and see her. She was not ready. She could not face him yet.

She turned and made her way back down the hall, leaving part of her childhood behind. She felt she had aged in that moment of revelation, and the feeling frightened her. Distracted, she found herself in the kitchen.

The room was as messy as she remembered, but that did not surprise her. She noticed the food on the dishes was hard and old, and wondered if, driven by his creative frenzy, Devon had forgotten to eat. Without conscious thought, she began to clean up. She knew he would not hear. As she gathered what fresh food she could find and put together a meal of beans, bread and cheese, her shock faded and a strange sense of calm enfolded her.

With a new sense of resolution, she took a plate of food in one hand and a mug of root beer in the other. Devon might rage and storm and order her out, but she did not intend to leave.

This time, when she paused in the hall, Devon sensed her presence and spun to face her. Illiann held out the food in explanation. "How long since you've eaten?"

He blinked and wondered where his rage had gone. He was not angry to see this girl who had crept stealthily into his home and his kitchen and his mind. He was startled to realize he did not think it odd that she was here. It came to him that he had been expecting her for a long time. He smiled crookedly.

"Too long. But I'm guessin' you know as much." He motioned her into the room, took the plate and mug and sat against the wall.

Illiann sat beside him, legs crossed under her skirt.

Devon had already begun to eat, his hands shaking at the strength of his hunger. "I don't know how long I've been here. I've no' counted the days. Time's different when I work -- sometimes so slow it's eternity, sometimes so fast it's the end of the world." He considered her, brow furrowed. "How did you know?"

"I didn't, exactly." She paused, twisting her finger in the end of her braid. "I just knew I had to come."

Outside, lightning illuminated a treacherous sky. "Did you come in spite of the storm?"

Illiann surprised herself. "I came *because* of the storm, to show you I'm not afraid." She looked away, embarrassed. "Besides, Papa mentioned he hadn't seen you, and with all that's going on, he couldn't understand why. Everyone was wondering where you were. Kit and Casey and Papa and everyone came by and knocked on the door, but no one answered."

He closed his eyes with a sigh. "No one was here."

Though she could not explain how, Illiann understood that though he had physically been in this room, his mind and spirit had been somewhere else, where hunger and stiff muscles and distant door chimes did not matter.

Devon sighed with weariness, which shone in his red-rimmed eyes and the unnatural whiteness of his skin. But within the exhaustion, there was satisfaction.

She contemplated him in silence. "You didn't go away. You came back to where you belong."

"Everyone except you wondered where I was, but you knew." He wanted to look away, just as he had wanted to turn so often from the canvas, from the colors taking shape and life beneath his hands, but the pain was too exquisite. "You know far too much, I'm thinkin'."

"No, I don't," she murmured sadly.

He shifted his weight. "Today you caught me unaware, but tomorrow, or any other day, I won't be rememberin' your face or your courage or your luminous eyes. I'll no' recognize the flecks of gold and green that make those eyes your father's. You should be after havin' your mother's eyes, you know." He paused. He was wandering down paths he did not wish to follow. "Sure an' the day will soon come when I'll turn my back on this again." He waved to indicate the white room full of light.

"And on me," Illiann murmured. "You'll turn your back on me." She was relieved by the thought, and oddly despondent.

"'Tis true you're part of this, since the day you wept with my paintin's around you and became one of them, Ellen."

She could feel him withdrawing, rebuilding the glass and stone wall that protected his dreaming self, his soul. "My name is Illiann."

Devon shrugged deliberately, carelessly. "But I shall call you Ellen." He took a last bite of bread and cheese and chewed thoughtfully for a while.

Illiann rose, crossed to the painting, and as she had that other day, examined the palette, the brushes, the jar of turpentine. She closed her eyes and sniffed, trying to separate the smells. Linseed oil and paint and varnish. She did not wrinkle her nose in distaste. Even with her eyes closed, her face was lit with eagerness and curiosity.

She opened her eyes and looked at the palette, touched the daubs of paint, rubbed her fingertips together, coming to know the texture, the smell. Finally, she turned to the painting. She reached out, but Devon's cry stopped her.

"Take care! 'Tis still wet."

Illiann smiled. "I can see that." She used one fingertip, brushed it gently over a tendril of flying hair. Her finger came away dark and fragrant with oil. She whirled. "Why will you turn away? How *can* you?"

Devon blinked. She was so innocent; she knew so little of real pain. Yet she burned with fervor just now, and her eyes were wet with unshed tears. "'Twill be necessary, me *Fand*, for keepin' me safe and sane."

"*Fand*? What does it mean?"

"'Tis the name of a woman from an old Celtic tale. It means gentle, but also stands for tear. Like the one on your cheek just now." He touched it with his fingertip, gently, as she had touched the painting.

She had not known it was there until he lifted it away and held it so the light struck it. He kissed his finger and the tear disappeared.

Devon's gaze held hers. "What does it matter to you if I've a mind to close this door and never open it again?"

Illiann was caught up in the lilt of his Irish voice and the web of her own confused yearning. "It matters. You belong here."

Devon took a swig of root beer and wished it were dark strong ale. "You're very wise for a girl so young."

Illiann straightened defensively. "I'm not a girl. I'm becoming a woman." She spoke the truth; she felt she had aged each moment since she opened the door and let herself in. She nodded toward the painting on the easel. "You know that."

"You'd best not be *too* wise, or you might become a fool."

Illiann smiled. "I'm not afraid of being a fool." She nodded toward the painting. "Was it really so difficult to start again?" Her eyes were grave, her hand poised in mid-air, as if she were waiting for him to fill it.

He leaned against the wall and stretched out his legs. "'Tis an odd thing," he mused. "It didn't hurt at all. It came back so sweetly, like it'd never left me."

"It didn't. You pretended it was gone, but it was there in your blood all along."

"Like the dance was in yours?"

Solemnly, she nodded. "When I watched you work, you were so vibrant. Every hair and freckle and muscle and nerve was breathing life and creation. I felt it all through me, like a shock. But it wasn't unpleasant. I was excited, and I wanted...something." In the back of her mind, she knew she should not be here, should not be telling him these things, should not speak truths that stripped her bare. It was too dangerous.

Devon was lost in his own thoughts. "As I said,'twas sweet. But the pain'll be comin' in time. Can't be helped, that. No more than you findin' this room and understandin' what it means. No more than you comin' here today."

His eyes glowed and Illiann felt a stirring of tension, apprehension and expectation. "You mean so I could keep you from starving?"

He reached out to touch her cheek. "I was no' starvin', *Aedh*. I had everything I'm needin', everything I'm wantin', everything I'm fearin' and everything I crave." He forestalled the question on her lips. "*Aedh* is a fire spark. *Aedh* is you."

The pulse in her throat throbbed, fragile and eloquent. "It's getting dark," Illiann whispered, too dazed to raise her voice and too hypnotized to move. "I don't hear the rain, so this must be real darkness, not just clouds and fury." She shivered and leaned toward him, so he saw the swell of her breasts beneath her shirtwaist. "It fed you, the painting; it gave you magic. But you'll begin to starve again, I think. You aren't just angry and in pain," she said, stunned by the realization, "you're afraid."

"'Tis the way to survive."

Illiann was so close he could smell her sweet breath, feel it caress his cheek. "To survive without living? Why bother?"

"Maybe 'tis true that you're no longer after bein' a child," Devon whispered. "I bother because, beyond the emptiness, there's always something lovely enough to tempt me to believe one day it'll be full again." He paused, holding his breath. "Something -- or someone." He lifted her hair away from her face and kissed her, very lightly, on the cheek, just touching the corner of her parted lips.

She shivered and her face grew warm with the heat of his breath.

"I shall call you Ellen," he repeated.

"I shall not answer." Illiann's voice shook, despite her resolution.

"Too late, me *Fand*. You already have."

Chapter 64

For the first time since their arrival in Victoria, Julian was without Saylah in the house at night. He guessed she was stranded at the Indian village by the storm. If she were, he was glad to know she had the sense not to risk crossing the inlet in the turbulent weather. But he missed her.

Now her voice came back to him in the beat of the rain, and he decided to go on an expedition to the attic, where their personal papers were stored. He was looking for a photograph of their wedding that he had been driven to find since the moment she left that morning. He wanted to reassure himself that Saylah was still his wife by finding in the faded image the emotions he had felt on that long ago day. It was absurd. He needed to see and touch the image of his wife, whom he'd held in his arms a few hours earlier.

On the second floor there was a latch that released the stepladder hidden in the ceiling. With a few sharp tugs, he freed it and the ladder slid down, revealing a narrow opening in the attic floor.

Julian hoisted himself through the opening and stood gingerly to avoid dropping the lamp he held. The room was large, echoing and dark, empty except for several trunks that seemed to crouch like hulking animals beneath their tarps. The rain beat heavily on the roof as if it planned to batter its way inside. Downstairs it had been too quiet. Up here it was too noisy; there was no escape from the rising fury of the storm.

He wasted no time, but threw the tarps off and began to look inside the trunks. He opened one after another, sifting quickly through the contents. Once or twice there was a flash of lightning through the dust-covered windows at either end of the barren room.

Julian paused when he came upon Saylah's wedding dress. This was the trunk he wanted. Running his hand over the patterned silk, he remembered how warm it had been the day they were married, though it was still winter. His new wife had absorbed the sun and given it back to him in her smile, in her shimmering green eyes, in the heat of the polished fabric. Now the silk was cold and smelled slightly bitter. But that would be the cedar and herbs Saylah had packed away in each trunk to keep the contents fresh. The photograph was not there.

Just a touch of fabric could take him so far back that he felt he was there, marrying her all over again, speaking his vows and rejoicing in hers. He was reluctant to let he memory go, but knew he could not retreat into the past forever. That's what his father had done.

Laying the dress aside, he plunged once more into the trunk and found some of his half-brother Theron's language books, his laborious translations of French words into English and back again. Julian reached in farther and closed his hand over a book bound in velvet.

He froze, unable either to drop it back into the depths or pull it out into the light. All at once, the night and the darkness were closing in on him. This must be his mother's diary.

On his knees in the flickering pool of lamplight, he realized it could not begin to warm the draughty attic or chase away the shadows.

He dropped the book and reached for something else. It felt like a manuscript and he took it out to find a thick stack of paper bound by string, with Theron's handwriting on the first dog-eared page. "Simone Ivy," Julian read, "May, 1859."

He frowned and stared at the words for a long time. He remembered that, in his second year of French, Theron had translated the diary as an exercise for his tutor.

248

If Julian ruffled the pages slowly enough to catch a few words, he would hear the echo of his mother's voice. It was a sound he had struggled for years to forget.

While the rain beat out its rage on the roof, Julian untied the string and turned several pages. A name caught his eye, and he could not look away.

Jamie stands, face turned toward the sky, though he does not absorb the light from the sun. Rather, I think the sun absorbs its light from him, for he is brilliant with dreams.

Julian was stunned. In an instant, Simone had brought the inspired father of his youth back to him. He had seen Jamie stand just so, before he lost his faith; he had felt the beauty of a sunset pale before the power of his father's dreams. But he had not tried to put into words that feeling of awe and incredulity. That his mother could have done so both shocked and dismayed him. The words blurred into wavering lines.

Though he wanted to close the manuscript, to bury it in the chest and forget it, he knew he could not. The allure was too strong, and it bent his will as easily as the lamplight chased the shadows. Unceremoniously, he sat on the floor and began to read.

Fear is a cold and comfortless thing, yet I hold mine close and feel its texture, its color, its very breath. It is all I know well and long, and so I clutch it, cling to it. Now, in the clear, clean light of dawn, I can say it. Does one fear most that which one does not yet know, or that which one knows all too well?

If there is an answer, I have not yet found it, and perhaps I should be grateful for that, as I am for the many blessings my Jamie has given me. I would be barren without him, without my son, whose wisdom at his young age impresses and saddens me. He has never known the carefree joy of childhood, and I would wish that for him. That and so much more. This family, this place are more than I had ever hoped to find, and if I found them, even less did I expect they would be mine.

Julian read the paragraph for the third time, caught up in his mother's powerful emotions. The words brought back her mellifluous voice, her many admonitions that he enjoy himself more and work less, that he be happy. The too familiar feelings of his youth washed over him, making his hands shake so he had to try twice to turn the page. He had to admit it was difficult to maintain the intensity of his resentment against her when her words were so poignant, her voice so lovely. He had once told Saylah and Illiann he had been listening for years as they read the diary out loud to one another, but he had been mistaken. He had not really heard at all—not until now.

It will happen. The past is never lost, escaped from, forgotten. Always it returns to consume and destroy. But until then, I shall lose myself in the enchanting quality of light—ever shifting, softer, kinder here than anywhere else on earth. The light which falls through the mist—muted and kind—breaks through the clouds: bright and pure. It sparkles on the water like fire on tumbled gems. The life-giving light in which beauty and fear thrive side by side.

"Papa?"

Kit's voice reverberated jarringly through the gloom, startling Julian so much that he dropped the stack of pages. He had been completely lost in and enveloped by these fragments of his mother's life, yet he knew little more now than he had when he first opened the chest. He resented that ignorance, that tale left untold, almost as much as he resented the spell Simone had cast over him. Afraid of what his expression might reveal, he picked the manuscript up and put it under his arm.

"Where are you? Are you there?"

The boy sounded panicked. He must be downstairs, shouting up the ladder.

"Up here. I'm just coming down, Kit. Wait for me."

Kit did not want to wait. He scrambled, crablike, up the ladder. The sight of his father caught in a circle of fluttering light which only deepened the darkness around him, did nothing to soothe the boy's nerves. "You look like a ghost or something. You scared me."

"I feel rather like a phantom. I don't really like it up here. Especially tonight."

Kit seemed frozen half in and half out of the attic and his eyes glittered.

"What's wrong?" Suddenly, Julian was fully alert.

His son swallowed. "Nothing really." He said it so casually that it was obvious he was lying. "I just wondered where you'd gone."

Still holding Simone's diary beneath his arm, Julian joined his son. No matter what Kit said, something had happened to upset him. Julian had been wasting time sorting through unhappy memories while his son needed him.

"Right," he said. "Well, I'm cold and I need to relax, even if you don't." Julian crouched next to the attic opening. "Maybe you'd do me a favor and keep me company."

The boy nodded in relief. "Sure. I don't mind." Once again, he spoke with too much care, revealing his inner turmoil in the things he did not say.

Chapter 65

Simone glided through the house in a fog, until she stopped before one of the few mirrors. She turned away to avoid its revelations; she did not need to see her face to know her skin was pallid and her eyes cloudy. Still, the thought woke her from her trance. She was looking for Mathilde, who was nowhere to be found. Could she possibly know why her mistress was seeking her? Was she hiding to avoid a confrontation? The idea was absurd. Mathilde did not believe in hiding. *Can't ignore those shadows lurking down the lanes. I turn and face 'em head on and shriek like a madwoman.*

With a renewed sense of purpose, Simone made her way down two flights of stairs to the isolated corner where the servant chose to keep her room. Holding her breath, she knocked sharply. "Mathilde? Are you there?"

The door was wrenched open and the servant stood gaping at her in consternation. "What're you doin' down here?" She blocked the entry with her bulk while trying to read her mistress' expression. "Hurtin' so much you're afraid to be alone? Grief can do that. Suck you dry until your bones collapse. Knew this might happen. Made cocoa and brioche for when you got home. Didn't eat a thing this morning."

"I would like to come in."

"Here?" The servant's mouth fell open. "But why?"

"I must talk to you, and I wish to sit. I imagine you may wish to as well."

Mathilde knew when she was beaten. The other woman's tone brooked no argument. She opened the door wide and stepped back.

Simone actually gasped at the chill austerity of the room, whichwas bare of any decoration. There was a small pallet for a bed, a single worn night table, a cross and a small wood stove for heat. It was not very effective. Shivering at the cold, she sat in the one chair: a battered oak rocker with cushions so faded the design was no longer discernible. "I don't understand. You know you may have any room you wish, any furniture, any hangings. Why do you hide down here in this…place?"

Shrugging, the servant plopped down on the bed. "Frills and feather pillows 'd be wasted on me. Make me think I have to behave. Can't have that."

"I see." But she didn't. Simone decided to get directly to the point. "Here is what I am wondering. After Claude's funeral, I went into the church to pray and saw an emerald necklace there."

"Aaahhhhh! De M's jewels." Mathilde nodded soberly "Wife's been at it again, I'll wager." She was uncomfortable under her mistress' intent regard. She remembered clearly her amused warning: I believe you are becoming obsessed.

"I do not think Madame de Marchand had anything to do with it. This necklace is one you tried to give me on my wedding night. I remember well how insistent you were that I take the gems." She took a deep breath. "I wonder, did you take them instead?"

There was a brief, breathless silence. The servant waved her arms to ward off the question. "What would I do with them?"

It's a puzzle, and I do love a puzzle, she had said, all innocence.

"I suppose if you were wise…well…you might keep them hidden for years, saving them in case I ever returned."Or perhaps, realizing I would never accept them, eventually, you might have decided to use the gems to punish Henri."

De M's an arrogant fool who never thinks of anyone else's pain, only his own.

254

"You might, for instance, have noticed that sometimes the rich leave small offerings of gems in the collection plate. That might have kindled the germ of an ingenious plan to present to the Church the jewels you had hoarded in secret for so long."

Mathilde's mouth fell open. "Glad you think I'm that devious. A great compliment, really." She brandished one blunt-fingered hand to deny the possibility. "But go to so much trouble just to make a man look ridiculous?" She frowned accusingly at the pitted lamp on the night table.

"Not—" she said, when Simone began to interrupt, "that it isn't proper. Man deserves such a diabolical punishment." She closed her eyes and shivered with delight. "Won't lie. Love to imagine those beautiful gems lyin' against cold stone instead of smooth white skin.

"But, and mind you, only guessing, *if* a person had been keeping the jewels after de M got an annulment, would've known they didn't belong to him. Never had, accordin' to the Church. Never married you, so never stole–inherited–all your worldly possessions."

Simone looked thoughtful. "They would have belonged to him if he had them in his possession. A court would never have given them back to me."

Mathilde raised her finger pointedly, as if instructing a recalcitrant pupil. "Didn't *have* possession, or why keep askin' for 'em back? Why chase you around the world if they were sittin' in a velvet bag next to his smokin' chair? Why bring you back? Nothing against you, Madame, but doubt it was out of affection. Might've been safe to give 'the jewels back to you, except de M's a cruel, mean-spirited man. Would've taken 'em away again, no matter he had no right."

Not once had Simone thought of that. The annulment had indeed freed her from all obligations. Henri's outrageous demands *were* proof he did not have the jewelry. She felt like an utter fool. "Why did you not tell me?

"Tried to. You didn't hear."

Now Simone remembered. *Must've gone soft in the head, accusin' you like that when the jewels don't even belong to him. Claimin' those gems belonged to his family. Ridiculous.* Why could she hear the words so clearly now, when she had ignored them then? "So you did. I suppose I was not really listening."

"Doesn't matter in the end, because de M *believed* they were his. Wouldn't have paid attention if you told him otherwise. Too greedy for anybody's good, if you ask me."

Simone thought she understood at last why de Marchand hated her so much. She had made a fool of him more than once, or so he thought. First by running away, and then by taunting him with her family jewels. You will not stop this persecution? he had asked in desperation. She had given him the only answer she could.

I cannot stop what I have not begun.

"Man ruined your life, Madame, and whoever had the gems helped him do it. All you ever wanted was happiness and a family gathered at your feet. To have taken those things from you would've killed me."

Except it hadn't. The moisture in Mathilde's eyes, the anguish in her gravelly voice told their own truth. She could not say the words, but they were not necessary.

Simone could not move. How self-absorbed had she been all these years, how complacent? How many like Mathilde and the Duc had cared for her, kept her comfortable, suffered her pain while tenderly nourishing her blemished soul?

She had been thoughtless and selfish, and thus had brought her nightmares crashing down around every one of those she loved. Too late, she realized what she had done.

Or was it, after all, too late? Could she begin again?

"Yes, Madame, you can."

She did not realize she had spoken aloud.

"You're strong, stronger'n you believe, stronger by far than your faults or weaknesses. Also kind and generous;

never forget your friends. Don't know what I would've done without you. "

What was it Mathilde had told her once? A fool, that's what you are. But God blesses such fools, because their hearts are pure.

Simone could only hope that it was true.

Chapter 66

While night fell unnoticed in the starless frenzy of the storm, Julian and Kit settled at the scrubbed pine table in the kitchen. The fire burned high and bright, dispelling not only the cold, but also the gloom. Sung-li had gone home long since, so Julian heated some hot chocolate and poured it into pottery mugs. Kit cupped his hands around the mug and felt the heat seep into his chilled fingers, then took two quick gulps, burning his tongue on the hot, creamy mixture.

"Careful, or you won't be able to taste the breakfast buns."

"Sorry," his son replied automatically. He was staring intently at the pages his father had dropped on the table, out of reach. "Isn't that my grandmother's book?"

Julian frowned. "Have you seen the diary before?"

"I heard about it, and I know it makes you sad." The boy took another drink to give himself courage. He had always wanted to ask about his mysterious grandmother. "Is that because she went away? Or just because she's gone?"

Julian was disconcerted. He had not realized Kit was perceptive enough to realize there was a difference between the two. "Both, I think. Because she left us at all, and because I missed her so much for such a long time."

"You don't anymore?"

"You can't mourn forever."

"You can't?" Kit was pretty sure his grandfather had done so.

Shifting his weight restlessly, Julian shook his head. "As time passes, you grow up, you learn more and begin to understand things that didn't make sense before. And then you can accept them."

"But you *don't* understand. I heard you tell Mama so."

Julian was suddenly impatient, but with himself, not his son. Kit should not have to ask these questions. The shadow of Simone should never have touched him. He cupped the boy's chin in his palm. "That's because I didn't want her to go, but she left anyway. I was only nine, and that hurt so much I wanted to curl up and hide. Imagine if *your* mama left and wouldn't tell you why?"

Julian regretted it the moment the words came out of his mouth. Kit went pale and still.

"I can't. I don't want to!"

"You don't have to worry about anything like that. I shouldn't have said it. Forgive me?"

Had his father ever asked for forgiveness before? Kit didn't think so. "That's okay," he said generously.

"Anyway, I thought we came down here so you could tell me about your problem."

The boy gazed into his hot chocolate, running his finger around the inside of the rim. "It's not really that important."

"You said that before, and I didn't believe you then, either. You were very frightened up there on the ladder. I'd like it if you'd tell me why."

"It's just…I don't want you to worry." Kit shrugged with elaborate unconcern. "Today Will and I were at the beach with Lord Byron, and he went mad growling at someone invisible. Will said he saw a man, and that he'd seen him before, but when we went to look, no one was there. Just some footprints."

Julian's was becoming uneasy. "What else? There's more, isn't there?"

"Well, after that, we went back to this place we go sometimes near Beacon Hill Park. It's like a fort." He would not meet his father's eyes. "But that's not important. Except…." He faltered and had to pluck up his courage all over again. "Except the man had been there. He had found our hidden place."

Julian paled and Kit hurried to reassure him. "He was gone already. We' weren't hurt." He flushed. "But the camera lens was scratched and some plates broken. I take good care of it, I promise. But this man—"

"Don't worry about the camera, Kit. It can be fixed. I'm more worried about you. Did you see who he was?"

"Not really. He rode away on a horse. Lord Byron tried to stop him, but he threw a rock and knocked him down." The boy grew angry at the memory.

"That was a cowardly thing to do. Is the dog all right?"

Kit nodded energetically. "His leg was swollen, but I put ice on it and he's better now."

Julian smiled. "You did well, my boy. But now, let's consider this. You said Will had seen the man before?"

"I didn't believe him at first. He's always pretending there's some kind of trouble. It's like a game. I don't know why. That's just how he is."

"Did he tell you what the man looked like?"

Concentrating hard, Kit screwed up his face and tried to remember. "He said he was really tall and strong and that he didn't have any hair."

"And this man never actually came near enough to touch you?"

"No. I think Lord Byron scared him away." He paused, cleared his throat forcefully, and added, "I wasn't scared, though. I'm tougher than that."

"Hmmm," his father said noncommittally. "I think it likely he only wanted to frighten you. Apparently he failed." Not that that was very reassuring. Kit had always been fearless, and occasionally reckless, and Julian did not like the sound of this. He raised his head when he realized the rain, which had stopped for a while, had begun its assault again. It fell torrentially, battering the windows and roof. It was warm and dry in the kitchen, yet Julian huddled close to the table, not so much as a defense against wind and rain, but more against the *wrath* of the storm, the threat inherent in its fierce attack. He did not like to think of Saylah out in this, though he knew she had survived much worse. He had to stop. "Do you think the man was following you or Will?"

"Maybe both of us. Why break the camera if he was only after Will? That wouldn't hurt him at all."

"No, it wouldn't." Julian felt ill.

You cannot protect your children from all harm. Saylah's voice echoed in his memory. And then his own. *I just want them to be strong and unafraid.* She had smiled compassionately. *You mean indestructible.*

"Papa?"

"Listen to me, Kit. What I want to do is lock you in the house so you can't get out to be threatened by anyone ever again."

"You won't, will you? I'd hate that."

"I couldn't make you a prisoner, even if I tried. I'll look into this until I find out who's behind it. But in the meanwhile, you must be very careful. You must take Lord Byron with you whenever you can, and watch and be aware. And please tell me the instant anything strange happens again. Do you promise?"

Kit shrugged. "Sure. But you don't have to worry. I can take care of myself."

Julian knew it wasn't true, but would never insult his son by saying so. He drew Kit close and hugged him hard. "You're very precious to me."

The boy was embarrassed, but didn't pull away. He knew it made his father feel better.

It occurred to him that this was the perfect opportunity to put his dearest wish into words. "I know something that'd help. If I had a bicycle like Will's, I could get away faster."

Julian considered. "You're certainly old enough to ride one, and I've seen how you handle the camera, so I know you'd take care of it, but I'm not sure we can afford one right now." The paper was doing well, but it would be a long time before it could provide a living for all the men who worked there. At the moment, their income came largely from freelance printing jobs, of which they had a good number, but they were still building a clientele for the shop. Julian still had income and savings from the ranch, but he was reluctant to let go of his back-up money.

Disappointment burned in Kit's throat, but he did not let it show. "That's okay. I can borrow Will's sometimes."

"I'm sorry, Kit. But I'll keep it in mind. And speaking of Will, are you absolutely positive this whole incident wasn't one of his games?"

"I don't think he lies. He's just always afraid."

Julian was sympathetic. "Why is that?"

"It's just—I don't think he's happy. I don't think he likes his parents much." His tone revealed how improbable he found the thought. "They're too busy and don't have much time for him. I wish I could help."

"It's quite kind of you to be so concerned about your friend. Maybe your mother and I can help as well. I want you to know that I think you've been handling well…everything since we came to the city. A strange school, Devon's injury, Sung-li's request, and now this. You're being very smart and very brave, and I'm proud of you."

Kit's chest swelled with gratification. He hated the warmth he felt staining his cheeks; it was stupid and childish, but his father didn't seem to notice. He was secretly glad when the doorbell clamored loudly enough to make them both jump.

Julian took a deep, steadying breath and headed for the front door.

Guardedly, he pulled it open, blinking in disbelief at the late night caller. Standing on his porch, cloaked and hooded and sodden with rain, was no other than Arthur Hart.

Chapter 67

That morning, Saylah had crossed the bay in the growing threat of the storm. The stirring motion of the wind-tossed sea, the bitter taste of salt in the misted air, the sting of the cold wind on her cheeks reminded her of the warning in her dream.

Having clamored up the ladder to the dock, she had settled her healing bag over her shoulder and set out through the woods. The trees were swathed in cloaks of white that diminished the sound of the wind through the branches, the chattering of birds, the rustle of small animals. The hush of morning had been profound.

The houses in the isolated village were shrouded in fog, heavy with the weight of the coming tempest. There was no movement, no raised voices, no echoing footsteps. The circle of houses was eerily silent, as if anticipating some grave event. Saylah sensed she would need all her skills today.

She headed directly to Old Grandmother's house, but before she could knock, the door swung open.

"Come in," Patal whispered. "We wait for you."

Over his shoulder, she saw that his grandmother was in bed with several blankets tucked in tight around her. Saylah's swallowed a gasp of surprise. She had not seen the woman look helpless before, and the sight shocked her. Old Grandmother's skin had a grayish cast, and she looked frail, with bones as thin as twigs and just as brittle. Her long silver hair was tangled and damp with her sweat. "You are ill."

"Last night I called for the loon to help me. I knew you would come."

She spoke with difficulty, stretching her lips taut with each word. Saylah realized the left side of her face was not moving; the features drooped as if they had grown heavy and awkward. She had seen the symptoms before, years ago when she worked with Doctor Helmcken. She turned to Patal. "When did this happen?"

He frowned. "It was after midnight and before dawn. There was yet no light outside." He glanced through the dirty windows at the overcast sky. "Just as there is none now." He blinked, battling for control. "She called out once, then fell out of bed."

Saylah touched his arm reassuringly. "I will need hot water, a kettle, some bowls and cloths and a cup."

Patal was grateful for something to do. He collected what she needed as she took out her mortar and pestle and laid the herbs and roots on the low table beside the bed. There was red cedar to steep for fever, Western white pine and Sitka spruce to clean and purify the blood, and larkspur to increase a sluggish pulse. Saylah had to force herself to concentrate. Though she had met the woman a little over a month before, had visited her only thrice in that time, she felt as though she might lose a dear friend. They understood each other effortlessly, and were comfortable with one another's dreams. Saylah had not felt this kind of connection since she was a young girl. She struggled to hide her alarm. It was not easy to appear tranquil when her mouth was dry and her hands had a tendency to shake.

"Now," she said gently, turning to Old Grandmother. "Do you have pain?"

Old Grandmother nodded.

"Are your limbs heavy? Can you move your arms and legs?"

Her patient lifted one arm, but the other lay still on the blanket. A bulge appeared at the foot of the bed on one side but not the other. "Do you feel numbness in your fingers or toes?"

"Yes. I do not like it."

"Then you must give yourself into my hands."

"I did so when first we met. You know that."

Saylah worked slowly but efficiently, bathing Old Grandmother in an infusion of skunk cabbage root, trying imperceptibly to move her arms and legs, feeding her broth and teas to ease her suffering.

As the hours passed, she fell into a natural rhythm of crushing herbs, setting water to boil, brewing infusions and coaxing her patient to try to move. She sat on the floor beside the bed, her hands always in motion, her voice mellifluous and serene. The reassuring flow of the stories she interspersed with instructions did as much to help Old Grandmother as the healing herbs. Gradually, the old woman began to respond.

Saylah knew sometimes it was days or weeks, even months, before a stroke patient got better, sometimes merely hours. Old Grandmother was lucky. Already she was lifting her arm and leg, only by an inch or two, but it was progress. Relieved and exhausted, Patal had finally fallen asleep on his pallet in the corner.

Just before the storm broke, Old Grandmother motioned Saylah closer.

"I am better now," she said, "and if you are right, I will grow stronger still." She paused, not because she had lost her breath, but because she wanted to choose her words judiciously. The thunder roared and splintered above the house, and when she spoke again, it was against the cadence of brutal rain against the windows.

"There is no need to burn the death root for me yet. But someday I will become one with the shadows. When that time comes, the People will need inspiration, someone to give them hope and reassurance. They need your gifts and your memories and your spirit. Are you willing to share those things?"

Saylah was speechless. She had played that role before, to her own sorrow and the desolation of her village. It would not be the same here; she was older and far wiser now.

But still she did not know if she was willing to take that risk again, as well as the risk of betraying her family, who loved her.

"Are you willing?"

"I am not unwilling."

"But not altogether certain?"

Saylah bowed her head. "As you say."

"You would be a fool to come dancing blindly into our chaos to try and turn it into order, a fool if you did not think long and carefully. And one thing you are not, *Ladaila*, is a fool." Old Grandmother brushed her cheek with bent and wrinkled fingers. "But never forget, as I do not, that you are, and always have been, a queen."

"No," Saylah murmured. "I am only a friend. And that is so much better."

In its outrage at the leaden clouds that tried to hold it captive, the rain drowned out their voices. Saylah realized the water would be too rough to cross the harbor safely. She would have to stay the night.

The old woman nodded. "I will have to be content with that for now."

"I know," Saylah agreed, "for already, through your silence, I hear your voice inside me."

Chapter 68

The rain fell so hard it stung Julian's face. The wind swept it into every undefended corner. Arthur Hart stood in the midst of it; the porch roof was little protection from the blowing downpour. Julian was so unprepared for this apparition that he forgot his manners. "What do you want?"

Hart shifted from foot to foot, his shoes squishing unpleasantly. "I, uh…came to give you a printing job. Couldn't wait until tomorrow."

Julian didn't believe a word of it. "Why didn't you come to the shop? I don't work at this hour of the night."

His guest looked miserable as the rain trickled down his face and inside his collar. Finally, Julian shook himself, as shocked by his own behavior as he was by Arthur's. "You'd better come in. It's beastly out there." As if the man hadn't noticed.

He took Arthur's cold hand and cursed himself for being such a boor. He was chilled to the bone. With some effort, Julian drew Hart into the foyer and shut the door behind him.

Kit was hovering curiously in the hall.

"Kit, can you do me a favor? Go find some of my looser clothes and bring them down. We have to wring Mr. Hart out and make him dry again."

"Okay." The only Hart Kit knew was Illiann's friend Laura. Maybe this was her father. But what was he doing here in the middle of the night? The boy could tell his father was wondering the same thing.

"Come into the kitchen. It's the warmest right now." Hart was shivering so violently that Julian was afraid if he released the man's arm, he would fall. He pushed an armchair in front of the blazing fire and lowered Hart into it.

"Sorry I kept you outside for so long. I can't imagine what I was thinking. I'll be right back. Don't move, Mr. Hart."

The man tried to nod, but couldn't find the energy. His heart was pounding; he could hear the frantic throbbing in his ears. His teeth chattered and he could not stop trembling. "Come on, old man," he muttered to himself. "There's work to be done. Pull yourself together."

Julian collected linen towels out of the cupboard, re-lit the flame on the stove and put the kettle on, setting out various selections of tea, along with lemon, honey and some of Saylah's herbs.

"Please let me take your cloak." When his guest offered no resistance, Julian swung the cape off his shoulders. Water ran in rivulets from the heavily sodden wool, and he took it to the sink and literally wrung it out. Next came the man's greatcoat, then his jacket and waistcoat. Everything was soaked through. Julian stripped off Hart's shirt and began to rub his chest and back thoroughly with a towel.

Kit soon joined him, and between them they managed to get Arthur Hart to change into dry clothes, drink several mugs of tea, and chew on some licorice root to stave off a sore throat. Gradually, he stopped shivering and the color returned to his face.

Julian sent Kit off to bed and drew a chair up to the fire.

"Better now? I can't apologize enough."

"No need. Haven't had anyone take such good care of me since I had the influenza several years back."

"Happy to do it. All I ask in return is that tell me why you came out at all in this ghastly storm?"

"Less chance of being followed. I came to warn you that Mr. Barrett wishes you ill. You and your printing business."

"You're serious, aren't you?" Julian's earlier anxiety returned tenfold.

"Absolutely. I came to you because I believe you're a good man, an industrious man, and I want to make certain no one can undermine you."

Suddenly Julian was uncomfortably warm, and a weight had formed in the center of his chest. Was it a coincidence that Kit had been threatened the same day Arthur Hart claimed he was worried about being followed? What, exactly, was going on?

The man opened a satchel to reveal a stack of soggy papers. "That's why I want you to do all our forms and flyers, and we have a catalogue coming up soon. We need to start work on it right away."

Julian was at a loss.

"I want to help protect you." Hart said it as if he knew he would never be believed, as though he were fighting a losing cause.

"Protect me from what?"

Arthur began to wheeze. He drank deeply from his mug of tea until the fit passed. "Your article was successful, and because of that, you have powerful enemies. It's a bad business. Very bad. Threats have been made. Ridiculous, certainly, but just the same--"

Julian shivered as gooseflesh rose on his arms and the hair stood up on the back of his neck. He indicated the briefcase full of papers. "If there really is danger," he was not quite ready to admit it out loud, "how will those help?"

"It's possible some of your clients will find it behooves them to go elsewhere, and you'll be better able to deal with every eventually if you're not worrying about income." He saw that Julian was ready to object, but Hart forestalled him. "Don't worry, it's real work. Aside from our regular flyers and advertisements, we're ready to start publishing in several major catalogs. We need copy, and type, design as well as massive printings."

Julian could hardly take it all in. He wondered what Devon would make of this. It was just the sort of thing his partner would revel in—shadowy threats, invisible enemies, unseen obstacles and secret allies. He would see those things as a challenge. Julian saw much more deeply than that. "I appreciate what you're trying to do—"

Hart interrupted his host before he could turn the offer down. "There's more." He cleared his throat repeatedly. "Much as I regret it, I must also entreat you to warn your partner."

It was the second time he seemed to have read Julian's mind. That was more disturbing than anything else.

"Mr. Fitzgerald has made no secret of his desire to destroy Robert Barrett, and that just isn't wise." He shook himself as if he had just awakened from a bad dream. "But I've said too much and stayed too long." He took his damp clothes from where they were steaming over the fire screen.

"Wait!" Julian had barely adjusted to the man's arrival and not at all to his message, yet Arthur was preparing to leave. "There're not dry yet. You'll make yourself ill. Besides, you can't leave now. I need to understand."

"And so you will, in time." Hart was suddenly nervous, and kept peering over his shoulder into the dark hall. "If I may impose upon you to allow me to take these clothes home, I'll have them laundered and returned." His tone was clipped and formal. "I really must be going. My daughter will be worried."

He left his briefcase by the fire and hurried out of the kitchen. With his hand on the front doorknob, he turned back. "Watch out for him, Mr. Ivy. He's dangerous."

Julian stood motionless as the door opened and closed. He could not help but wonder who Hart thought was most dangerous: Barrett or Devon. He was not really certain he knew himself.

Chapter 69

Illiann could not escape the rhythm of the drums. Twice she rose and went to the window, and when she drew the casements inward, she thought she heard the melancholy cry of the loon. The drumbeat grew louder, demanding of her things she did not understand.

Shivering under her heavy quilt, she covered her ears, but the sound would not go. It wound its way through her thoughts and fears, wove a fine-spun web about her dreams.

Illiann rose and put on her robe and slippers, then hurried through the sleeping house toward the kitchen, praying someone would be as restless as she, that they would have fed the fire until it roared, obliterating the specter of storm and loon and lonely drum.

When she reached the kitchen, she was disappointed to discover it was quiet and the fire had been tamped down for the night. She started when the door swung open. Suddenly the room was full of light. Sophia stood with a lamp in her hand, regarding the girl without surprise.

"You couldn't sleep either?" she asked softly.

Illiann shook her head.

Sophia could see the girl was upset, but could not think how to soothe her. "Are you concerned about your mother?"

"Yes." It was such a relief to admit it. "It's awfully cold and wet and windy and we don't really know where she is. None of us has ever been there."

"You know how strong your mother is. She's had a lot of practice taking care of herself." Sophia busied herself gathering tinder from the wood box. People used to say the same about *her*. "I'll build up the fire. Things are always clearer when you're warm and dry."

Illiann was grateful for Sophia's presence. "I'll make some hot cider."

When it was ready, she and Sophia sat side by side on the stone hearth. "I had a dream this morning. It wasn't about Mama, but when I woke up…I can't explain it. I just knew something was wrong. I tried to tell her, but—" she broke off. Her mother had already known about the danger; she was certain of it. But that did not make her feel any better. "I don't understand. I don't know what to do."

Sophia felt inadequate. "Nor do I, Ilya. Just when I think I *do* know, the clouds shift, the shadows change and my resolution has been washed away in the rain."

For some inexplicable reason, the girl remembered the heat of Devon's lips when they brushed the edge of hers, and how that feather light sensation made her tingle all over. A minute ago, she had been chilled through. Now she was too warm. She was shocked by the abrupt change in the direction of her thoughts, and even more disturbing, the sensations in her body. Impulsively, she asked, "How do you know when you're in love?"

Sophia was so startled by the question that she dropped her cup of cider. She did not ask the girl if *she* were in love. Her flushed cheeks and luminous eyes told their own story. With an effort, Sophia regained her composure and replied, "I suspect it's different with every person." She took a breath and added, "How do *you* feel?"

Illiann grew pensive, hands locked around her knees. "Frightened and happy and confused and excited." She could not believe she was saying these things to her mother's friend, but she found she could keep them inside no longer. "That sounds silly. I can't be all those things, can I?"

"You'd be surprised. You obviously feel something intense and compelling. But you need to realize that love is often cruel and destructive, especially when one is young. I can't tell you to ignore your feelings. You'd have to be inhuman to do that. But please, please take care. Don't be reckless or hasty. Take your time. Think things through."

"Did you?"

Sophia blushed. "No. I simply followed my heart, no questions asked, no doubts allowed."

PART THREE

Chapter 70

"What are we going to do about Kit?" Julian asked his wife.

"I do not know. I have been trying to think how to keep him out of danger, but my thoughts just tumble in all directions."

The morning was dim, the air cold, wet and motionless. The watery sunlight was alternately exposed and obscured by shifting clouds. The couple sat on a boulder at the narrow beach a few blocks from their home. They had come to get away from the gloomy house the morning after the storm. Both were a little off-balance and they were trying to pull themselves together with this hour alone on the sand. The sea was unnaturally still, it's thunder muffled by the heavy air, and Saylah found that it made her uneasy. "This feeling is unfamiliar. I cannot name it."

It's called helplessness." Julian rested his cheek on top of her head, and the fragrance of cedar mingled with sea salt teased at his nostrils. His own thoughts were chaotic and unsettling; he was ashamed to realize he was glad Saylah shared his confusion. "It was so much easier on the ranch, where the only peril came from nature. We always knew instinctively how to prepare and protect the children from that. But here there are dangers we never imagined. I feel weak and foolish because I can't keep my son safe anymore."

"You are neither of those things. You know that in your heart, do you not?" She was pleased that she managed to sound confident, despite her agitation.

Her husband sighed heavily. "I try to. It's just that I'm afraid for him. He shouldn't have to pay for what I do."

Saylah looked up. "Are you certain that is what is happening?" Her intuition told her it was so, but she had to ask.

Considering, Julian gazed at the unnaturally silent sea. "Robert Barrett thinks I'm not concerned for my own safety, so he's sent his thugs after Kit. I don't like to think what else he might do." He shivered at the touch of the mist on his skin.

"You are certain he would resort to violence?"

"No doubt in my mind." Pensively, he rubbed the rough whiskers on his chin; he had not yet shaved that morning.

"But would he actually attack our son? How will it help him, in the end?"

"Perhaps by making us more wary and more cautious. Barrett must think he can frighten us into silence." He gave her a lopsided grin.

"Then he does not know you, does he?" She regarded him, brow furrowed. "You are certain Barrett is behind this?"

Julian rubbed his forehead to try and erase the lines there. "Who else has anything to lose if I keep publishing *The Voice*?"

"I have no answer."

"Neither do I." Taking her hands, Julian tried to warm them with his. "But one thing I *do* know. I came here seeking excitement, and I've certainly found plenty of it. At the moment, I could do with a little less." Still, his hazel eyes sparkled and his cheeks were pleasantly flushed.

Saylah smiled. "Perhaps we have both found too much of what we sought. But just now we must think only of Kit. Our only choice must be to confront Mr. Barrett."

"He won't take kindly to being threatened. He's not very tolerant."

"Then we must be calm, because *he* is not. His rage is our greatest weapon against him; it makes strong men reckless."

"How do you know so much about people?" He did not expect an answer; Saylah had always sensed many things. And she always trusted her instincts.

She slipped his arm around her shoulders and leaned her head against his chest. "I have learned, my Julian, that sometimes you know better, or Ilya does, or even Kit."

"Is that so bad?"

"No, I am glad for it. It is just…sometimes I forget to remember how things change." She put her hand over Julian's heart. "Do you love me?"

He was as shocked as if she had struck him. "You know I do." There was a tiny flicker of doubt in her eyes, but it disappeared in an instant. "You need never doubt me, *ladaila*."

The Salish endearment was like the touch of his lips against hers. "Of that I am certain. Only sometimes I doubt myself."

He smiled charmingly. "I assure you there are much better things to do with your time."

Chapter 71

"Ah, there you are," Simone said. "We must begin packing at once."

Mathilde raised a suspicious eyebrow. "Packin'?"

"Yes." Her mistress touched her silver cross, a faraway look in her eyes. "I made a promise to Claude just before he—" She paused to swallow her still fresh grief. "I told him I would go to Vancouver Island to see my son. After all he has done for me, after all we have been to one another, it is the one thing that remains that I can do for him." Her eyes were misted with melancholy, but she tried to do as he had wished and look only toward the future. "Besides, it is long past time for such a trip, is it not?"

The servant endeavored to sound calm. "Said so often enough, but you're too good at paying me no mind. Had, alas, given up hope." She heaved an exaggerated sigh.

"I am sorry to have spoiled your sunny temperament. I can only pray that you will soon recover in the fresh air of the Canadian wilderness."

"Takin' me with you, is it?" Mathilde's tone was acerbic, but she could not conceal her relief. "Just as well. Leave me alone and I'd have no one to bully. Too dreadful to contemplate."

"I should not like to make you suffer unduly. But in return, I shall ask you not to argue when I say there is something I must take care of before we go. It is time and long past time." Simone sounded very determined. "I must settle things with de Marchand, once and for all."

"Guess the grief must've addled your brain. Courtin' trouble's what you're doin'. Not that you care what I think." Her mistress was taking a huge risk. Mathilde was certain de

Marchand was going to be angry, and she was well aware of what happened when he lost control of his temper.

She had first learned that lesson on his wedding night, when he woke from a drunken stupor to find his new wife missing. He had not hesitated to take it out on Mathilde. She still bore a scar low on her neck where de Marchand had struck her without bothering to turn his signet ring away.

Simone sank into the wingback chair as if suddenly exhausted. "You are afraid for me. You are thinking of that night."

"Aren't you?" Mathilde spoke to the ceiling, because it was easier.

"Almost never." But she was lying. Even as she spoke, she could feel herself being sucked backward in time, to the dark night she had struggled so hard to forget. She shuddered at the insistent memory.

De Marchand had torn off her wedding gown and tossed it on the floor, devouring her with hands and eyes and grasping mouth. She could barely breathe though the haze of wine and foul breath and the weight of his body holding her down, cutting off her breath. She tried to focus on the pattern of firelight on the wall, but she could not ignore him or pretend it wasn't happening. All at once he groaned twice, grunted and raised his head. Surprised by the lack of motion, she opened her eyes to find him staring down at her, his gaze clouded and angry. Her body was damp from his sweat and something else she did not wish to identify. She closed her eyes again, praying fervently for him to go away.

He rolled off her, but did not go far. "Come, my wife. Open your lovely eyes." The invitation not romantic; it was a command. She was momentarily distracted when she heard the door open. She scrambled to draw the covers up to hide her nakedness, but her husband held them away.

"That's right. Don't hide such pure beauty."

Simone's eyes opened wide at the sound of her father's voice. What was he doing here, witnessing her shame and humiliation?

"You look just like your mother," Alphonse Destranges repeated, as he had many times in the past year. "Just like her, only more beautiful."

Simone attempted to swallow, but there was a blockage in her throat. She flinched when he leaned close enough for her to smell his wine-soaked breath. He was unsteady on his feet, and his hands were trembling. She realized what it was then, that dreadful look in his eyes—lust. She turned to her new husband pleadingly. Surely he would protect her from such defilement. But he shrugged and looked away, picking up a brandy bottle from the bedside table and taking a long drink. For a moment, the three of them hung suspended in time—de Marchand with his back turned, clutching his liquor bottle, Destranges unconsciously licking his lips, his need and yearning evident on his face, Simone lying huddled, her body exposed, terror in her eyes.

Then Destranges broke the spell. He lunged for her, grasping her arms and drawing her toward him, seeking to distract her with his mouth while he ran his hands over her downy soft body.

She was aware all the time of de Marchand sitting on the far side of the bed, unmoving, apparently unhearing. He had abandoned her.

"No!" She pulled away, sickened. Bile rose in her throat when her father dragged her back, creeping his fingers toward her breasts, and then lower.

Struggling wildly and aided by his drunken state, Simone broke free, knocking him backward. She ran, looking frantically for an escape. There were three doors, but she had never been in the room before and had no idea which one might lead to freedom. With her father on her heels, she opened the nearest and plunged through, pulling it closed and taking the key, suspended from a ribbon on the doorknob, in with her. She drew the ribbon taut as she fit the key in the lock. Then she collapsed, shivering, on the floor. Too late, she realized she was in a small closet, with no light to ease her nightmare. But perhaps, after all, that was better. She did not want to see.

She could hear her father outside, scratching at the door and whimpering. "Don't run from me, *ma petit*. I've taken care of you, always. I need you. Your mother left me alone, you see. The world has been cold and cruel since. But now you have become a woman. You can ease my loneliness. I have waited so long. Please come out. Please!"

He paused, waiting for her response, then began to pound on the door. "Listen to me! I'll get to you. I'll break the door down if I have to. Do you understand?"

She shuddered uncontrollably, and her heart began to beat in time with the menacing rhythm of his fists. She had seen him drunk before, but never like this. When the knob began to turn and the door shook, she scrambled backward into the depths of the closet, where things she could not see fell on her head and shoulders. She held her breath, praying the door would hold. Eventually, her father gave up.

"Simone!" he bellowed, and then he seemed to slide to the floor. Hearing the thump and his ragged breathing, she huddled, terrified of making any sound. She had begun to think she might be safe when he whined through the crack at the bottom of the door. "Come out, my sweet, dear girl. Come to me and let me hold you. Come, come, come."

Time and again his voice faded in a hoarse whisper; time and again he waited, then began once more. It went on for hours, and now and then he rose to shake the doorknob violently. "Let me *in*!" he demanded. "Now!"

For hours she listened and prayed and tried to make herself as small as possible, while her father sputtered and threatened and cajoled. She barely dared to breathe, and her heart beat wildly, then dully, then, she was sure, ceased to beat all together.

Finally, she heard him sag where he sat. For the first time, she approached the door and pressed her ear to the wood, listening. She heard nothing but the sound of labored breathing. She tried tapping, to see if it aroused her father, who was snoring loudly. Nothing. She tried again. She bent down and peered through the crack under the door. She could see him slumped in the dim light, unmoving except for his chest, which rose and fell with his sputtering breath. He was either sleeping heavily or unconscious.

She decided it was time. Easing the door open an inch at a time, she slipped into the room. The smell of wine and vomit assaulted her. Her father lay in a pool of excess. She choked on her own bile, refusing to give in to the reflex. De Marchand was passed out on the bed, breathing heavily, and she thanked God for that. She realized she was still naked, and grabbed a shirt tossed over a chair.

Stumbling in her haste, she nevertheless managed to find her way downstairs. All she could hear was an internal voice screaming, "Run! Run! Run!"

Since that night, she had run for years, gone as far away as she could get, and been forced to come back, but she had not stopped running until this moment.

Chapter 72

Robert Barrett kept his attention focused on the papers on his desk when Saylah and Julian entered his office. He was annoyed that his secretary had let them in, and he did not intend to give them the courtesy of a pleasant greeting. He didn't look up for so long that the silence grew heavy and forbidding.

Which is precisely what he intended, Saylah thought. He wanted to make them uncomfortable, perhaps even angry, but that would not happen. She nodded at Julian, who suppressed a rueful smile.

"What is it?" Barrett said with the slightest tilt of his chin. He kept his gaze on the papers stacked before him, as if reluctant to prize himself away from his work.

"We need to speak to you," Julian said somberly.

"What, *now*? After the damage has been done? It's a bit late for polite conversation, Ivy."

"So it is. In fact, that's why we've come. To tell you we don't like you trying to intimidate our son."

At last Barrett looked up. "Now you're speaking nonsense. I really don't have time for your paranoid fantasies."

"Do you not?" Saylah asked, scrutinizing him openly. "I think perhaps you do."

He shifted under her compelling green gaze. He could tell at once that she saw too much. He had better take control of this interview, as he was used to doing. "No, I can't. All I know is that your husband here has jeopardized my livelihood, my success, my very life with his preposterous stories about the 'poor and unfortunate' of Victoria. His ambition makes him think he can speak for others, but he doesn't know even half the truth."

The intensity of his concentration on Saylah was unsettling, as if Julian were not standing beside her.

"I know you've threatened to burn my newspapers, and even my shop. Then you sent Arthur Hart to warn me. You've threatened the workers and Devon Fitzgerald and anyone else you could frighten, and now it's my son Kit."

"I have no interest in your son. He's of no use to me. In fact, he's merely a vague annoyance, rather like that fly you see buzzing at the window. It's far too easy to swat it, and thereby ease my annoyance. No challenge in it." He tried to keep his tone level, but could not conceal his anger at being accused like a criminal across his own desk. "This is not just an office," he told Saylah, ignoring Julian pointedly. "It is my retreat. Everyone knows that, and no one dares threaten its sanctity. Not even my wife."

"Do you mean to say that no one has ever disagreed with you in business? That surprises me considerably, since you are so caught up in every facet of this city's wealth." Saylah was somewhat surprised by her sharp tone, but did not regret it.

He leaned forward, hands fisted, black eyes glittering. "It is not wise to provoke me, Mrs. Ivy. Please don't make that mistake."

"You have said quite clearly that Julian is already your enemy, that he has threatened all you value. That was not a mistake; it was a necessity."

Julian was startled by his wife's attack. She was usually so calm and self-contained. But usually her children's safety was not at stake. "Listen, Barrett, I'm warning you right here and now to leave my family alone. This has nothing to do with them, and it's only going to make me more firm in my resolve."

Robert Barrett leaned forward until he was bent nearly in half. "Don't you dare threaten me. Not ever!" he practically barked. "Unlike my partner, I am neither a weakling nor a fool. I'd keep that in mind if I were you." He was shaking and his cheeks were flushed with fury.

In spite of his determination to remain calm, Julian took a step toward the massive desk. "Nor am I," he said heatedly.

Purposefully, he took Saylah's arm and propelled her out the door, so he would not have a chance to strike the man. When they'd reached the safety of the wooden sidewalk, he slowed down. "He's so angry," Julian said. "I wonder why. Or maybe he's just mad."

Saylah considered. "I wonder if *he* even knows why. Does he not remind you of someone?" She regarded her husband closely.

"Devon, of course. He also thrives on the force of his rage."

"Both men may be angry, but I think, more than that, they are afraid."

Julian stopped without warning and she nearly collided with him. "Would fear make Barrett threaten our son?"

"It might. It might make him do anything. It is more powerful, even, than anger. But you should know that, Julian, for you have lived it."

"What are they afraid *of*?"

"Each other perhaps? I do not know. But I felt Robert Barrett's fear as strongly as I once felt my own. You must remember that a man who is angry can be unwise and even cruel, but a man who is afraid is far more dangerous. We might think we know what he is planning, but we cannot, because he does not know himself. That is what worries me."

It took a great deal to worry Saylah, and Julian was wise enough to take her observations as a warning. "So you don't think he'll stop harassing us?"

"I do not know for certain that he has begun."

Her husband was not precisely certain what she meant, but he could feel her uncertainty, and it disturbed him. "I will be watching," he assured her. "I'll be ready."

"But that is just it. I am not convinced you can be."

"I'm not afraid of Robert Barrett."

"I know," Saylah replied. Under her breath, she added, "Perhaps it would be wiser if you were."

Chapter 73

"Kit, I need your help."

The boy turned, startled by the sound of Sophia's voice. At his side, Lord Byron woofed affectionately.

She stepped out of the shadows wearing a close-fitting jacket of soft blue wool, a tam of the same fabric with a huge fat tassel on top, a pair of blue wool trousers that fastened just below her knees with shiny silver buckles. Her stockings were patterned and slightly paler blue than her trousers and coat, and her long auburn hair was fashioned in a loose braid. She was balancing a shiny new bicycle awkwardly by the handlebars.

Kit knew it was rude, but he gaped at her. He had never seen a woman wearing trousers before, and though his mother often wore unusual clothes, this was altogether shocking. "Um, hello."

Sophia grinned. She had bought the bicycle and the cycling outfit for many reasons, not the least of which was hearing Kit express an intense desire to have one of each. She also wanted to use it to get around the city, to feel more independent and self-sufficient. She was envious of the ladies who went about Victoria in their tennis and hunting outfits, riding streetcars and looking delightfully free and unencumbered.

"I didn't mean to startle you, but I want this to be our little secret." She glanced about ostentatiously, as if someone might be eavesdropping. "I waited until everyone else was gone."

As he began to recover from his shock, Kit stared at the bicycle hungrily. It was a real beauty. "I didn't know you could ride, Mrs. Ashton."

Sophia smiled at his unconcealed excitement. "That's just it, you see. I can't. That's why I've been looking for you."

He was still too unsettled to understand. "What for?"

Having decided his young master would be staying for a while, Lord Byron settled at Sophia's feet.

She motioned Kit closer to the tree, where she leaned the bicycle precariously, then sat down on the stone bench at its base. She patted the seat next to her. "For one thing, I miss riding horses as I used to do at home. I want to ride along the beach and listen to the waves against the shore, but here we are in the middle of the city, and I'm helpless."

Kit had never known a less helpless woman, except for his mother. And they weren't exactly in the middle of the city. The Bay was barely two blocks away, the beach a few minutes, and Beacon Hill Park a few more. There were many houses on the peninsula, but much of it was still forest, and the paths were endless and winding, but he did not argue. "So that's why you got a bicycle?"

"Exactly why. But since I don't know how to ride, I wondered if you'd teach me."

Kit blinked and chewed his lip nervously. He was afraid both she and the bicycle would disappear if he closed his eyes. "Me? But I...it's not...I'm just learning how. I don't think I could teach an adult—"

At the distress in his voice, Lord Byron raised his head.

Sophia leaned toward him. "Do you think we're that much thicker than you youngsters?"

"Oh, no, ma'am. I didn't mean that. It's just that Will and I can fool around and fall over ourselves and tumble in the dirt, but you're a lady." He blushed furiously.

"Well, thank you, Christopher Ivy. That's quite a compliment. The thing is, I really want to learn, and you're the only one I know who can teach me."

The boy was pleased and flustered all at once. "Devon Fitzgerald knows how. He might be better than me."

"Unthinkable. I much prefer you. You've always been careful and thoughtful when you want to do something right. I trust you."

Kit ducked his head in embarrassment, but he was charmed by Sophia's winning smile and measured compliments. Besides, she looked so odd in her new clothes that he didn't feel he was actually speaking to the very old woman he knew her to be. "Besides, this is such a wonderful bicycle, it'd be a shame if it ended up rusting in the shed."

Sophia nodded. "That reminds me. I won't be able to take it out often, and I don't want it to be neglected. I wonder if you wouldn't mind riding it for me every day?"

Kit swallowed a whoop of joy. "Are you sure? I mean, it's yours, and I don't think Papa—" He let his breath out in a disappointed sigh.

"I'm sure he will realize you're doing me a favor. I suspect he doesn't disapprove of bicycles at all. I wouldn't be surprised if one day he gets you one of your own."

"If you really think it'd be okay." He seemed to come to a decision. "When do you want to start?"

Sophia gazed up at the branches of the cherry and smiled. "We can have the first one right now. After that, I'm going to be awfully busy at the shop with your father, so it might be only once a week."

Kit beamed at her. "That's too bad, isn't it?"

"Hmmmm," she murmured noncommittally. "But I shall try to live with my disappointment, secure in the knowledge that you'll be putting it to good use in my absence."

Catching the flicker of something in her voice, the boy tilted his head curiously. Just for a moment, he wondered if she had bought the bike for herself at all. But, of course that was silly. She had a cycling outfit, didn't she?

Sophia rose and straightened her cropped jacket. "Shall we begin?"

The dog barked enthusiastically and Kit wondered, not for the first time, if Lord Byron actually understood what people said. His tail was wagging with what Kit could only assume was delighted expectation of a new adventure.

Chapter 74

Simone stood, hand raised, at the top of the majestically curved steps that lead to de Marchand's chateau. She had barely knocked once when the massive door was opened and the man himself stood on the threshold.

"What is it?" he asked suspiciously. She had entered this house several times against her will—on their wedding night and after her return to Rouen, but she had never come by choice. He could not quite believe his eyes. "Is something wrong?"

"I would like to come in," she murmured. She wanted to reassure him that she had not come to make a scene.

He backed up, allowing her access to the glittering foyer of his family home. "Shall I ring for tea? Or sherry?" He was hoping for the latter; he was so unsettled by her unexpected appearance.

Simone shook her head. "I will only be a moment. I have come to speak to you."

That in itself was extraordinary. She had not entered his house of her own free will in over thirty years. "Surely not out here in the hall? At least come to the drawing room."

She entered the room ahead of him. "Henri," she began, "I have come to say that I am returning to Vancouver Island, and this time I am staying."

"I always knew you would one day."

He sounded resigned, and that surprised her so much that she almost lost her train of thought. "There is no point trying to stop me. The jewels are gone, so there is no longer any reason to hold me here." She raised her chin defiantly, not knowing what to expect. She was not even certain why she had come, except she felt some strange and morbid obligation to the man.

"It does not matter about the jewels. It hasn't for some time."

Simone was stunned. "If that is true, why did you keep demanding their return? Why did you keep me here like a prisoner?"

De Marchand cleared his throat twice before answering. "I couldn't bear to let you go. I didn't want to lose you."

"You did not want...." She repeated n disbelief. "You lost me on our wedding night. Did you not know that? And all you have demanded from me since is the return of your fortune."

"That was only an excuse." He began to pace, running his hand through his well-coiffed hair and destroying the hairdresser's careful work. "I had to blame you for something, and I made myself believe I only wanted the jewels you'd taken from me, but really, I wanted much more." He could not look at her, though he could imagine the color draining from her cheeks and rushing back again, as it did when she was upset.

"Perhaps you do not recall the first time I saw you. You were playing piano and singing in your father's drawing room. Your voice was so lovely and pure and your expression so completely without guile." He remembered clearly her pale complexion, the small movements of her graceful hands, and the hint of a smile that lay hidden beneath a young girl's sorrow.

Simone's eyes widened at the regret and affection in his tone.

"I was already jaded and bored and deceitful, but that image of you made me stop and think. I wanted you: your purity, your grace, your youthful enthusiasm."

"Then why destroy those things, allow them to be strippcd from me on our wedding night?"

Staring at a spot on the wall above her head, he continued. "When I heard your father was looking for a husband for you, I was exultant. But he thought I was too old, though my family and my fortune tempted him. I was determined, and, finally, he gave in, but I had to strike a deal with him. He wanted to hold you, just once."

Illness overwhelmed her. "You made a bargain for my virtue?"

"I was cruel back then, and that cruelty was my strength, or so I thought. More than anything else, I was, and am, a coward. Just as your father was. That's why he took his life, you know. He could not bear the guilt—or the loneliness. It never occurred to either of us that you might go. We didn't think you had the courage. I was wrong about so many things."

Simone was struck dumb. She could see the anguish in his eyes. She would never have guessed he could feel such a thing, let alone reveal it to her. "What are you saying?"

He continued to pace, limping a little, as if he had gout in one knee. Why had she never noticed that before? Why had she never seen him as vulnerable and entirely too human? *Perhaps it did not suit me to do so*, she thought. *Perhaps I felt safer thinking of him as an implacable villain rather than merely a man.*

"I don't know. I suppose I'm trying to tell you I have been the worst kind of selfish fool. You see, in those days, I valued your innocence above all things. It beckoned to me as powerfully as would an invitation to your bed. Because of that, I determined to destroy it when I made you mine. I wanted to obliterate the life you had lived before me, to insure that you were bound to me body and soul." De Marchand paused in front of the floor to ceiling window, clenching and unclenching his fists as he stared out at the grounds. "But I couldn't let you know how I felt. My need for you was a cancer, a weakness. I hated it, and therefore, you."

"Then why did you hold me here, even after the annulment?"

His back was so rigid she thought it might snap. "Because I couldn't bear to let you go. I never wanted the annulment. I only wanted you." His back was so rigid she thought it might snap.

In spite of herself, Simone pitied him in that moment. "I...do not understand."

"Of course you don't. How could you?" At last he turned so she could see his face. He looked very young and the mask of hauteur he usually wore was gone. "The Duc de Montagne gave me no choice. But I couldn't simply allow you to be happy when you'd taken so much from me."

She started to speak, but he held up his hand. "Please, let me finish. The truth was, I was jealous of your happiness, because I couldn't share it. Which is why I could not bear for you to be in touch with the man who had stolen both my bride and my happiness. I was jealous, Simone, crazed by your joy with that man. That's why I collected every letter you ever wrote to Jamie Ivy. I paid a boy to intercept them."

De Marchand fumbled with the door of a small cabinet, reached in and produced a thick stack of letters, tied by a wide ribbon. He offered them to her, and she reached out only far enough to take them quickly, then backed away. "He never received them?"

"No. But I want you to know I did not read them; I did not have the strength."

Simone's head was swimming, but one thing clear; Jamie and Julian had not responded to her letters because they had never seen them. What must her silence have meant to them? Her heart sank as she realized the kind of barrier that still stood between her and her son. It was bigger than the ocean, bigger than the miles of Canadian wilderness, bigger, even than her own fear and doubt.

Seeing that she was incapable of responding, de Marchand filled the awkward silence. "I wanted you to suffer as I was suffering. I did not let you go because, no matter how pointedly you ignored me, how furiously you fought me, how often you denied me access to your family fortune, I always, always loved you."

"It is difficult for me to believe that."

"For me as well, especially when I realized I didn't care if I ever saw the damned jewels again. I never thought I could be so weak and ridiculous."

"You will no longer try to hold me here?"

"I have not had that power over you for a long time. You called my bluff, you see. You refused to be broken. You survived and I did not. The joke was on me, in the end, don't you think?

"I am sorry, Simone." He stared, transfixed, at his age-spotted hands.

"As am I. We have lost so much, stolen so much from one another."

He shrugged, spreading his hands wide in a gesture of surrender. "I can only ask that you forgive me. I have nothing else to offer." He did not realize he held his hands outstretched as if expecting her to fill the empty palms.

She looked at the floor to avoid the sight of his desolation, but she could not deny it. Neither could she force herself to reach for his hand. "I forgive you, Henri. Because I must, because I can, or so I am beginning to believe because to bear you ill-will would only be to burden myself with the feelings of the past. I am done with such suffering. It is time. For both of us."

"Thank—"

She put a finger to her lips. "Do not say it. And do not think me good or kind. I do this for my own benefit, not yours." It was over. She was weak with relief at an unexpected sense of liberation. What had the Duc said just before he died? *You are a prisoner of no man, but only of your own imagination.*

He had been right, as always. He had known her better than she knew herself. She might have believed all love was self-serving and brutal if not for Jamie and Claude. She might never have known love at all.

That thought, more than anything, told her she was finally free.

Chapter 75

On Sunday morning, Illiann found her mother in the sunroom at the rear of the house, seated at the small oak table that served as a desk, alternately gnawing at the end of a fountain pen and scribbling furiously. Saylah's hair was tied back with a ribbon, and her feet were bare, as usual.

Except for the wall shared with the house, the rest of the room was made of panes of glass, supported by narrow oak beams. Though the glass was cold, the room was not, bathed, as it was, in every trace of winter sun. The girl thought her mother looked most at home here among the brightly colored cushions, wicker furniture and thriving plants and flowers. The only solid piece of furniture was the carved cedar cabinet where Saylah kept her stories when she was not working on them, as she obviously was at the moment.

"Come, Ilya," she said without looking up. "I have been waiting for you."

Illiann jumped; she thought she was watching unobserved. Her mother looked disheveled, dusty and quite happy. The girl could not help but smile in response. She settled on a fat red cushion on the floor, raising her face to the sun.

"I have not seen much of you since the storm, and I have missed you." Saylah considered her daughter, resting her fountain pen absently on a stack of clean paper instead of in the inkwell. They had not spoken again of her daughter's warning the morning of the storm, nor of Illiann's hurt and disappointment that her parents had ignored it. "I wonder, are you all right?"

The girl certainly looked well; her cheeks were slightly flushed and her dark eyes glistened softly. "Sophia said you seemed upset the other night. I think we all were, but for different reasons."

For a moment, Illiann could not find her voice. Sophia had promised not to tell, but the girl's heart raced at the realization that she might not have been unable to resist Saylah's intent questioning. Her calm air of self-assurance and her concern and empathy intimidated people. Illiann said the first thing that came to mind. "I was, a bit. Did you know Papa was reading his mother's journal? He went to the attic and brought it down. It's not like him."

Saylah regarded her daughter doubtfully. "It is certainly strange, though I am glad to hear it. But that is not what is unsettling you."

"Well, no. Not exactly."

"Was it the drumbeat from your dream?"

"Yes." It was the truth, just not all of it. Though it seemed like long ago, she had not forgotten what her mother told her: *For the People, a dream is a warning or a promise: a prophecy.* "It haunts me because I don't know what it means."

"Neither do I. I just know that the drums also call me."

"If you don't know what it means, how can I possibly guess?" To the Salish, dreams are a responsibility. You must train yourself to hear the voices of the spirits, untainted by your own fears and hopes. *"I've never even seen a Salish village,"* Ilya added longingly.

Saylah grew pensive. "The place I visit now is very different than the villages used to be, but still, there is something in the air and the sea and the earth which belongs to their past. Why do you not come with me and see for yourself?"

Illiann had been hoping for the invitation for so long she had begun to think it would never come. "Do you mean it?"

"I told you I would show you someday. As soon as Old Grandmother is better." She frowned, but tried to hide it from her daughter.

The girl was not fooled. "You're worried about her, aren't you?"

Saylah brushed her daughter's cheek affectionately. "Yes. My friend is ill and I cannot cure her. I can only wait. So, foolishly, I worry, expecting a dream to give me a sign."

Illiann realized she too was feeling helpless—about Devon and the things he made her feel—waiting for a signal that would tell her what to do. Just a week before, she would have asked her mother, but now, when she tried to speak, the words would not come. She was engulfed by a wave of insecurity. "I'll go with you. Of course I will."

"I am glad," Saylah murmured. She was certain the girl was keeping something from her. Certain as well, that, at fifteen, Illiann had reached the age when a mother's questions suddenly become too difficult, or too painful, to answer.

For the first time since her daughter was born, Saylah had to restrain herself from trying to read Illiann's thoughts. Instead, she must wait patiently for the girl to find her woman's voice and learn to trust it as she had once trusted the voice of her childhood.

Chapter 76

Edward Ashton woke to bright afternoon light. He was appalled to realize he had fallen asleep in the middle of the day, but then he had not been sleeping well at night. Stretching, it came to him that he actually felt rested for the first time in weeks. He noticed Sophia's letter lying on the Persian rug beside the uncomfortable blue velvet sofa on which he had unaccountably drifted off.

"That's why," he said out loud, having become weary of the silence. Scooping up the brief missive, he read it again.

Dear Edward,

I have pondered your letter long and thoroughly, with both my mind and my vulnerable heart. Here is the conclusion at which I have arrived: I am trying very hard to believe you; I miss you; I am willing to wait until you feel able to tell me the rest. I shall remain with the Ivys for the moment.

Yours Most Truly,

Sophia

Edward smiled despite his wrinkled waistcoat and shirt, the collar and cuffs askew. He had been growing out a beard, since he had felt too weary to attend to his toilet, but today he decided to shave and have the housekeeper trim his hair.

Today, for the first time in months, he heard the chandelier whisper; the crystals touched each other sweetly, singing in the shimmering light.

Chapter 77

"Damn!" Devon swore when he caught his finger for the second time on the nail he was trying to extract from an awkward spot on the galley press. He watched the blood well up, bitter red, and sucked at it angrily.

"What's the matter with you?" Julian had to shout over the sound of the presses turning out page after freshly inked page. "You've been restless all morning, just waiting, it seems to me, for a reason to make trouble."

On the composing table between them lay the plate for the latest edition of *The Voice*. The lead story was about a Scottish family of servants, the fifth in the series. They had done articles about the Salish, the workers at the corset factory, the women whose lives were often limited to moving between house and garden and dock, where they bought their fresh fish. Julian was working on a new one about the black stevedores and the sailors, and one about the Chinese.

"I don't know what you're talkin' about. I'm fine and calm as the Irish sea of a January afternoon."

Julian had never seen the Irish Sea, but he had a feeling it was anything but calm in January. "Come on, man. The truth. I've told you before, I can't help if you don't tell me what's on your mind."

"Mayhap," Devon snapped, "I've no need for your help." He spoke more sharply than he intended, because he knew he was being irrational. "I can no' stand this inaction. I want to be up and doin'." His friend's constant admonitions to 'be patient and not act recklessly' were useless against Devon's restlessness and anger.

"I know how you feel," Julian said.

Devon raised a quizzical reddish eyebrow.

"I do, whether or not you believe it. But I still say we need to take care." The presses stopped within seconds of each other, and his voice rang too loudly across the room. "I promised Kit we wouldn't just stir up trouble without having a plan, some kind of solution."

"'Tis for Kit then, is it? No' for me or yourself?"

"It *should* be for the people we write about. And anyway, that's beside the point."

"What *is* the point?" Ever since the day after the storm, Devon had been unusually subdued, mostly because he felt guilty for that brief but poignant interlude with Illiann.

Sometimes he sat staring at the painting of the girl of dance and flame that had risen from his imagination, knowing she was all too real, wanting to touch her, then turning away abruptly, as if, by doing so, he could shut her out of his mind. He was afraid his feelings were so transparent that Julian could read them like the lines of type that passed through his hands each day.

"The point is that we got the workers all stirred up and left them without a course to follow or a leader to guide them."

Once again, Devon forced his thoughts away from Illiann. "You've an idea?"

Julian shook his head. "I keep thinking I should have, but I can't seem to gather my thoughts together long enough to form a strategy."

Casey snorted from behind the silent presses. "Coulda told ye that, but ye were no' askin' me."

Both men turned to glare at him.

The forceful opening of the door, which revealed several red-faced men in flannel and jeans, saved Casey. They were muttering amongst themselves, but they quieted when someone made his way to the front. It was Devon's friend, Davy O'Reilly. He held his cloth hat crumpled in his hands and cleared his throat dramatically.

"You tell 'em, Davy. There's a lad."

"It's just…we were wonderin'…we're wantin' to stop Barrett and men like 'im, but we'd not be knowin' how. We've come to ask for help."

Devon and Julian avoided Casey's accusing stare and focused their attention on Davy and the twenty or so men who had crowded into the shop. Julian collected himself first.

"To begin with, we must take it one step at a time. Stopping all men who exploit their workers is rather an unrealistic goal, so, for the moment, we'll have to work on Barrett alone."

The men shouted in approval, but Julian barely raised a hand and they fell silent. "And I don't mean through violence. If you caught the man and beat him, frightened him, even killed him, someone else would just take his place. We need to be smarter than he is. We need to think this through."

"We been thinkin'!" one man called out. "We're tired o' that and we want action."

"I know you do." Julian strode toward them, unfazed by the rage the men were ready to unleash at the first provocation. They saw he wasn't afraid and admired him for it. "I say you all come in and find a place to stand or sit, close and lock the door behind you, so we won't be interrupted, and we'll talk this over."

Devon stared in astonishment. He would have thought Julian had been planning this for days if he didn't know better. But that was Julian for you. He usually knew where he was going, and almost always how to get there. He had the ability to think on his feet, while Devon only knew how to bellow. His heart raced with anticipation. Something was going to happen here; he could feel it in the tingling of his fingertips and the chill bumps on the back of his neck. He didn't like not knowing what it was, but he was enjoying the sensation immensely.

Everyone worked to clear the tables and stools, perching on desktop and rolling table and chair, some sitting on the floor, some leaning against the wall. Casey had the good sense to take the galley and plate for *The Voice* to the storeroom and wrap them carefully in oilcloth.

Devon could not resist the expectant gazes turned toward him. He swore he would not fail them twice. "Since Barrett doesn't seem to listen to words, 'tis time for something more drastic, eh, lads?"

"You bet!" one man yelled, and "that's it!" called another.

"Obviously, Barrett doesn't care what the public thinks," Julian interjected. "He's guided only by greed and anger." *A man who is angry can be unwise and even cruel,* Saylah had said, *but a man who is afraid is far more dangerous.* "You can't scare him by threatening him physically; he's got enough thugs to protect him. You do have an advantage in Arthur Hart. He's troubled by his partner's behavior, and I don't think you have to fear reprisal from him."

"What're we s'posed to do, then?"

Julian rubbed his chin between thumb and forefinger. "Well, if you can't, or shouldn't, threaten him with violence, how about with stillness?"

Devon was intrigued. "What are you sayin'?"

"I have an idea," Julian said.

Silence fell, and he proceeded to create a scene with voice and hands and his own compelling passion. By the time he was finished, he had won over every man in the room. Even Devon, who had tried to resist with all his hostility and frustration.

In the end, the Ivy charisma and eloquence were more powerful and seductive than one Irishman's bitterness.

Chapter 78

After a choppy ride across the bay, Saylah and Illiann approached the clearing where the Salish missionary village lay. Illiann was excited to be on an excursion with her mother, especially because, at last, she would get a chance to see the Indians up close. Besides, it had been a long time since she'd spent the day in Saylah's company, and she meant to enjoy it to the fullest.

Saylah paused at the edge of the forest to allow her daughter to take in the scene, and Illiann was glad. She was shocked by what she saw, and did not want her mother's friends to see it.

The houses were weathered and looked as frail as if they had been built from straw. The people scattered about were dressed in White man's clothes; most of the flannel shirts and wool skirts and denim trousers were ill-fitting. The deeply bronzed faces looked tired and drained. Then someone looked up idly and recognized Saylah; the news of her arrival spread quickly. The children came running from their desultory games to gather around her, and the adults moved with sudden energy toward the square in the center of the village, marked by a jumble of multi-colored boulders.

Illiann felt their vitality spring to life at the touch of Saylah's hand and the sound of her dulcet voice. Watching in silence, the girl was amazed that this world she had only imagined had been just across the harbor all along. It was not that she didn't notice the poverty and misery of these people; it was just that, somehow, Saylah made it fade, as if her very presence diminished its importance.

Her healing bag open, she moved among the Salish, and they listened gravely as she doled out herbs and ointments, bandages and plasters. Quietly, the People made way for Illiann, accepting her help because her mother told them they could.

Finally, the girl noticed a regal old woman in a billowing white blouse and dark wool skirt, who could only be Old Grandmother. Saylah had described her shimmering white hair, her wise black eyes and wrinkled face battered by the sun, as well as her noble carriage, which had not been damaged by the stroke from which she was beginning to recover. She sat at the edge of the square on a throne of a chair carved from a huge oak stump, the seat low and flat in front, the back rising behind her like frozen tongues of colorless flame.

Eventually, the others began to return to their chores, and the old woman rose with agonizing slowness. Saylah was at her side in an instant, balancing her weak left arm on her own shoulders, though she had to lean down to support the tiny woman. Old Grandmother walked with a distinct limp, but her eyes were alive and aware, and her expression made it clear that she was ignoring the infirmity of her body, and so should everyone else.

"My loom is set up at your favorite spot on the beach," she told Saylah. "I've told them to leave blankets and food so we can enjoy the blessings of this day. Come," she added, "I have promised you a story."

"So you have," Saylah replied. "My daughter and I have looked forward to this day."

As the three stepped from among the rushes and goldenrod to the shell-scattered beach, Saylah breathed deeply and moved toward the foaming waves as if mesmerized. She reached back to take Illiann's hand, drawing her daughter into the magic. The sunlight marked a shimmering pathway across the gray-green water, and the clouds drifted soundlessly over the lapping waves. Illiann sighed with pleasure. Like her mother, she loved the sea, lapping soothingly against the pebbled shore, undulating with familiar shifts of color and light. She was caught up in the salty tang of the wind, the whisper of water on stones, the shimmering green-white foam.

The girl took the pins from her hair and unwound it, letting the thick braid fall down her back. She would have unwoven that as well, but the wind was too high and wild. Saylah did not seem to care; she loosened her long, black hair and let the wind toss it about her face.

Saylah spoke quietly, so she would not disturb the tranquility which enveloped them. "There is something sacred here that renews the spirit." She smiled down at the sparkling shells like tiny, incandescent footprints in the sand. Such small miracles inspired her, and she sensed they would also inspire Illiann.

The two stood side-by-side for a long time, matching their breathing to the rhythm of the sea. Then Old Grandmother coughed, and the spell was broken.

Saylah settled on the ground, her skirt gathered around her knees, her bare feet crossed. Illiann followed suit, watching, intrigued, as Old Grandmother settled herself behind the sturdy frame of a loom on which a long, glimmering fabric was being woven. The many textures and colors flowed together, blue-green blending with sky-blue and shimmering silver, then separating as the waves of the sea flowed together, swelled, then parted in a crash of foam and radiant hues that glittered like tiny rainbows from the slightest touch of the sun. As the woman sent the shuttle flying through the threads, then packed in the new line of weaving, the girl noticed the extraordinary differences in the threads, which created a remarkable pattern. She had never seen anything like it before.

"What is it?" she asked, as her mother had once asked.

Old Grandmother smiled. "It is intended for a sacred purpose. There is only one who is worthy of receiving its blessing. Just as a young girl was blessed long ago when the Changer first made the world and it lay in utter darkness."

Her eyes took on a dreaming cast, and her expression softened, making her look younger and less worn. "Sensing something was missing in that vast blackness, Raven came to steal the moon, the stars and the sun from the chests of a rich man, and so showed the people for the first time what their world looked like, and the People were amazed and full of gratitude."

She glanced up from the loom, but her gaze was fixed on something invisible and far away. Her fingers moved the shuttle effortlessly, preserving and expanding the pattern of the threads.

"Once the daughter of He Who Had Hidden the Light saw the brightness of day, she began to fear that the long black night, which had lasted many years, would return, and the riches of the earth would be lost in eternal darkness.

"Raven appeared, showing her how the light of the new day sparkled on the water of a clear stream in vivid bursts, and bid her gather them in her hand and follow the light from stream to river to the pulsing sea.

"All along the way, she gathered the sparkling light from the water into her hands, until near sunset, when the light began to fade and the girl's fear began to grow. To distract her, Raven sang, 'Do not fear the night, my daughter, but take these fragments born of light and water and spin them into threads. And when you have done this, set the threads upon a small but sturdy loom, warp and weft, and begin to weave yourself a robe.'"

Illiann stared at her mother. Saylah's expression was unguarded, and her face was naked with yearning, her eyes focused on a distant vision at which her daughter could only guess. She leaned forward, as if pulled by an invisible force, smiling slightly, face serene and beautiful. A pain tightened Illiann's chest and she tried to catch her breath, not certain why it was so difficult.

"'When you have finished this robe,' Raven said, 'place it about your shoulders and feel its softness, its uniqueness and its power. It will protect you always from the darkness, because it is woven of the light."

Saylah had begun to tap out a rhythm with her palms on her knees, and she matched it to the old woman's voice and the meter of the loom. She swayed with the beat of her makeshift drums, and the cadence gradually wormed its way into Illiann's head and changed the pulse of her blood. She knew that insistent rhythm, and it held her prisoner.

Old Grandmother watched mother and daughter covertly, twined her gnarled fingers together and groped for the thread of her story. "When she found it, she began to roll it between her deft and aged hands, and from the thread came words which Raven chanted. 'This robe will protect you from the many darknesses—the darkness of night, the darkness of man and the darkness that is deep inside yourself. And as the threat of darkness disappears, so will your fear turn to ash and be carried away on a wind, for the power of light bound with water is strong, and you shall be strong and safe forever.'"

In that moment, Illiann felt the impact of the past as she never had before, poignantly, intensely, with a sense of awe and gratitude. Her gaze was fixed on Saylah in a kind of wonder laced with apprehension.

There was a quality to her mother's stillness that Illiann had never experienced. Her eyes were closed, her lips slightly parted, a beatific expression on her face.

Illiann was startled when Old Grandmother touched her on the shoulder and sank down beside her.

"It must be difficult to see her like this."

Her voice was full of compassion, her eyes of wisdom, and her smile of kindness. Inexplicably, Illiann felt tears rise in her throat. "I always knew she yearned for the magic of her childhood, but—" She paused. "Until this moment, I didn't really understand…" She broke off, unable, or unwilling, to put her feelings into words.

"How deep the longing went?" Old Grandmother suggested.

"Maybe. But it's more than that. I thought I knew how she'd be with her People; I'd imagined it often enough. But it seems I didn't know her at all."

"It upsets you to see how powerful the truth is."

Illiann nodded. "It frightens me." Just then, she was terrified of losing her mother to the past that had engulfed her, taking her to a place where her daughter could not follow.

Old Grandmother slipped her arm around the girl's shoulders. "You see more than most, I think. You have begun to understand that Saylah lives always in two different worlds, and it is hard for you to accept."

"I've know it for a long time, but I never *felt* it until now." Her eyes burned and her spirit ached. "Still, it's good to see her happy."

She hesitated. "I don't mean she's *un*happy at home, only that she's different here, at peace." It was difficult to admit that simple truth, but Illiann had never lied to herself about her mother, and Saylah had never learned to lie to herself.

Old Grandmother whispered, "You have a generous heart, *Ladaila*. I understand now why your mother is so proud of you."

Illiann knew from her mother that *Ladaila* meant 'dear little one', and she was touched that the wise old woman had addressed her so affectionately.

All at once, she understood with a new, intense awareness what Saylah had meant when she told her daughter that, above all, she should follow her instinct and the dictates of her heart.

Chapter 79

Robert Barrett was in an exceptionally ill humor Monday morning as he approached the iron works. He'd had a fight with his wife, Diana the night before, though even in the light of day, he was not certain what had caused it. She seemed increasingly short-tempered of late, and he could not shake the feeling that her annoyance had something to do with the men at the Works. The thought was so absurd that he tried to dismiss it, but it would not leave him. The workers had been grumbling louder every day. That was clearly Julian Ivy's fault. He had never met a man with such understated confidence and no apparent fear. It was a deadly combination, and a challenge, to a man like Robert Barrett. Hart had only added to his partner's troubles, had even suggested he listen to the workers' complaints. Barrett rolled his eyes in disgust and nearly tripped over a loose board in the sidewalk.

The worst thing was that the low grumble of dissent had stopped abruptly a couple of days ago, and he found it unnerving, though he would never admit it. Barrett was not allowed the weakness of being uneasy; he had to be always resolute and unshaken. Anything less was cowardice, and he would not stoop to being a coward.

A few raindrops fell; he heard them as they struck his top hat. The road out near the works was already one long ribbon of mud, and the wooden sidewalks had long ago warped from harsh weather and lack of repairs. Another storm would only worsen the conditions. He glared upward, shaking his gold-tipped cane at the cloud-filled sky. He was tired of the rain. To him, weather was an inconvenience created to test him. "Too sunny yesterday, too cloudy today," he muttered toward the dark billows above him. "Can't ever get it right, can you?"

When a young boy stopped to stare, he lowered his cane and turned away, sweeping his cape about him as if to block out what the boy had seen. Looking forward with grim determination, he covered the last few yards to the door of the factory in long, impatient strides.

It was raining in earnest by the time he stepped over the raised wooden threshold, and he was relieved to get in out of the damp. He was also relieved at the comforting sounds of the works running along smoothly—the furnaces snapping and spitting fire, the machines creaking and cranking, the air filled with the smell of oil and hot iron and sweat. The men talked among themselves as they worked, and the low hum of their voices contrasted with the growls of the machines and the iron they were striking, shaping and finishing.

One of the men glanced up and saw him, stopped what he was doing, and signaled to the man beside him. He repeated the gesture to the man beside *him*, and so on, until, one by one, all the workers stopped mid-motion. They did not look at each other, but stared somberly at Barrett. Their hands were suspended in the air for a long moment, as if his sudden presence had frozen them where they stood. Slowly, almost rhythmically, they let their arms fall to their sides, where they clenched their fists, but made no other move.

Barrett was brought up short by the sudden stillness. He had not realized how much of the sound in this place was made by the men. He had always thought the machines more powerful. He looked around distrustfully, but no one moved. The silence was absolute, except for the roaring furnaces with their white-hot flickering light. Every head was turned toward him; all eyes were staring.

The light cast by the furnaces, which threw half the faces into shadow, half into unforgiving light, turned the room into a static kind of hell; Barrett suppressed a shudder. He felt an unspoken danger pressing against him, hostility so intense it was palpable. The antipathy in the workers' sullen gazes was suffocating, and he had to struggle to breathe. Their faces were expressionless, but their silence was more volatile than violence. The air might as well have been laced with gunpowder.

For the first time in his life, he was struck dumb. For the first time, he had a sense of the people as one living, breathing force more dangerous than any he had faced before. It frightened him, and because he did not approve of fear, except in others, it also enraged him. These men, who were completely dependent on his largess, who were close to starvation and living in filth, had no right to make him feel this way. He shook with disbelief and fury, trying to gather his wits about him in order to strike back, to put them, each and every one, back where he belonged—underneath Barrett's thumb.

Minutes seemed to stretch into hours as he searched for the words to puncture the inflated silence, but they did not come.

Perplexed by the silence below, Arthur Hart appeared at the top of the stairs.

He stood there, stunned, and tried to assess the situation. Though it appeared no one had spoken a threat or wielded a weapon, the air positively crackled. The tension hit him like a blast of scorching air. Barrett was hemmed in by animosity, trapped—there was no other word for it—in the middle of the floor. Hart had never faced a situation this explosive, and he could see his partner was about to strike a match. Barrett knew no other way to deal with a challenge.

What if I do nothing? Hart wondered. *What if I let him blurt out his fury?* But he knew he could not do that. If Barrett were hurt, the men would be the ones to pay the price.

Hart tried to focus on practicalities. "Ah," he heard himself say in a voice that pierced the silence like a sharp, cold blade, "I forgot I promised you a break in mid-afternoon." He tapped the side of his head, as if to shake loose the memory, and tried not to pay attention to the sudden current in the air. He had to plow ahead, regardless of his own queasy stomach and shaking hands. "Forgive me for my absentmindedness No time like the present, I always say. O'Reilly, Moran, Sanders, Davidson—could you each take a several men and go off one group at a time?"

When he first spoke, most heads had turned in his direction. Others maintained their scrutiny of Barrett. But as Hart went on, more and more eyes sought him out. He had been good to the workers before Barrett came, sending his wife with food and bandages and blankets when they were most needed. Lately, since Julian Ivy's article had come out, he had begun to give them breaks when he knew his partner would not be in. They had a silent agreement that they would not speak of the concession; they knew Hart would be in trouble if Barrett found out. Yet there he stood, revealing it himself. Now he was in more danger than they. His smile and jolly tone were forced, but he did not back down. Gradually, unwillingly, men turned back to their stations and, one by one, began to work again.

Barrett was enraged. He had never felt threatened as he had by these insignificant men and boys. He didn't like feeling that Hart had been smarter than he, that his partner had actually rescued him. He did not like feeling vulnerable, so he attacked the only person in the room he was sure would not fight back.

"Are you mad, Hart? Giving in to them like that? Next thing you know, they'll be telling *you* what to do. You're damned lucky I have an urgent errand elsewhere." He favored Hart with a withering look. "Do try and hold the place together for another day at least. As for me, I've much more important things to do."

Released from the force that had held him immobile, he turned on his heel, his taut muscles aching from holding them so tightly in check.

The men nodded to each other, and a few smiled tentatively. They had brought Barrett to an utter standstill and frightened him as well. They had succeeded at long last in getting and holding his attention. Though Julian Ivy had spoken of it with great zeal, not one of them had ever, until that moment, understood the power of silence.

Chapter 80

"Why do you keep looking over your shoulder? It's been a fortnight since we saw him." Nevertheless, Kit coasted to a halt on Sophia's bicycle and glanced back down Government Street the way he and his friend had just come.

"You know why," Will insisted.

Kit thought maybe Will was bored. The last two weeks had been unexciting, without a whiff of danger, or a glimpse of the large bald man. "You worry too much."

"Maybe." Will did not sound convinced. He stopped, balancing his bicycle as he glowered at the pedestrians.

Kit narrowed his own gaze and grabbed Will's elbow. "You're right. He's there. I saw him." The boys had left Lord Byron at home so they could ride their bicycles around downtown, but now he wished the dog was there.

"Where?" Will had been expecting the reappearance of the man they had dubbed Baldhead, but he had not been expecting Kit's panic.

"In front of the general store. Maybe it's nothing to do with us. Maybe he's just doing some shopping."

"Sure he is."

Kit frowned. "I know how to find out."

"How?" Will was alert, if skeptical.

"We'll turn down Fisgard here and see if he follows."

"What if he does?"

"Then we'll try to outwit him."

Will shook his head as they remounted their bicycles. "That's dumb. He's huge. What if he catches us?"

"He won't. We're smaller and lighter. I used to see big men on the ranch who could practically lift a horse out of its stall, but they couldn't run as fast as the tall, skinny ones, and they got tired sooner." He began to pedal furiously.

"Yes, but what if he *does*?"

"What's he going to do in the middle of the street with all these people looking on?" Kit glanced back and saw Baldhead emerge from the crowd, heading in their direction. The afternoon sun glared off his pate like a warning. "Come on!"

They headed toward the harbor, almost to Henry Street, along the wall that bordered Chinatown. Will was so nervous he swerved to the side, when a door opened and a Chinaman appeared waving at them to come through the narrow opening in the wall. Will had not guessed the door was there.

Kit was unfazed, however. He turned and bumped over the threshold, looking back to make sure his friend followed. Once they were inside, he stopped abruptly, just as the door slammed shut behind them. They had entered Chinatown, a different world from the one they knew. "I was photographing here the other day with Su-ling and her brother, Yuan Chao. This is him. This is my friend, Will."

Yuan Chao bowed, acknowledging the introduction. "Come, I will show you how to lose yourselves here."

Kit had the feeling people were watching, but he had spent a long time here two days before, and had gradually grown used to the sensation. The street was extraordinarily still, but he knew there were life and breath and many secrets behind the ordinary façades along both sides. He recognized a vegetable seller, his wares drawn quickly inside the store's blank face when he heard the boy's commotion. Beside him was an apothecary, also closed and silent.

"You must go." Yuan Chao directed the boys to turn down an alley too narrow for their bicycles. As they dismounted, another man appeared and began to wheel them away. "He will keep them safe for you," Yuan said.

"Where...are...we...going?" Will demanded.

"Don't know. Away from Baldhead."

"Yes, the giant man," Yuan Chao agreed. "He comes behind you. You wonder why I have let you in. It is because you have friends here, Young Master. They will help you to elude this Smith." He bowed again, addressing Kit formally.

"We do not care for him. He tricked many into coming to the Island to work when there were strikes at the coalmines. He said he would protect us. When the regular workers turned on us, he stood by laughing, and many died. He has no reverence or respect for anything but money." He tilted his head, listening. "I hear him coming; you must go."

Kit felt ill. He was just beginning to comprehend the danger he was in.

Overwhelmed by a sense of unreality, Will was barely listening, though when Kit tugged on his hand, he began to run, more out of instinct than fear. He had never been beyond the outer walls of this section of Victoria, and had never imagined the intricate alleyways, courtyards and corridors they passed through. Whenever they hit a dead end, another secret door was cracked open and another alley revealed.

After a few wild minutes, they stopped to catch their breath. By then Will had begun to notice the smell of cooking oil and vegetables and fruit, of bitter herbs and the sickly sweet odor of opium. He had heard of the opium dens where men and women went to escape their troubles, where pipes and pallets were provided. He knew they were nearby but out of sight.

Kit was preoccupied with flickering movements on the balconies and down the corridors, and a rising whisper, first of panic, then of anger. He was overcome by a sense of foreboding as he dragged in deep, ragged breaths, one after another.

A panel slid open in front of them, and the boys ran through the opening, into the heart of a winter courtyard, and beyond it, to a path of flat stones across gravel. By then they could hear Baldhead crashing along somewhere behind them, so they clutched their aching sides and moved faster. They scrambled down blind alleys, over fences, piles of bricks and washtubs and under lines of laundry strung across the corridors. Red in the face, dripping sweat and gasping for breath, they hurried through smoky kitchens, hidden nooks and graceful courtyards.

The tenor of the whispers overhead increased and Will glanced back, eyes widening in fear when he actually caught a glimpse of Baldhead coming. He nearly filled the narrow street, could easily have made the walls shake as he passed by, but he did not pause to test his strength. "Come *on!*" Will cried.

Fortunately, Kit had been right about their pursuer's size; he seemed uneasy in the close quarters and winded by the exertion. It was true that he was strong, but he was not nimble. He used his strength to intimidate, and did not have the kind of endurance the twisting alleyways demanded.

Once or twice, Kit actually thought his heart was stuck in his throat; he could feel it throbbing there, choking him, and he was sure Will was not doing any better, but they did not dare stop. The boys were negotiating a carefully tended rock path when Will came up too fast, crashing into his friend so they both went down, sprawling against a brick wall with a sickening thud. Kit grabbed his head, and Will his wrist. Both were scraped and bleeding, and so tired and aching that they did not want to rise.

Will was shaking so hard his teeth chattered. "What does he *want?*"

Through the pain that seemed to echo through his head, Kit listened intently for the sound of the man's footsteps, but could not yet hear them. "My father thinks he just wants to scare us," Kit whispered.

If possible, Will withdrew farther into the shadow of the wall, so his expression was completely hidden. "But why? I don't get it."

"*I* think because of Robert Barrett. Because my father made him angry. Shhhh! Here he comes."

They stood, limping forward so they could see beyond the tiny opening at the far end of the alley. Kit looked at his friend. "Ready?"

Will managed to nod slightly, but he was very pale and his breathing was heavy and uneven.

Suddenly, a Chinese boy appeared in front of them. "You tired?" he said. "Come. Shortcut."

Using most of their remaining strength, the boys stumbled up a steep staircase, at the top of which a door hung open. Kit's head ached horribly, but he did not want to complain. This was his fault after all, he thought.

By the time they reached the top of the stairs, Kit's blurred vision was settling back to normal, and he tried to take a couple of deep breaths. The open door beckoned, but when he glanced back, he saw Baldhead appear out of nowhere and hurtle up the stairs behind them. Kit managed to pull his friend into a covered corridor, but the man had grabbed Will's other arm and he wrenched it brutally. Will cried out, kicking and grasping at the railing to try to break free.

Kit refused to let go, and all three tumbled into the passageway and out the far door, which opened onto a balcony overlooking an empty street. He braced himself against the railing and kicked out as hard as he could toward the man's knee. To his surprise, Baldhead went down with a grunt. He loosened his grip on Will momentarily, and Kit took the opportunity to drag his friend away. Baldhead rose and tried to come after them, but he lost his footing, and the rail cracked beneath his weight. He hovered on the edge for what seemed like a long time, swayed forward, back, forward again, and then hurtled backward off the edge and onto the street below.

The boys did not wait to see what happened next. They ran, gasping for breath, down the length of the corridor.

When they finally emerged into daylight again, they found themselves staring down at Baldhead lying in the street, right leg bent at an impossible angle. He was bellowing in pain, calling out, "My leg! My leg! I need help."

Kit shook off a chill at the sound of the man's pitiful cries. He was not so frightening now. That was when the boys finally began to shake, knowing they were safe. Battered and bruised, but safe nonetheless.

"Kit?" Will's voice came out a squeak, and he cradled his left arm close to his chest. The last of the color had drained from his face and Kit thought he might actually faint.

"Come on. Let's get out of here."

Will was not listening. He was staring down, open-mouthed, at Baldhead on his back in the dirt. It was the first time he had looked the man directly in the face, and even through the dust, his rough features were clear. He stiffened and gulped back an exclamation, scooting back as far as he could go, pressing his body hard against the wall. His face, already worn from exertion and pain, was drawn.

Kit sensed movement in the street below, and peered over the railing to find the Chinese had begun to appear soundlessly, first one by one, then two and three together, until a large crowd had gathered. He did not understand how so many people could cause so little noise; it made the gooseflesh rise on the back of his neck. The crowd was staring at the injured man, eyes glittering with animosity.

The boy sagged under the weight of that knowledge. "Maybe we should help him." He turned to Will, hoping for reassurance, but Will had problems of his own. He clutched his left arm to his chest, though he could not stop the swelling or the bruising that had begun to stain his pale skin. He needed to get home, and quickly.

Kit was aware that he did not owe Baldhead any kindness. Still, having been trained by his mother, he found it difficult to turn his back on anyone in pain.

The Chinese had begun to whisper among themselves, and as the seconds passed, the whisper increased to rapid-fire Chinese. He could not understand the words, but he heard the ominous message clearly. This man, whom they hated, who had mistreated and used them, was suddenly at their mercy.

The air was full of menace, and Kit's blood ran cold. He had meant to trick Baldhead, to show him the boys were not afraid of him, and that they could outrun him if they chose to. But he had not meant to trap him—helpless—in the midst of his enemies.

Carefully, he helped Will sit and lean his head against the wall.

"What're you doing?" Will demanded.

Kit crouched down beside him. "He's hurt and they're angry and I'm afraid they might do something crazy. Maybe even kill him."

Will peered at him through swollen eyes. "What did you *think* would happen?"

Flushing, Kit shook his head. "I didn't think. That's just the problem. And I can't leave him like this."

"He wouldn't care if it was you down there."

"I know. But I still have to help him." As the sweat on his body turned cold, he clattered down the stairs to the street.

The buzz of the crowd was growing louder, and their rage became a living force. It almost broke him, but he forced two deep breaths into his lungs and pushed his way through the tightly packed bodies until he stood in the center, beside the injured man.

Silence descended abruptly, and it was more chilling than the talk had been. "You've been really great, helping me and my friend get away from this man. But he can't hurt us anymore, or you, and I'm asking you not to hurt him. *Please!*" He knew it was a feeble attempt, but he could not think of clever words the way his father did. He could smell their collective breath as if he stood nose to nose with them. He swallowed dryly, pulse racing. They could crush him in a second if they wanted. But he didn't back down.

Yuan Chao appeared like a puff of smoke from the tainted air, and translated what Kit had said. "He is right," he added in English for the boy's benefit, before repeating it in Chinese. "This man works for Robert Barrett. He is what they call a 'right-handed man.' And Robert Barrett has much power and influence. He would find a way to harm us much greater than the harm we could do to his man here. You know it is the truth."

A hundred voices rose in protest, creating a threat so powerful that it shook Kit to the soles of his feet. What had he been thinking, challenging a crowd like this?

Yuan Chao exchanged angry words with several men, pounding his fist against his hand, talking himself breathless.

Kit tried not to move, hoping they would forget he was there.

Finally, after what seemed to him an hour, the voices began to fade and heads to nod as the Chinese backed away.

Yuan Chao turned to Kit. "I promise, he will not be hurt."

Baldhead, who had remained silent, was furious that he could not wave his fist and threaten, frightening these people into submission. Never in his life had he felt helpless, yet here he lay, pain streaking up his leg, making him gasp, unable to move, being defended by a ten year old boy. Someone would pay for this. He swore it.

Kit barely had time to take a breath before the crowd broke up, disappearing back into their shops and homes as soundlessly as they had come. The silence they left behind was more eerie than their roar of rage. He still found it difficult to draw a steady breath.

Will moaned, shattering the stillness, and Kit shook himself awake. He had to get his friend to safety. As he remounted the stairs and draped the boy's arm around his shoulders, he glanced back at the street one last time.

Baldhead lay there, face ashen, leg torn and bleeding, and there was no sign that this city within a city was inhabited. Not one face behind dusty glass or one whisper above the afternoon breeze. Nothing. They would not hurt him; they had promised. But, Kit realized, neither would they help him.

Chapter 81

When Agatha appeared in his study early that evening, Arthur Hart was taken aback. It was the only room in the house that he had made his own, and his wife had never liked it. The glossy mantel – Agatha had wanted marble, but he had insisted on good solid oak -- was crowded with his pipe stand, a hand-tooled ash box for his tobacco, a miniature of his mother in a startling silver frame beside another of Laura and her mother. There were fishing lures and some small black, gray and silver rocks, as well as other oddities he had collected over the years, and finally, a wrought iron rack for a pistol and hunting knives fashioned at the Works by one of his father's finest craftsmen.

The library table was scattered with foolscap and dried inkpots, pens that had stained the blotter with irregular black puddles, books piled haphazardly, while the stags head book ends served as paper weights. His desk chair, also inherited from his father, was well-seasoned oak, creaky and stiff on its wheels.

Agatha said it was shabby and undignified, and more than once had tried to discard the chair when he wasn't looking. Laura always helped him rescue it before it was hauled away. He could feel his wife's discomfort, her itch to put things in order, every time she came in.

Today she did not seem to notice the clutter; she simply stood, hands clasped, her coiffure askew and her violet gown slightly wrinkled. "What is it, my dear? What's wrong?"

"I was…just, ahem, I was wondering how…things are at the factory."

Her husband stared at her curiously. "Well, if that's all, then you needn't worry."

"But I do, Arthur. You've stopped talking to me, and that's worrying."

Curiosity shifted to suspicion. "You were never interested before."

"But now people are talking."

"Are they? I hadn't noticed." He sounded either bored or unutterably weary.

"They're saying that you've gone soft, that you've been giving these people ideas."

"I assume you're referring to the workers at the factory."

"Of course I am. The situation is dangerous, Arthur. There are too many of them and too few of us."

"And naturally, in your view, *we* are more important."

She did not seem to notice the edge in his voice. "We have to be. Don't you see that? We can't give them even the smallest victory; they'll never be satisfied until they have it all. And what's more, you don't care. I wish just once, you would think of your daughter and your wife instead of your pride."

That stung, and he let her see it. "I'd never knowingly hurt you or Laura. You must know that." The slightest lift of his voice at the end made it a question, not a statement.

"I find it difficult to believe that, when you're turning the works upside down by allowing the men time off and standing idly by listening to their problems."

Arthur narrowed his eyes. "How do you know about that?

Agatha seemed to find a sudden absorbing interest in the webbing on his old cane chair. "I told you, people are talking. I've heard rumors. For heaven's sake, everyone has."

He waited silently for her to continue.

"Everyone's worried that if you relent, you'll give the men the upper hand, and the dissatisfaction will spread like the influenza. They might even strike!" She risked a quick glance, but could read nothing from his rigid features. "That's what happened at the mines. We can't risk it, Arthur. Not again."

Arthur was troubled less by her panic and more by the fact that she was remarkably well informed.

"If you must know," he said, packing his pipe with tobacco in order to keep his hands busy, "I'm acting out of pure selfishness. Tired and unhappy workers make mistakes and have unfortunate accidents and end up disrupting the other workers and sometimes even bleeding all over the handwork. Now *that* would indeed be a shame, wouldn't you agree?"

It took a great effort to keep his voice level, and she recognized it. Finally.

"You're just trying to appease me."

He tilted his head in acknowledgment. "Sad, but all too true, I fear."

Agatha was puzzled by his attempt to restore their usual precarious balance. For some odd reason, it made her ache. "I'm sorry. I know you've never meant any harm to anyone. I can't think why I attacked you like that."

He knew her fear was real and that she was rarely able to escape its influence. All a once, he felt sorry for her. At least he felt something, and that was quite a little victory in itself.

He took a step toward her and she threw up her hands in a kind of surrender neither of them understood. "Have a little faith in me, can't you?"

She nodded wordlessly, though she knew that of all the things he might have asked for, she could not give him that.

Chapter 82

"You've been hiding something for weeks, Illiann Ivy," Laura said accusingly, "and I'm about to burst with curiosity. Tell!"

She had waited to say it until the girls sat cross-legged and barefoot on Illiann's bed, their shoes and stockings discarded on the floor, though she'd been wanting to for the longest time. "You're not leaving this room until you give me an answer." Her tone was harsh; she puffed up her chest and drew her lips into a thin grim line, holding her hair in a tight chignon on her head.

Illiann smiled. Her friend looked and sounded quite a bit like her mother, just as she had intended. "You really shouldn't do that."

"I'm waiting, miss." Laura released her hair, allowing it to fall untidily down her back, then opened three buttons on her wilted blouse, which was already partially untucked, and gathered her skirt carelessly into her lap, exposing her bare knees. Her cornflower blue eyes sparkled with inquisitiveness.

Illiann was reluctant to respond, but she had kept her secret for so long she ached with it. "You have to promise—"

"Of course I do." Laura was up on her knees, knuckles pressed into the duvet. "Stop delaying. Tell."

"You're becoming a nag," Illian warned with a grin. When she had an object in mind, Laura hung on tenaciously until she got what she wanted. "Lucky for you, I was planning to tell you anyway." Which wasn't exactly true. "You see, there's this…man."

Her friend's mouth fell open in disbelief. She had expected anything but that.

"I went to his house after school one day."

"His *house*? Without a chaperone?" Suddenly Laura sounded like her mother without trying, and she did not like it.

"We just, you know, talked."

Arms folded, Laura regarded her dubiously; she could not help it. "Really? About what?"

Illiann was uncomfortable under her friend's penetrating gaze, but she needed to go on. "His past and his painting and…things."

Intrigued, concerned and not a little envious, Laura prompted, "Who is he, then?"

"I don't want to say," her friend replied carefully. "And I can't tell my parents. They wouldn't like it."

"Not even your mother? You tell her everything."

"Not this." The time Illiann had spent with Devon felt forbidden and exciting and clandestine, and that was part of its appeal. "Mama and Papa think he's angry or scared or something. I think they're afraid he might explode."

"What do *you* think?" Laura was troubled by Ilya's's admission.

"I think so too, if someone doesn't help him understand himself."

"That's what you want to do? Help him?" Laura was incredulous. She had never had a beau herself, but she was under the impression there were much more pleasant ways to enjoy one than by being helpful.

Illiann's eyes glowed with unusual intensity and she blushed. "Sort of, but that's not all--" she broke off in confusion. "Sometimes he makes me so angry I want to knock him over, but other times I feel desperate and excited and I *ache* when I think of him. I just feel *different*."

Laura tried to take it all in. She could not sort out her own feelings, and she did not want to let her friend down. "So, you just talked. He didn't hold your hand or *anything*?"

"Well…he did kiss me, but only on the cheek. His lips barely brushed the corner of my mouth. And he touched my cheek with his fingertip."

"Illi-*ann*!" Laura wanted to launch into a dozen more questions, but Lord Byron began to bark downstairs just before the girls heard a sharp tattoo at the window. "Someone's throwing rocks to get your attention. Maybe it's your beau."

"Stop it! You promised." Illiann slid off the bed, facing her friend, arms crossed.

Laura had never seen her look so flustered. She sighed with disappointment. "You're my best friend. I'd never betray you. Especially not about something this important. Even if you *won't* tell me his name."

As another smattering of pebbles rattled against the glass, Illiann hurried over to the window. "It's just my little brother." She was both relieved and intensely disappointed. Lifting the sash resolutely, she leaned out. At first glance, she had noticed Kit was disheveled and dirty, but now she realized his face was scratched, and the sweat dried on his arms was streaked with blood. "What happened?"

Kit raised his finger to his lips in alarm. "Quiet. Are Mama and Papa home?"

Perplexed by her brother's furtive behavior, Illiann leaned out farther and saw his friend Will hovering in the shadow of the horse chestnut tree. "Mama's with the Indians and Papa's working late at the shop. Why?"

"Come down and let us in—the back way—and I'll tell you. We need help, Lily."

He had not called her Lily for years, and it told her how upset he really was. "Of course." She kept her tone matter-of-fact, though she was more than a little troubled by the boys' appearance. In addition to their obvious injuries, they looked as if they had been dipped in a dust bath.

Laura joined her at the window. "Golly, what happened to you?"

Kit blinked at her suspiciously. "What're *you* doing here?"

"Don't be rude," Illiann said. "She's my friend. You know that."

He flushed in embarrassment, rubbing his toe in the dirt. "Sorry."

"Never mind," his sister told him, taking control. "Meet us at the back door." She dragged her healing bag out from under the bed and hurried downstairs, Laura at her heels. She was unusually silent.

Lord Byron was already there, wagging his tail in welcome. The door was on the latch, which was why Kit hadn't come in on his own. "Su-ling has gone on an errand; we're the only ones here." She had grasped Kit's sense of urgency.

"Sit," she instructed the boys. They did so, far too meekly, she thought. It was not natural. The dog moved around them in agitation, sniffing one, then the other and whining softly in sympathy.

Illiann glanced at Will's arm and headed for the small icebox. She chipped some off the melting block at the bottom, wrapped it in a towel and settled it, as gently as she could, around the wrist and forearm. Dark, ugly bruises were already coming up, some of them looking suspiciously like the imprint of fingers. "Laura, can you get a kettle on the boil? I'm going to need hot water for teas and infusions. Stop squirming, Will. I know it's hard, but try."

Laura was astonished and impressed by the change in her friend. Before Kit appeared, Illiann had been laughing, light-hearted, teasing about her secret. Now she was brisk, efficient and tender. Laura filled the kettle from the pump in the sink and placed it on a burner, encouraging the water to boil with her hands, though she knew it was silly. She wanted to feel useful.

Meanwhile, Illiann dragged over a pitcher of cool water and a large bowl, seating herself between the two boys.

"Now. Tell me what happened." She began to clean the dirt off Will's face, and the towel came away rusty with dried blood.

Kit's mouth went dry. "You can't tell Mama and Papa."

Illiann gaped at him. "They might notice on their own, don't you think?"

Kit ignored her. "We, um, fell off our bicycles."

"Excuse me?" Laura was trying to stay in the background, but she could not stop her exclamation of disbelief. She had suffered her share of childhood accidents, and she could not imagine a tumble from a bicycle that would cause this much damage. The boys were covered in scratches and newly formed bruises, and they looked as if they had been dragged through the street in the wake of a carriage with shaky wheels.

"Bicycles?" Illiann was dubious.

"Head first!" Will added a bit too quickly. "Owww!" he cried when Illiann tested his wrist to see if it was broken. The blood drained from his face.

"Only sprained," she muttered to herself in relief.

"We hit a rock. A big one," Kit elaborated.

Illiann met Laura's gaze, raising her eyebrows in incredulity.

"What, both of you?" Laura shook her head. The boys were obviously lying.

"*Must* have been big," Illiann observed as she swabbed their scrapes and bruises with cottonwood, then witch hazel. "But then, why didn't you see it before you hit it?" Her tone was deceptively mild.

"It was really wide, like this." Kit held his arms about five feet apart. Lord Byron tried to insinuate himself beneath his master's hand, but the boy hardly noticed. He was watching his sister.

She focused on Will's arm, propping it carefully on a rolled up towel, then shifting the ice slightly. "Try to keep still. The tea and the infusion will help with the pain, but it will take a little while. Can you stand it till then?"

Will nodded, biting back a groan. He glanced guiltily at his friend.

"I don't think you finished your story," Illiann suggested.

Laura could only admire her friend's patience. She must be afraid, worried, but she didn't show it; her hands were steady as she moved confidently from healing bag to kettle to herb packets to the boys' tender skin. Laura's own hands were trembling with excitement, curiosity and concern for the boys, who looked suddenly small and helpless.

"It was hidden by pine needles in the forest. The rock, I mean."

Illiann regarded him pensively. The dog followed her example, thumping his tail on the floor in disappointment because Kit had not noticed him.

"If that's all it is," Laura said, recognizing her friend's dilemma, "why can't you tell your parents? And, since I'm assuming Will doesn't want his to know either, what's he going to tell them when he gets home?" She had experience with this kind of thing, and didn't want Will to be as unprepared when he faced his parents as he obviously was now.

Kit was stumped, but Will saved him from answering.

"I don't want to go home! I can't." He was so agitated that he stood up, forgetting his injuries in his panic.

The girls exchanged another telling glance. "Why not?" This time Illiann could not keep the surprise out of her voice. The dog went to Will, nearly tripping the boy with his bulky body.

Arm hanging limply, Will rocked back and forth, torn between pain and guilt. "Because of my stepfather." He took a deep breath and plunged ahead. "This is all my fault. Because of him. It wouldn't have happened—" He broke off.

"What do you mean?" Illiann asked.

Gulping down air, Will stared at his feet and mumbled, "My stepfather is Robert Barrett." He sank back into his chair, as if waiting for the earth to open up and swallow him.

Kit sat back on his heels, staring at his friend in astonishment. "The one who's been threatening my father?"

Will nodded miserably. "I guess you won't want to be my friend anymore."

Kit sputtered, "Don't be stupid. You don't even like your stepfather."

Rubbing her temples, which had begun to ache, Illiann put her hand on her brother's knee. "Robert Barrett aside, you're going to have to tell us the truth, Kit. I know you don't want to, but I need to know. Please."

Laura felt she was intruding on a private moment. She had always wondered what it would be like to have a brother or sister. She watched Illiann's gaze meet Kit's, kindly, probingly, and he looked back at her, trying to be hostile, to shut her out, but unable to do so. Laura felt a jolt of envy.

"Will you promise not to tell? And you, Laura?" His expression was full of pleading.

"I want to, but I have to know what happened first."

Laura nodded in agreement.

Resigned, Kit sighed hugely. Then, a few words at a time, he explained, leaving out some pertinent details. In this version, it seemed that Baldhead had forced them into Chinatown, and they had had no choice but to run.

The girls were horrified by his account of the Chinese gathering in the street, although Kit had toned it down considerably. Will felt compelled to interject his own belief that his friend had been very brave and righteous in defending Baldhead against the mob, and Laura and Illiann could only nod, speechless.

"You promised not to tell." Kit watched the girls' faces intently for any sign of rebellion.

"Not precisely. I said I needed to know the truth first. Besides, they should know you're in danger."

"They already do, and they can't change it. It'll only worry them more."

He was right, but his sister wasn't certain it was enough.

Chapter 83

The Ivys' dinner table was crowded that evening. Devon had joined the family, as well as Will and Laura. Lord Byron lay in the corner, front paws crossed, head raised at a regal angle. His nostrils were extended and his ears at attention.

Illiann had had to change her gown at the last moment, because the skirt was stained with blood and dirt and bits of herbs. She paused in the doorway, observing the group fondly. She was particularly grateful to see everyone together and at ease, though Kit's secret weighed heavily on her mind. She was not used to hiding things from her parents, and this made two things she could not tell them.

There were exclamations all around about the boys' injuries, and Saylah examined both to be certain they did not need further attention. She was pleased to see what a fine job her daughter had done, and smiled at Illiann as she hovered in the shadows just beyond the candlelight.

"What happened?" Julian asked.

Once more, Kit told the story of hitting the rock on their bicycles and pitching headfirst over the handlebars. "But the cycle's all right," he told Sophia, anxious to reassure her so she wouldn't decide he was reckless and refuse to let him ride it again. "It's a little dirty, is all. Nothing to worry about."

"Kit, I'm not at all worried about the bicycle. I'm worried about you." The sight of his swollen and discolored face made her wince. Just promise you'll be more careful of *yourself* in the future, and I shan't say another word. All right?"

Kit nodded with enthusiasm. "I promise."

"Are you after bein' certain you don't have a concussion?" Devon demanded. "Goin' over the handlebars could well break your head."

"I can assure you, no heads were broken." Laura wanted the subject dispatched quickly; if the discussion continued much longer, she was afraid someone would say the wrong thing. The more she thought about the boys' misadventure, the more anxious she became. She wasn't certain why; she just knew something was not quite right—other than the fact that the boys had been chased down and threatened.

She was grateful to be sitting at the Ivys' table instead of her own. Here there was noise and concern and laughter. At home she would have been left alone with her own troubling thoughts. She caught sight of Lord Byron and smiled, forgetting her anxiety for a moment. She could just hear her mother's horror upon hearing about his presence. "You ate with an *animal*? What kind of barbarians are these people?" No doubt she would insist on stripping off her daughter's clothes and washing her repeatedly from head to toe. Laura smiled to herself.

"That is a blessing," Saylah said pensively. She was a little uncomfortable about Kit's story, but she was not certain why. The injuries did not disturb her unduly; Kit and Will had been wise enough to go to Illiann and get them seen to. Still, there was something in her son's manner that bothered her, but she could not define it. Both boys were flushed with excitement, which glowed beneath their bruises—excitement because they had survived without crushed skulls, she assumed, *and* because they were the center of attention.

She exchanged glances with Julian, who covered her hand with his. "They could have been badly hurt," he whispered. "We should be grateful they're able to smile about it."

"I should have been here to take care of them," she whispered back. She felt guilty about spending time with Old

Grandmother when her family needed her. She could not deny that she was worried about the old woman, though Old Grandmother was healing better than expected at her age. Nor could she deny that she would have been visiting the village even if her healing skills were not needed. What troubled her was that, since the stroke, Saylah was finding it difficult, if not impossible, to read Old Grandmother's thoughts, which had once been so clear. That had never happened before, and it frightened her. The one thing she had always been able to depend on was her intuition. Now she could not guess what Kit or even Illiann was thinking, and she knew her daughter best of all, except for Julian. It was more than a little disquieting. She felt inadequate, and that was not a feeling she was used to.

"Is there cider?" Sophia asked.

Illiann was still standing in the doorway. I'll get it."

As she turned away, the servant, Su-ling grasped her arm and drew her into the pantry. Earlier, apparently unfazed by the discovery of Will's parentage, Saylah had insisted on sending a note to the Barretts, telling them their son was hurt and would be staying for supper. Su-ling had delivered it to the Barrett's Chinese cook, who had given it into the hands of the housekeeper, as the couple was out for the evening. Su-ling had hurried back to the Ivys', but had been busy cooking and had not been able to speak to Illiann until now. Her brow was creased with worry.

"He's only bruised, though he'll be stiff and sore in the morning. His friend's wrist is badly sprained, though. He'll take longer to heal." She observed the Chinese girl curiously. "You heard what happened today?"

"Yes."

"Already? It was barely three hours ago."

Su-ling smiled. "Sometimes when a story is not yet finished, we Chinese have already heard how it ends. But that is not why I brought you here. I wanted to tell you your brother is very foolish," she paused, then added, "but also very brave. My people will speak of him with admiration for some time." Her eyes sparkled. "Some of the men felt very small in the face of Christopher's courage."

In spite of her apprehension, Illiann felt a flicker of pride "Will they blame him because they were embarrassed?"

"I think instead they will add this to the list of Master Barrett's sins, which are already many. It would never have happened if he had not sent the man after your brother."

A chill ran up Illiann's spine. Had the man really been after Kit, or was it Will he had been chasing on behalf of Robert Barrett? Although it struck her as odd that the man should go to so much trouble. After all, he could keep a close eye on his stepson at home. Or perhaps, as Will claimed, Barrett had been watching the two of them together. She shivered.

"Something is troubling you?" Su-ling asked.

"Many things. I don't like what's happening, but I don't know what to do. How can I protect my brother?"

"That is easy. You cannot. You can only be here when he needs you, as you were today."

"Ilya? Are you coming?" Saylah called from the dining room.

Su-ling pressed Illiann's hands between her own. "Go. I have made a feast in honor of your brother and his friend. You are pale, Young Mistress. You must eat."

"Coming," Illiann called, squeezing the servant's hand in return.

When she found her place at the table, she saw what Su-ling meant. There was roast pork, roast chicken, a noodle dish with scallops, water chestnuts, carrots and snow peas, new potatoes drenched in herbs, spinach, Brussels sprouts, and rice flavored with fragrant spices. As a special treat, she had made a platter of golden dumplings.

Laura glanced up as Illiann sat beside her. "Look at this. It's amazing. How on earth did the cook manage it all in such a short time?"

"Su-ling is very talented," Saylah replied. "Though she seems to have outdone herself this evening. You shall all have to take food home or it will spoil."

Devon managed to look aggrieved. "Sure, an' 'tis quite a burden. But if we must, then so we must. The loads we carry for the sake of friendship."

Until that moment, Illiann had been so concerned about Kit that she had ignored Devon. But the sound of his Irish lilt and the sight of his lopsided smile, as well as the twinkle in his turquoise eyes, made the breath catch in her throat and her stomach clench. She remembered vividly the last time she had seen him, sitting on the floor of his studio. She remembered the touch of his lips on hers. Aware of a break in the conversation, she looked away quickly, afraid everyone was looking straight through her skin and bones to her rapidly beating heart.

Devon kept his eyes on Kit, though, to his distress, he felt Illiann's presence like a wave of heat that left him chilled. However, he did not intend to let her—or anyone else—guess that.

Everyone had begun to pass the heavily laden dishes around the table. Between the rice and the spinach, Laura caught a glimpse of Illiann's response to Devon, and his to her. *So*, she thought, *is this the man my friend spoke of?* She knew the answer at once. Though the spark between them was gone as quickly as it had come, it shone brightly, undeniably for a moment. Laura smiled into her napkin.

Aside from the possibility of discovering Illiann's secret, she was enchanted by the camaraderie, the casual atmosphere, and interest each person showed in all the others. Everyone spoke; everyone listened, asking questions, smiling, laughing sometimes. She felt she'd always been a part of the family, that accepted her warmly, merely because she was Illiann's friend.

Will was equally delighted. He had fallen into a kind of trance, a result of excitement, relief and the herbs he'd been given. "At home I eat alone," he'd confided to Kit. "My stepfather never eats till late, and my mother's often out with friends. When she's home, she tries to wait for him, but usually ends up eating alone, like me.

"That's awful," Kit had exclaimed. It had been much easier to talk about Will's neglectful parents before Kit knew his stepfather was Robert Barrett. Now the mere thought made him queasy. How had Will managed to survive in that house for so long? "I'd hate it if we didn't have our dinners together. Don't worry. It'll be fun. You'll see."

Will did see. It seemed he had been holding his breath in apprehension from the moment they sat down, but now he released it in a gusty sigh. He liked it here.

The talk died away as people began to eat, but Devon could not sit still. He did not like silence; it made him nervous. Besides, he was eager to discuss what had happened at the iron works that afternoon. He hadn't had a chance to bring it up in the face of the concern over Kit and Will's accident.

"Did you hear," he asked the table in general, "that Hart's workers made a stand today? Followin' our Julian's advice, they were. Fell silent to a man when Barrett walked in, refused to move or look away. Frightened 'im half to death, I'm hearin'. Hart tried to calm 'em down, but Barrett barely got out with his skin intact. Those two have no' the first idea what they're dealin' with. Blind as bats, but much more dangerous. We'd best be watchin' our backs after this."

Laura went pale, her stomach clenching at the sight of the food on her plate. Devon had expressed a thought that had haunted her since Kit first told his story. Was her father somehow involved in this? She didn't believe it for a minute, because Arthur Hart was a good man, an honorable man.

"Laura?" Sophia said softly. "What is it? Are you ill?"

Without looking up, Laura cleared her throat. "You'll probably want me to go now." She found it ironic that although, when Will said the same thing a few hours earlier, she'd known the Ivys would not judge him for his parents' flaws, she felt certain she herself would be rejected.

Everyone turned to stare. "Why on earth would we want that?" Julian asked.

"Because Arthur Hart is my father, and I suppose that makes me your enemy."

Saylah was aghast. How could they all have forgotten that this girl was intimately involved in the conflict brewing among the workers in Victoria? She glanced at Devon, who had the good grace to blush, making his already ruddy cheeks glow. "To begin with, your father is not our enemy. Julian says he is a good man. We are all just caught up in a lot of turbulence right now, and no one knows quite how to end it." Saylah spoke calmly and kindly, as was her wont.

"Second, you are not your father, any more than I am mine. We each have our own flaws and strengths and weaknesses. Yours are, I'm sure, uniquely yours."

Illiann nudged Laura, mouthing, "Told you they wouldn't mind."

All at once, Julian leaned forward, very serious. A knot tightened in Laura's throat..

"No man is my enemy, unless he has no care for kindness and fairness and resorts to violence to settle his battles."

Will's mouth was so dry he knew that water wouldn't help.

"Your father," Julian continued, addressing Laura, "is a far better man than that. Isn't he, Devon?"

Devon hadn't been expecting the question, and didn't really want to answer. He knew his enthusiastic little story had changed the tone of the conversation completely, and he hadn't meant to do that. Reluctantly, he admitted, "Aye, weel, he seems to care about the workers, 'tis true. I'm thinkin' he'd no' want to hurt 'em, would even protect 'em if he could. But he can't. Doesn't know how. It won't matter in the end, because money'll always win out over humanity."

Saylah wanted to object, but Julian spoke first. "I begin to wonder if you even *want* humanity to triumph. Seems to me that you know Arthur Hart is a good man trying to do the right thing, but you consider that a weakness. Don't you?"

"To a man like Barrett, 'tis just that. 'Tis time and long past time to go beyond gestures like today's, to make the owners recognize and respect how much power these men have."

His cheeks were flushed deeper than before, his eyes snapped, and the curly hairs of his beard quivered. He had obviously been waiting a long time to speak up.

"I'm tellin' you, 'tis time to frighten the bejesus out of 'em." His voice shook and he drummed his fingers on the table, willing Julian to listen for once. When he glanced up, Illiann was looking at him, and their gazes locked for an instant. He turned away abruptly, but not before he saw the question, the dread on her face.

Lord Byron stood, alert and faintly threatening. He was not used to this kind of animosity at the dinner table.

All eyes were on Julian and Devon, except for Laura's, so only she saw that moment of electricity and distress between the Irishman and Illiann.

Julian shook his head. "Devon, *listen*, won't you? The workers can't just take a deep breath and a shot of whiskey and face down Barrett and his thugs, fists raised."

"Why not?" Kit interrupted indignantly. He spoke a little too loudly and everyone turned to stare at him in astonishment. This was not like Kit at all. The boy began to squirm in his chair. Now that he had their attention, he didn't want it. He had been foolish to blurt it out like that, but after his face-off with the Chinese, he wondered if his father was right. "I mean, it might work, mightn't it?"

Julian and Saylah stared fixedly at their son. He was too uncomfortable and far too passionate and it made them uneasy. "It might work for a little while, but it would only be holding off the inevitable."

"There're lots more workers than owners," Devon pointed out obstinately. "The few could be overpowered by the many."

Julian suppressed a sigh of frustration. "Barrett has more power and money, and he can bring in weapons and reinforcements and slaughter the men in cold blood if he wants. Don't you understand yet, Devon? He's *not afraid of us*."

Waving the admonishment aside, along with the last of his caution, Devon replied, "I don't care. He'll crumble in the end. He has to."

"You mean you *want* him to."

Illiann focused furiously on eating the single dumpling left on her plate. She was frightened for Devon—and for herself.

Resting her chin in her hand, Laura considered her friend in silence. Devon had not looked at Illiann again, but it was the *way* he didn't look, the intensity of his determination not to look, that intrigued Laura. The brief current between the two was palpable. When she saw how angry he was, how stubbornly unyielding, she understood why, if this were indeed Illiann's mystery man, the girl did not want her parents to know.

Devon was not the sort to make a girl happy, or, indeed, to give her any peace. He quivered so intensely that she felt he might self-destruct at any moment. Suddenly, she was afraid for her friend, because she knew too well, from spending a lifetime yearning toward the very things her mother feared, how alluring and irresistible were the forbidden and the dangerous.

She had thought Illiann was safe, but she wondered now if any of them were.

Chapter 84

Julian insisted on riding home with Laura in a hansom cab, to make sure she was safe. His kindness and concern astonished her, and she thanked him graciously before jumping out of the cab and up the steps to her own front door. She was aware that he waited to see she had gotten inside, and that only impressed her more. She smiled and waved from just inside the door, then closed it quietly.

Agatha Hart was in the sitting room, pretending to write letters. Laura could see the wavy lines and circles of ink on the otherwise blank pages.

Her mother glanced up without bothering to hide the worry in her pinched features. "I didn't realize you'd gone out."

Her tone was mild, but Laura was immediately wary. Her mother kept a strict accounting of where her daughter went, for how long and how often. It was one of the things that drove Laura mad. That Agatha should be regarding her with disinterest, while gratifying—because the girl did not *want* to talk about where she'd been—was also a disturbing breach in Agatha's strict code of behavior. Laura narrowed her eyes as if that would make her understand. "I mentioned it yesterday. Had dinner with a friend." She said it so casually that she felt certain her mother would pounce, but she didn't.

"That's lovely, dear. I'm sure it was jollier than we were tonight."

Something was not right. "Where's Papa?"

Her mother raised a hand and gestured absently toward the back of the house. "Somewhere, I shouldn't wonder. He was at supper, in any case, so he must be about, mustn't he?"

Laura hesitated, but Agatha waved her away. "Go along and find him. I must get back to my correspondence."

Though she knew it was cowardly, Laura did as her mother bid her. A weighty feeling she could only call dread was building inside her, crowding her chest so her heart could only manage to beat sluggishly.

"Papa?" she said when she found him in the winter garden.

Her father turned, startled by the sound of her voice. For some time, he had been lost too deep in his own troubled thoughts to notice anything around him. "What is it, Laura?" He managed to sound calm, but just barely.

His daughter wasn't fooled. "Is something bothering you and Mama? She's acting strange, and you look...different."

"Not to worry, my dear. I'm sure it'll all come right in the end."

"You don't believe that. I can see you're upset."

Her anxiety shook him out of his distraction. "Of course I am. It's all this politics and the other disturbances." He did not elaborate. "I don't quite know what to do."

That was enough of an invitation for Laura. She rested her hand on his arm. "What's going to happen, Papa? Will it really be all right?"

She sounded like a child pleading for a father's blind reassurance, regardless of reality. But he knew she was no longer a child, and she deserved the truth. Besides, she was no fool. She would know if he lied. "I honestly don't know. I can't predict the future anymore. I can't even imagine it. All I do know is that I need you to stand by me." He did not add that her mother did not seemed inclined to do so.

She swallowed dryly around the lump in her throat, straightening her shoulders as if to convince him she was not afraid. "You know I will."

Something in her tone alerted him to danger. Arthur Hart peered at his daughter through the dim light of the moon. "There's something else, isn't there?"

"It's a secret, and I promised not to tell the Ivys, but I have to tell someone."

Her father drew her over to the chilly garden seat and settled beside her. "What happened?"

So she told him about Kit and Will and the bald man in Chinatown. "It sounds like Mr. Smith, doesn't it? And he works for Mr. Barrett."

Hart was shocked. He'd known there was trouble brewing, but he never thought children would be in danger. "You're sure about this?"

"Oh, yes. I helped bind their wounds. And one thing Kit Ivy is *not* is a liar. Still...." She trailed off.

"Still?" Arthur encouraged her patiently.

"I don't know, exactly. It doesn't sound right. To have those boys followed, possibly injured, is a stupid thing to do. It won't help Mr. Barrett. I know he'll do anything to get what he wants, but if this became known, it would only turn people against him who might have been on his side otherwise."

"You don't believe Barrett hired Smith to follow Kit and Will?"

"Do you?"

He rubbed his chin thoughtfully. "Much as I'd like to blame him, it doesn't seem to make sense."

"Then who did do it? And why?"

"Smith's very loyal to his boss. Maybe he did it on his own."

Laura raised her eyebrows skeptically. "If he did, which I don't believe for a minute, his leg is broken now, so it should stop. But I'm worried about those boys. Christopher Ivy is too fearless for his own good. I'm afraid he'll really get hurt."

"Too much like his father, I gather. Not used to fighting forces stronger and meaner than they are, except perhaps, for Nature."

"Well, at least that's good training." Laura was clutching at straws.

Hart shook his head doubtfully. "For something like this? I'm not so sure."

Chapter 85

Saylah and Julian were discussing what to do about Will when the doorbell rang. The boy wanted to spend the night, which they did not mind, but they had not yet heard from his parents, and that worried Saylah. She could see in Will's pale blue eyes how little he wanted to go home, and she was caught between a sense of duty and profound compassion.

The front bell gave her a temporary reprieve. Julian picked up an oil lamp and followed his wife to the door, as had become his habit. He never knew what kind of threat might appear on his doorstep without warning.

The door swung open to reveal, in the gloomy half-light, a woman of about 60 in an expensively made but extremely plain gray wool gown and heavy coat. Her iron gray hair was pulled into a tight bun, and her face was creased with concern.

"I've come to take Master William home," she said stiffly.

The Ivys did not know what to say. Surely this could not be Diana Blanshard Barrett, the celebrated heiress?

The woman saw their confusion and hurried to reassure them. "I'm Mrs. Brown, the Barrett's housekeeper. I received your note—" she held it up to prove it, "and couldn't get here to pick him up until now. I'm sorry if he's been any trouble. You say he's hurt. Should I send for the doctor?"

"Will is no trouble at all." Saylah could see the woman was prepared to do battle, though she could not imagine why. "And a doctor is not necessary. I am a healer and his injuries have been seen to."

Julian took the woman's elbow and guided her inside, away from the chilling cold. The lamplight revealed the deep lines in her face and the weariness in her eyes.

"A healer?" Mrs. Brown looked suspicious, as any proper Victorian would.

"Yes. When I was young I studied with Dr. Helmcken. I have tea and some tinctures to send home with him, but perhaps I should show his mother how to administer them?"

The housekeeper nearly lost her composure, but she caught herself in time. "I should think I would be the one administering if anyone does. Mrs. Barrett leaves such things to me as a rule."

Julian was wise enough to hold his tongue, though he was surprised by this revelation.

"And his parents," Saylah asked quietly, "are they—?"

"Still out. They often are of an evening. All those dinners and social engagements, you see."

"Then who takes care of Will?" There was no criticism in Saylah's tone, but her perplexity was evident.

"The cook sees that he's fed, of course, and the upstairs maid takes care of his things. The rest generally falls to me, I suppose."

"You suppose?" Julian could not help himself. Kit had told him Will was lonely, but it had never occurred to him that the boy lived such a solitary life.

The housekeeper raised her chin stubbornly. "Mr. Barrett is, of course, only the boy's stepfather."

As if that's an excuse for neglecting him, Julian thought. He could tell by the tension in Saylah's shoulders that she agreed, and, like him, was restraining herself from expressing that opinion out loud.

"And Mrs. Barrett?" she murmured instead.

"Mrs. Barrett is out a great deal. Naturally, she does what is right by her son, as any mother would."

The Ivys were not convinced.

Saylah believed she had begun to understand Mrs. Brown's guardedness. No doubt she did not enjoy defending her employers' behavior towards their son. Perhaps Saylah could help, if only a little. "We want very much for Will to spend the night. I did not think to include that in my note, did I?"

"No. Had you done so, I would have informed you that it's impossible. His mother likes him home first thing in the morning, when she has time to spend with him."

Behind Mrs. Brown's inflexible statement, Saylah sensed the slightest disapproval, which she tried valiantly to hide. "I see." She was not yet ready to give up, and looked up at her husband as if she might find the answer in his face.

Just then, the boys popped their heads around the dining room door, curious about the whispers in the front hall. "Why're you standing in the hall? It's cold here." Then Kit caught sight of their guest. "Oh!"

"Mrs. B?" Will looked confused, but he nevertheless managed a lopsided grin of greeting. "What're you doing here?"

The housekeeper froze at the site of the boy's battered face and the sling from which his left hand protruded— swollen and dark with bruises. She cried out, forgetting her place and her purpose, and opened her arms. "I'm so sorry, Will. Poor mite."

The boy did not hesitate, but hurled himself into her embrace.

"'S'all right," he mumbled into her coat. "Ivys took care of me. Oh!"

He struggled free and she realized she had squeezed too tightly. "Sorry, lad. Mrs. Ivy will show me how to treat your injuries. Shall we go home now? It's late."

"You came to get me?"

The astonishment on Will's face made Saylah and Julian ache for him. He had not expected anyone to notice his absence, let alone try to take him home. His eyes grew damp, but he blinked the moisture away. He was obviously fond of the housekeeper, which was reassuring, and besides, they could hardly keep him here against her will. Still, they felt they were letting their son's friend down somehow.

"We've become very fond of Will, Mrs. Brown," Julian murmured.

Saylah added, "Please take care of him and see that he is safe."

The woman nodded. "I will. I'll try."

With that they had to be content.

Chapter 86

Exhausted, and not entirely certain why, Sophia slid between the linen sheets, settling the rose-colored duvet up above her collarbone. Closing her eyes with a sigh of pleasure, she let her head sink into the down pillow she had brought from home. "Sleep is a lovely thing," she murmured, welcoming the caress of the covers on her arms and legs. The cool sheets were a perfect contrast to the warm duvet that enveloped her body. She was unusually aware of her skin, long untouched by human hands, and the small frissons of sensuality that kept both awake and alive—and lured her toward sleep. For the first time in a good while, she felt that she was not alone. She fell asleep with a tender smile on her face.

~ * ~

Her dreams became entangled, one with another. Sophia felt them grasping her arms and feet while she struggled wildly to get free. She sat up abruptly, shaking the images away. She grew still in the portentous darkness left behind. She heard a warning but did not understand it. When she caught her breath, an image of Kit and Will flickered through her blank mind. That must be it, she thought, not yet daring to speak out loud.

Shivering, she nodded, and that's when her husband's face filled her head. She'd been wrong about the boys. The warning was for Edward.

"I have to go home," she said. "*Now.*"

Chapter 87

Illiann dressed hurriedly in the dim light from her low-burning lamp. Dawn had barely begun to extend wispy fingers of light through the edges of the curtains, but she was determined to get out of the house early. Opening her door as silently as possible, she crept down the hall, braiding her long hair as she went. She tiptoed with elaborate care past her parents' room, button-top boots still in her hand, and cracked open her brother's door.

Slipping inside, she closed it quietly behind her.

"Kit? Are you awake?"

The only answer was a groan from beneath the mound of twisted bedclothes.

She padded across the room and leaned over, drawing the quilt back to reveal a tousled dark head. Her brother had pulled the covers up so far that only the top of his head was visible. "Kit," she whispered, "I need to talk to you."

"Wha?"

It was more a grunt than a word. Kit was pale, but she could barely tell beneath the swollen abrasions and bruised skin. She had known he would look worse today, but had not imagined how much. He squinted up at her through swollen lids.

"Oh, Kit!" Her heart melted at the sight of him, curled into a tight ball in the center of the bed. He looked so young and vulnerable. "How do you feel?" She knew it was a silly question, but it tumbled out anyway.

"Hurts everywhere," he croaked. "Cold."

She tucked the covers around him, then knelt before the fireplace and stirred the smoldering ashes, adding kindling and two logs from the basket beside the hearth and using a small bellows to get the flames burning again.

"It'll warm up soon," she whispered. She took a step toward the bed, but the sound of movement from her parents' room stopped her. With a quick kiss on top of her brother's swaddled head, she took her shoes and slipped out as silently as she had come. She did not want Saylah and Julian to see her.

When she cracked the door open and saw how gloomy the morning was, she called Lord Byron. She did not want to be out there alone.

The black Shepard appeared, wagging his tail, sniffing at her curiously. This was not part of her usual routine, and change was always exciting to him. "Come boy. We're going for a walk."

She guided him outside before he could bark in anticipation and stopped to hug him tightly, burying her face in his thick, soft fur. She was grateful for his company.

Usually, she met Laura at the end of Crescent Street. Her friend came from Dallas Road—the grand houses that fronted the San Juan Straits—and the Ivy house was halfway between the Harts' and Miss Chadwick's. But it was too early.

Lord Byron seemed to sense the need for quiet; he only woofed softly in delight as they turned onto the sidewalk. He kept looking up at his mistress as if she might have more pleasant surprises up her sleeve.

Once she was safely away from the house, the girl was not certain where to go. Miss Chadwick's would not be open yet, and besides, if she went on, Laura would wonder where she was. Her dilemma was solved when she caught sight of her friend coming toward her through the misted dawn light.

"I didn't think you'd be up yet," Laura called. "I hardly slept, and I couldn't stand to stay in bed a moment longer." She leaned down absently to pet the dog. "Say, you look terrible. I'll bet you couldn't sleep either."

Illiann was so glad to see her friend that she wanted to cry. "Not much. And then I checked on Kit. He looks dreadful. I think he feels worse than he expected."

Laura nodded soberly as they turned toward the James Bay Bridge. "So do you, don't you?"

"I don't like lying to my parents." She felt so guilty she ached with it. Her family had always been honest with one another, and she'd been proud of their mutual faith and trust. Now she had broken that trust.

Lord Byron tensed at the sound of her distress, and she soothed him unconsciously.

"*You* didn't lie."

"I did in a way, because I didn't tell the truth."

"But you promised Kit. Besides," Laura pointed out with firm practicality, "you didn't tell them the truth about Devon either."

Illiann stopped in her tracks. "That's different. Kit's in danger. I'm not."

"Are you sure? Devon Fitzgerald seems pretty dangerous to me."

"What do you know about Devon?"

Rolling her eyes, Laura replied, "I was there last night, remember? I saw how *you* didn't look at him and *he* didn't look at you. I'm not stupid, you know. And neither are your parents."

"No, but they believed Kit." She was glad to shift the conversation back to her brother.

"Did they? I mean, completely?"

Illiann paled and her stomach lurched. "I hope so."

Laura decided to take a new tack. "What difference does it make, anyway? I lie to my mother all the time."

"What about your father? You tell him the truth, don't you?"

"Sometimes. But sometimes I just can't. He worries about me too much."

Illiann shivered. She was covered from head to toe with dew, which had begun to soak into her skirt and hair and even her wool coat. She brushed at it futilely. "I'll bet your mother worries too. Maybe even more than your father."

Laura remembered her mother's odd behavior from the night before. "Maybe *everyone's* worrying too much."

For the second time, Illiann stopped short, remembering to shift her grip on Lord Byron's collar. "Do you really think so?" Her expression was pathetically eager, though she knew the answer before she asked. Suddenly, she was desperate for someone to tell her everything was all right.

"No, I don't. Not for a minute."

Laura sounded so miserable that Lord Byron pushed his wet nose into her open palm in an effort to reassure her. The gesture touched her so much that she knelt beside him, wrapping her arms around his neck and buried her face in his coat, dusted with dew. She did not want Illiann to see how frightened she really was.

Chapter 88

The sun hovered barely above the horizon, wrapped in early morning fog, when Diana Blanchard Barrett heard the door across the hall open and close and footsteps creeping stealthily across the carpet. Her husband was up earlier than usual, which didn't surprise her. She guessed that he particularly wanted to avoid her this morning.

Throwing on her wrapper, she waited a few minutes to give him time to get downstairs, but when she heard the front door close, she followed him. She, too, moved on tiptoe, not wanting to wake Will after what he had been through. She rarely thought of her son in the morning, when she was usually busy trying to shake away the lingering affects of too much food and wine the night before, but today was different.

Bare feet sinking into the thick carpets, she made her way to the front bay window and knelt, opening the velvet drapery only enough to see out into the gray, dew-soaked morning. She expected to see the carriage drawn up and waiting for her husband to climb in, but it was nowhere in sight. She caught a glimpse of him glancing over his shoulder toward the house, then to both sides, as if wary of a waiting assassin—or a witness.

Diana held her breath and waited. Presently, over the pounding of her pulse in her ears, she heard an odd thump-thwack, thump-thwack, and saw a man appear from behind the carriage shed. He glanced about constantly, moving surreptitiously, if awkwardly, on the makeshift crutch he carried. His right leg was splinted and heavily bound, and though she could not see his face, she knew perfectly well who he was.

Barrett approached him and they bent their heads together, while the hobbled man gesticulated wildly. Diana's husband nodded, scowling, and began to give hurried instructions. She didn't need to hear the words; she had seen him do it often enough—to the servants, the workers, even his partner Arthur Hart, and, of course, to his stepson. He had not yet dared to instruct her, but she was waiting. Barrett pointed, stabbed his finger several times in the palm of his hand as if making a critical point, and Diana let the drape fall closed. She had seen what she needed to see.

Chapter 89

Kit awoke shivering and lay for a moment in frigid misery before he heard low voices and poked his head out of the bedcovers. His mother was kneeling in front of the fireplace with her back to him. Her long black braid, frayed from sleep, brushed the floor behind her. The smell of herbs and the welcome sound of the kettle boiling made the room seem warmer than it had, and the sight of his mother brought tears to his eyes. He wanted to weep and was ashamed of his weakness. He was nearly a man, and supposed to be brave, yet the sight of Saylah at the fire undid him.

"Where's Lily?" he asked, voice husky and raw.

Saylah turned, and Julian, seated on the bed, sighed with relief. "So you're awake after all. We thought you might sleep all day."

Kit jumped at the sound of his father's voice. He had not realized Julian was there. "What time is it?" he asked, breathless.

"It does not matter, my son." His mother was as shocked by his appearance as Illiann had been earlier, but she hid her surprise well. She and Julian had begun to wonder about their son's story, remembering all too clearly when Kit had last been in danger, when a stranger had followed and threatened him. The more they thought about it, the less certain they were that he had told them the truth. "Did your sister build up the fire for you? That was kind."

"But where is she?" Kit sounded desperate.

"She left for school a long time ago," Julian told him. "It's nearly 10:00."

Kit regarded his father blearily, eyes still crusted with sleep. "Ten? I'm late. I have to get ready."

"Not today. I want you to stay home and let your injuries heal."

The boy jumped up and threw the covers off, though the sudden movement made him dizzy.

"You got pretty banged up yesterday." Julian paused, choosing his words with care. "More than I would have thought with a fall from a bike." There was the slightest edge in his voice.

Kit froze, glancing back and forth from his mother to his father. They were watching him warily. "What do you mean?"

"It's just that we were wondering if perhaps you forgot to tell us all the details." Julian was angry at the possibility that his son had lied, but also disappointed and anxious.

"I think you might well be in shock, that awareness has come upon you late because of the excitement yesterday. It kept you too busy to realize what had really happened."

For a moment, Kit could not breathe. Did they *know* what had really happened? He collapsed back onto the bed and drew his cold feet beneath him. "I don't think I forgot anything," he murmured, afraid he might actually vomit on the sheets as he lied to them yet again.

Saylah sat on one side of the bed, Julian on the other. "Maybe you should think a little harder," his father said firmly.

Kit sat on his hands to hide their shaking. "I don't know—"

"Christopher," Julian interrupted, "stop it. Now."

The boy had only heard his father use that tone once before. He couldn't remember what he had done, but he did remember that he hadn't been able to go riding for several days afterwards.

Chewing his lip, Kit looked away. This was getting too complicated. He was tired and hungry and aching and confused, and he wanted to curl up in his father's lap while his mother crooned and fed him warm tea and buns, because most of all, he was afraid. Saylah was right. Yesterday he'd been too excited to feel fear, but it had crept up on him during the night, and now he could not shake it. He was finding it difficult to keep his voice steady, and his guilt only made it worse. Not only had he lied; he had forced his sister to do so. He'd known she would not betray him.

When Illiann looked in on him that morning, he had expected resentment or irritation, but she had felt only concern. That made him feel terrible. In a way, he was glad his parents hadn't been fooled.

Saylah's anger evaporated at the sight of her son, lost amid the jumble of covers, skin pale and eyes glazed. He looked so young and helpless. She was taken aback, because Kit had always been fearless. He had fallen from a horse, a fence, and once the roof—when he climbed up to try to rescue a bird—and though he had complained dramatically of his injuries, he had always been ready to take another risk as soon as he felt better. Nothing seemed to subdue or concern him. "Please Kit, tell us what really happened. It cannot possibly be worse than what we have imagined."

The boy had his doubts, but he could not hold out anymore, so he told them the truth, or at least, part of it. He said that Baldhead had chased them through Chinatown, he but did not mention the mob or Baldhead's broken leg. Instinct kept him silent on those details.

Saylah and Julian were stricken. Their anger had been subsumed by fear.

Julian rose and went to the window, staring blindly out at the street below. He was more than furious at Robert Barrett. What kind of man *was* he to torment children because of what their father believed? He was also consumed with guilt, but it did not make him want to give up the cause. Instead it made him determined to go forward, gave him a new sense of urgency. He pressed his forehead against the cold glass, but did not shiver at the chill that went through him. It was no colder or tenacious than his fast-burning rage.

Hand fisted around her son's quilt, Saylah found she could not speak. Julian's guilt was nothing compared to hers: she who was supposed to be so sensitive to her children's problems, had been distracted by other things, things that should long have been relegated to the past. She should have known something was wrong, sensed that just because her son had not mentioned the bald man again, did not mean he had disappeared. She should have guessed Kit was in trouble; she should have stopped it from going any further.

Kit was terrified by his parents' silence. He had never seen them struck dumb before, and the sight fed his fear as dry wood feeds a fire. "Don't lock me in my room for the rest of my life!" he blurted out.

Vaguely, Julian remembered making such a threat. He wanted to reassure Kit, but did not know how.

Even Saylah was stymied. They could not condemn the boy to what amounted to a comfortable prison at the age of eleven. She went to stand beside Julian, seeking his warmth as well as his wisdom. "We will not lock you up," she said. She looked up at her husband and some silent communication passed between them. "But it is not safe for you to go out alone anymore, or even with Will."

"For the time being," Julian added, "you must have an adult with you, and limit your trips to those to and from school and the print shop."

"That's not fair!" Kit wailed. "Why can't *I* have any fun just because Robert Barrett doesn't like *you*?"

Julian grew pale and cleared his throat. "You're right; it's not fair. You shouldn't have to fight my battles for me. But we also can't put you at risk, until—" He broke off.

"Until what?" his son demanded.

Julian and Saylah did not look at each other, though the urge was strong. They knew they were thinking the same thing. Until Robert Barrett saw sense and stopped persecuting children. But men like Barrett never saw sense, or if they did, they chose to ignore it, unless it was to their advantage. So when would Kit be safe from Julian's enemies? Not when the problems with the workers at the iron works were settled. That would anger Barrett more, make him more malicious. They very much feared that it would not be until he was gone from Victoria—or dead.

Chapter 90

Diana Barrett waited, utterly still, until her husband climbed the steps and opened the front door. As usual, his expression revealed nothing of his thoughts, but that did not matter. She knew enough already. He was startled when she stepped out of the shadows to confront him, and that pleased her perversely. "I've always known you would go to any lengths to get what you want, but it never occurred to me that you were cruel enough to go after my son."

"I don't know what you're talking about. Surely it's too early in the morning for this," Barrett said in annoyance.

"I think the timing is perfect. And though I don't, for an instant, believe you're not aware of what's happened, you'll find our Chinese cook is remarkably well informed about some agitation in Chinatown yesterday. I'm certain Mrs. Brown would oblige you by describing Will's various wounds, though I suspect you already know the details. Besides all that, she says my son cringes at the sound of your name as if you were the devil himself."

"You had to find this out from the cook and the housekeeper? I don't suppose you've spoken to the boy yourself. You so rarely bother."

Diana paled and her husband read the danger in her striking violet eyes. He really didn't want to fight with her just now, but he was too tired to be wise. "My dear, you know Will has always been over-imaginative. Don't tell me he's finally taken you in?"

Diana was stung by the implication, and angered by his accusation that she neglected her son—particularly because she knew it was true. She hated it when Robert pointed out her faults; he seemed to do it most often when she pointed out his. "Is he imagining his wrist, so swollen that he has to wear a sling? Is he imagining the bruises?" When he didn't answer at once, she continued doggedly, "Will is my son, Robert. I can't believe you would stoop so low."

"Then don't believe it. You don't have to, you know."

Ice hot anger raced through her, making her skin tingle. "How can I not, when I've seen the evidence with my own eyes? He's a child! He and Christopher Ivy both. You must have lost your mind if you think threatening them will accomplish anything positive."

"Let me assure you, my dear, that I have not lost my mind. You should have that much faith in me, at least. Anyway, what could I possibly gain from frightening children? I never act without purpose. You of all people should know that."

"Oh, I know. At least I used to. That's why I don't understand. This was a cowardly act. Are you so desperate—"

"I am *not* a coward, Diana. Don't *ever* say that again. And I am never desperate. I am most certainly not afraid of the paltry men who attack me. They are not worth my anger." Uncomfortably, he remembered that day at the ironworks: the uncanny stillness, the air that had crackled with the threat of violence. He had, for a moment, been afraid, but he would never admit that to anyone, certainly not his wife.

"Did you, or did you not, tell Smith to follow those boys? To lead them into danger? Explain it to me."

He went rigid. "I should not *have* to explain, especially to you. You should believe in me, regardless."

She would have laughed if she weren't so upset. She was no fool; she knew what it took to survive in the business world, and integrity had very little to do with it. "I *do* know you, better, I'm ashamed to admit, than I know my own son. And I'm telling you now that you'd best leave Will alone. He's innocent, and no matter how much you deny it, that's something you and I have never been."

Chapter 91

Tugging on the stiff collar of her violet traveling suit, Sophia Aston walked away from the country post office, head held high. Though she was only 5'5", she knew she seemed much taller in her military patterned skirt and jacket with the dark violet epaulets on her shoulders and matching braid down the front, which continued to the bottom of the decorous skirt. She was aware that those in the crowded country store were watching her intently. That only reinforced her long held conviction that the store-owner/postmaster, Riley MacTavish was a hopeless gossip.

Not only did everyone who passed his counter know that Sophia had left her husband weeks ago—though not the reason why, because Riley had been unable to lay ears on that particular piece of information—they also knew about the mysterious letter Sophia had stuffed into her bulging reticule, along with the other mail for the ranch. Now they watched, as if staring alone would answer the burning questions in their slightly open mouths.

Sophia climbed up onto the wagon seat of her neighbor, George Hendricks, who happened to be passing and had offered her a ride home when she left the coach at the junction of Salish Way and Jamison Avenue—the only two paved streets for some distance around. And hence the natural setting for the country store and post office; the stables and blacksmith; the Anglican church; the school house and the small local office for overseeing Indian affairs, which was currently empty.

Looking back once, Sophia smiled to herself.

"Not what you're used to in Victoria, I shouldn't wonder," George observed mildly.

"No, not at all." She paused, then added, "It's good to be home." And with that, she left thoughts of the city behind her and turned her head toward the ranch—and Edward. Letter or no letter, mystery or no, she was looking forward to seeing her husband.

~ * ~

Edward was waiting for his wife on the settee in the front parlor, showered, shaved, hair combed, suit pressed and top hat hanging from one of the hooks by the door. He had removed his suit jacket and replaced it again several times before he heard Hendricks's wagon pulling up outside. Happening to be jacketless at that moment, Edward decided to throw himself into a more casual look and promptly removed his cravat as well. He hung both beside his hat.

"Edward?" her voice floated to him from the other end of the house.

He opened his mouth to reply but felt as though he had stuffed his cravat down his throat, rather than disposing of it properly.

"Where are you?" she called, and then, suddenly, she was there in the far doorway, poised for an instant in dusty beauty, before she ran toward him, lips parted in a smile she was obviously trying to fight, silver-streaked auburn hair tumbling from it's pins and falling over the epaulets on her shoulders.

Edward caught her in his arms and held her tight, as tight as he could without breaking her. "Sophia, my love. You're home." He buried his face in her hair and fell silent.

"I am, Edward. Home at last." She had seen his smile, his relaxed body as she ran to him; he was no longer haunted. He was ready to tell her the truth. *Then what brought the nightmare that sent me flying back to him?* But she thought she knew the answer. It was pressed against the side of her reticule. But she would not show him yet. *Let us have a little time together,* she begged the empty air. Just a bit to get to know one another again.

Chapter 92

In her dream, Saylah rose from the river, humming. The water streamed down her back, chilling her as she stepped onto the bank. A warm glow enfolded her, dissipating the darkness and revealing the snowbound world around her.

What should have been the stark branches of aspen and beech were covered in shimmering silver leaves, and the needles of pine and cedar edged with glitter. The pond was luminous, the water rippling softly in the whisper of the night breeze. Peace settled around and within, and she knew she was more than safe—she was blessed.

Her heart soared, and she listened for the name racing through the sky on the back of the wind, but it eluded her. Still she smiled, content. She knew that one day soon she would slip into the name and it would fit her like a robe. It was so near she could feel it like a chill and a caress upon her naked skin.

Chapter 93

The Astons ate a sumptuous feast of caviar, then salmon with fresh made noodles in a lemon cream sauce; green beans from their garden, seasoned with thyme, rosemary and garlic; followed by poached pears in rum. Afterward they retired to the sitting room. A small fire burned in the fireplace, made of marble imported from Italy. Both Edward and his wife had brought glasses of red wine, and now they leaned back, staring into the flames.

Though she hated to disturb the peaceful stillness between them, Sophia finally turned to her husband. "It's time that we talk, don't you think?"

He sighed, but only briefly. "It's more than time." He put his hand on her shoulder—to keep himself from flying apart, not her.

"First," she said hurriedly, "I have something to show you." Reaching into the mail crowded in her small purse, she drew out a letter and handed it to Edward. "What do you think of this? I believe it's from Simone Ivy."

He stared at it while the color drained from his face, then came surging back. Moving his lips once, then again, he managed, "When did you—"

"Just today at the post office. I didn't like to ask how long it had been there, since so many people were there and listening. It looks somewhat old, but I suppose that's from travelling all the way from France." When her husband did not respond, she added, "It's addressed to Julian. After all this time. An eternity of silence, and now, suddenly, this? I don't understand that woman. To send nothing, not even a note to let them know how she was, to ask how they were. Yet all that time…" She finally ran out of breath.

Edward was flushed and obviously uncomfortable. "Perhaps it was not an eternity, after all."

Shocked by his troubled tone, as well as his off-color complexion, Sophia nevertheless replied automatically. "Of course it has been. How can you say that?"

Edward stared at his feet. "I can't…believe this letter has finally come, and now of all the times she could have chosen. Now, when I just—"

A chill ran down Sophia's neck. "You just what?"

He struggled to gain control over his voice. "I don't know if you remember how, after—Simone—left, Jamie asked me to pick up his mail—his and Julian's. He couldn't bear the disappointment when…if she didn't write."

"And she didn't, so it was just as well."

Edward swallowed drily. "You remember the dreams that started last summer, how I used to…go to the…cellar before you left? How I searched the chests and behaved like a lunatic?"

For the first time, Sophia began to fear she did not want to know his secret after all. "I remember," she said tonelessly.

"I didn't know why at the time, honestly." The blood left his face again. "I had forgotten. I made myself forget."

His wife waited in silence.

"But then one day after you left me, I stumbled on something in the cellar, and it made me remember everything." He paused to see if she would comment, but she didn't. He reached for her hand that lay still and unresponsive in his. He tried to get up, but she pulled him back down again.

"Just tell me the truth, Edward."

He finally found the courage to look into her eyes— the violet eyes that drew the honesty and faith from deep within him. He nodded once. "Simone did write to both Jamie and Julian, for years, about every six months or so. But

I was the only one who knew, so I kept them, but I hid them away."

Ever so gently, Sophia withdrew her hand, her own face pale with shock. "Why? Edward, why? You knew their hearts were broken. Those letters would have poured salve on the wounds."

Her husband thinned his lips into a straight line. "Because I knew she was going to get my friends in trouble. Evil people were after her for a long time, powerful people from the Catholic Church. I assume that eventually they caught up with her. But first they threatened Jamie and Julian. Just having her in their home was dangerous."

He collapsed, arms and knees inward, as if his bones had given up. "For Jamie and Julian's sake, I hate to admit it, but I was glad when she went away. She was the one thing from which I could not protect them."

Running her finger around the garnet necklace at her throat, Sophia eventually asked, "So you kept her letters to protect them as well?"

"Yes."

"From what *exactly*?" she pressed.

Edward was caught off guard. "From the danger if she should ever return. From the pain of remembering. From the hope that things would change." He took a deep breath. "It was selfish of her to write."

"And of you to keep the letters. Why didn't you tell me back then? Why didn't you ask my opinion?" she demanded, unable to hide her hurt and frustration.

"Because I was afraid and ashamed. I didn't realize I'd pushed it so far back in my mind that I lost it. I knew I had betrayed them as much as she had, and I could bear anything but that."

"So you forgot." It was not a question. "And the nightmares and wandering was your mind trying to remember."

"I believe so."

His wife was quiet for so long that Edward feared he had lost her for good. "And now we have this new letter. Have you found the old ones?" Sophia asked.

He nodded, waiting for her decision.

"Then we must go back to Victoria and you will have to tell Julian about both." Sophia's voice was soft but firm.

Edward glanced up, full of hope. "We? You'll go with me?"

"I'm your wife. Of course I will. I understand how you felt, how Simone embodied danger, but you don't know what she said afterward. It's time to find out. It's time to learn to forgive yourself."

"But you left me. I was devastated."

"No, Edward, you left me. You shut me out, refused to talk to me about your troubles."

"I didn't realize what was wrong until just now. The guilt was building and giving me no peace."

"You couldn't say that to me?"

"No, Sophia, I couldn't."

"Why not??

"Because I was ashamed. I thought you would never forgive me. For that—for everything.

Sophia took her husband's hands in hers. "I know more than you think, my love. Despite this unkind, even cruel decision, I've always forgiven you. You are a good man who let fear overcome your common sense. I know your heart, even if you don't."

Chapter 94

The streetcar rattled to a stop and Illiann climbed down, dragging her satchel behind her. She was on her way to the shop, the only place where she felt at ease. She could see Julian, Casey and Devon gathered around the galley press. Devon was gesticulating, the others listening intently. Illiann's heart began to pound. She felt lightheaded and found herself smiling, while at the same time, feeling wary and apprehensive.

Devon looked up as he made a grand gesture and caught sight of her watching. He froze, his lips parted but unmoving.

Apparently surprised by his sudden silence, the others turned toward the window to see what he was looking at. Without thinking, Illiann backed out of their line of vision. She knew Devon would come as soon as he could get away. Again, she was not certain *how* she knew; she just did.

He appeared after an endless few minutes, guiding her farther away from the shop window.

"I can't believe what I just did," she blurted out.

Devon regarded her in concern. "Nor I. Are you all right?"

Illiann was perplexed by the question. "I'm fine." But she wasn't, not really.

Devon did not seem to believe her. "Weel, be careful, Ellen, is all."

She was stunned that he, of all people, would say such a thing to *her*. "My name is Illiann."

He was scowling, as he so often did, and the fitful sunlight trailed shadows and light across his face, revealing more than he would have liked, she was certain. "Told you I'd call you Ellen." He glanced back once, then took her arm to hurry her along. "Let's get walkin' before the cold turns us to stone."

They turned toward the small park across the way, walking side by side without touching, practically without breathing.

In trepidation Devon crouched beside Illiann as she settled under a gnarled oak, clasping her hands around her knees. Her school uniform was severe, her blue wool coat merely serviceable, yet on her they were charming. Perhaps it was the contrast of her golden skin with the starched white blouse, or the black hair that fell to her waist, gleaming against the rough wool. Or perhaps it had nothing to do with her clothing. Perhaps it was her expressive hazel eyes and sinuous grace that made what she was wearing irrelevant. Those eyes, which, at the moment, were looking up at him, wide, deep and shadowed. "You're upset," he said. "I can see it."

"*I* am? What about you? You go along glaring at the world so fiercely that I'm surprised people don't run from you in terror."

"*You* didn't."

Illiann felt him searching her face. She stared down at her hands in an attempt to hide what he'd already discerned. "Well, but I have no common sense. If I did, I never would have discovered the world hidden behind your locked door."

"'Tis a shame, that. I was never after invitin' you in." He meant it absolutely, and yet....

Illiann looked up. "Didn't you? I rather thought you did."

He decided to be wise this once and change the subject. "That's as may be. But I was talkin' of your mood. You can no' hide that you're unhappy. Tell me why."

She rested her chin on her knee pensively. "I never realized how safe I felt on the ranch. It was as if our family were separate from the rest of the world, protected, that everything I needed or wanted was there. Mama and Papa never doubted their course—or each other—at least that I could see.

"Now they're afraid, both of them. It seems everyone I care about is uncertain or frightened or angry or confused. Especially me."

Devon leaned against the tree, raising the collar of his overcoat to keep out the chill. He and Illiann were hidden from passersby by the fir and cedar and the trunks of tall birches, but it was not the gaze of strangers he feared.

Illiann turned to face him. "In Ireland, when you were a child, did you ever feel the way I did about the ranch? Safe, I mean, content?"

"I'm no' what you'd call the contented type."

His tone was even, but she saw the storm brewing in his eyes. "What is it, Devon? Tell me."

He swore silently, because he had revealed himself to her again, and it had taken no more than a moment's glance. "I'm goin' mad with waitin' and stayin' calm and bein' wise. We're so close to Barrett, we could bring him down in half a day if we had the men behind us. And they're ready. They're tired of the stallin' as well. Your father's a good man, and has more patience than ten of me, but patience never won a war like this one."

"How do you know? It's not over yet."

"'Tis that's drivin' me mad. I'm thinkin' if Barrett's wise, he'll run and slip out of our grasp. I can no' let that happen."

"What if you have no choice?" As always, she was discomfited by his fury and impatience.

"But I do, can you no' see that? 'Tis why I came here, because I *do* have a choice. I never did at home."

"Tell me about your home." She knew it was a dangerous request, but all at once she had to know, and she suspected it was time for him to tell her. "Surely you must have some good memories."

He didn't like looking back; it could only be destructive. He wanted to turn her down, to avoid even the risk of remembering old sorrows. But somehow, inexplicably, he found himself saying softly, "I do recall sittin' on a wooden stool by the peat fire while my mam wove the tartans and cloth she sold."

Not daring to move, Illiann waited.

Devon felt he was drowning, and the water rose higher with every word he spoke. "She was always sittin' by the window to catch the sun, and the peat fire lit her face. She was gey bonny then, at least to me. But that was before."

She could feel his reluctance to continue; she ached with it. Illiann reached out to trace the softening curves of his mouth. "Before what?"

"Before Deirdre—and Barrett." He stopped, lips pressed tightly together.

"Please, Devon, tell me. I'll never ask again; I swear."

He shifted his weight as if his foot had fallen asleep. Except Illiann suspected it had not. He simply could not sit still for long without growing restless. She did not mind this time, because his voice had softened, and his Irish lilt grown stronger, and there was tenderness in him that she had not seen before.

"You think it'll make you happy to know the truth, don't you? 'Twill only hurt you, Ellen, though no' as much as it hurts me."

"Maybe. But maybe it will help you to let it out. You've been holding it inside for a long, long time, I think." She touched his shoulder lightly, trying to ease the tension there.

"If you want to know, I'll tell you, but you'll regret it in the end, I promise." He wasn't sure whether he wanted to punish her or himself. Before he could talk himself out of it, he said, "I loved Deirdre all my life. We were engaged when she was fourteen and I fifteen. Soon after we found she was with child, and we were to be married at once. But Barrett took her away." It all spilled out too easily; he had thought he would choke on the words, but instead he could not seem to stop them.

"What do you mean, he 'took her'?"

Devon heaved a deep breath, and though he was looking at Illiann, his gaze was fixed on an image beyond and before her. "Seemed Barrett had other plans for Deirdre. He kidnapped her and gave her to the local laird."

Illiann stared at him, bewildered. "*Gave* her?"

"For his mistress. 'Tis a feudal practice, that—the laird takin' the gift of a young girl's virginity. Except, of course, he could no' do what had already been done. I think Barrett wanted to make a fool of him."

Shuddering, Illiann cried, "But it's almost the twentieth century. He can't get away with that in the modern world."

"'Tis no' the modern world I'm talkin' of, but Ireland. 'Tis what comes of clingin' mindlessly to the past."

He glared, and she realized he was accusing *her*.

She wanted to object, but he did not give her the chance. "The laird soon knew she was pregnant, but thought 'twas his child, so he kept her by him. 'Twas six months later she finally got away. 'Twas a cold night, and she fell more than once, and in the end, our child was born on the moor— dead. Deirdre could no' bear the loss. She took…." He could not go on.

Illiann felt a chill that had nothing to do with the season or the wind or the damp grass on which they sat. She rested her hand on his. "She took her own life?"

The words were so soft they might have been a sigh in the breeze, but he heard her and nodded without meeting her eyes.

She left her hand where it was, unmoving, hardly daring to breathe. She was shocked by how badly his grief hurt her. He was right; by sharing his story, she also shared his sorrow. "I'm sorry."

Devon let out his breath in a long, sad sigh, and it was as if all the life left his body along with the air. "'Twas my fault she died. I should've known she needed me. I should've found her sooner, should've kept her safe from the beginnin'."

Illiann knew there was nothing she could say to convince him otherwise, but she wanted so much to try. "Don't—"

"The laird went after Barrett and named him an outlaw. " Devon interrupted. "He'd committed many crimes in his day, and suddenly they caught up to him, every one. Barrett had to run for his life – 'tis why he went to Scotland and changed his name—but before he went, he took his rage out on my family. Bought our land for back taxes and threw us off. Broke my parents' hearts, so he did. They died soon after from grief. I should've stopped that too. They'd no one else to stand up for them. I could no' stay in Ireland after that, and I knew Casey had come here, so I joined him, thinkin' I could leave the past behind. Instead, I found Barrett, rich and greedy and more powerful than ever. 'Twas no' a moment I ever want to live again."

"Oh, Devon." She squeezed his hand, then raised it to her lips and kissed his knuckles gently.

For a moment, he was rigid as stone, and then he flung her hand away. He leapt up and turned his back, calling, "Go away! I don't want you!" Even *he* could hear how petulant he sounded, but he didn't know how to go back. She had seduced him into telling the truth, tricked him into revealing a pain so deep there were no words to describe it. His grief, his guilt, his bitterness: she had seen them all.

Illiann did not flinch. Her eyes filled with tears, and she struggled to keep them from falling. He would think they came from pity, and she could not bear that. Not just now, when he was so vulnerable.

He turned, drawn by her silence, and saw the moisture in her eyes. He wanted to shout at her, to hurt her, to send her away, but he knew he could not bear her absence. He felt a desperate tearing inside as he knelt to take her in his arms. "Ellen! Don't hate me. Don't let me hurt you! Not ever."

Illiann ran her fingers through his hair, clinging tightly. "I won't, Devon. I promise."

Unable to resist, he kissed her, gently at first. But as she leaned into him, desire raged through him as fiercely as his fury had a moment before. She was warm and willing, lovely and pure. He raised his head. "Ellen," he began.

"Shhhhh," she murmured. "I know. Don't let go of me, please."

Her dark gaze was so alluring that he almost lost his balance; it was like a blow so sharp it would not let him catch his breath.

Their lips met again, hungrily, sending heat after chills along her arms and legs. She shuddered; the touch of his hands and his lips was so sweet it made her ache.

Illiann leaned her head against his chest and put her arms around him, consumed by his sorrow, his warmth and his erratic heartbeat. "Don't forget where we are," she whispered, though it took all her will-power.

Why, he wondered, was she always wiser than he? "I'll no' be forgettin'. But tell me why, whenever someone touches your soul, even with a breath or a whisper, your body longs to follow?"

"I don't know," she said. "It's never happened to me before."

It was that which finally broke the spell.

Chapter 95

The watery sun lapped at the windows of the solar where Saylah sat cross-legged on the floor, a few of her Salish stories scattered around her. The dream of the magical winter landscape, surrounded and enhanced by the song of the water, had driven her here for the past two mornings. One door of the cabinet hung open; the other was locked and she could not find the key. Even in the dim light, she could see clearly enough to recognize each of the few stories from the open half of the cabinet. She welcomed her silent friends composed of ink on paper. These pages held for her no fear, no sense of failure or frustration. Among them she could escape, for a time, from the sense of helplessness that had begun to overwhelm her.

She was seeking comfort in the legends and traditions of her people. There was magic and ritual and justice in them. She picked up a story and pressed it to her cheek, trying to feel the impression of the pen, the color of the ink, the age and texture of the paper—a warmth and yearning more dangerous than passion. She was swept up in the voices of her people and the rhythm of the past in the beat of their hearts and their hypnotic drums.

"Hello, my love."

She looked up in surprise at the sound of Julian's voice. She had not sensed his presence before he spoke, and that was unusual. "Hello," she said, reaching for his hands.

He drew her to her feet. She stepped carefully outside the ring of parchment and bits of wrapping paper and scraps, leaning into him in one fluid motion.

Julian kissed her and murmured against her lips, "I've come home for the midday meal so we can have it together."

With a tender smile, she indicated the stories at their feet. "Shall we eat in the sitting room and take these with us? I believe some of them are from when the children were small."

"That sounds like a lovely way to spend an hour or two."

Together, they gathered the bits and pieces, which Saylah put into one of her wide pockets before the couple settled in the sitting room.

Reaching into the pocket, Julian took one out. It was done in Kit's youthfully awkward handwriting. Saylah ran her fingertips across her son's first effort at copying down a Salish legend. The page was splotched and stained and crumpled, nearly unreadable. "Kit was so proud when he brought me the story of how Raven rescued Man from a giant clamshell." The boy had drawn a crude shell at the bottom of the page, with imperfectly round heads poking out around the edges. "He told me he couldn't do Raven," she said, smiling at the memory. "'He's too hard,' he told me, biting his lip because he was afraid I would be disappointed."

Julian smiled with her. "What did you tell him?"

"I said it was beautiful, and he could tell I meant it." Kit had smiled up at her with Jamie's luminous liquid brown eyes, and thrown his arms around her, squeezing as tight as he could, then fled in embarrassment.

Saylah smiled through unexpected tears. Kit had been so young then, yet she had known with certainty he was safe. Now she did not know what to believe, except that the familiar world of the ranch had disappeared into the thunderclouds that came and went with such ferocity over the city of Victoria. Either Julian or Devon had escorted Kit to and from school for the past week, and Devon was always willing to take the boy from school to the shop in the afternoon.

There had been no further sign of trouble, no ruffians lurking, no threatening glances or whispered warnings. Still she was unsettled by a sense that some nameless menace hung over the household, invading every stronghold of peace and familiarity.

Though she tried to disguise her discomfort, Julian glimpsed a momentary flicker in her eyes. He clasped her hand and kissed her again, balancing Kit's precious story with care.

"Madam! Sir!" Su-ling appeared in the doorway, startling both Ivys. "Mrs. Ashton has returned. And brought Mr. Ashton with her. And they have a priceless dragon chest."

Saylah regarded the Chinese girl curiously. She had never seen her flustered; usually she took everything in stride, but just now she looked unnerved.

"What's wrong?" Julian asked before Saylah gathered the words.

Su-ling took a breath and drew herself upright. "Not wrong, Mr. Ivy, Madam. I am just surprised to see both together. And the chest—I never see one so fine."

"We've asked you to call us Julian and Saylah. But for now you'd best show the Ashtons in."

Saylah was as surprised as the young Chinese girl to hear that Sophia and Edward had come to call. All the way from the ranch, and without letting the Ivys know. It was so unlike the other couple. But she stopped herself from wondering further, though her curiosity about the chest consumed her. She glanced over at Julian, who also seemed intrigued. "And, Su-ling, if you would kindly set the table for four. The Ashtons will be joining us for the meal. If we have enough."

"Of course, Mad—Mrs. Saylah." Su-ling took the opportunity to hurry from the room.

In what seemed like an instant, Edward and Sophia had taken her place. Both the Ivys rose to greet them, hands outstretched, though Julian intentionally headed for Sophia, greeting her warmly, while he merely nodded at Edward. The man had been Jamie Ivy's enemy for years, though Julian couldn't say why, but he had never warmed to Edward.

Saylah kissed Ashton on the cheek because his hands were full. He was carrying a laquered box of Chinese design, about two and a half feet long and one foot wide. "Good day, Edward. May I take that for you?" With a tilt of her head, she indicated the box. To her surprise, he took a step back, obviously distressed.

"No. No thank you. I must keep it…must hold onto it."

Julian raised an eyebrow as he took their coats and hung them on oak coat tree he had carved with half-Indian, half-whimsical designs. He had enjoyed carving since he was young and had used a small knife to make a squirrel for his mother.

"Sophia, it is wonderful to see you again," Saylah said in a normal voice, then whispered, "Are you all right?"

Hugging her close, Sophia replied, "It's good to see you as well. Edward and I are here to talk to you and Julian." She put a slight emphasis on 'Julian', which intrigued the Ivys all the more.

Su-ling appeared in the doorway, and the Ivys spent the next several minutes inviting, and convincing, while the Ashtons regretted and at last agreed. Then everyone seated themselves at the table, and Su-ling served them chicken and dumplings.

Sophia smiled at the girl. "The dumplings are particularly succulent. I have missed your unique cooking.

Blushing with pleasure, Su-ling backed into the kitchen.

As they ate, Edward updated them on the still successful running of the ranch they had left behind. Julian and he discussed apples and barley and livestock while the women remained silent, because all four knew they were only passing time until the Ashtons revealed reason they had come.

Edward kept the Chinese box on his lap until Su-ling cleared the bowls away.

Sophia was thinking she would have to begin the conversation, when her husband placed the chest on the table.

He touched it with reverence and met Julian's curious gaze. "I brought this for you."

Taken aback, the other man shook his head. "Why? I don't understand."

"Because it belongs to you. It always has."

"But I've never seen it before." Julian took Saylah's hand. He had a bad feeling about this.

Moving her chair closer, his wife leaned against his side.

"No, you haven't. Nor have you seen what's inside. But maybe you should have." Edward glanced down at the table and took a deep breath.

Sophia touched his arm. "Just tell him. It will be easier for you both."

Everyone was staring at the lacquered Chinese box, with carvings of dragons on the tops and phoenixes on the sides. It was intricate and beautiful, and clearly expensive, as Su-ling had claimed.

"Yes, please say what is inside," Saylah suggested. She knew the answer would upset Julian; she also knew he needed to hear it. Her skin tingled with anticipation.

Edward rose and began to pace, stomach tight and throat dry. "It holds letters from Simone. Three years of them. From approximately six months after she left." He kept his head averted so he would not have to see the expression on the younger man's face. "I always went to get the post, so…I kept them…kept them from you and Jamie."

Julian sat frozen in his chair. He did not move because he could not. He was slightly dizzy and nauseous. He forced himself to speak. "In God's name, WHY?"

"Because she brought danger. She was a threat you couldn't survive. Because she broke both your hearts.

Because there was no hope, and I didn't want you to think, even for a moment, that she was coming back. I was protecting you." Breathing harshly, he took the ornate box and handed it to Julian.

"Protecting us?" Julian was incredulous. "*Protecting* us!" He did not know what else to say. He was furious with Edward, but his heart was beating with relief and muted joy. His mother had not abandoned them after all. She had written for three years. His anger at her had abated as he listened to her diary for so long, then read it for himself. He had even come to understand. But he was still wounded. He ran his hand over the fragile, yellowed envelopes, confused and heartened and outraged all at once. He wanted so badly to draw them out, to hold them in his hands, to unfold them slowly, discovering the old mysterious messages they contained. He wanted so badly for them to heal him.

He rested one hand on the letters with profound regret. Perhaps these words had no power to do that; perhaps nothing did. Until Simone left, he had only known the loving, tender things she did for him. He had never known her as a woman with flaws and weaknesses and pain. He had sensed she was haunted by sorrow, but he had not understood it. Her silence had protected him, even though it also broke his heart. It had broken *her* entirely, from what he had come to see of late. Did he want that for himself?

And Edward. Damn the man! Who the hell did he think he was, to take the power over three lives and use it to keep them apart? He felt Saylah slide her arm around him and squeeze.

"It is late, my love, very late, but it is a gift to you just the same," she told him.

"I was mistaken, I was wrong," Edward declared. "I should never have made that decision for you. I know that now. I'm sorry—for that, for everything. I know it's not likely, but I hope you can forgive me."

Looking up at him, Julian saw the dampness in his blue eyes, the downward slope of his shoulders, the grip of his fingers on the table. Edward was sincere, at least in his shame. Julian wondered if Simone would have forgiven him. "I will try."

Ashton's shoulders came up just a bit and he half-smiled. His throat was still parched and raw, but somehow he had gotten through. He put his hand on Sophia's shoulder and she smiled up at him.

The four rose from the table, the box now securely in Julian's hands, and adjourned to the sitting room, where Su-ling brought them tea. Sophia stopped on the way at the coat tree.

Julian, still in turmoil, anxious with curiosity, wanted to read his letters at once.

But no sooner had everyone settled onto the settee and two over-stuffed chairs, than Sophia announced, "That's is by no means all. There is one more. It came in the post just before we left." She handed it to Saylah, because her hands were empty. Then the Ashtons crept out of the room and disappeared beyond the front door.

Saylah gasped, paused, blinked, then turned to her husband. "It is from France, from your mother, and dated barely three months back. I would recognize the handwriting even if her name was not on the envelope."

She had longed for this voice, tried to conjure it out of dust and dried out petals, prayed for it to sound once more. She glanced at Julian, who had gone pale and still. He nodded.

Gingerly, she used one finger to lift the flap. More gingerly still, she unfolded the pages inside, smoothed them on her knee and, sick at heart, began to read out loud.

My Dearest Julian, Beloved son:

You will perhaps say I have no right to address you thus, be insulted, even, that I address you at all after so many years of silence. But I speak the truth from my heart and my own bared soul—the only way I know to reach for you now, be you listening or waiting or lost to me long since. Your truth, your heart may be closed against me, your soul forever a mystery to my hungry eyes. If this is so, I will bear it, as I have lived through so many years and challenges, joys and tears without you.

There are many things I did not—could not— tell you before I left Vancouver Island, in part because you were too young to understand; in part because I was a coward, afraid to expose my flaws and betrayals to the lustrous light protecting me there. I have more to tell you now, and so I am returning to the one place I ever truly called my home. To explain, to see you—if you will allow me that great favor— and for other reasons of my own. For you are right if you think me selfish and weak; I am those things and more.

Things change so much, do they not, dearest Jules? I hope there is still time to learn what we might otherwise miss and mourn for the rest of our days. But there, I have crossed a line and attributed unto to you feelings you may not have. No doubt you are a proud man—even as a boy you were proud, and fierce with your pride—and will probably not wish to see me, nor will you believe me when I say that I have missed you every day since I last saw you, but it is true.

Still, I must take this chance, even knowing you might reject me. If that should be your choice, I will accept it and go away again, though I will do so with great sadness and reluctance. I ask of you only one thing—that you find it in your heart someday to forgive me or, if not that, then perhaps to wish for me a little peace. I wish you all the joy and tenderness you once gave me so unreservedly, and that your own family be stronger and more enduring than was ours. It is what you deserve. The only thing you deserve more is the truth, which is the single thing I have to offer. That, and my unchanging love for you. In spite of the pain I have caused, I hope someday to be allowed to know you as a man, as Jamie's son, and, finally, as my own.

I must tell you that I will always be grateful for the years we had together, for the joy you gave me, and even the regret. It is a poignant ache that I could never wish away, any more than I could wish away my life on your beautiful, wild island.

Always,

Simone

Saylah realized, as she stared at the letter, that for all these years, in all her knowledge of the woman with the flower-scented room and the lyrical voice that rose from the pages of her diary like a caress, she had been clinging to a ghost more tightly than Julian himself, and yet she had not known it.

She clutched Simone's letter in rigid fingers. For years, she had imagined this moment, when the woman of dream and smoke might actually take human form. Saylah turned to her husband. "Julian—"

He was standing, fists clenched. The lid of the Chinese box on the simple tea table was tight closed. "It's too much," he said. "I don't want to know."

"Surely you don't mean that. I saw how you stared at her letters just now, as if you wanted to absorb them through your skin. How you read the English translation of the diary, searching for her in every line. It seems to me you very much want to know."

"Because you think you understand every beat of my heart and pulse of my blood?" he demanded. Because you're always so damned wise?"

Shocked at the bitterness in his tone, Saylah nevertheless remained motionless.

Julian moved toward her until they stood a breath apart. "How can you possibly know something I can't begin to understand myself?"

She stood against his anger. "I did not say I know. I said 'it seems'."

"You forget how long I've known you, how young you were when we met. How you believed the world would not continue to turn without you here to heal it."

Turning on her heel, Saylah headed for the stairs.

"Saylah, wait. I'm sorry. I didn't mean to hurt you."

She paused only long enough to say, "Did you not? Then why did you say it? Is that how you will greet your mother? With cutting memories?"

"I told you, I don't want to see her."
But he was talking to the empty stairs.

~ * ~

Hovering in the hallway, hand on the half-open door, Illiann sucked in her breath in disbelief. She had never heard her parents argue like this before. Always, at least within her hearing, they had been loving and kind to one another. Her chest hurt at the lingering resentment in the air. She had known all along that her father had been deeply hurt by Simone Ivy. But she'd thought he was getting better.

Enveloped by guilt, she hung back, not wanting to see Julian just now. Because she was thrilled. She had spent years daydreaming about the Frenchwoman, imagining what she was like, the sound of her smoky voice, the scent that must still linger about her. Now she was going to find out at last.

She knew her father was still angry with and confused by Simone. Illiann wondered now if he were also afraid.

Still, she could not quash her anticipation over his mother's imminent arrival.

How was it possible, she wondered, that she could want so much something which her father did not want at all?

Chapter 96

Kit was concentrating on hanging photographs of Chinatown at perfectly even intervals along the fishing line in the darkroom, when a flurry of motion caught his attention. Unexpectedly, Will burst through the curtains, out of breath and clutching his side.

More startled than he cared to admit, Kit dropped the print in his hand and just managed to catch it before it hit the floor.

"Have to talk to you!" Will gasped. He stopped, wrinkling his nose. "What *is* that smell?"

"Sulfur and silver nitrate and other stuff for developing the negatives and prints. It won't poison you unless you stay here too long." Kit sloshed the next print in the fixer with extra vigor and the chemical splashed up onto his leather apron and splattered Will's shirt.

The boy raised hands and eyes to the heavens with his usual melodramatic flair. "First you try to kill me by dragging me through Chinatown with a crazy man behind us, and now you're trying to poison me."

The tongs slipped from Kit's hand as he turned to face his friend. "My parents are right; I should be more careful. You might have been killed, and me too."

"From this?" Will knew very well what his friend meant, but was trying to distract him. He looked and sounded like he was confessing a mortal sin. Will remembered how *he* had felt when he confessed the identity of his stepfather, how relieved he had been at Kit's dismissive comment; *That's just stupid.* "Now *you're* being stupid," Will insisted. "It was only a joke. I didn't have to go with you, you know. It was my choice."

"I didn't really give you one, did I?"

"Stop it right now, Christopher Ivy! We're both okay, and even Baldhead is still limping around somewhere. Why do you have to start trouble again?"

"I've already done enough. I acted like an irresponsible brat."

"That sounds like your parents talking, not you." Will became agitated. "You didn't tell them the truth, did you?"

Peering warily at the curtains that separated the darkroom from rest of the shop, Kit whispered, "Only some of it. They guessed it was more than a fall from my bike. But I didn't tell them about the end."

"They'd chain you to your bed if you did."

"They almost have. I can't go anywhere unless Papa or Devon or Mama is with me." His tone was dejected, but it hadn't turned out as badly as he'd thought. He got to spend more time with his father and Devon, and he enjoyed being in the shop nearly every day, listening to the men joking and cursing at each other, and having time to work on his photographs.

With elaborate glances in all directions to reassure himself they were alone, Will lowered his voice dramatically. "That's kind of what I have to talk to you about." He peered over Kit's shoulder at the print coming up in the tray. It was a Chinese winter courtyard, and despite the dormant flowers and shrubs, there was a grace and elegance about the place, a kind of peace in the drifts of snow across the boulders and the frozen pond. "Hey! I've been there!"

In spite of himself, Kit smiled. "You were in most of these places." He pointed to the hanging of images of Chinese shops and bridges and narrow alleys.

"I didn't think I'd remember anything from that day," Will mused. "But I do. That's weird, isn't it?"

"Where've you been, anyway? You haven't been at school."

"My mother kept me home."

"Don't you mean Mrs. Brown?"

"No, that's just it." Will's voice was so low Kit had to lean closer to hear it. "My mother sort of took over. She's there a lot more now—doesn't even go to parties much. And she watches me all the time, like she's afraid if I go outside, a beam will fall on my head or something." He held up his bandaged arm. "Because of this. She's been acting real strange since that night. Asked me what happened, and I told her about the bikes, but I think she knows I'm lying."

"What makes you think that?"

"Because she asked me three more times. I can tell she doesn't believe me. Besides," once more he looked about for conspirators, "she hardly speaks to my stepfather, and if we're in the same room, she stands between us."

Kit was astonished that Will's mother, who had shown so little interest in the past, was being so vigilant. "To keep him away from you?"

"I guess so. Like she thinks he's going to attack me right in front of her. And he doesn't like that one bit. He glares at her a lot. One time I even thought he looked sad, but I must've been wrong."

Rubbing his chin thoughtfully, Kit murmured, "If your mother does know, *how* does she?"

Will shrugged. "She's got lots of friends. And our cook is Chinese. He never liked my stepfather much. Maybe *he* told her."

Just then, Julian stuck his head in. "Good to see you, Will. How're you feeling?"

"Much better, sir." He didn't add that while his body was healing, his nerves were strained to the limit.

Julian could nevertheless see the shadow in Will's eyes, just as he saw it in Kit's. He knew he looked in on his son too often, but he could not stop himself. He also knew the boy was plagued by remorse for not having told them the truth from the beginning, and Julian tried to ease that burden, because it had long since ceased to matter. The lie had not been malicious, but merely misguided.

As long as Kit was working in the darkroom, Julian knew he was safe and happy, but could not rid himself of a nagging worry. Why hadn't they been watching the boy more closely? How could they possibly have let it go this far? Julian was struggling so hard with his own guilt that he could no longer see beyond it. "Kit?"

"I'm okay. You know, working away, keeping busy." He was trying to sound cheerful, though he clearly wasn't, which was very unKit-like.

Will noticed his friend did not turn to look at his father. That was peculiar. Usually Kit was thrilled to have Julian nearby, but now he was nervous and uncomfortable. Acting guilty was what he was doing.

"We're taking a break in a few minutes, and wondered if you boys would like to join us. Julian brought cakes from Johnson's."

"Really?" Kit's mouth watered. "Okay, maybe."

Julian hesitated, wanting to push the point, but he saw Kit's hand had begun to tremble and decided to leave it alone. "Well, you're welcome to, anyway." He disappeared before his son could see the hurt and confusion on his face. He wished Saylah were there. Without her, this was much too hard.

"I'm sorry," Kit said, half to Julian and half to Will. "This whole terrible thing is all my fault. I'm sorry."

"If you ask me," Will declared, "it was Robert Barrett's fault, and after that, Baldhead's. If you want to blame yourself so badly, maybe you should go home and yell at your mirror, because I don't want to hear it, and I bet your family doesn't either. It happened, that's all, and nobody can change it, no matter how miserable you are. So stop it."

It sounded easy, when he put it like that. Kit wondered if he was capable of doing this the easy way, but he decided to try. He was tired of feeling bad all the time.

Chapter 97

When Mollie, the housekeeper at the boarding house Nellie Howard owned in Victoria, burst into Nellie's office without knocking, the owner dropped her pen, making an ink stain on the page onto which she was entering the figures for the week.

"Two ladies have arrived, Ma'am," Mollie cried, out of breath. "Foreigners!"

Nellie tried to subdue her irritation. "So? We have foreigners coming through the port all the time."

"Not like these." Molly dropped her voice and spoke in a reverent whisper. "They're French, and one is so elegant, she looks like a queen." She paused. "The other—" she wrinkled her nose in distaste.

Molly had finally caught Nellie's interest. "Yes?"

"The queen asked to see you special, ma'am. Said she knows you."

Nellie rose, intrigued. "Does she, now? Did you get her name?"

Scratching her dark hair, the woman tried to remember. She had been so flustered by the unexpected arrivals that she could barely remember her own name, let alone a stranger's. Except it had been kind of familiar. "Ivy," she cried in triumph. "Simone Ivy."

Nellie Howard stared in disbelief. That name was from a past so distant she had put it out of her mind long ago. Or thought she had. Back in the days when Simone and her husband used to visit the Royal Oak Inn, owned jointly by Nellie and her husband John Thomas Howard.

The proprietress remembered with a shudder the last time she had seen Jamie Ivy's wife.

~ * ~

Two tall, muscled men with beards and a priest had come seeking rooms for the night. After they were taken care of, the stable master had come to her, looking grim, and taken her down to the carriage. "In the back," was all he said. Nellie was shocked from the top of her curly red chignon to the bottom of her calloused feet to find Simone Ivy in a small luggage compartment, bound and gagged, wearing only a chemise and drawers.

No! she gasped when Nellie removed the gag. *You must leave me be. They will hurt you if they find out.* She swallowed with obvious pain. *They are very strong, Nell. Very.*" Simone fell silent, a determined set to her jaw.

Nellie had ignored her. With very little difficulty, for Nell Howard was a big-boned woman, she snuck Simone up to her and John's suite of rooms for a bath and a soft bed. *I cannot stay, it is not safe for Jamie and Julian. I must return to France with these men and face…what I must face.* She yawned and Nellie made certain Simone went off to sleep.

When all was silent, John took a long walk and did not return. The following morning, the priest and his accomplices discovered a lady dressed in mourning clothes and a heavy veil seated in their carriage. She refused to speak, but Nellie had no such problem. *You will take her to the ship as she is, sitting upright and unhindered. Had she asked me to stab you while you slept in the night, I would have done so, but Mrs. Ivy has a kind and guilty heart, it seems. Do not touch her again. Ever.* Nellie had ridden with them, just to make sure.

When the carriage arrived at the docks, the men, especially the priest, had the clear intention of binding Simone again, once Nellie had gone, but her husband John Howard was waiting for them. Tall and thin, but strong as either of the bearded men, he told them softly and clearly, *I've spoken to the captain and paid Mrs. Ivy's passage. She will stay in a cabin near his, while you will be at the back of the ship and farther below. If you speak to her, harm her, touch or threaten her, he'll put you in irons. Yes, even you, Father.*

The captain stood beside him, nodding.

As John and Nellie made their way back to the Royal Oak Inn, she kissed him, right in the middle of the sidewalk.

~ * ~

"I'll be down shortly," she managed to respond to Mollie at last.

Molly ducked in a half-curtsy and disappeared, leaving the door ajar. Swaying slightly, Nellie stopped by the sideboard to pour herself two fingers of whisky, and though it was barely eleven in the morning, drank it neat. "Stopping loitering, Nellie," she admonished herself. "No point in avoiding the inevitable." She simply didn't know what to expect. Straightening her shoulders, she started toward the stairs. In spite of her own warning, she stopped halfway down when she caught her first glimpse of the two women.

She was stunned at how well Simone looked after so long, after how they'd last met. Her black hair was streaked with silver, but her figure was perfection. The only obvious difference was her haunted grey eyes. Simone had aged, yes, but she was still graceful, beautiful and elegant, still quiet and self-contained. Why was she here? Did she even know Jamie was dead? How on earth could Nellie tell her something like that?

Simone glided forward, hand extended, smiling. "I do not know if you remember me—"

"I remember," the other woman interrupted, then found herself at a loss.

"I have come to Vancouver Island to see my son, Julian," Simone explained. "My companion Mathilde and I would like to stay here for a day or two while we make arrangements to go to the Ivy ranch."

Nellie was jolted back to reality and the cold, piercing light of morning. She had thought fleetingly of Jamie and Edward when she heard this woman's name, but had forgotten about Julian. Now that she tried, she had trouble connecting the man she knew with this insubstantial vision of a woman. Ice blue and silver, ethereal and charming—a stark contrast to the other woman, clearly a servant, who might have sprung directly from the earth. Mathilde, as Simone had called her, was quite extraordinary, with her battered felt hat crushed in her hands, her spiky gray hair standing on end and her bulky, shapeless gown, which clearly showed the wear and tear of a long sea voyage. Somehow Simone managed to look as if she'd just come from her boudoir, except for the smudges of exhaustion beneath her eyes, and the lack of color in her pale white skin.

The wind had risen off the water, and it rippled their skirts and tugged at their curls. Nellie's unruly hair used to be brilliant red, but in the last ten years it had turned iron gray. Her figure, always buxom—gawked at and desired by the men who frequented the Royal Oak—had filled out, making her round where she used to be enticingly curved.

The woman was waiting, though she showed no sign of impatience. With difficulty, Nellie collected her thoughts. "Julian doesn't live on the ranch anymore. Moved to Victoria at the end of the summer with his wife and two children. His wife's a healer, a Salish woman. Some sort of royalty or other, I think. Julian owns a printing business just a few blocks away. You can see him tonight if you want."

Simone took a step back, obviously shaken. She had thought she would have more time to prepare herself, pictured meeting her son in the familiar surroundings of Jamie's beloved ranch. But here? So soon? In a city she didn't recognize? She pressed her hand to her stomach to stop its churning.

"Lovely thought, that," Mathilde chimed in, having overcome her momentary astonishment at the whole situation. "But just in off the ship. Nasty journey. Sea persecuted us like we'd done it some wrong. Don't like to complain, but back achin' somethin' horrible. She bein' delicate," she tilted her head to indicate her mistress, "bet hers is too."

That brought Simone to her senses. Thank god, as always, for Mathilde. "Perhaps you have a chamber where we could bathe and rest? We would like to take it for several days, since we do not know our plans precisely."

Nellie's head was swimming, and for wont of a better plan, she led the way to her best chamber, throwing open the door with a flourish.

The large window allowed the sun to spill in, dappling the duvet and the pale rose rug with dancing sunlight. The fireplace was white marble, the walls soft blue, and the graceful looking—if less than comfortable—furniture upholstered in burgundy and dusty rose. The drapes were blue velvet, the lace under-curtains pink.

Simone smiled as she looked around, Mathilde peeking out from behind her. Then she stopped. The colors were different, but she recognized the furniture. Nellie must have brought it with her from the Royal Oak Inn. Before she stopped to think, she murmured, "At this very table, I sometimes supped with Jamie."

"And Edward Ashton, if I'm not mistaken."

Simone had actually forgotten Edward in the years since she left the island. Perhaps because her memories of him were unpleasant.

Nellie saw the look on her guest's face and immediately regretted mentioning Sophia's husband. She backed out hurriedly. "I'll have your trunks brought up."

As the door closed behind her, Mathilde regarded her mistress, hands on her generous hips. "And who, exactly, is

Edward Ashton?" Her tone was accusing, as if Simone had intentionally duped her.

The other woman did not notice Mathilde's tone. "No one," Simone said firmly. "Just a man without a conscience."

Chapter 98

The presses rolled, whirring and clicking and thumping in a rhythm that had become familiar, even comfortable to Devon. Julian had gone out, and Casey was working in the back, so Devon had the shop to himself. He could feel the thunderous expression twisting his face, but could not seem to make it go.

When something clattered in the other room he jumped, cursing, so startled that he dropped a tray of type and the letters scattered on the floor. "Sorry," he muttered, as Casey reappeared, grinning sheepishly.

Before he could lose his nerve, she folded her arms and faced him squarely. "I hope ye know what ye're doing, boyo. I hope ye've thought it tru."

Devon squinted at his friend in surprise and bristled at the criticism. "Julian sendin' you to do his dirty work, is he?"

"Julian knows nothin' about it, for which ye should be tankful." Casey could see Devon was ready to do battle, but did not intend to let him provoke a fight. He had seen the lad and Illiann meet on the street the other day. They had looked at each other like strangers rigid with mistrust, and had turned away with a furtive backward glance at the shop window, too carefully, as if afraid of what would happen if they touched.

"If Ivy finds out about this, well, I'll not guess what might happen." Casey didn't know much about the girl, but everyone knew Devon was fire and gunpowder in equal parts, and that he might explode at any moment. Casey did not want Illiann to get burned.

Truly alarmed, Devon tried to think of a way out. How did the other man know he was stalking Barrett? He had been at the shop every day, working on the new editions of the paper—gathering information and background and personal stories, and helping Casey keep the equipment running smoothly, but apparently Casey had guessed he was also involved elsewhere.

He had followed Barrett more than once, and seen him meeting in the shadows with Smith, gesticulating and pointing out the men trailing into the iron works every morning. Barrett would then disappear, but Smith—broken leg and all—would linger, harassing the men, calling out threats so vague they seemed harmless. Except they were not, and the workers knew it. Devon saw that the men wanted to fight back, but they were still trying to avoid violence, as Julian had suggested. Devon wanted to shout at them to have at it, to knock Smith from his crutches and leave him helpless in the mud—the way young Kit had done. He wanted to tell them fear was Barrett's most effective tool, the only one he really understood.

"Are you even listening?" Casey demanded. "All I'm sayin' is, you should think carefully about seein' Ivy's daughter agin, so ye don't end up hurtin' her. He'll come after ye if you do. Ye're smart enough to know that."

Devon gaped at him. Ellen not Barrett. Somehow Casey knew about Ellen. That frightened him far more than the chance that Julian might find out about his reckless behavior with Barrett. Though Julian was not a man of violence, in defense of his daughter, he might be capable of anything.

Chapter 99

"How exciting," Laura exclaimed, arms outstretched like rigid wings. "No one in my family has ever disappeared mysteriously, let alone returned inexplicably decades later. I can't wait to meet your grandmother. Can you?" She placed one foot in front of the other and pretended to lose her balance.

"Be careful," Illiann warned. "This is a cliff, not a fallen log." She glanced at the thrashing sea below and shivered, but did not step off the footpath that meandered dangerously close to the edge.

Looking back over her shoulder, Laura grinned. "As if I didn't know that. Besides, a gust of wind could carry me over just easily as a missed step." As if to illustrate her point, a current of blustery air swept her skirts up around her knees. She let them twist and twirl, turning her head into the wind. She noticed Illiann had not answered her question.

"If you're trying to reassure me, you're failing desperately."

Laura moved out of the chilly gust and smoothed her skirts down. The last two words had struck her hard. Just last night her father had used them to describe his own problems. *I don't know where to turn*, he'd said. *The men grow more restless every day, and yet I offer them nothing. And your mother…she's become a stranger. I fear I'm failing desperately in every part of my life.*

Not with me, she'd murmured.

He'd touched her cheek and smiled with infinite sadness. *I hope not.*

Don't be silly. I'm proud of you, Papa, of your integrity and your honesty and kindness. Proud of the way you worry about the men and their families, the way you try to help them.

He'd begun by smiling, but was frowning again when she finished. *But that's just it, you see. I* can't *help them. I don't know how.*

His daughter thought about it, lips pursed. *Why not ask* them? *I'm pretty sure they know what they need.*

He stared at her in astonishment. *Ask them,* he repeated in wonder. *So very simple, when you think of it. But what if they won't tell me?*

Perhaps you should take someone with you. You know, to be a buffer between you.

He looked at her warily. They both knew there was only one man in Victoria who was likely to succeed at such a task. There was no need to say his name.

"What's wrong?" Illiann asked Laura suddenly. "You're awfully pale."

"Doesn't matter. It'll pass." Laura had been delighted to go walking along the cliffs with her best friend, who never failed to distract her. "Besides, you didn't say. Aren't you eager to meet the illusive Simone?"

"Well, yes." Illiann was ashamed of her impatience. "It's just…it's hard for my father."

"And your father's stubborn. We all know that well enough." There was no criticism in her tone—just resignation. Laura decided it was time to change the subject. "Well, what about Devon, then? If you won't let yourself get excited about your grandmother, surely you will about him." She was teasing, trying to get a reaction out of her friend.

"I don't talk about him anymore. He has nothing to do with my life." Illiann bent her head and strode forward along the narrow trail.

Laura could not see her eyes, but she was fairly certain Illiann was lying. What frightened her was that her friend had felt compelled to deny Devon so emphatically. Their relationship might have been a flirtation before, but now it was much more serious. Laura wasn't sure why the thought bothered her so deeply; she just knew that it did.

Chapter 100

Saylah was restless. All morning she had paced through the front rooms, unable to concentrate. She had planned to visit Old Grandmother today, but Kit had a holiday from school, and she wanted to stay with him. And there was something else, something more illusive, keeping her at home.

Watching her, Kit began to feel her agitation. It was not like his mother to pace. "We could take a walk down to the beach, Mama." He knew it was a risk to suggest going out, but he was desperate to go somewhere besides school and the shop.

Smiling affectionately, Saylah sat beside him. "I would love to, even now, with everything that is going on. I would even make a picnic. But I sense that I should stay here."

"Did you have a dream?" he asked.

Saylah ruffled his hair, forgetting that he had grown too old for such displays of affection. This time he did not object. "I do not think so. I just…feel as though I am waiting, though I cannot guess for what."

Kit, who had grown up a great deal in the past weeks, nodded solemnly. "That must be hard. I wouldn't like it."

"No, I do not think you would. You, my son, would go rushing out in search of an answer, because the suspense would drive you to distraction." She rose abruptly, then stopped as if caught in an invisible lacery of threads, and gazed toward the front hall.

"Is someone there?" Kit spoke in a whisper so no one would overhear.

The bell chimed and, released from whatever spell had held her briefly, Saylah hurried to open the door, Kit at her heels.

A short woman stood on the doorstep in a lumpy purple gown, with iron-gray hair sticking out from beneath her felt hat. She was examining the bottom of her disintegrating lace-up boot. The heel was practically worn away, and the ball of her foot, in its black and white striped stocking, was fully exposed by the hole in the sole. She held the porch railing to balance herself and poked at her toes, wiggling them as if to make certain they still functioned. When she was finished with one foot, she turned her attention to the other, only to find it in similar disrepair.

Saylah managed to hide her astonishment, but Kit stared unabashedly. "Who're you?" The words were out of his mouth before he realized how rude they sounded.

The woman raised her head, still holding one foot in her hand. "Me? Nobody much," she said in heavily accented English. "Been sent with a massage."

Kit grinned at odd accent and misuse of the word 'massage.' She must mean 'message.'

"What happened to your boots?" Saylah could not help it; she was worried about the poor woman's feet.

The woman regarded her keenly, not bothering to hide her curiosity. "Worn 'em for ten years. More comfortable this way. Can't bear stiff new patent leather ones that bind your toes in a knot and wear your heels to the bones." She sighed heavily, releasing her foot at last. "Still, may've waited a bit long to replace 'em."

"I could make you some new ones out of doeskin." Saylah lifted her skirt to reveal her own soft boots.

"Mama!" Kit was horrified. "You don't even know her," he whispered. "She'll think it's charity."

Saylah could hardly believe she had made the offer. She thought it was partly because she could not bear to see anyone suffer when she had the means to help, and partly because, for some odd reason, she admired the stranger's brusque but straightforward manner.

The woman pursed her lips, regarding Saylah through narrowed eyes. "We'll see about that," she said under her breath, but loudly enough so mother and son could both hear. She should have been offended by the offer of new boots, but wasn't. Perhaps it was Saylah's warm smile or the guileless look in her moss green eyes. "Not the time or the place, though." She thrust out her hand, and when Saylah took it, shook vigorously. "Mathilde," she said. "Used to have a sewername, but forgot it long ago. Mrs. Julian Ivy, isn't it?" She glanced at Kit who was grinning at her second misspoken word. "Must be your son, Christopher. Mistress asked me to bring a note. Terrified to come herself, but then, who wouldn't be?"

Mathilde narrowed her eyes even more, so they nearly disappeared into the wrinkles around them. "Mr. Ivy not at home? Just as well, I say, though no one cares if I do or don't. Tellin' you right here and now," she instructed the carved door knocker, "better not break her heart. Have me to deal with." She drew herself up to her full height, and though her size was not intimidating, her resolution was.

"Whose heart?" Kit was fascinated but bewildered.

Recognizing that further explanation was required, Mathilde fished in her bulging pocket, brought out a grimy square of folded paper and handed it to Saylah.

Curious beyond enduring, Kit tried to look between her fingers, but could not make out the words on the crumpled paper.

The note was addressed to Mr. Julian Ivy in a flowing hand. The world around Saylah grew still with waiting. The wrens froze in their ringing songs, the warblers fell silent, and the ruby-crowned kinglets ceased their chatter. Even the breeze stopped, leaves half-turned in mid-air. The hairs on Saylah's neck were lifted by the cessation of movement.

She knew that handwriting. There could be no doubt. Julian's mother had come home at last.

Chapter 101

The bell over the door jangled, causing Julian to look up from the paperwork on his desk.

"Good morning, Mr. Hart," he said. "What can I do for you?"

"I wish to speak to you privately." He glanced at Devon, who grumbled under his breath.

Glad for the excuse to abandon forms in favor of human company, Julian shook Hart's hand warmly.

Devon turned his back and pretended to be absorbed in his work. Julian was disturbed by this uncharacteristic behavior. He had once thought Devon too loud and passionate, but now he missed the Irishman's fire. And since he was under no illusions that the fire had burnt out, he could not help but wonder what was smoldering beneath Devon's mildly irritated manner. He was up to something, and it could not be good.

Julian turned his attention back to Hart. "Just the man I want to see."

Devon hissed like a boiler about to burst, but said nothing.

"Let's talk in here." He guided his guest to the tiny office, which was also the composition room.

Hart relaxed visibly once the door was closed behind them. Running his hand around his collar, he sighed in relief.

Circling his shoulders to loosen the tight muscles, Julian indicated that Hart should take the more comfortable of the two chairs.

"You look tired," Hart said spontaneously. He realized too late that his observation was impertinent.

Elbows on the desk, Julian leaned forward. "These aren't easy times for any of us." He paused, his hazel eyes unfocussed. "Sometimes I get up at night and wander to keep uneasy dreams away." He did not know why he admitted it to this man, of all people. He had not even told Saylah about the nightmares.

Inevitably, Kit was running. Sometimes Simone swooped down like a beautiful, avenging bird from the sky to abduct the boy, and sometimes the workers lined the road with red-hot pieces of iron, threatening to hurl them into Kit's path. Julian obviously had too much on his mind. He did not say that thoughts of his mother tormented him, or that he felt a distance growing between him and Saylah, which both frightened and angered him. He wanted his wife on his side, not Simone's, but even as he thought it, he knew there should be no sides to take.

"What did you want to see me about?"

"It seems to me, though you might not agree, Mr. Ivy—"

"Julian, please."

"Julian then. From what I've seen, we're both interested in the welfare of the people at the ironworks." He did not wait for a reply. "That being the case, I want to ask a favor."

Hart decided to plunge in before he lost his nerve. "I know we have to treat the workers differently. At this point, we can't go back to the way it used to be. I'm simply not sure what it is we should do." He put down his teacup and leaned across the desk. "The thing is, I was wondering if you might come speak with the men as a kind of mediator, don't you know. Find out what they want, what they might settle for. Perhaps you can get them to tell you what they won't—or feel they can't—tell me. Make them see I want to listen, to reason with them."

Julian was astounded. He knew Barrett would never agree to something like this. Hart was forging ahead on his own. "Are you sure it's me you want? I mean, it was *The Voice* that stirred up the trouble in the first place."

"That's precisely why I *do* want you. Besides, the trouble was here long before you came to Victoria. You just pointed it out, gave the men a voice, as it were. That's why they trust you to tell them the truth."

Julian looked thoughtful.

"I think this might be exactly what the men have been waiting for," Hart pressed. "A chance to talk to someone who genuinely cares about their plight. They'll probably listen to you. And at this point, when everyone's muttering and steaming under their breath, it could be the outlet they need."

Julian nodded pensively. "Let me think about it. I realize we have to act fast."

"I need hardly add," Hart murmured with a wary glance over his shoulder toward Devon bent over the Fairhaven press, "that I want this kept between us. If word got out...." He trailed off, but he had said enough.

"I understand." Julian had become quite good at keeping secrets, though it had not been his choice. He rose, and Hart with him. "Arthur," he said, "I shall do my best."

Chapter 102

At loose ends because Illiann had gone home early to help her mother, Laura headed downtown to Johnson's, her favorite bakery. She was hoping a sugar bun would soothe her edginess.

She was licking her fingers in satisfaction when she noticed a man across the street was limping. Despite the hat pulled low over his face, she recognized Mr. Smith at once. Her heart began to pound.

Though she knew it was foolish and even perilous, she crossed the street and began to follow him. She was not certain what she was after; she simply felt compelled to do it. He could not move very fast, and she slid in and out of groups gathered on the sidewalk, keeping her head low and hoping he wouldn't notice.

When he turned down the alley off Kane Street, she looked both ways, as if someone were following *her*, then slipped into the shadows behind him.

She gasped when a muscled arm reached out and grabbed her around the shoulders, holding her arms immobile. Her heartbeat increased and the pressure in her chest made her gasp.

"Whaddaya want?" a gravelly voice demanded in her ear.

His fingers dug into her shoulder and his foul breath assaulted her nose. "I just," she tried and failed to catch her breath, "I want to know who hired you to follow those two boys." What on earth was she thinking? As if he would tell *her*.

There was a pause during which she could hear his heavy breathing and the odor of his breath mingled with the smell of sweat, and perhaps a hint of fear.

"Don't know what'cher talkin' about."

"I think you do. I think you know perfectly well," she said in her most intimidatingly formal tone.

Abruptly, he whirled her to face him. "You're the Hart brat!"

Facing him up close, she could see his menacing expression, the way his muscles bulged beneath his flannel shirt and denim trousers. Laura suppressed a shudder.

Smith peered at her from beneath bushy eyebrows. "Afraid of me, are you? Makes you smarter than some I could name." He shifted his weight and grimaced in pain. "Those boys, now. Too stupid to know when they're beaten."

"It seems you're the one who was beaten." Did she want to die? If not, why was she pushing this ruffian so hard, she wondered?

He heard the disdain in her voice, grasped the collar of her coat and twisted until she began to choke. "Don't play with me. I got no sense of humor."

Though she had to struggle to speak, Laura did not hesitate. If Kit and Will could face this man unafraid, then so could she. "Just tell me who made you do it."

Eyes mere slits beneath the shadow of his hat brim, he considered her for a long time before answering. "I work for Barrett. Ever'body knows that."

Something in his voice made her wary. "So he's the one, just like they all think?"

Suddenly his lips split into a wide grin, revealing his crooked teeth. "Whadda *you* think?"

His smile made her uncomfortable. "I think it's an odd thing to do, for someone as powerful as he is."

"You listen to me, girl. You'd better stop askin' questions, or this could turn into your worst nightmare."

With an effort, Laura drew herself up, though his grip on her coat kept her from straightening completely. She wasn't frightened now, just confused, and angry that he'd managed to intimidate her. "You wouldn't dare touch me."

418

He shrugged. "Wouldn't have to. There's more'n one way of gettin' what ya want," he said obscurely. Unexpectedly, he thrust her away, releasing her collar with one last twist. "Leave it alone's my advice. Don't be stupid like those kids. I don't like stupidity; makes me nervous." He turned awkwardly and lumbered off.

Stomach queasy and skin clammy, Laura watched him go. His smug certainty bothered her, and that single crooked grin. She could have sworn he was laughing at her. And that just didn't make any sense.

Chapter 103

Two nights later, Julian stopped outside the print shop to lock the door. Caught up thinking through Arthur Hart's request, he was nevertheless acutely aware of the shadows upon shadows that crowded the street. Black on dark gray on obsidian, bush upon tree upon eaves upon porticos. Foolishly, he was neither threatened nor surprised when one shadow dissolved, raced past, then reappeared like smoke, from the ground up, beside him.

"I apologize. I didn't mean to frighten you," Edward Aston said.

Julian was wary. "Didn't you?"

Pausing for an instant while he decided how to respond, Ashton shook away his ghosts. "No. I really am sorry. I'd just like to talk to you. It's important."

"I thought you'd gone back to the ranch."

"No, Sophia and I are staying in town. No doubt you're disappointed."

"Saylah is waiting." Julian felt uneasy and wished the man would go away.

"She will wait," Edward said quietly. "You know that."

Julian felt more than a little abashed. "You're right, of course."

"Where would you like to go? There's a public house just down the street, but it can get fairly noisy around this time."

Reluctantly, Julian suggested the inn around the corner. "The bar is much quieter."

~ * ~

To his chagrin, he found himself seated across from Ashton at a secluded table in an eating establishment with chandeliers of candlelight and tablecloths of fine linen. He was not quite certain how he had come to be here, until he remembered how smoothly his former neighbor often got what he wanted.

Edward tried to order wine, but Julian refused, so instead Ashton ordered ale for both of them, then sat back and waited.

Julian watched him in silence, noticing how he tapped his fingers on his knee without ceasing. He also kept swallowing as if his throat were dry. Finally the drinks arrived and Edward sighed with obvious relief. He took a large swig of the dark amber ale and downed a third of it at once.

Ivy began to sweat. What did the man want this time? Julian had not yet recovered from their last confrontation, though to tell the truth, the shock of Ashton's betrayal was not nearly as intense as the shock of discovering Simone had written for so long and was coming toward the Island even as they sat in these sienna-colored padded armchairs.

Downing the rest of his ale and motioning for another, Edward began. "This is not easy for me to say—or you to hear—but you need to know."

Julian held his glass in both hands and waited.

"It's about Simone. I think it's time to tell you how she left—and why."

Ivy could not seem to escape the subject. "Some priests took her away, I think. They seemed angry at something she had done. She was always afraid of the priests." Silence fell and lingered like a hot, distasteful breath between them.

"Perhaps she was more afraid of the thugs that were hunting her for the fathers," Edward suggested. "They were sent from France to take her back and make her pay for her sin."

"What sin?" Julian held his breath. "I've always wondered."

Ashton looked away. "How would I know? Besides, it doesn't matter all these years later."

Leaning forward, Julian knocked his glass so the ale rose over the edge. "It matters to me." He grabbed the glass without thinking and looked closely into Edward's face. "And I think you *do* know." A knot of both hope and fear formed in his throat.

"Julian, my friend, can't you just let it go?"

"No! I can't. I been confused for too long. You said you came to tell me what happened. Please do as you promised." Odd, Edward had never called his 'friend' before.

Feeling defeated, Edward stared into the liquid in his glass. "One of the priests mentioned once that he thought Simone had been..." he paused and sighed, "...married before."

"Before what?" Julian frowned. "Before she came here, you mean? Before she married Papa?" He could barely breathe or think. But how hard was it to come up with the answer? Her sin had been bigamy. He had never guessed that. Never guessed he was a bastard, Simone Ivy's—or whatever her real surname was—illegitimate son.

Edward plunged ahead, afraid of the silence and the pain on his friend's face. "The Bishop of Rouen came to Vancouver Island, bringing with him desperate men who did not care how they achieved their goal." He ran out of breath and determination at the same instant and took a long pull of his drink. "They threatened her, but more important, they threatened you and Jamie. I couldn't bear to stand by and do nothing, knowing how dangerous they were, to wait, knowing what might happen to you all."

Raising his eyebrows, Julian tried to assimilate the hollow feeling in his chest—the feeling of having been betrayed by his mother in the most fundamental way, and what Edward was telling him now, but he had to struggle.

"I once saw the thugs beat a man senseless for refusing to answer their questions, while the bishop and priest looked the other way," Ashton continued doggedly. "They were full of rage and determined to find your mother, and I didn't want you hurt. I had to protect Jamie and you from their viciousness and insanity. I was terrified for you both."

"Sooooo…." Julian rolled the word on his tongue, "let me guess. To protect us you told them where she was." His tone was flat. He could see Edward had been genuinely afraid for them, but was not certain that made a difference. Except it did. A small one anyway.

"Jamie would never have recognized or acknowledged the danger, or gone up into the mountains to hide, as his wife was prepared to do. He couldn't see what she'd done to him. He wouldn't open his eyes to the truth."

Julian sat motionless, remembering Simone's letters, the entries in her diaries, the poignant quality of her voice.

"Jamie was oblivious. I made a deal with the bishop and that priest. They promised not to harm her if I told them where she was. Jamie was—well, you know how he reacted."

"He must have sensed you had something to do with her leaving."

"Not at the time. Years later we ran into one of the men who helped take her away; he said something, and Jamie guessed. He asked me why only once, and I explained that I wanted the two of you to be safe. That I sensed Simone did not belong here, that they would have found her in time in any case. After that he never said a word about Simone. Just drifted away. He never forgave me."

"Perhaps because he sensed your motive was partly selfish: to punish her for making Jamie and me and herself happy," Julian said without thinking, but he knew somehow it was true.

Ashton was shocked by the accusation, but recognized its veracity at once. He was not going to argue; he had hurt his friend enough.

"I warned her they'd be coming. All her concern was for Jamie and you. Would you be all right? Would you know how to heal? Would I look after you and make certain you were safe? She knew you would hate her for abandoning you, and feared the hate would poison your lives. She asked many promises of me, and I kept every one. Of one thing I am absolutely sure. Your mother loved you and Jamie as deeply as it is possible to love anyone. It tore her apart to leave you." His eyes were damp, and before tears formed, he added, "I was certain she'd run and hide herself somewhere on the island until they gave up. But—"

"She gave herself into their hands," Julian interrupted.

"I never understood why."

Ivy considered for a long moment. "For the same reason you revealed her: as punishment for having allowed herself to be happy." He was hearing an echo, and not just in the words he spoke. "In everything she wrote, her guilt loomed over her, threatening her 'paradise', she called it. She knew something terrible was coming. Always."

"I won't ask you to forgive me this time. There's no excuse." There was no plea in Edward's voice, just deep regret and sadness.

Julian sipped his ale thoughtfully, gazing into the past, as he had been for so long. But now he had glimpsed— no, lived in—the present, and Edward's choice, even Simone's had happened long ago. "Not today, in any case," Julian replied, shocking himself. He turned to meet Edward's eyes in the deepening darkness. "I can't imagine why I said that, except…. *Maman* would have gone to those priests on her own when she could bear the guilt no more. She knew, you see, she always said—no dream, no illusion so sweet, no paradise can last forever. In the end, the waiting would have crushed her."

Chapter 104

"Julian?" Saylah hurried toward her husband as he came through the door and glanced around blankly. It was dark outside and the wind was howling. He tilted his head, listening. His face was pale, and she took it in her hands, standing on her toes until her lips barely touched his.

"I don't know what to believe anymore. I don't know what to feel." He was dazed and had trouble finding the words. Ironic, he thought, that earlier today he had felt confident, resolute and certain of his strength and his course. Now he was confused and shaken.

"You are home now; the children are home; I am here and you are safe. Please tell me what has happened."

He focused on her face, on the light touch of her hands against his cheeks, on the nearness of her warm, familiar body. Gradually, the sickness in him receded and his rigid muscles relaxed a little. He rested his forehead against hers, breathing in the scent of fir and heather and clean, fresh air.

Saylah waited, knowing he would speak when he was ready. They held each other in silence, tightly, so the world became no more than their two bodies and the empathy between them.

When Julian could breathe normally again, he went to close the parlor door, then guided her to the sofa, where they sank down, facing each other.

"What is it?" she asked quietly.

So he told her. "Simone married another man first."

Saylah could not take it in. "Surely not willingly?" She rubbed her temples, thinking. "Else why did she leave him? Why was she running? What was she running from?

I'm certain it was something horrible. All that melancholy, my Julian. All that certainty it would end."

"But she married Papa, and she knew exactly what she was doing." Julian shook his head, his expression a judgment. "She allowed herself to have a son."

"And paid for it every day with fear. You know she did, you've seen it yourself in her diary and letters." Saylah fell silent for the longest time. "Besides if she told Jamie the truth (and you do not know if she did), if she tried to leave him, do you think he would have let her go?"

Julian remembered the expression in his father's eyes when he used to watch Simone play the piano, the way he stood listening to the rustle of her skirts, smiling at so ordinary a sound. Or had that been Julian himself? Both had loved her and she them. Edward was right about that. No matter how she'd come to them or why she'd gone, Jamie would have stayed with her, married or not. He would not have hesitated to make that difficult choice. "But I was never *given* a choice. I believed in my mother, and now I am—have always been—a bastard."

"Do you think that matters to me?" his wife asked. "Or to Illiann or Kit? It makes no difference to the man you are: husband, father, hero, lover."

"It makes a difference to them," he hissed, waving his hand toward the front door. "Society."

"But we've never cared what they thought, not one whit. It is none of their concern, and They will never know."

He knew she was right, and yet it meant something to him. "I could forgive almost anything but that." He thought of how Edward had tried to spare him the knowledge. He'd never thought of the man as kind, but he clearly cared about the Ivys.

"Why can't my mother's sins ever be simple—good or evil, black or white? Why, around every corner, is there always a new shadow or unexpected turn of fate? Just when I think I've figured her out at last, I'm proven wrong. I am her fool just as my father was, and I can't even hate her properly." He frowned. With a heavy sigh, he rested his chin on top of his wife's head. "I need some time to sort this out."

Saylah leaned back, hands on his shoulders. "Time is what you do not have," she said gently. "Simone is here in the city. Her servant came today with a note."

For a long moment, Julian refused to believe, but Saylah's earnest expression convinced him. "Here," he repeated numbly, "now." He rose to wander the room as if seeking a clear path in an overgrown, treacherous forest.

"How?" he asked. "How could she let this happen?" He sat down again with a thump.

His hands were trembling, and Saylah twined her fingers with his. Neither her herbs and tinctures nor her deep compassion could heal Julian's wounds tonight. But she could try.

"I might have one answer, though I do not know if it will reach your wounded heart and pride. I know you have never read it, because just yesterday I discovered it was stuck to the front of the diary. It took me a long time to peel it away."

"I can't listen to her tonight. That's asking too much of me."

Saylah nodded, disappointed. "If you say so."

"You doubt me? You want to force it on me?"

"Of course not," she said. "As you say, you are not ready to hear it."

Julian felt duped by his wife as much as all the others. When he finally spoke, his tone was weary. He kept his gaze fixed on the floor. "Why do you always defend her?"

"Because you always blame her. As long as I have known you, you have railed at your mother and ached for her and damned her and adored her, and it has burned out a place inside you that I cannot heal. You have questions for her, and accusations, but she has never heard them, so they do not haunt her, only you. I want you to meet her face to face, as a living, breathing woman, and free yourself at last from her ghost."

She paused, but still he did not raise his head.

For good or ill, his wife was right about one thing. For years he had been clutching his uncertainty and anger close, working hard to keep it burning so brightly that it blurred his vision. He knew one could get scarred from such heat—look how badly it had changed his father. And in a different way, his friend Devon. "Because it's familiar, and I don't want to let it go."

With a silent prayer, Saylah reached over to brush her fingers across his cheek. "I know. I have always known. But Julian, my love, think of this. You forgave Jamie long ago. Why can you not forgive Simone?"

Only then did he look up and meet her gaze. "Because, after all this time, I don't know how."

Chapter 105

From the moment Arthur Hart left the print shop two days past, Devon had been watching and waiting. He could see Julian was troubled, and not inclined to take Devon into his confidence. Nevertheless, he was determined to learn what his partner and Hart had talked about; he could smell expectation like unlit gunpowder in the. He had asked around, but no one seemed to know anything.

In his office, Julian stood with his back to the window overlooking the shop. He rolled one shoulder and then the other, taking deep rhythmic breaths. He repeated this routine over and over without moving from his original position. Finally, he took a stack of papers from the desk and straightened them methodically. Taking one last, decisive breath, he folded the papers and slipped them into his jacket pocket, opened the office door and, without a glance to right or left, he left the shop.

Devon was not far behind him. He slipped out the back way, easily catching sight of his partner heading west and then north. He stayed back, moving cautiously, determined to stay close, though he had a good idea where his friend might be going.

He hoped he was wrong. If Julian had set out for the ironworks alone, he had intentionally left Devon behind because he did not trust the Irishman and no longer had a need for his dedication and his passion for those who had been mistreated.

Devon could think of no other reason, and the knowledge hurt. When he saw Julian take the wobbly curving sidewalk west toward the factory, he stopped as suddenly as if a wall had risen from the earth and he had slammed into it head-on. He found he could not breathe, that his temples throbbed and his limbs ached. He had feared this was going to happen from the moment Hart entered the shop the other day, but he had not really believed it in his heart. Not until this moment when the bright sun burned his eyes, filling them with moisture that blurred his vision and left him powerless.

That was one thing he had sworn never to be again.

In a red haze, he left the sidewalk and took the long way through weeds and over swampy ground to reach the ironworks. No one saw him; that day, at least, no one was looking.

Chapter 106

As usual, Laura met her friend on the way to school, but this time Illiann stopped in the middle of the sidewalk to face her.

"I overheard Papa telling Mama he was going to talk to the workers today. I know it's not right, but I want to skip school and go there. We could find someplace to hide and listen."

Laura was astonished. Usually she was the one who got them in trouble because she could not bear to miss any excitement. "I was going to ask *you* if you'd come with *me*," she said. "Papa told me all about it. Of course, he'd kill me if he knew." She linked her arm through Illiann's. "Come on. I know the perfect places to hide, one upstairs and one down. They'll never even know we were there."

Illiann's stomach rumbled with nerves. "I hope not. Papa's angry enough about Kit. I don't know what he'd do if he thought I was in danger too."

"You worry too much. I've told you that before. We'll slip in and slip out again, unnoticed. It'll be all right. I promise."

Illiann was doubtful, but she did not intend to let that stop her. "I'm coming," she said. "You couldn't *make* me stay behind."

"Thank God," Laura muttered. "It's about time."

Chapter 107

Smith had not spoken to Robert Barrett the night before, but he was sure his boss would want him to check into the murmurs he had heard yesterday among the men at the ironworks. Smith had been making his presence   and therefore Barrett's—known among them, harassing them on the way to work, tampering with the machinery in small ways that would not stop production, but would certainly make their jobs harder. He hovered when they took the breaks Hart had been granting them, listening shamelessly so they could not speak freely. But yesterday, he had come upon a group of troublemakers, and they hadn't known he was near. He hadn't been able to make out precisely what they were saying, but he gathered something was going to happen today, and they were excited about it.

A sure sign that whatever it was dangerous for Barrett. He should have made a point of seeking out his boss and informing him that more trouble was brewing, But Barrett had been ill-tempered and short with him lately, and Smith hadn't wanted to risk another reprimand. He felt bad enough with his damned bum leg; it throbbed all the time and didn't seem to be getting any better. He was depressed and bad-tempered himself, and Barrett didn't seem to care. "Shouldn't have gotten yourself into that situation. It's your own fault. I can't help it if you're going to make a fool of yourself in front of a helpless kid. Remember, you made me look like a fool as well. You're lucky I didn't break the other leg. I still might, if you keep annoying me."

The memory was bitter, and Smith spat it out in the middle of the sidewalk. He did not like to admit it, but he was a little afraid of his boss these days -- he, who had always been the biggest, the strongest, the most feared among his peers. Now he was hobbling and helpless, but he still knew how to intimidate people.

Though apparently not Julian Ivy, who had not backed down from his pledge to assist the troublemakers in their lunacy. He refused to think about that; it rankled too much, like a nettle caught inside the bandage on his leg. Today would be different, he swore to himself. It had to be.

He made his way stealthily toward the ironworks, despite his pronounced limp. He would be Barrett's eyes and ears in secret, and he'd know the workers' plans practically before they did. He'd report everything to his boss, who would remember to appreciate him then. If he didn't…well, Smith was getting tired of being blamed for everything that went wrong.

He just might have to prove himself in some other way.

Chapter 108

Julian had never been to the iron works, and he stopped short in the massive doorway, trying to adjust to the sight. The cavernous room, into which the print shop would have fit many times over, glowed eerily with the unnatural light from the huge furnaces and gas lamps along the walls. He smelled sweat and oil and hot shavings and an all-encompassing heat that seemed to pulsate through the air, making the scene appear to shift in the heavy vapor. The machinery creaked and cranked, surrounded by crowded benches full of men who worked steadily at striking, flattening, twisting the iron into shape.

He could not imagine working in such a place, day after day, hour after hour with no promise of reprieve. Devon had told him about the conditions, but even his friend's vivid description had not prepared him for this.

He was still standing there when Hart came rushing forward to greet him. He drew Julian halfway up the stairs, so they could address the entire factory. One by one, the workers laid down their tools and turned to listen.

"Most of you know this man!" Hart shouted. There was general murmur of agreement. "He's Julian Ivy, and he has kindly acquiesced to my request that he talk with you this morning. You all know why he's here." The murmur became a rumble. "I hope you'll take advantage of his willingness to listen. As for me, I'll be up in the office and I shan't interfere. Take as long as you like." He thumped the other man on the back and disappeared up the stairs, closing the door to the office with a distinct click.

Though the unearthly glow of the furnaces distorted the expressions that changed moment by moment in the odd half-light, Julian was not intimidated. He made his way through the crowd, shaking hands, asking questions, bending his head to hear the answers above the machinery and furnaces and the beating of the iron.

By the time he had made a circle and crossed the room in both directions, some of the more vocal men had gathered around him. He recognized several of them, Davy O'Reilly in particular, as the ones who had come to the shop to ask advice. He suggested it might be more efficient if he spoke with perhaps twenty people who represented the varying opinions in the factory, rather than try to communicate with the nearly two hundred and fifty men who worked there. There was some muttering at this, but most could see that Julian was right. They quickly chose the men who had risen as leaders during the recent troubles, and Davy led the group to an abandoned office on the ground floor.

Julian perched on the ancient desk covered in empty files, discarded stacks of paper and iron shavings. The room was stale and chilly after the heat and motion in the factory. Julian lifted his hand, covered in soot, and realized his trousers would be ruined, but he had more important things to think about. "So," he said, "I'm beginning to get the general idea. Why don't you give me some specifics?"

"We want more breaks," Davy called out, "long enough to go out in the sunlight."

"More money," another added. "We're nearly starvin' now, and us with wives and kids to feed."

"Protection if we're hurt. A broken hand can ruin a family forever."

"The thing is," he said thoughtfully, "we need to make certain this agreement works for all of you—for Arthur Hart as well as the workers. He's willing to change, but it might require a compromise."

"What about Barrett?" Davy practically spat the name. "He'll no' be makin' a compromise. He don't care about us, just about makin' money."

"Yeah!" a couple of others agreed. "Eve'body knows Barrett's the one with the power. Hart won't stand up to 'im."

"That's not fair," someone else declared. "He's stood up for us more than once."

"Get rid of Barrett!" Davy bellowed. "Tis the way to solve all our problems, right enough."

He was only half-serious, but others picked up his cry. "Get Barrett out. That's the only way."

The same thought had occurred to Julian soon after Arthur Hart left the print shop. He had been pondering the question, partly because he knew in the long run this answer was the only one that mattered, and partly because he wanted the distraction. The men were right; any agreement with Hart would fold under Barrett's influence. He had broached the subject with Arthur when they met the day before to make their plans.

'Is there any way you could buy him out? It seems to me that as long as he's around, he'll continue to make money and the workers and you will continue to suffer.'

Arthur had shaken his head miserably. 'I don't see how it could be done.'

'There must be a way,' Julian had said, in that persuasive voice which took its charisma from his father and it's conviction from his mother. 'All we have to do is find it.' It was hard to doubt words spoken in that voice, even if facts and precedent were against them.

Chapter 109

Devon crouched in the shadows just inside the back door, watching Julian make his way through the building. He had to admire his partner's easy, open manner and the way he listened attentively, unafraid to meet the gazes of those he approached. If Devon hadn't been so furious, he might actually have applauded his friend.

He watched, unseen, as the men chose their leaders and the group trailed off to the other end of the factory and disappeared. For a while after they left, there was silence, though the men found it difficult to focus on their work. They were anxious and shifted from foot to foot, tapping their fingers restlessly, unable to stay still.

"Hey!" someone said in a loud whisper. "Why'n't they do it out here? Don't want us to know what they're sayin'?"

"I was thinkin' that too," someone else replied. "Didn't make no promise or nothin'. Could be getting nice fat raises for themselves and ignorin' what we want."

Devon decided it was time to speak up. He came out of hiding, aware that Hart would not see him from the office, and Julian was locked in on the opposite side of the works. "You *should* be askin' those questions, I'm thinkin'."

The workers were startled until they recognized Devon with his flaming red hair and beard, and his tall, heavily muscled body.

"It's that Irishman!" a young man cried. "The one sellin' the papers." He turned to the others nearby. "He's on our side, sure enough."

"That I am. Now, you know Julian Ivy's my friend, but I'm worried today is more like a surrender than a victory."

He knew it was just the spark to ignite the men's simmering indignation. "You're Ivy's partner, ain't ya? Why'n't you in there wi' 'em?"

Devon thought quickly, but not carefully. "'Cause I was no' willin' to go along with this." Which was true, in a strict sense. "I'm thinkin' we could do better. But we have to show 'em we're ready to fight. They have to know we *won't* surrender."

Throughout the factory, pockets of discontent had been forming, caused by intense nervousness, uncertainty, and the tedium of inaction. The workers had begun to mutter among themselves, until they noticed Devon was speaking. Gradually, the faces turned from the office door to the sight of the Irishman exhorting them with passion and resolution. "True, you've had reason to trust Hart in the past. But he's under Barrett's thumb right enough. 'Tis *him* you must get rid of, him who's holdin' you back. You know he'd stoop to anything to keep from givin' up a single sovereign. Don't let 'im get away with it. He needs to hear all your voices, no' just a few."

"He's right! Damned if I haven't said the same. We've no idea what's goin' on in there." A man waved toward the abandoned office, "or there," he gestured upward toward the new one. "Only here, right where we stand."

Mutters turned to rumbles and rumbles to shouts, as the discontent found focus and exppression.

Devon nodded to himself. This group had the makings of an army who would fight for their rights until the last man was heard and Robert Barrett was sent packing in disgrace. And that was all he wanted.

Chapter 110

Laura and Illiann hung back in an alcove at the top of the stairs. From there they could watch what was going on below, as well as keep an eye on Arthur Hart in the glass-walled office. Both girls had been disappointed by the morning so far. It seemed to take Julian forever to walk through the factory, doing nothing more exciting than talking and listening in an atmosphere of nervous expectation. Then he had disappeared into that room, and the stillness had grown oppressive. Laura yawned, and Illiann sat, arms around her legs, knees beneath her chin, her eyelids drooping. She had not slept much the night before.

"Hey," Laura said, poking her friend in the arm. "What's that? At the side door. See?"

Illiann glanced up idly. "I don't know. Wait, yes I do. It looks like some women and children trying to keep out of sight."

Narrowing her eyes, Laura peered into the shadows. "I'll bet they belong to the men who work here. I'll bet they heard what was going to happen and couldn't wait at home to find out."

"That could be." Illiann cursed her gored skirt when she tried to move and caught her foot on the hem.

"Shhhhh! You want my father to find us?"

Illiann shivered at the thought. "Sorry. Those women must want to be part of this." She stopped when something else caught her eye. She nudged Laura and pointed toward the back door.

Conversation had sprung up again after a long stillness, but now the girls realized it was more than casual. Anger raced across the crowd like a frission of electricity, and those around the back door added gestures to their complaints. That's when Illiann saw Devon and her mouth went dry.

"Who's speaking back there? Isn't that—" Laura broke off abruptly.

"Yes," Illiann replied. "He wasn't supposed to be here. I heard Papa telling Mama. He likes to make trouble too much." Her words were muffled, because she spoke to her knees and would not look up.

For once, Laura did not know what to say. The implications of Devon's presence and the threat in his demeanor were immediately obvious to her. Besides, she had heard him at dinner that night. He had made it clear that he did not believe the problems here could be solved with talk. She glanced at her friend, who looked pale. Her hands were clasped so tightly around her legs that the color had drained from her fingers.

Devon began to pace back and forth as, one by one, the workers turned toward him. The girls could not hear what he was saying, but they could see the crowd react. Their shoulders tensed and their expressions became hostile. That hostility spread as quickly as sparks raced through tender, and the already stuffy air in the factory became heavy with disapproval.

"Dear God, what is he doing?"

"It's simple," Illiann said miserably. "He's starting a war."

Laura had come here hoping for excitement, and suddenly she was sick with fear that she would find it.

Chapter 111

Smith ducked behind a wagon when the women and children began to appear. Only about twenty all together, but certainly enough to cause trouble, which Smith sincerely hoped they meant to do.

Once they were inside, he retook his position outside the building and behind the open door. Through the crack at the hinges, he could see what was happening without being seen.

He wanted to shout out their stupidity to workers who seemed to swallow Ivy's charming approach hook line and sinker. It made Smith sick to his stomach. Coddling the masses was all it was, and the ultimate in stupidity. He had heard how dangerous Ivy was, but had not really understood until today. He did not incite; he seduced, and seduction was much more dangerous than violence. Even Smith, who had spent his life doing violence, knew that.

His leg ached viciously from standing by the time the men went off to confer. He was about to leave in disgust when he heard voices asking pointed questions. Aha! Discontent. Now that was something he understood. He returned to his vantage point just in time to see a commotion at the back door. He recognized Devon Fitzgerald at once— the man who had been following Barrett, threatening all kinds of things. Normally, Smith would have been angry at Devon's appearance, but he soon saw that today, the Irishman was doing his work for him. Whipping up already unhappy men, exhorting them to make themselves heard, reminding them of their misery and helplessness.

Smith sniffed appreciatively. He smelled hatred in the air, and once it erupted, Barrett would have the excuse he needed to silence these angry voices forever. For once, Smith himself hadn't had to do a thing but watch gleefully from the shadows.

Chapter 112

Hart was moving a thick folder from the desk to the filing cabinet when he glanced down. His hand froze in mid-air. Many of the machines had been abandoned, and the men were clustered toward the back of the factory, nodding vigorously and calling out, some waving their arms, others their fists. He could not quite see what held their attention, but whatever—or whoever—it was was clearly feeding their frenzy.

He saw a few men pick up pieces of iron and wave them about like swords. This was exactly what he had always feared would happen one day. In less than an hour, someone had destroyed the men's reluctant, thereby baring their raw fury.

Arthur Hart was not a hero; in fact, he was terrified. But he had to try and stop this from becoming a riot. He pushed his fear down and made for the door.

Chapter 113

By the time Julian emerged from the abandoned office, dissatisfaction had swelled into rage, and many of the men carried weapons and called out curses. They were still mostly turned toward the back, though Hart stood at the bottom of the stairs, trying to get their attention. Davy O'Reilly had no such problem.

"What the hell?" he shouted in a booming voice reserved for communicating over the noise of the machines. "Are ye all mad?"

The closest men heard him and turned, the red coals from the fire reflected in their eyes. Their jaws were set, their expressions belligerent. "You're one a them now, ain't ya? We're tired a hearin' yer voice. Time to listen to ours." He thrust out his piece of iron, the tip glowing red-hot.

Julian was stupefied. When he left, the men had been anxious but calm. Now the room seethed with bitterness. The eerie glow of the furnaces had become a conflagration with more than enough power to consume every person in the building.

Arthur reached his side unimpeded. Julian feared that was because the workers wanted the two of them exactly where they were. Someone closed the doors behind them, and they were trapped against a huge blank wall of darkness. Half the men with him went to try and open the doors; the other half stepped automatically in front of the owner and the man he had brought here to ease their burden.

Davy felt the waves of fury undulating through the room, which seemed suddenly small and overcrowded, with little air left to breathe. "What're ye doin'? They're tryin' to help us."

"You maybe. Not us. Never did listen to us."

"Yeah! You're always the one to speak up. You and the others. Maybe they give you enough to keep the bunch of you quiet, and we get nothin'!"

"'Tis a lie!" Davy shouted back. "'Tis for us all!"

"Prove it, then. Prove you've got Barrett in hand, 'cause if not, you ain't doin' us no good."

Davy looked out on the crowd of faces he no longer recognized, and knew it was too late. A fuse had been burning here for a long, terrible time, and now that someone had lit it, it would not go out until the world exploded around them.

Julian and Arthur looked at each other in disbelief.

"We're going to die," Hart choked. "They're going to kill us. You can see it in their eyes. It won't help them, but they don't care."

"Or don't realize it yet." Julian's stomach churned. There was no way out of this, no way to argue or cajole or charm or influence these people. He was speechless, and in his speechlessness, powerless. Finally, inescapably, he understood in his pounding heart and numbed brain that there were kinds of danger in the world that he could not overcome. The depth of his own arrogance astounded him. Why had he never seen it before?

As the crowd surged forward, he put his hand on Arthur's shoulder. It was a useless gesture, worse than nothing, but still, Arthur looked up at him and smiled, as if he too believed, foolishly, misguidedly, that Julian Ivy was invincible.

Chapter 114

Devon wasn't sure when things had gotten out of hand. From his spot on a worktable, he saw the doors close and knew that, not only had it gone too far, but also that it could never go back again. What these men were doing-- protecting themselves, they thought, from an enemy who was not even present, let alone an immediate threat--would alter the lives of everyone irreparably. And it was all his fault. Julian had had it under control, and Devon had been unwilling to let it to stay that way, because that would have made him wrong, and his friend right, and that was a reality he simply could not face.

"We can't trust you two. You ain't our friends."

He heard the words clearly despite the noise. He had meant to excite the crowd; it's what he was good at. He had meant to win them over to his side, to convince them not to give in. Once again, he had set out to charm and mesmerize without asking himself what the consequence would be.

Worst of all, he knew that if Julian had been there a few minutes earlier, he would have been able to quiet the disgruntled workers. He would have had the patience and the wisdom to stay at it until he convinced the angry men that violence was not necessary. Devon could not do it; he did not even know how to begin. He knew how to incite rage—he was very good at that—but not how to control it.

He saw Julian recognize the mood of the crowd, look to see that the doors were closed behind him and realize that he was caught. He saw Davy make his feeble attempt to settle the mob, saw Hart speak in a murmur he could not hear. Finally, he saw realization dawn on his friend's face, saw him put his hand on Hart's shoulder and stand straighter. The men he had come to help were going to kill him, and he knew it. What he did not know, would never know, was that Devon had put the weapons in their hands.

Chapter 115

Smith stared, slack-jawed, as the men surged forward. He could not have planned a better outcome. He was pleased with himself for having judged the crowd's mood correctly. He doubted that Fitzgerald had intended this kind of insurrection. Nevertheless, the cocky Irishman had played right into Barrett's hands.

Not only would Smith's boss have a reason—practically an obligation—to exact vengeance on the workers, but they would kill both Arthur Hart and Julian Ivy and save Barrett the trouble. How lovely, Smith thought, that Barrett could come forward in righteous indignation, stamp out the lingering vestiges of this rebellion, put the men in their places, and punish them for their transgressions. He would do it in Arthur Hart's name. And Ivy's. And of course, Fitzgerald would be killed in the melee.

His boss had told him once that the best way to win a battle was to let your enemy dig his own grave, and when he stood at the edge, you'd need only one finger to tip him in. Devon had certainly dug his grave, and many, many others, and Smith and Barrett did not even have to push them in. They were already falling so fast that no one could have saved them even if they tried.

Chapter 116

Having forgotten they should not be there, Illiann and Laura were leaning over the railing, watching with horror the scene unfolding below. They had ducked back into the alcove when Hart rushed down the stairs, but they felt the tension building and could not remain hidden for long. Fortunately, no one was looking at them. Almost without exception, every eye in the room was focused on Julian and Arthur standing alone facing the mob, which had suddenly lost its wits. The men who had followed Julian into that tiny room now stood between him and their friends and co-workers, brothers, cousins, fathers and sons. For a long, painful moment, time stood still.

The girls grasped the railing so hard it should have broken beneath their combined weight, but it held. Danger pulsed around them, brighter *and* more shadowed than the weird, flickering light from the furnaces. The growls and snarls that rose from the men's throats, combined with the force of their makeshift weapons, were terrifying enough, without the bulk of over two hundred furious souls bent on exacting revenge for what they had never had, on the people who had never had it to give.

At the same moment as Julian stiffened, Illiann gasped, realizing those men would not stop until someone was dead. And her father was their principle target—he and Arthur Hart. Laura felt as if the moisture had been drained from her body, and without that moisture, her bones creaked and her muscles clenched and she could not free herself from the waking nightmare that enveloped the two people she most loved.

She turned to Illiann in panic. They stared at each other, unmoving, for what seemed like hours, trying to think, to move, to scream.

Finally, Illiann found her voice. "We're as strong as Kit."

Laura shook her head. "We have to be stronger. We have to be willing to die." The roar from the ground floor emphasized her point.

Illiann did not have to answer. She simply could not stand by and watch them murder her father.

The girls acted on instinct spurred by terror. "We have to get their attention."

"They won't hear us." Laura looked around wildly and saw a barrel outside the office door. She was fairly certain it was full of water. She cocked her head, and Illiann understood at once. Together, they tilted the barrel on its side, rolled it to the top of the metal stairs and pushed it as hard as they could.

The heavy barrel picked up speed on the steep stairs, thundering downward until the men below paused to look that way. Slowly, the girls followed in the barrel's wake, walking steadily, although they were shaking and trying not to choke on the fetid air. They did not look to either side, but directly ahead at the men with their backs to the unyielding doors.

The crowd stilled for an instant in disbelief.

Illiann knew exactly when her father saw her. He had been standing very straight, not resigned, but unable to fight the inevitable. When he turned to see where the racket was coming from and his gaze settled on his daughter, he flinched for the first time. He mouthed the word, 'NO!' though it was already too late, and suddenly he looked ill.

The girls paused unconsciously at the twin looks of horror on Julian and Arthur's faces. "If the men don't kill us," Laura whispered, "our fathers will." It was her last attempt to pretend this was a normal day and not the end of the world.

The mob was holding broken pieces of iron and hot ingots from the furnace, but they stopped moving to watch as Illiann and Laura crossed the empty space between the workers and their chosen adversaries, until the girls stood, each at her father's side.

"You said you can't trust these men, but you *can*," Laura shouted.

"They're as much Barrett's enemies as you," Illiann added.

"That makes them your friends. And we're not going away, Illiann and I."

"And if you do this…thing…no one will be your friends, not even your wives and children." Illiann had noticed that some of those who had crept in earlier were hovering near the side door, looking confused and desperate. They had come too see their husbands and fathers find new hope and a new plan for the future. They had not come to condone murder, but until the girls appeared, they had not known how to stop it. Now they came forward quietly and turned to face the rioters. They did not have to speak; their appalled expressions said everything.

Illiann became aware of her father's fingers digging into her shoulder, but she did not dare look up. Not yet. She could feel her heart pounding in her throat as the silence lengthened, on and on, the men with weapons raised, their quarry with hands hanging at their sides.

It seemed the entire cavernous room was holding its breath, waiting for an explosion, which the overbearing silence muffled and, at last, snuffed out. The workers retreated, dropping their hot, mangled pieces of iron one by one.

At long last, Julian began to breathe again.

Illiann glanced accusingly at the table in back where she'd last seen Devon, but he had disappeared.

Chapter 117

Devon had crept inside that morning, feeling hurt and self-righteous and determined. He crept away feeling ill. He knew now that he had wanted violence when he saw where Julian was going. He had wanted vindication, a salve to his injured ego, proof once and for all that he knew the men best.

Julian might have died, and Hart and Laura and, God forgive him, Ellen. He had been terrified as he watched her cross the room and join her father, appalled that he had caused the furor which she had faced with only another fifteen year old girl at her side. Now all of Julian's family had stood up against Barrett and made themselves his enemies.

Illiann might think the danger was over, but it was not. His fault. His weakness and his damnable pride had kept him from protecting the people he loved. Again.

~ * ~

Smith limped away, disappointed in the outcome, but not entirely discouraged. Julian Ivy was talking again, and the men were listening again, probably out of embarrassment at what they had almost done. The damned girls had shamed them into silence. Still, knowing that violence smoldered gave Smith hope. He could use the incident to Barrett's advantage, and his own. He could make everyone happy at once. He barely noticed the mushrooming ache in his leg as he limped awkwardly toward the concealing woods. He had plans again, and they burned in him as his strength and fearlessness used to do before Ivy destroyed them both.

Chapter 118

In her dream, starlight fell from the sky to linger on the surface of the water, on her skin, on her long black hair. She heard a noise in the wind, a voice, too distant to recognize, too indistinct to understand.

She saw the loon beside her, head tilted toward the sky. It too was listening to that distant voice. It too was trying to understand.

Slowly, Saylah began to see through the bird's eyes and hear through its ears. Only when her senses blended and became one with the silent loon, twice touched by starlight, did she hear the sound and sense of the name whispered on the back of the wind.

"Samaya!" it called softly, making her tingle with warmth and expectation. "Samaya!" it cried, demanding her attention, her acquiescence. The wind swirled around her until the name was more than sound, but also touch and sight and smell. It was the loon, the sheen on her own golden skin, the starlight moving on the pond. It was the water itself, and the stillness, and the trees that rose majestically. It was all she knew and all she felt and all she needed.

~ * ~

Saylah sat up abruptly, disoriented. What had awakened her, and why was she sleeping when it was full light out? Endless minutes passed as she tried to remember, tried to name the alarm that was pulsing in her head.

Gradually, she remembered she had not slept well the night before, had been bedeviled by nightmares she could not recall when she awoke. She rubbed the sleep from her eyes, concentrating intently. After everyone had left that morning, she had returned to the bedroom and opened the carved cedar chest against the wall, removing the partially finished set of boots she was making for Simone's servant, Mathilde. She knew she would feel better if she were busy. Then, on impulse, she had dug deeper into the chest, lifting out the memories of her childhood—the drums and stones and carvings which the Salish held sacred, and which she had not touched for many months.

Sitting in the middle of the floor with her task and her treasures around her, she had begun to drift and had climbed back into bed and fallen deeply asleep.

She knew the dream had been soothing, joyful, even, but she could not get it back. "Something is wrong," she whispered, rising from the tangle of covers. "Very wrong." The blood was singing in her ears as she stood uncertain and unmoving, a captive to her own ignorance. She did not know what to do or where to go or who was in danger; she just knew in her soul that the danger was real. She whirled, once, twice, as if seeking the answer beside or behind her, but there was nothing. Not even the voices of the past, though it lay at her feet.

She was drawn inexorably toward the open French doors to the balcony. She was desperate to feel the sea air on her face. Sadness twisted her heart, along with panic, and she turned toward the water, as she always did when she needed comfort. But she could not see the ocean through the fog today, could not hear its gently undulating water.

She was intensely aware of the echo of the voice in her dream. Even now she strained to hear the name, yearning and praying to the breeze that brushed past with fleeting promises. She listened, as she had been taught as a child, with her whole body and all her senses, but the sounds of day defeated her.

The air was cool and touched with the scent of the sea, but that did not calm her. She gripped the railing and tried to still the images tumbling in her head. She forced herself to breathe slowly, but every breath was painful, and she felt, suddenly, very much alone.

Because she knew no other way, she began to dance backward in time to a day when the spirits would have heard her prayers, and answered them.

Chapter 119

Arthur Hart took Laura home, wondering what he could possibly say about the incredible risk she had taken. Once the men had dispersed, he had hugged her over and over, so tightly that they both gasped for breath. "Don't ever do anything that foolish again," he said when they reached the front door. Afraid to leave her alone for a moment, he had insisted on walking her right up to the porch.

"I had no choice," she told him for the fifth time. "I couldn't just let them…." She trailed off, unable to speak the words.

"You had a choice." Arthur gazed at his daughter with pride and despair. "And you were brave enough to make it. I have never admired you so much, or wished so much that I could thrash you senseless."

Laura knew her father too well to believe him. "You wouldn't have done that."

His expression grew stern. "I will, Laura, if you don't stop this reckless behavior. This isn't the first time you've gotten yourself in trouble. I sometimes wonder if your audacity isn't just a means of driving your mother mad."

His daughter swallowed dryly. He was too close to the truth for her comfort.

"Any more dramatic incidents," he continued, "and I promise you won't be smiling impertinently any longer. Now go inside and lock the door."

Laura's mouth fell open in disbelief. Her father's perception knocked the air out of her. She hurried inside, intimidated by his anger for the first time in her life.

Arthur waited until he heard the bolt slide into place before he turned away.

Laura leaned her cheek on the cool surface of the door. All at once, she was back at the factory, the angry glare of the workers following her as she crossed the endless expanse of that hellish room. All at once, the numbness fell away, and the full force of her terror washed over her in waves. Her skin grew clammy and she began to shake; she had to grab the doorknob to keep from falling. She tried to breathe deeply to calm her stomach, but it continued to churn. Slick with cold perspiration, she turned, lurching toward the basin in the dining room, where she was sick again and again.

By the time the maid reached her, she was huddled, shivering, against the sideboard, unable to speak a single rational word.

Chapter 120

Julian opened the bedroom door silently. Su-ling had said Saylah was asleep, and it was so unlike her that it made his hand unsteady on the knob. Momentarily, he was relieved to see wife standing on the balcony, looking out over the lapping sea, swaying, dancing to a music only she could hear. Her long black hair fell well below her waist, and the breeze caught it, lifting the dark strands gently, revealing the line of her waist and hip. He realized she was wearing her light summer wrapper, and the outline of her body was clear against the afternoon sun. All across the bedroom floor were reminders of her past. For an instant, he thought she might have conjured them with her dance.

Memory came back with an intensity that stunned him. The first time he had seen her like this, she had been bathing in the river, and, still wet, had flung her wrapper on without fastening it. The moisture on her skin made the fabric cling, revealing every curve and hollow. He had watched, captivated, not only because she was slender and lovely, but also because she was serene and perfectly comfortable with her body. She seemed more at ease half-naked and dripping than when she was fully clothed. She had smiled to herself, singing Salish songs.

For an instant, Julian felt that if he reached out, he could touch the young Saylah—lithe and unafraid and free. He needed to touch her, to remind himself that he too had once been young and that perhaps, after all, he would live to be old. Sometimes he forgot how much he loved her, loved to watch her and craved the stillness in her that he had never learned to feel.

She sighed, and he felt the ragged breath all through him. She lifted her arms, palms upward, reaching out and up toward the sky, but her hands remained empty. At first he was dazed by the sensual movement of her body, drawn in by the call of his own need, so intense that he ached with it. But as he approached and caught a glimpse of Saylah's averted face, he realized something was not right.

Once before, long ago, she had danced and showed him her soul and her spirit and the rhythm of her celebration. Now she was revealing herself to him again, but this time she seemed incomplete, as if she were reaching for something beyond his grasp or understanding. Did she hope to find her spirit in the salt-laden air, or was she struggling to keep it from drifting beyond her grasp, leaving her half-made?

His eyes burned, raw and dry. He had looked forward so much to coming home to her, to rejoicing because his death had not come in that warehouse of weird, disturbing light. He had looked forward to the way she felt in his arms, the way she listened with all her attention and affection, as if she were absorbing his words, not simply hearing them. Though in the last months, a vague disquiet had come over her. He had felt it like the whisper of tiny beating wings, but not once had he insisted that she tell him what was wrong. He had not given her the attention and care she gave to him so freely.

Now that he saw her reaching, every quiver of her body revealing her yearning, he felt he was reliving the moment long ago when he had seen his mother in her rose and silver gown. It had been her birthday, and he had given her a cougar he had carved, meticulously and lovingly over several months. He remembered the tears in her eyes when she saw it, the way she had caressed it tenderly, as if it were alive and she could feel its warmth in her fingertips. She had risen suddenly and looked away, or tried to, seeking the support of a nearby oak, her hand pressed against the rough bark. Her pellucid skin and graceful body were fragile, lovely and completely out-of-place.

Julian felt an unwanted jolt of recognition. He had always known his mother did not belong at a wild ranch on a barely settled island. He had always known that one day she would leave. He had simply prayed and hoped that she would prove him wrong.

As he prayed now that Saylah would prove him wrong.

He realized she was concentrating on something on the balcony railing, lifting, rubbing her fingers together, closing her eyes and tilting her head. He caught a glimpse of her stones, her magic stones to which she prayed and from which she gathered part of her serenity and certainty. Each one had a different meaning, and he knew she was seeking guidance. He watched her fingers move over the smooth surfaces, jealous that they were feeling her touch and he was not. He called her name, quietly, more than half afraid to break the spell.

Turning, the questions and doubts still misty in her eyes, Saylah gasped at her husband's drawn face. "Something happened. I felt it, but I could not understand. Are you—?"

"Safe," he said. "Alive. Thank God and Illiann."

"What do you mean?"

It was not easy for him to admit. "Our daughter rescued me at the ironworks. If not for her and Laura, I'm fairly certain I would have been killed."

Saylah's eyes darkened as if a veil had fallen over them. "Your life was at risk, and I did not know?"

"It doesn't matter. It's over now." He knew she would not be reassured.

"But it *does* matter. I should have known. I should have been there."

"I didn't need you there." He realized his mistake too late.

Saylah swayed, as if she could not stand against those simple words. "It has always been my choice to be needed. It is who I am and what I do. Without it—"

"You are not without it. You never will be." He crossed the room in three strides and took her in his arms. They held each other, trembling, afraid to let go.

"Oh, Julian, please forgive me. I should be feeling your fear, not my own."

"I don't want you to feel my fear. I want you to make it disappear as you always do, with your hands and your lips and your generous heart."

"Yes," she said, and kissed him.

Rarely in their marriage had Saylah allowed Julian to see her need. It always took him by surprise, and touched him deeply, because he knew how hard it was for her to admit weakness. A few hours past, he had realized how defenseless he really was against the world and its evil. It struck him, as he held his wife close, that she was even more so.

Chapter 121

"I don't believe you!" Kit stared at his sister, wide-eyed.

"Shhhhh! They'll hear you." Illiann actually glanced over her shoulder, as if her parents might be watching.

"Well, they already *know*, don't they? It's not like the last time."

His sister grasped her elbows, arms crossed defensively beneath her breasts. "But it *is*. It's just like the last time."

Kit frowned, puzzled. "What's wrong, Lily? You saved Papa's life. You aren't afraid of him, are you?"

"Not…of him. Of them. I feel like their eyes are following me, like they're just waiting to…I don't know." She broke off, flustered, feeling sick to her stomach. "Didn't you feel that way about the Chinese?"

Her brother had worked hard to forget, but for her sake, he wanted to remember. "I don't think so, but I kept dreaming of Baldhead, and that really scared me." He would not have admitted it to another human being, but he sensed that Illiann needed to know.

"Yes," she said, "me too."

Kit was not sure whether she meant she too was afraid of Baldhead, or that she would dream of the men at the factory, but he realized it didn't matter. "I wish I could've been there."

"No, you don't. I promise."

"But don't you feel…strong? Aren't you proud of what you did?"

He wanted her to be; she could see it in his eyes. "I'm glad we're both alive. I'd be stupid if I weren't. But, Kit, you didn't see the expression in Papa's eyes. He wasn't afraid, or at least, he didn't show it. He just stood there, unflinching, as if he'd known all along that it would happen, and he'd made his choice. Until he saw me. He went positively gray, and he looked old and…powerless. Our Papa." She hugged herself, shivering.

Kit sat back on heels, shocked and numb. He wanted to say again that he did not believe her, that his father had never been powerless in his life, and never would be. But he knew Illiann would not make it up; he could see the truth in her ashen face. He wished he had stopped her before she put that image in his mind, but it was too late. Now they were *both* frightened and dismayed. Without conscious thought, he put his arms around her and hugged her tight.

Illiann hugged him back, grateful beyond words for the simple, heartfelt gesture. For the first time in her life, *she* needed Kit and not the other way around.

Chapter 122

Richard Parnell shook his head mournfully as he closed the door of the boardroom behind him. The directors sat in chairs upholstered in gold brocade, their faces reflected in the gleaming surface of the mahogany table that dominated the room. The heavy drapes—burnt sienna and copper designs on a tawny velvet background—were edged with thick gold cording and drawn open just enough to let in a bit of daylight. Jonathan Douglas was pouring a cup tea for Harold Blanshard from the sterling silver service, while Stephen and Frederick Johnson leaned back, cigar smoke curling around their shoulders. No one looked at Parnell until he cleared his throat several times.

As the youngest and least distinguished member of the Board, and also the bank president, he had the task of actually handling the paperwork and the patrons and trying to make certain neither impinged upon the regal solitude of the other members unless the matter was urgent. Which it was.

Harold Blanshard, Chairman of the Board of Directors, and its oldest member, glanced at Parnell over the rim of his fine china cup. "Yes?" His raised eyebrows and his chilly tone suggested Parnell would be well served to rethink his arrival, which disturbed the tranquility of the hushed and gilded room.

"It's Arthur Hart," Parnell said, for once without preamble. "He wants us to lend him the money to buy out Robert Barrett, using the iron works as collateral."

If possible, Blanshard's eyebrows rose higher. "Can't be done. You know that. The Works is already mortgaged."

Parnell cleared his throat again, nervously. "Yes sir. I seem to remember your son-in-law wanted the cash for another venture, but I don't recall it ever getting off the ground. In any case, it appears he did not tell Mr. Hart. I should have thought such a large loan would require both signatures, but it seems Mr. Barrett signed it alone. With your approval." Only the slightest rise in inflection at the end of the sentence implied a question.

"You didn't tell him that, for God's sake!" Frederick Johnson raised his considerable bulk out of a chair, glaring at the hapless manager with glassy blue eyes.

"Of course not. I am not an imbecile. It's just that I have to give Hart some explanation. I told him we'd apprise him when we've come to a decision."

In the silence that followed, Jonathan Douglas gazed speculatively around the table. "Barrett's become a bit of a problem of late." His tone was mild, but the other members gawked at him in astonishment. As a rule, one did not malign the president's son-in-law, particularly when the question of money was involved. Everyone waited breathlessly for Blanshard's response.

"Hmmmm." He leaned his head against the chair back and steepled his fingers under his chin. "Indeed. Bob's rather too sure of himself, I'm afraid." His son-in-law would have cursed the man, had he been present. He hated being called Bob. Diana said she thought it was because it reminded her husband of being a boy, and he did not want to remember. Which was, naturally, why Harold Blanshard used the nickname as often as possible. "He's been throwing his weight around, intimidating people. Not the done thing, by any means." What he meant was, one never 'threw one's weight around'; one distributed it calmly and ever so subtly, like a proper gentleman. Which Robert Barrett was not. He had sensed that even Diana was unhappy with the situation, and could only wish she had realized her mistake long since, before her husband gained so much power and influence. It was not, of course, Blanshard's own fault that he and the other board members had never once turned down a request from the man, and none of *them* cared a fig for Diana.

And then there was the money. Barrett seemed to make it without effort, fortune after fortune. Odd that he had had the temerity to ask for that mortgage on the iron works. Odder still that they had funded it.

Stephen Johnson concurred. "He's stirring up the men at an appalling rate, and seems to have forgotten to whom he owes his current good fortune."

'To himself', Parnell thought derisively, but he wisely refrained from expressing that opinion. "It seems to me that it might be in our best interest to keep one of Victoria's largest businesses viable." He did not know what had made Blanshard turn against Barrett, but he could only be grateful he had finally done so.

"How are we to do that?" Frederick Johnson inquired, "When Barrett holds the reins?"

"*We* hold the reins," Blanshard said sharply. "It might behoove us to stop funneling the profits into Bob's pockets, and aim them toward Hart instead."

"Are you saying we should call in the loan?" Douglas was horrified. "If I'm not mistaken, Barrett will have worded the thing so Hart has to pay if off, and we all know he can't do that. Can barely keep his wife living in that mansion and wearing her Worth gowns."

"If I may?" Parnell asked. When they did not object, he continued, "I've been hearing things today—well, I do have my sources. One must, mustn't one, in order to keep ahead? They say that if Barrett remains a partner in the company, the workers will riot. Which, as I'm sure you're all painfully aware, would be terribly disagreeable and inconvenient for the other business owners. On the other hand, Hart seems to have gained the men's trust. It seems to me that it would be far preferable to settle the matter with Hart, privately, if you see what I mean. Quietly and peacefully. In order to cause as little trouble as possible."

The members nodded. They were always in favor of a quiet solution to any unpleasantness. And they certainly did not wish to be the instrument of further unrest among the workers in Victoria. They lived in terror of strikes and riots. They did not want their placid, comfortable lifestyle to be disturbed by such distasteful events.

"However," Frederick Johnson pointed out, "the fact remains that we have no surety for the loan. I don't see how it can be done. Although I, for one, do not wish to live out my days with that ill-mannered person lording it over me while he counts his piles of money. Far too common, in my humble opinion."

"There's nothing humble about you," his brother Stephen countered. "But you're right, as it happens. Life was much more refined before Bobby Barrett came to town."

Barrett would have cringed at his father-in-law calling him 'Bob', but he would have lunged at Johnson's throat for his casual 'Bobby', which would only have served to prove the man's point. Not that Barrett cared a whit for Johnson's opinion, or anyone else's. It was that disregard for the attitudes of others which made him most dangerous to these affluent, inflexible, pious and self-important guardians of Victoria's welfare.

Chapter 123

Julian had just stepped into the hall when Kit came barrelling toward him.

"Papa! The lady who talks funny is waiting in the parlor. The one who brought the note."

"Mathilde?" Julian vaguely remembered Saylah was making her a new pair of boots; she had mentioned the woman would be coming to try them on. "Where is your mother?" he asked Kit.

"I don't know. Shall I go find her?"

"Please. I'll see to our guest in the meantime."

"Would you be Mathilde, by any chance?" he asked as he opened the parlor door.

The woman, who had been concentrating on a pine branch on the sideboard, turned abruptly, arms crossed over her ample bosom and lips pursed. She stopped at the sight of him. "Aha!" she cried as if she had surprised a child stealing forbidden candy, "you're Mister Julian Ivy." She was flustered, but managed to sound the slightest bit accusing. She drew herself up, which accomplished little, but made her feel better. "Wife told me to come try on my new boots. Been three days since we got here, my mistress and me. 'Course you'd be too busy to notice time was passin', I'm sure. Important man like you."

Julian narrowed his eyes. "I hardly think—"

"Not impatient, mind you. Not my mistress, anyway. Not a kinder, more tolerant soul to be found, if you ask me. 'Course you wouldn't, 'cause don't want to know. Can't blame you, mind. Her disappearing like that without a word." She examined the frayed toes of her shoes. "Don't know why your wife thinks I need new ones. Barely broken these in."

Thrown off by the change in subject, Julian tried to think of a response, but nothing came to him.

"Perfectly good pair of sturdy boots," Mathilde continued relentlessly. "No need to toss them aside like an old servant you've no use for anymore. You wouldn't do that unless they were relatives, I s'pose."

"Now see here! You can't come into my house and accuse me of all kinds of things you know nothing about." He knew he sounded childish, but he could not believe this was happening. The day had already held too many unpleasant surprises.

"That'd be rude. Just makin' chatter. Mistress chides me for it often. Says I always have an opinion, whether one's required or not. Mostly not, it seems." She heaved a heavy sigh.

Inexplicably, Julian wanted to smile. He could tell she was just getting started, and for some reason, he refrained from stopping her.

"Told her to come here, just the same. 'Go see the boy! Tell him what's what. 'Course, she tried years ago. Wrote you over and over, but never got an answer. "'Wastin' your breath,' I said, but she's a stubborn one and kept right on."

Clearing his throat, he chose his reply with care. "I only laid eyes on those letters a week past. I had no idea they existed until then." Julian reproached himself for feeling guilty. "A friend, er, acquaintance of mine intercepted them." Wondering why he had even spoken of Edward's deceit, he noticed that, for the first time, Mathilde was staring at him directly

"Thought it was that blackguard, deM. Would have sworn he never let them leave France."

She was speaking is complete sentences, too. Apparently Julian had startled her deeply. "Who, exactly, is deM?" He was trying to be patient, but his curiosity and her odd manner had begun to wear on him.

"The monster Madame's father married her to when she was fifteen. Things happened that night that'd make your skin crawl. Ran away as soon as she could. He tracked her down tho'." She stopped to take a breath.

"Got her excommunicated and broke her heart. Again. Used to drift around the house like a ghost. Depressed me no end, but did I say a word of reproach? Only on every second Thursday, and she never listened anyway. Church finally granted an annulment, tho' not before time. Gave her a little peace to know her real marriage to your father was all tidy and legal after all."

She eyed him to see if he understood the implications.

Slowly, Mathilde's message penetrated, but Julian did not feel the relief he had expected. Confounded by so many disparate emotions that he could make no sense of them, he foundered.

"Punishes herself for deM's failings and cruelty." She snorted in disgust. "Doesn't need anyone else blamin' her for things she couldn't help." She stood, arms akimbo, chin jutting out at an obstinate angle. "Understand what I'm sayin', Mister Julian Ivy?"

He should have been angry, but instead, he was sad, and that bothered him. "It would be difficult to miss your meaning. You might just keep in mind that I don't respond well to being threatened."

"Suspected as much. Stubborn, like your mother. If I were her son, I'd want to see that for myself. Completely up to you, of course. Wouldn't dream of interfering."

"In that case, I'd be interested to see what you *would* dream of doing." When he heard the door open and his wife came in, he turned, grateful for the reprieve.

As if Saylah had heard every word and understood his every thought with a single glance, she nodded and took his hand. He stared at her serene smile and something started to shift inside him. He'd been cradling excuses to his chest like as if they were armor, piling them up like a weapon to keep an enemy at bay. But with Saylah's hand tight in his and the heat of her body near, he recognized his excuses for what they were: cowardice. He was afraid Simone would be a stranger, and so he did not wish to see her. He would rather have his memories, old and tattered as they were. "Mathilde," he said, "would you kindly carry a message for me?"

Chapter 124

"Illiann? Are you all right?" Saylah found her daughter in the sunroom. She and Julian had made love that afternoon, and by the time she went in search of Illiann, the girl was fast asleep. Apparently, she too had slept fitfully the night before, and the incident at the ironworks had drained and exhausted her.

"I just wanted to see them." Illiann indicated the hand-written pages on the tabletop. "To remember what it was like to feel—"

"Safe?" her mother offered, settling crossed-legged onto the floor.

Illiann looked up, eyes damp with tears. "Yes. Safe." The word tasted sweet, though she knew it was a lie. "I don't know why I didn't see it before—the danger, I mean. I suppose I didn't want to."

Slipping her arm around her daughter's shoulders, Saylah murmured, "That is because you did not have to. Not until today. Believe me, Ilya, it would have happened sometime. I am only sorry that it had to be so abrupt and so very painful. I know you saw many things this morning that will haunt you, perhaps for a long time. But you are resilient, my daughter, and you will grow stronger because of these things. Even the sight of your father's fear."

Illiann looked up sharply. Had Kit betrayed her? What she saw in her mother's eyes reassured and frightened her both at once. Of course Saylah knew how she felt. She always did. Relieved that someone understood, Illiann rested her head on her mother's shoulder. "I didn't want to see that. Ever."

Tenderly, Saylah tucked a stray hair behind her daughter's ear. "I know you did not, but it was time. You are nearly a woman now, growing every day, and sometimes growth means learning that, like you, your parents are only human. Julian is the strongest, bravest man I have ever known, but he is also warm and giving, and he loves us so much. You would not wish that part of him away, would you?"

"No. He'd be a different man then, a stranger."

"Exactly. And it is the sensitive side of his nature, the part we most cherish, which makes him fear for us so deeply. He needed you today, and you were there to save him. He gave you a glimpse of his vulnerability, and in return, you gave him his life. That is not a coincidence, my Ilya. It is nothing less than a miracle."

Chapter 125

With no warning, and a great deal of huffing and puffing, Mathilde sailed into the suite of rooms at Nellie Howard's. "Ah! There you are." She came to a halt in the sweep of light shining through the window, unaware of how unflattering it was to her robust figure and craggy face. She would not have cared if she had known; she had more important things on her mind. "Where d'ya think *I've* been?"

"I cannot imagine," Simone replied. "I cannot even try."

"Visitin' your son. Of course, was only there for the new boots." She pointed woefully at the old ones she still wore, while holding the new pair in her other hand. Cutting Simone off before she could ask why, Mathilde told an empty place on the shelves, "Can't wear these beautiful new ones. Ruin 'em in no time." Reverently, she placed the new boots in a square of oak, then whirled on Simone.

"Appeared out of nowhere. That surprised, I tell you. Never expected to see *him* there."

"Did you not?" Simone went pale. "In his own home in mid-afternoon? It does not seem very odd to me." She was more anxious every day she did not hear from Julian, and more inclined to turn around and return to France, but she did *not* want Mathilde forcing her son into a meeting he did not wish to have.

"Nice boy. Not averse to sarcasm on occasion. Has a sense of humor. Like that in a man."

"Please stop torturing me and tell me what he *said*."

Mathilde cleared her throat thoroughly. "Said never saw your letters years ago. Hidden from 'im. Doing us the great honor of meeting you after supper." She made a mock curtsey, sweeping her arm out wide and nearly toppling forward when she bent at the waist. "Told him he was too, too generous. He actually smiled. Consider that a victory."

Simone was momentarily speechless. "Are you certain?" she asked at last.

"Quite. Told him he'd be coming here, downstairs parlor. Safer that way."

"Why? Do you think he might strike me?" Simone leaned forward anxiously.

Mathilde rolled her eyes. "Honestly, Madame! He's your son, and a gentleman. Wouldn't even think of strikin' a woman."

A fist clenched and unclenched inside Simone. Mathilde had never defended Julian before. She had not precisely attacked him either, but she had had very little good to say about him.

Her mistress was not willing to give up on her original question. "But he was angry with me, was he not?"

"'Course he was. Wouldn't you be? Thinkin' you'd been cast off and forgotten all those years. Don't worry, though. Won him over eventually with my multitudinous charms." She actually pirouetted to demonstrate those charms, but Simone continued to frown.

"Best take some wine to clear your head. Not thinkin' straight."

"Suppose I were to refuse? Should you send me to bed without my supper?"

It took the servant a moment to grasp that Simone was mocking her. When she did realize it, she collapsed on the sofa, faint with relief. "Thought you were never goin' to stop frownin' and worryin'. Now, listen. Been out talkin' to people. Your son in a bit of trouble. Can't seem to help 'imself. Too much like you." She tapped her finger on her lips. "Worked people up into a frenzy, I hear. So, time for you and me to figure out a way to help our boy through this."

Over the years, Mathilde had referred to her son by many names, from MISTER JULIAN IVY (all in capitals

476

and with a snort of disdain) to 'that Ivy boy' (coolly and dismissively) to 'he' and 'him' (as anonymously as she could manage). In the last few hours, he had gone from Julian (with humor) to 'your son' (with some flicker of warmth) to, finally, 'our boy'.

That, more than anything else, gave Simone hope.

Chapter 126

After her talk with Saylah, Illiann left the house on an errand she had been planning, and avoiding, all day.

She walked, because the afternoon light warmed her blood, and because she needed to be moving, though she did not allow her thoughts to wander; it was too dangerous. She knew her parents would not approve of her errand, but she put that knowledge aside.

This time she did not bother to knock on the front door, but opened it without ceremony. She knew where she would find him. There was only one place he went to hide.

Devon was standing before a painting of a violent sunset, which he was covering a streak at a time in black paint, hiding the passionate ferocity that cried out from the part of the canvas he had not yet ruined.

She stood in the doorway, horrified. If he was capable of blotting out his soul on canvas, he was capable of destroying anything. But she already knew that, didn't she? "You could have gotten my father killed today."

He gasped. He had not known she was there. "Tryin' to scare me senseless, are you?"

"Maybe. Just like you frightened me." Her voice shook, and she plunged ahead before she lost her nerve. "I *saw* you, Devon. I saw you working the men into a rage. Why did you do it?"

He answered without thinking. "Because 'tis what I do. 'Tis all I know."

"That's not true. Look around. You know all about capturing beauty with paint."

He shrugged his broad shoulders. "'Tis wasted on the likes of me. I'm no' good enough. I never was."

She suspected he was not talking just about painting. He looked beaten down, despairing. But this time, she would not be drawn into his pain. This time, she had her own. She gave her head a little shake. "Did you want my father dead? Is that why you were there?"

His stomach clenched as if she had struck him. "Now, that's blasphemin' pure and simple. Julian's my friend, and well you know it."

Illiann regarded him in silence.

"I'd no way of knowin' that would happen. I didn't think they'd go that far." His cheeks were flushed and his heavy red eyebrows bristled. His thick, curly hair was tangled and streaked with paint, his flannel shirt soaked in sweat.

"You didn't think at all, did you?"

His nostrils flared with anger that she was scolding him like a wayward child. "Mayhap I was driven to act, to do somethin' besides stand by watchin'."

"Even if you couldn't control it? Or didn't you care?" She swallowed a gulp of air. "I don't know you at all, do I?" She stepped back, her expression guarded.

"'Course you do." He tried to smile, to reassure her, because even her chiding voice was better than the silence in which he had been living, but the color in his face betrayed his agitation. "I told you everything."

"I thought so once, but it's not true." A sense of unreality made her head swim. She grabbed the doorjamb to steady herself. "I never thought I'd see you cowering in back, hiding in the shadows. Why didn't you help my father? *Why*?"

Devon reached backward and slashed another black stripe across the disappearing sunset. "'Tis what I've always done: stand back and let people I care about die because I don't know how to save them." He closed his eyes to shut out the sound of his own self-pity. "I don't know why I drove the men mad. I'd not be knowin' why I left them that way. I could no' stop myself. Must be I lost my mind for a time."

Illiann's brown eyes filled with tears of frustration, and the color came and went in her cheeks. "At least my father faced the mob head-on. I used to think you were brave, because you burned so brightly and wouldn't back down, but you're not."

She was calling him a coward without saying the word. He did not wish to consider whether she was right. "And there *you* were, Dad's frail, courageous lass, facin' the bad men for his sake. Like to wrung my heart, it did."

Illiann could not believe he was mocking her about *this* of all things. "What's the *matter* with you?"

With an explosive breath, he shouted, "You could've been killed! What if I'd lost you, too?"

She blinked, but her vision was blurred, and the images in her memory grew vivid and all too real. She had refused to see them since the incident, but they were stronger than her will to ignore them. Once again, the men were crowding forward, glowing iron in their fists and murder in their eyes. Once again she stood before them, waiting to be crushed by the molten fire. She could hear her father's shallow breathing and feel his fear like a fist in her stomach. She smelled death in the air, and it made her feel faint, but she had to keep standing, head high and face blank so they would not see her terror. She swayed, teeth chattering.

Devon took her elbow. "You're cryin', me *fand*, and shakin' as well."

"No, I'm not." The words came out a whisper as perspiration trickled down the side of her face. The room was stuffy and began to spin. "I'm all right. Have to be, for Papa's sake."

"'Tis no' your responsibility to save him, Ellen. No' again. He's got your mother now, and friends. They're older. They'll know what to do. You're only a child."

"I'm not. I'm a woman. Mama said so." She heard the words, but the voice was not her own. "But I can't…do this anymore. I can't."

"Ellen!"

Her legs crumpled and he caught her in his arms, carrying her into the hall toward the parlor. "'Tis shock," he murmured, uncertain whether she could hear, but he needed the sound to stave off panic. "Delayed, no doubt, but shock just the same." He put her on the sofa, dragging a faded quilt from the back of a chair. He wrapped it around her and cradled her against his chest, feeling her shivering all through his body. He could not remember what else he was supposed to do. She was so cold, and her eyes were empty. How could he have been so stupid? Why hadn't he noticed she was in trouble? He had provoked her and mocked her when he should have been holding her and protecting her.

"Ellen, listen! Hang on, lass! Don't be driftin' away from me now. Look at me. If you don't I might be after startin' to sing, and you don't want that." He laid his cheek against hers, shocked by the chilled, clammy skin.

He remembered hearing that people in shock should be kept warm. He held her close and tucked the quilt tighter, but he could not seem to chase away the cold. Something warm. He needed something warm. He found a half-empty bottle of sherry on the bookshelf, and wrestled the cork out with his teeth. Then he sat with her on his lap, propping her head against his shoulder and, using his free hand, tipped the bottle against her parted lips. She coughed when the sherry hit her throat, but did not spit it out. He gave her some more, and she coughed violently, then lay back, dazed and exhausted.

She was still shivering, so he carried her into the bedroom and took the blanket off the bed, wrapping it around the quilt. He stirred up the coals in the wood-burning stove and sat beside her, trying to give her his warmth. He had not felt so helpless since he was a child trying to help his father work the plow.

He talked to her all the while he rubbed her hands to warm then. He jumped when she raised her head and said, "Devon? What're you doing here?"

She mumbled, but he understood her. She must think she was at home. He touched her cheek, which was sleek with sweat; the skin beneath felt slightly warm. "I live here, lass, more's the pity. But there you are. It can no' be helped."

"'S' hot." She tried to dislodge the blankets, but they were wound too tight.

"Here, let me."

Illiann watched warily while he freed her, watching the red hairs on his sunburnt hands in fascination. When he tossed the covers aside, she breathed a sigh of relief. Her insides were quivering, but she could see more clearly. She sat up abruptly and the dizziness returned. They were in his bedroom, on his bed. That wasn't right. Besides, she was so angry with him that it was choking her.

"What are you *doing*?" She scooted away from him, backing against the wall, eyes wide. Somewhere inside, she knew she was being unreasonable, but she could not control her panic.

Devon stared at the discarded blanket, stunned by the depth of his disappointment. For the second time in half an hour, he felt like a helpless child. "You went into shock. I was tryin' to help."

"Oh." She remembered now. The sound of his voice, the warmth of his arms, the threat that he might begin to sing.

He looked up and she met his gaze, caught, as she so often was, in the turquoise depths of his eyes. Her heart began to race and chills rose on her arms, but not from the cold. They stared at one another, unable to look away, and the silence sizzled between them. Slowly, inevitably, they leaned forward, compelled by everything that lay unspoken between them.

Illiann realized he was going to kiss her, and some deeply buried instinct snapped her awake. She remembered why she had come, and why she had to go and not return. "Don't touch me. You're dangerous. You don't care who you hurt." She maneuvered around him and slid off the mattress. Her legs were wobbly, but she managed to stand.

"Ellen, don't be doin' this to me. Not now." He could not bear her enmity; he needed her to love him.

Crossing her arms, she shook her head. "What about what you've done to me? To my family? Pretending to be our friend, when all you care about is yourself? Just like you pretended to befriend the workers. But you don't care about them either. You don't even care about justice, do you? Except for yourself. Except if it's revenge for what you've suffered."

"Stop it. You don't know what you're sayin'."

"I do now, finally."

He winced at a fresh surge of guilt. He had been hiding from it since he left the iron works that morning, but could not escape it anymore. "Does Julian know…that it was me?"

Illiann stopped, arrested by the torment on his face. "No."

"Are you goin' to tell him?"

He was pleading; all his fire had burned out. He had gone too quickly from rage to surrender, and she almost pitied him. He would have hated that. "I don't think so. It wouldn't do any good. But you have to promise you won't turn on him, on us, again."

"Would you believe me if I did?"

Illiann hesitated. "I don't think you're a liar; I just think you're frightening, and that ruining Barrett won't make you stop hurting."

He rose from the bed, using his size to intimidate her. "As usual, you don't know what you're talkin' about." His icy tone and practiced sneer told her all she needed to know.

Illiann felt a desperate sensation, like a tide pulling her out to sea. "You aren't listening. You don't even trust me. Why can't you do that, just once?" Her voice nearly broke. "I think you'd rather trust your own demons. They're probably better company."

"Considerably better. Especially right now."

She turned away and started down the hall.

Against his will, Devon followed her. He had meant to offend her, to drive her away, leaving him to his private and familiar hell. But as he watched her go, something snapped inside him. "Ellen!" he shouted, "Wait!"

She did not hurry her step, but neither did she pause.

Devon thought he might suffocate in the suddenly airless hall. He could not let her go. "Ellen!" he cried again. "Ellie!"

She kept walking, one foot in front of the other, each step taking her farther away, until, while he stood, speechless and bereft, she opened the front door and closed it carefully behind her.

Chapter 127

When Julian entered the parlor at Nellie's, Simone was sitting half-turned away, head bowed. For a moment, in the subtle play of lamplight and starlight, she looked no different than she had the last time he had seen her. Though her hair was streaked with silver, he saw only the dark curls he remembered brushing his cheeks as she bent over him while he studied, or at night when she kissed him before sleep. Her figure was still slender, her hands soft, the fingers long and graceful.

He had thought she would be unrecognizable, that time and betrayal would have transformed her into a stranger. But she was, incredibly, painfully familiar. He had known she was here, had come specifically to see her, but he knew now that he had not for a moment, believed it would happen.

She heard him and turned, and he was struck dumb by the sheer impossibility of standing a few feet from the woman whom, alive or dead, he had believed with heart, soul and mind he would never see again.

Saylah was right; Simone had become a ghost, no more substantial than the smoke that drifted upward when a candle was blown out. Once, she had been the candle itself, but the wax had long since melted away. She could not possibly be real.

And yet she was. He could smell her delicate scent, hear the rise and fall of her breathing, the slight rustle of her skirt as she moved. Her face, which he had dreamed of time and again, was undeniably compelling, even to him.

He had tried to believe he was ready for this moment, but he had been wrong.

Like him, Simone had thought herself prepared. Like him, she had lied to herself. She had been certain that Julian would look like his father, and was mute with the realization that her son's face was a stronger, broader reflection of her own. His hair was lighter, but just as thick and wavy, his eyes hazel instead of gray-green, though in the low light, the green shown more brightly. He had her lips, but firmer, and her cheekbones. She did not care to see *herself* in the mirror, but she did not turn away from this reflection, though it frightened her as her own never had.

What if, after all, he rejected her apology? What if this man she did not know never unbent from his frozen silence and, wearing her face and carrying her hope in his hands, he simply turned away? It would be as if she had rejected herself, blamed herself past all forgiving, as she had done most of her life. She had survived many things, but could not survive this.

She wanted to say so, but knew it would not be fair to her son, who might not be *able* to forgive her. She had always known Jamie would do so; it was not in her husband's nature to hate and punish, only to grieve. But Julian was too much like her.

He was holding a rich-looking laquer box, which she stared at fixedly, trying to hide her nervousness. Still standing, he clutched it for a long moment, then opened the heavily engraved lid and held it out to her.

Inside were some very old letters. She recognized her handwriting as it had been when she was younger. Beside them lay a bound book; it took a moment longer for her to realize it was the diary she had kept from the day she met Jamie Ivy. The one she had left behind, hoping her husband and son would read it and understand how much she loved them—how much it hurt to know she must lose them in the end.

She touched the edges of the envelopes slowly, as if trying to remember what she had written inside. "What do you want to know?" was all she could manage. She had imagined many things, but never this. She wanted her son to see her as she was now, in the present, but his eyes and his interest seemed fixed on the past.

He raised his head at the sound of her voice, transfixed by the entreaty in her eyes, the tenderness. "I want you to know I never got the letters when you sent them. Just recently…" He paused to clear his throat. "And the diary. I never knew you tried to touch…to keep in touch. But I do now." Still something was holding him back.

Sensing his remoteness—after all, he had not yet sat down—Simone replied with care, "It has been too long and too strange between us. We do not know one another. There is so much I need to tell you."

"These tell me a great deal." He closed the box and seated himself across from her. He was not sure why, but he wanted to do her a kindness, at least one, in the midst of his own uncertainty. "The diary was a gift, but I didn't realize it for a long, long time. We read it often. My daughter Illiann and my wife Saylah practically know it by heart."

Eyes moist, Simone looked up at her son. "I did not know if you ever found it. Thank you, Julian."

He knew she was grateful for more than the knowledge that her granddaughter and wife had cared enough to memorize her diary. He half-smiled. "You used to call me Jules. Remember?"

Her face relaxed into a hint of the radiant smile of her youth. "Yes," she said. "I remember everything." She had not seen it before, but it was true—every moment had come back to her, an unexpected gift, and perhaps, if she were lucky, if they both were, a promise.

The night she had left the ranch came back to him unexpectedly. *Forgive me,* mon petit, *but I must go away,* she had said. *Because of things that happened a long time ago—things too dangerous to tell you. I must go to keep you and your father safe.* He had asked plaintively, *Why are you leaving me?* And she had answered, *I am not leaving* you, *Jules, but I must go back. Back to where I started but did not end.* She had tried to kiss him, but he had turned his head away. *Please, Jules, let me remember you loving me. I shall have to live on memories from now on. Will you not give me a kiss to hold onto? Will you say goodbye, at least?* He had not answered, and finally she had kissed the back of his neck and left him. He remembered she had been weeping. He had forgotten all about it.

Suddenly, without planning or reflection, he spoke, and was startled by the sound of his own voice. "I thought you were…I didn't believe you would ever come back."

"Neither did I. But then my friends made me open my eyes and see that by punishing myself, I was also punishing you, that if I were ever to find peace, I would have to find you first and hope that one day you might forgive me."

Julian was transfixed by her accent, once so familiar, now so achingly exotic. Her mellifluous voice reminded him of Saylah's, each word spoken fully, no contractions, the lilt of a foreigner speaking English when it was not her natural language.

He could not doubt her sincerity. Her eyes were wide and clear, her expression full of regret and hope. Six months earlier, he might have been filled with irritation instead of sympathy, but that was before he realized he was human, and so was she. "I can't deny that it hurts to see you, flesh and blood and bone, and know all these years that you were somewhere I couldn't reach."

"I know," she said, surprising him again. "I always knew. For a long time I thought it was better for you to think me dead. Better for everyone. But that was because I was afraid."

"Of what?"

Simone frowned. "Of you. Of the truth. Of your anger and bitterness. Most of all, I was afraid of how you would judge and condemn me for what I had done to Jamie and you."

He could no longer hold it in. "Then why, in God's name, did you do it?"

She was silent for a long time. "The only way I could have avoided hurting you both so badly, the only way I could have stopped it, was by not falling in love with your father at all." Her eyes glistened with tears and she faced him squarely. "And, Julian, no matter how much you curse me or rage at me or blame me, I can never regret that moment. You and Jamie were the greatest joys of my life. I will tell you everything you want to know; I will tell you the whole truth, ugly as it is, but I will not wish away my memories of the only paradise I have ever known.

"If you cannot forgive me for that, then you might as well turn away and leave me now."

Julian was knocked off-balance by her passion. The last thing he had expected, the only thing he could not allow, was to see the torment in her eyes and hear the anguish in her voice.

He felt compelled to do precisely what she said, to turn on his heel and walk away without a backward glance. Not because he could not forgive her, but because he understood. Despite the grief, frustration and heartache his father had caused Julian, never to have known Jamie Ivy was unthinkable. In baring her own soul, Simone had also touched his; he could see his own reflection in her eyes, just as surely as if she were a mirror. The sensation was more unsettling than any he had ever known, even the fear of losing his life.

"I am arrogant, certainly, and proud, but even *I* know that whatever has come between us, whatever I have suffered, I can never wish I had not been born. You gave me many gifts, *Maman*, before you went away, but my life was by far the most precious. I don't what to do or say to make the pain go away, but I do know this; you do not need forgiveness for being happy. No one does."

Simone closed her eyes briefly. "Thank you, Jules," she whispered. "That, above all, was what I needed to know."

Chapter 128

Saylah slept lightly, dreaming of the river, but the water was drifted by a thin haze that muffled its song and disguised its beauty. The starlight failed to penetrate the gauzy film hovering over the chilly night. She felt numb, and strained to hear the whisper in the breeze that had comforted her before. Instead of the name, Samaya, the wind carried the acrid odor of smoke, which settled about her, leaving ashes on the blurry surface of the water.

She awoke abruptly and drew her knees to her chest, rocking and rocking, until she realized the smoke from her dream had lingered, drifting through the still, dark room, carrying with it the smell of fire.

"Julian!"

He sat up beside her and did not need to ask what was wrong. The bedroom was dimmed by smoke that curled through the darkness in a serpentine haze. He and Saylah rose, went to the window and looked down, coughing on the bitter air. Below, an eerie yellow light flickered in the sunroom. "Fire!" Julian shouted, racing for the door.

"Kit, Illiann!" Saylah called as they stumbled into the hall. "Get up."

The hall was free of smoke, for which the couple was grateful. The French doors to their bedroom had been open, and the room was directly above the sunroom. Perhaps that was why the smoke had spiraled upward and not reached the rest of the floor.

"Get the fire brigade," Saylah told Julian. "I will get the others."

Together, they peered over the banister, but could not see any flames.

"You'll be all right?" Julian asked.

"Yes. Go. Be safe."

Her husband did not have time, but he bent to kiss her anyway, and she touched his cheek as he turned away.

She called out again, but the children were already out of bed, tying their robes haphazardly, rubbing their crusted eyes in confusion.

When they were all together, Saylah said, "There is a fire in the sunroom."

Illian's eyes widened with a question as they met Saylah's.

"We do not know anything yet. We must put the flames out and see to the damage before we even begin to wonder how—"

"I know how," Kit declared hoarsely. "Barrett did it, or sent Baldhead to do it for him. I looked out the window before I came out and saw someone running away. And he was limping."

"Are you certain? It is dark tonight." His mother was herding them downstairs, looking for smoke and flames, but finding none until they reached the back of the house. Something was wrong with Kit's theory, and her instinct prodded her to listen, but she had more immediate concerns. They had to put out the fire.

There was smoke in the hall behind the kitchen, but the flames seemed to be contained in the sunroom. When Saylah started to open the door, Illiann wanted to scream at her to stop, but it was too late. Her hand had already closed around the knob. She cried out and leapt back as the hot brass burned her palm, but it did not stop her for long. While the other three ran for buckets to fill at the pump, Saylah plunged into the thick gray-yellow mass of flame and smoke. She could not tell how big the fire was; it seemed to fill up the night around her. She choked and gasped in the thick, acrid air, going back for water when she heard Illiann at the door.

"Stay there," she shouted, taking the bucket from her daughter's hands, "and bring more water. More than one would be dangerous in here." As she always did, as she had since she had been a child, she took charge, and as they always had, her children followed her instructions.

When she had poured three buckets in the direction of the flames, though the steam rose around her in clouds, it became clear that the fire was not a large one. She stumbled out the door, taking huge gulps of air. "I suspect it started in the center of the floor," she rasped, "so it must have been set deliberately. But I do not think it was meant to destroy. The door was left closed, and only one window cracked open. That is how the smoke escaped.

"But why?" Saylah asked, feeling useless and inadequate.

"Like Kit told you, to warn us." Illiann's voice was strained and her eyes shimmered with tears from the stinging smoke. All at once, she was back in the factory, mesmerized by the weird glow of the furnaces and the choking fear in the air.

Saylah took another bucket and disappeared into the room.

"I know it was Baldhead," Kit added stubbornly. "He was dragging his leg like it was broken."

Dumping a sloshing bucket onto the remaining flames, Saylah sniffed and wondered why more of the smoke had not cleared. Then she heard a crackle, and instinctively turned toward the cabinet where she kept the Salish legends. She cried out for the first time in pain, took off her cloak and threw it on the floor. She was not aware, as she opened the doors, that the latches burned her hands. All she could see were the flames dancing across the crowded shelves.

At her cry, the children realized something was very wrong. Something more than a small fire meant as a warning. They crowded around the door, waving their hands before their faces to clear the smoke.

Saylah fell to her knees and tried to beat out the flames with her cloak. Illiann and Kit tried to help, but it was too hot and they backed away. Their mother did not seem to notice the pain. She struck at the flames again and again, with her robe, her gown, her naked palms. She continued to do so until Kit tossed a bucket of water over it all and the fire died out, sizzling.

The smell of wet ashes filled the air. Kit and Illiann choked on it, backing away from the billowing smoke. Saylah remained unmoving in the middle of the cloak. Slowly, she picked up the curled and blackened remnants of the stories she had worked so long to collect and transcribe. She was aware of no sound, no smell, no heat, no light, of nothing but darkness and a coldness deep inside.

Julian came running from the fire station, the horse-drawn engine clanging loudly in his wake. He found his family at the back of the house, gathered around the sunroom, stricken and silent.

Illiann explained that the fire had been small and contained and there was no other damage.

Julian sent up a prayer of gratitude. Everyone was safe, and the house would not burn after all. He sent the fire brigade away and looked for his wife to rejoice with her.

Then he saw Saylah kneeling in the soot-stained room with charred fragments of paper in her hands. She was black and sweating, her hair was loose, and he could smell burnt flesh. Illiann came up beside him and whispered, "Her stories. All of them."

Julian could not speak; something had lodged permanently in his throat, cutting off the flow of air, or so it seemed to him. If this were another warning—and what else could it be?—it was his fault. He did not doubt that Barrett was responsible.

He had warned the man to leave Kit alone, but he had not really understood the danger. Now he did. Now that it was too late. What was it he had told Saylah? *I'm not afraid of Robert Barrett.* And she had replied, *Perhaps it would be better if you were.* He always listened to his wife's advice, but that warning he had chosen to ignore.

He knew there was nothing he could say, no comfort he could offer. The work of Saylah's life had been destroyed, and he had not been able to protect her. He had promised once that he would do so, that he would protect her solitude and her past and her magic. That he would never let anyone intrude on the stillness inside her which he valued most of all. But he had failed. He did not have to see her face to know what he would find there.

Saylah did not hear Julian arrive. She heard nothing, except the slow eroding of her faith. She had not ceased to believe when her people turned away from her and doubted her; she had not ceased to believe when her mother or Jamie died, or when she left her People behind. But now, with the ashes of her stories in her hands, she began to doubt. Her past, her dream, her People's history and rituals were nothing more than ashes, carelessly destroyed by a man with a black heart.

She was too numb to take it in. When she finally looked up, there was no anger in her eyes, no blame, just infinite sadness -- and that was the worst accusation of all.

Julian was hit by a physical pain, which he welcomed, because it gave him something to fight against.

Still silent, still apart, Saylah gathered the edges of the cloak, enveloping the remnants of her memory, lifted the bundle and turned to go inside. Her bent head spoke of resignation. Julian realized that, though he hated her anger, it would have been infinitely better than this.

This woman, stained with smoke, burned and battered, clutching the useless bundle in her arms, moved in a world he could not enter, could not even approach, just as she had when they first met, and he had envied and condemned her Salish beliefs, because he coveted so desperately the stillness and wisdom with which they had blessed her.

Where was that blessing now, when she needed it most?

Chapter 129

Keeping a sharp eye on the back door she had snuck out of a few minutes earlier, Laura Hart tackled the rusty lock on a gate at the rear of Miss Chadwick's School for Girls. Rust flaked off on her hands and settled on her once immaculate white blouse, but she did not care. She wiggled and tugged until, at last, the padlock came loose. With a last glance over her shoulder, she pushed the creaking gate open just wide enough to slip through. Once on the other side, she put the lock back in place so it would appear to be untouched.

Laura was on her way to the Ivy's. She had been unusually nervous since the day at the factory, and when Illiann did not show up at school that morning, she had panicked.

The sick feeling in her stomach intensified when she turned onto Crescent Street. She could see that a large, heavy vehicle had made deep ruts in the mud, and wondered if it could be the fire brigade. There was no reason to think they had been to the Ivy house, but she could not resist the urge to run faster.

As Laura came upon the house, she felt it was wrapped in an odd, unpleasant stillness. Desperate now, she leapt up the steps and pulled the bell.

No one came for the longest time. When she was about to give up, Su-ling cracked the door open, opening it wide when she saw who it was.

"Miss Laura, it is good you have come. The family is most upset."

The servant's hair was pulling loose from her long braid, and her hands, arms and face were covered in what looked like soot. Her clothes were wet and stained.

Laura froze for an instant. She had been right; it was a fire. "Where—?"

Su-ling pointed toward the back of the house, and Laura ducked under her arm. Long before she reached the sunroom, she could smell wet ashes and singed fabric. Her chest felt tight with dread.

Everyone was gathered outside, covered in soot, wearing damp and ruined nightclothes.

Illiann looked up and caught a glimpse of her best friend.

"Laura, you shouldn't be here," she cried. "You'll get in trouble. You know your father said —"

Paying no attention, Laura threw her arms around Illiann's neck and squeezed hard. "What happened?"

Leaning briefly against her friend for support, Illiann choked back tears. "Someone set a fire in there. Mama got here in time to put it out, but…." She trailed off.

Laura tried to quell her panic and squeezed next to Kit, who greeted her absently, to look inside the sunroom. The curtains had burned, and the rug, but it did not look like the house itself, or even the structure of the room had been damaged. It could be cleaned and repaired and redecorated so no one would guess what had happened here. Why, then, this grim assemblage hovering outside?

She leaned forward to get a better look and saw several charred pieces of paper floating in a pool of black water at her feet. "What's that?"

Julian stared at her blankly, but gradually he nodded in recognition. "My wife's stories were destroyed."

Laura turned to Illiann in disbelief. "The ones you told me about? The legends?"

She did not require an answer; their faces said enough. With sudden nauseating clarity, she realized this could not have been an accident. Overwhelmed by the smell of leftover fire, by relief that the family was not injured or dead, and by horror at their unspeakable loss, Laura went into the garden and was sick among the winter flowers.

The others looked as if they wanted to follow her example, but they seemed compelled to linger at the sight of Saylah's tragedy. She was nowhere to be seen, yet her spirit permeated the room, the hall, the very air.

Laura took a deep breath and prayed for strength. She could not share their pain, could not even begin to understand it, but perhaps she could wake them from their trancelike grief. Rolling up her sleeves, she went in search of Su-ling. "I need a mop and some cleaner and rags. And we'll need the buckets filled with water."

Within half an hour, she had galvanized the Ivys into mopping and wringing, wiping and rinsing. Su-ling brought hot tea and cinnamon buns, and they nibbled and sipped, sparingly at first, but gradually with more energy. They were grateful to have something useful to do. Most important, they were, with their own hands and the strength of their bodies, destroying the physical signs of the fire, and therefore, the power of whoever had laid and set it to bring them down.

~ * ~

Illiann was so exhausted she could not think. Her muscles ached and she coughed, knowing the others were suffering just as much. Not until she was sweeping up the last scraps of parchment did she realize there simply were not enough, even with the pile in Saylah's doeskin cape.

"Oh!" the girl cried, "I'm such an idiot!"

Everyone but Saylah raised their heads in surprise when she dropped the broom where she stood and raced upstairs, her feet pounding like noisy drums.

She was gone for less than five minutes before she came thundering back down and out to the sunroom, shouting, "Mama, look what I have! I was so upset I completely forgot."

Saylah turned with blank eyes, rigid and unbending, until she saw what her daughter held in her outstretched hands.

Chapter 130

Devon was smoldering. He was trying to paint, but he could not concentrate. He paced around a blank canvas, threatening its purity with a paint-heavy brush. He motioned shapes and textures in the air, leaving the white expanse unmarked. He wanted to paint out his frustration, but did not want to see what that frustration looked like. He had spoken to no one for several days, and now even his brushes would no longer speak for him.

He had moved the portrait of Ellen out of sight, or thought he had, but it kept turning up to stare at him accusingly. He did not want to look into her eyes and remember what he'd last seen there.

Gripping his head in both hands, he forced his fingers back through his sticky hair and cursed helplessly. He could not stand it; he wanted his fury back again. He eyed the whiskey bottle he'd propped on the lip of the easel, then swept it up and took a long swallow. There was only one way to drown out Ellen's voice, and that was to listen to the very demons she said he preferred.

Since he'd first come to Victoria, he had been planning for war against Barrett, but now his army was ready to surrender before a single blow was struck. How had he fallen so quickly from general to unwanted intruder in this campaign? He tried to believe it was from the moment Ellen called him a coward, but he knew that was not true. It had happened because he had pushed his soldiers they did not need to fight, and in doing so, had endangered every one of them. *I don't think you care about the workers. You don't really care about justice, do you? Except for yourself.* Why could he not shut that voice out as effectively as he had shut *her* out? Everywhere he turned, the portrait of her taunted him — an example of what he was capable of, a condemnation of what he had become.

"Damn you, Ellen Ivy. Leave me alone!"

But she wouldn't, because she was right; he was caught in the past, driven to punish Barrett for his sins. He had tried to use the anger of others, but the others were not angry *enough*. Devon was obsessed by a rage so deep and fundamental he could neither ignore nor control it.

You've a silver tongue for sure, Devon Fitzgerald, but I'll not give you my heart to break, Eileen the barmaid had told him what seemed like decade ago. Why should he remember it now? *Neither will I sit home and wait while you shout your anger to the world, and me alone, waitin' for a knock on the door and the police to tell me they've killed you at last.* It was Ellen's fault. If she were here, she would tell him the same. Why did it always come back to Ellen?

He was losing his mind; he could feel his self-control slipping away. Rage was his muse and his destruction. *You came to Victoria to die,* the barmaid had added, *and don't be thinkin' I don't know it.* It wasn't true.

He stabbed the brush into the canvas, but it held, leaving an uneven sphere of red where he ground it in over and over.

Dropping the brush in disgust, he threw back his head and took another drink, wondering if he craved the rough burn of the whiskey down his throat, or the oblivion he might find if he drank enough.

This time the voice was his conscience. 'You're a fool!' it shouted, 'with no purpose an' no future'. A coward, jest like the girl said.'

He had failed his family and Julian and Ellen, and worst of all, himself.

There was only one way to make up for that failure, to convince himself that perhaps there was some small reason for his living.

He would have to kill Barrett himself.

By the time he had finished that bottle and the next, he realized he had silenced Ellen at last.

Chapter 131

When Arthur Hart arrived home, his wife was waiting for him. He could tell she was ready to do battle, but then, so was he. For the first time since Robert Barrett had come to town, Arthur felt strong enough to stand up to him, and that meant being ready to stand up to Agatha.

She stood rigidly beside the rickety chair he loved so much, scrutinizing her husband warily. Her shoulders were tense and her fists clenched, as if she were expecting a blow. "I've been waiting at home all day to speak to you. What have you been doing?"

Arthur took a deep breath. "I went to the bank the other day to ask for a loan with which to buy out Barrett. I just checked again but they haven't yet made a decision."

His wife turned pale. "Exactly when did you intend to tell me you'd taken leave of your senses?"

"I've rediscovered them, more like. Barrett's been the source of our troubles for too long."

Sighing, his wife shook her head impatiently. "You seem to have forgotten that we need his money. We've barely enough of our own as it is. How will you manage to pay a loan as well?"

"He won't be taking his share out of the profits, and, in any case, I suspect he's taking more than he should be. I've thought this through carefully, Agatha. I know what I'm doing. Believe me." He knew it was a mistake as soon as the words were out of his mouth.

"Why should I? Look at all the trouble you've caused, letting Julian Ivy stir up the workers until they went mad and threatened to kill their benefactors, the other owners worried and frightened, our own future in danger. Isn't that enough for you? And let's not forget those horrible boys leading Mr.

Smith through Chinatown and leaving him to the mercy of the Chinese."

Her husband was confused by the leap from their inevitable ruin—as Agatha saw it—and Christopher and Will's misadventure. "I think they were rather brave, actually. Something was niggling at him, but he could not decide what.

"You think this is a game, don't you?"

"No. It's dead serious."

"It certainly is," his wife agreed. "Mr. Smith could've been killed."

"I hardly think that likely." Why did Agatha care, anyway?

"How would you know? You weren't there. The Chinese were all around him like locusts, ready to swarm."

It sounded to Arthur like she *had* been there. He had thought more than once lately that she knew too much, that perhaps someone had been keeping her informed.

For once, his wife sensed the direction of his thoughts. "I've told you, people love to talk, especially about ugly things, and there are too many of those since Julian Ivy came to town. I'm sure someone was bound to do something eventually, and now they have, by setting that fire."

Hart felt a prickle of foreboding on the back of his neck. "You said you were at home all day. How did you know about the fire?"

She decided to take the offensive. "*You* never tell me anything. I had to find out what was going on somehow. If left to yourself, you probably wouldn't even have mentioned the fire in the Ivy's sunroom this morning."

Quite suddenly, he understood. Nausea rose in his throat. "Ivy thought *Barrett* had the children followed, but he didn't, did he? Any more than he hired Smith to set that fire. It was you." He said it flatly, coldly. "Wasn't it, Agatha?" He grabbed her by the shoulders.

His wife knew she was cornered. She sensed the violence building in her usually meek husband, and it actually frightened her. "I'd do anything to protect my family. Do you hear me, Arthur? *Anything!*"

He'd been hoping she would deny it, but she seemed almost proud of herself. "What kind of person *are* you?" He no longer knew. "Julian Ivy has become my friend. How can I ever face him again?" He was not talking to her, but rather to the acrimony holding them apart. "Leave them alone, Agatha, all of them, or I swear, I'll—" He broke off when she winced and he realized he was squeezing her shoulders so tightly that she would have bruises later. He released her abruptly. "What were you thinking?"

"I had to get Ivy's attention," she declared with false bravado.

He could not believe what he was hearing. "And then what? What if Christopher had broken his arm, or worse, his neck? What if the whole house had burned down instead of just the back room? What if the fire had killed someone? That would make you a murderer. Did you consider that?"

Agatha faltered. "That wasn't what I intended. I just meant to frighten the boy, so he'd run home and cry on his papa's shoulder. I didn't know what else to do. I was terrified."

"Did you think, even for an instant, of Laura and me? Of how this might affect your own family?" He knew the answer, but he had to ask.

Her façade was beginning to crumble, and it unsettled him. Always, she had been an unwavering tower of strength. Her sense of propriety, of order and necessity had never even slipped in all the years he had known her. Now, for the first time, he saw the frightened woman she really was.

Agatha wrung her hands. "It was wrong. I know that, but it's too late. What can I do about it now? What do you want me to do?"

She had never before asked for his help; she had demanded, suggested and tried to coerce, but never simply asked. She had struggled to build her protective walls so carefully, and having done so, had believed herself to be invulnerable. What she had really been was desperately alone. He pitied her, but that did not mean he could forgive her.

Agatha realized she was losing control. She had been holding on tightly, trying to keep things from changing; she was so dreadfully frightened of change. But just now, she was more afraid of looking into her husband's eyes than she was of anything else. She could not bear his disgust.

"You'll have to apologize to the Ivys," he said without inflection.

"No!" she cried, and then, quite firmly, "I don't apologize to anyone."

"Perhaps it's time you learned. The Ivys could have you arrested. Don't you realize that?"

"You would never let it happen." She tried to sound confident, but a thread of apprehension crept through. She felt she might be ill on the spot. "They don't even have to know it was me. You won't tell them." Her inflection made it a question.

It was the closest to pleading that she had ever come. Arthur shook his head in defeat, but Agatha did not understand why.

"No, I won't. But you will. And you'll promise them, as well as your daughter, whom you seem to have forgotten altogether, that nothing of the kind will ever happen again." She started to protest, but he shook his head. "I'm not giving you a choice. If you're very lucky, perhaps they won't report you to the police."

Agatha was aghast. Her husband had never spoken to her in such a tone. The expression in his cool blue eyes was implacable, his stance unyielding, his words clipped and precise. She did not doubt that he was serious. "You can't make me do it. The humiliation…."

He didn't blink or flinch or speak, and his silence told her he would not change his mind. She was not going to survive this after all.

A choking noise caught them both off-guard. They looked up to find Laura frozen in the doorway, staring at them in horrified disbelief.

Chapter 132

The waiting, the not knowing, made the Ivys feel on edge. They had heard nothing from the police after their brief visit the morning of the fire. "I didn't really expect to," Julian said in irritation, "but I suppose underneath I was hoping they would find something."

"I do not think such proof exists," Saylah replied. "I do not know that we will ever understand who did it or why."

"I *told* you, Mama. Weren't you listening?"

"Yes, Kit, I was. And I believe the man you saw was Mr. Smith. But I wonder if that matters, in the end? I wonder…." Her eyes clouded over and she gazed across the room at shaped and colored windows she could not make out in the low light. "Though my instincts speak to me, I do not understand what they are saying."

The only thing that brought them pleasure was Illiann's revelation of the secret she had kept so well for many months.

~ * ~

"I wanted to make a more formal set of your legends and stories. That's why I asked for the typewriter," she explained, once her mother recognized she was holding an uneven stack of paper and parchment, and what they meant.

"But how…?" Saylah had asked. "I go to the cabinet often to add to them and read them…."

"But only the right door has been working. The other was stuck for a long time, and then the key was missing." It dangled on its leather thong from her finger. "I've been taking some of the stories upstairs to my room, leaving some so you wouldn't suspect. Then I replaced the ones I'd finished and took others." Illiann smiled because she had managed to do it without her mother—who sensed so much—guessing.

Saylah hugged her daughter tight, ashes and all. "My child, you are a miracle. I thank you from the depths of my soul." She turned to Julian. "I had forgotten the legends I put in my pocket the day the Ashtons came. Those are safe as well."

"So very few are actually lost." Julian sighed with relief and pulled his wife into his arms. "Illiann, I'm so proud of you. To think of such a remarkable gift for your mother to begin with. And now, well, it's astonishing."

"I can only believe that somewhere in her heart she sensed they were in danger." Saylah smiled at her daughter with love and gratitude and the secret knowledge that Illiann, too, was touched with magic. It was a day for miracles after all.

~ * ~

Saylah and Julian had invited Simone and Mathilde to dinner, and Kit, for one, was thrilled. Everyone was prickly and afraid, and it was getting on his nerves. They would have to behave if Julian's mother came. It would be rude not to. He was looking forward to that.

"I know this dinner will be difficult. I don't want to delay."

Illiann could tell he was nervous; he kept glancing toward the door.

"We could use the distraction. We need to remind ourselves that there are those who care about us, and who will be hurt if we turn away."

His daughter could not help thinking he was not referring to Simone.

"Is Laura coming?" Saylah asked. Both Illiann's friend and Devon had been asked to join them.

"She didn't respond. I've been over to see her three times, but she won't come out. It's like she's hiding from me." Devon had not replied either, but she was grateful for that.

Saylah sat beside her daughter on the settee. "Perhaps she is afraid to face you, because you are the only one who knows exactly what she felt that day at the iron works. Perhaps she thinks seeing you will bring those feelings rushing back, and she is not yet strong enough to let that happen."

Illiann looked up doubtfully. "But she was here after the fire. She's the one who made us do something, 'instead of standing around looking mournful'. Her exact words. So it can't be that. Maybe she's angry because she had to work so hard to clean up the mess."

Julian sat on the arm of the settee and rested his hand on her shoulder. "She wanted to be here, sweetheart. I think she was happy to be able to help."

Kit wrinkled his nose in disgust. "Only a girl would be *happy* to clean. It was disgusting. I had to throw out my favorite nightshirt."

Illiann wanted to hug him in reassurance, but she knew he would be embarrassed. Only a *boy* would feel that way, but there it was. "We have to talk about it, Kit. We can't just pretend it never happened."

Kit glared. "We can too. Don't be stupid."

"Illiann is right, my son. I am touched and grateful that you wish to spare me pain, but we have to go on. We are alive and safe, and for now that must be enough for us."

The doorbell rang, effectively putting an end to the conversation, and everyone crowded into the hall.

Mathilde came in, stamping her feet to shake the rainwater free. "Weather's hateful," she announced without preamble. "Has a grudge against us, I swear. Tried to speak to Him about it," she gazed heavenward with a soulful expression, "but, as usual, too busy to listen. Irritating, but then, *He's* not afraid of me."

She was followed by the most beautiful woman Illiann had ever seen. She wore a blue gown overlaid with lace and trimmed with seeded pearls, and her dark hair was piled in curls on her head with ropes of pearls as adornment. She moved so gracefully that Illiann actually looked to see if her feet were touching the ground.

"Mathilde, you've already met my son and my wife. This is my daughter Illiann. *Maman*," Julian had not intended to use the word, but it slipped out, "this is Saylah. Saylah, Illiann, Kit, my mother."

Simone could not take it all in. "Christopher," she said. She had expected Kit to look like his father, but instead he was the image of Jamie. She took the boy's hand and shook it solemnly. He grinned at her with Jamie's smile and she was lost.

She turned to the girl, who was extraordinarily lovely, and looked as if she did not know it. "Illiann. I am so happy to meet you. Mathilde had told me all about you. She is quite good at collecting information." When she kissed the girl's cheek, Illiann leaned closer, drawn by the scent of roses, which she knew so well.

"I've waited a long time," she said. "But I knew you'd come. Mama did too."

In trepidation, for she had heard much about the mystical paragon her son had married, Simone turned to Saylah. Before she could speak, the woman took her hands, murmuring, "You are very welcome. As Illiann says, we have waited a long time. But then, we had your diary to tell us what was in your heart, so I do not feel that we are strangers."

All at once, Simone knew with a certainty she had rarely felt before that everything would be all right. Saylah's voice was as comforting as a healing balm. How had she calmed so many doubts and fears with a single touch? "You are more than kind, but generous as well." She wanted to return a small part of the gift her daughter-in-law had just given her. She turned Saylah's hands palms up. "Is this from the fire? I cannot believe anyone would dare." Her gray-green eyes were solemn. "I wish there was something I could do to help."

"You are here. That is enough."

Resplendent in a burgundy velvet gown that looked incongruous on her stocky figure, Mathilde dug her elbow into Simone's side. "Told you so, you ninny. Just people like any others. Bettin' they're just as curious as you."

Su-ling took Simone's cloak and Mathilde's heavy wool coat. Mathilde watched her suspiciously as she disappeared with them over her arm. "Not goin' far, are you? Chill in the air this evening." She glanced at Julian. "But not, I hope, in here."

"The fire is burning robustly, as you see. I'm sure it will do."

"Do what, I'd like to know?" She gave him a conspiratorial wink.

Illiann stared, though both Kit and Saylah had told her about this odd woman. The servant was such a contrast to her mistress, yet, strangely, they balanced one another.

Simone could not help taking Saylah's hands once more. "You have such kind, intelligent eyes, such wisdom. I can feel it."

"Best stop there or you'll swell her head." Mathilde crinkled her nose critically. "Spend dinner watchin' it float above the table. Not a pretty sight."

"Ignore her," Julian said. "The rain must have knocked her on the head."

"Not deaf, you know, just ugly." Mathilde raised her hand to forestall an argument. "No need to deny it. Looked in a mirror once when I was five. Nearly scared myself to death. Don't think I ever got over the shock."

"Indeed," her mistress said. "I fear it turned your mind, or surely you would not have stayed with me for so many years."

Kit looked from one adult to the other in confusion. Mathilde acted more like a friend than a servant, and Simone clearly enjoyed it. But then, they were both French. That probably explained it. When Julian took his mother's arm and led her into the parlor, Kit tugged on his sister's sleeve to keep her back. "She smells good, doesn't she?" he whispered. "I mean, so does Mama, but it's different. I think she's too pretty to be a grandmother. I don't even think she's really a mother. If Papa says so, I guess we have to believe him, but—"

"Honestly, Kit," Illiann interrupted. "You're terrible." But she was smiling. "Doesn't her voice make you want to cry? It's like she's speaking music."

"Cry? Music?" Kit shook his head in disgust. "You're just being a girl."

Illiann screwed up her face in her best imitation of Miss Reynolds. "I most certainly am not. I am a young lady, and you would do well to remember it."

It was good to have something to laugh about; she had begun to wonder if that would ever happen again. To finally meet the mysterious Simone in the same evening made it especially nice. She only wished Laura was there to share it.

Chapter 133

"Where was Devon tonight?" Saylah asked when everyone had scattered. "I have never known him to turn down a meal cooked by Su-ling. He has practically become a member of the family."

Her expression told Julian she felt more than she was saying. Perhaps she had had a premonition of some kind.

"I am worried for him or about him; I do not know which. I am plagued by misgivings."

"So am I." Julian could not shake a vague sense of anxiety about his friend. "We barely spoke to one another for days before the incident…." He was still troubled by the memory. "And I haven't seen him since. If I know our Devon, this silence doesn't bode well."

"It does not." Saylah was pensive. "I wonder how he feels now that there is no longer an enemy to conquer, now that the workers have found a way to make peace?" She rested her head on Julian's shoulder and he put his arms around her. "Besides, I miss him."

"Yes. As irritating as he can be, his energy and passion are contagious. Though we've certainly had more than enough excitement without him." He stroked his wife's hair and drew her close, though he could not possibly hold her close enough to ease her sorrow. There was so much to fight and so much to fear in their once protected world, that they clung together constantly, whether they were touching or a room or street or blocks apart, as if that would prevent the earth from continuing to shift beneath their feet.

"Go and find him," Saylah murmured. "And when you have, I will be here waiting."

He was inexplicably relieved. Since the fire, he had been afraid every minute that she might disappear, and what sounded like a casual promise was much more than that, because Saylah never lied. Over the years he had come to depend on her honesty as much as he depended on her love and strength of will. "Thank you," he said. "I'll be back as soon as I can."

~ * ~

He went out into the night, checking first at the shop, which was dark and deserted, as he had expected. He looked in at the bar his friend frequented, but Devon was not there. It was easy to tell; there was no redheaded giant with a booming voice dominating the murky rooms. Finally, Julian reached Devon's house, but no one answered the door.

Noticing it was not locked, Julian hesitated, then pushed it open and ventured into the hall. He stopped to listen, trying to pinpoint a sound that led him to the untidy bedroom. A candle burned on the bedside table, partially revealing Devon's body sprawled at an angle across the mattress. He was snoring ferociously, and a bottle of cheap whiskey lay empty in the hollow of his arm.

'As if it were a lover he couldn't bear to let go of,' Julian thought.

The Irishman's hair was matted and his beard ragged; his clothes were grimy, stained by food and liquor and a number of smudges that Julian could not identify. Devon had not bathed, judging from the odor rising from the bed, and had probably not left the house in days.

Julian did not need to be omniscient to understand that his friend was despondent. The careless angle of his body suggested he had stumbled onto the bed without looking, no doubt exceedingly drunk. There were several bottles scattered down the hall and on the bedroom floor, indicating a serious intention to find oblivion in a drunken stupor.

Why did Devon have to be so obstinate? Why hadn't he come to his friend? Julian might have been able to help. But for now, there was nothing he could do. He decided to let the Irishman sleep it off. He would drop by the next day to see if Devon was awake and able to talk coherently. Perhaps Saylah or Illiann would bring some herbs to treat a hangover.

He had turned to go when he noticed light streaming into the otherwise dark hall. Intrigued, Julian followed it to an open door he had not noticed before. He looked in and his mouth fell open. The oil lamps here were large and bright, turned up high to illuminate the canvasses against the white walls, on easels, on the floor. Brushes were gathered on stools and small, waist-high tables, standing in cans of turpentine beside oil and palettes and endless tubes of paint. Everything—tables, cans, brush handles, palettes, the floor—was stained with color.

The canvasses were a revelation. He drew in his breath in admiration and surprise. There were green landscapes touched by mist and racing water, golden ones emblazed and made vivid by the sun, blue and emerald and silver ones of the thundering sea or windblown lakes. There were portraits of people Julian did not know, powerful interpretations that breathed with life and character. No image was static; every painting shouted rather than murmuring, raced rather than standing still.

The paintings spoke with Devon's voice, but through color instead of sound. They revealed the depth of his passion and the need in his soul for the comfort of beauty.

Overwhelmed, Julian did not notice at once that one of the easels had been tipped over, while one was balanced precariously at an unnatural angle. A palette lay face down on the floor near tubes of paint twisted so hard that the color oozed from the wrong end. Several of the paintings had been slashed across or marred by violent streaks of black. And therein lay the other side of Devon's volatile nature—the need to destroy, to explode, to let loose the demons that bedeviled him.

Julian felt sick. The drunken man asleep in the other room was the one who had wreaked havoc on this refuge, tainting the living light with shadows and desolation. It made him want to weep. He had known Devon was in trouble, but never guessed he was in such pain.

Automatically, he reached for the leaning palette to right it. His hand froze above the canvas nearby. For a moment, he did not comprehend what he was seeing — did not want to comprehend. But he could not turn away; he was transfixed. The painting was of Illiann with her Indian drums, whirling through the air as if unattached to the ground. She was alive and passionate and lovely—magnificent in every way. Devon had captured the girl so skillfully that her soul shown from her dark brown eyes.

Revealed on the canvas was the vivid perception and gifted touch of a man consumed by passion, amazement and feverish yearning.

In other words, a man in love.

Chapter 134

"What can we do?" Simone asked the textured wallpaper. Beside her on the settee was a stack of copies of *The Voice* that she had read twice front to back. She now understood why her son was in danger. He seemed to have no fear of other men, just as his father had had none.

"Been doin' some reconnoiterin'," the servant replied to the mantel clock. "Can't prepare for an attack if you don't know the enemy. Father always told me that. 'Know your enemy,' he said. 'The better to get out of his way.' Need a plan. Can't just sit here like toads waitin' for a fly to come along."

The servant plopped down in the wingback chair and put on her most solemn expression. "Been thinkin'. Nearly killed the other day. Too brave by far, our boy."

Simone was awash with the kind of fear she thought she had left behind in Rouen. Now Mathilde was echoing her thoughts. "Do you think his life is still at risk?"

"Don't know. Do know his future depends on whether Barrett's out or in." She had already explained about Hart's request for a loan. "Everyone's waitin' to see what the bank does." She was busily picking the threads from her gown. "Could be our cue," she said, ever so casually. "Have to be blind not to see it."

"Perhaps then I am blind. What are you talking about?"

"Seems to me helpin' Hart'll help your son. Gets the loan, pays off That Man, makes workers happy, saves his family. McC loses power, stops harassin' Julian, who feels he's accomplished something. All falls together nicely."

The whole thing seemed simple and clear, which made Simone suspicious. She could not help noticing how quickly Mathilde had substituted the villain 'deM' with the villain 'McC'. "I do not see how."

Mathilde became preoccupied with the pattern on the carpet, tracing the edge of the flowers with her toe. "Problem is, Hart's not got the capital." She hummed tunelessly, a sign that she was hiding something or avoiding something. Or both.

"Ahem! Well. Yes. Was thinkin', if only we'd some of your mother's jewels, could put 'em in the bank for safekeepin'. Bank wanted to use 'em as collateral for Hart's loan, wouldn't hurt anybody, would it?"

"There are no more jewels." Simone clenched her fists in her lap and waited.

"Might not've told you everything when we left France." Mathilde had not mentioned, for example, that in one of the trunks, she had hidden away a leather satchel, which, while it appeared innocuous on the outside, in fact contained the remainder of the jewels in question. Simone had assumed they'd all been given to the Church, and Mathilde had let her think so. Her mistress had never been rational about those gems, which she'd paid for with her virtue and her faith. Even her mother had only paid gold. Besides, they'd never been de Marchand's to begin with.

"Might be a few left over. Maybe quite a few. Must've forgotten." She continued to trace the flowers in the carpet. She did not dare look up; she could feel her mistress' anger drilling a hole through the back of her skull.

Simone opened her mouth to protest, then thought better of it. "It is something to consider," she said circumspectly.

Mathilde took this for enthusiastic agreement. "Only for your son's sake, to protect his family. No personal gain whatsoever."

For the second time, her mistress thought of objecting; for the second time, she did not do it. "I can see that you have thought long and hard upon this. I am grateful, as always, for your unique kind of wisdom. I thank you, Mathilde. Over the years, you have made my burden considerably lighter."

The servant sniffed uncomfortably. "Prefer derision to gratitude, if you don't mind. Goin' to think you've grown senile. Lock you in a room with a bare mattress and a bread crust, see if I don't." Her eyes were damp, but no doubt that was from the dusty carpet.

"If you were to do so, I suspect you would be bringing me wine and roast chicken within the hour. Cursing a blue streak, I am certain, pretending the stairs were too high and too curved and too worn for your poor feet, in spite of your new boots. You cannot help yourself. You are too soft-hearted to let anyone suffer if you know how to stop it."

"Soft-headed, more like. Same as you."

Simone's eyes were also damp. "I hope so. I should very much like to believe I am like you in even the smallest way."

Chapter 135

"I don't like it," Julian declared. "He's too volatile."

"You do not know that Illiann shares this feeling of Devon's, or if she is even aware of it." Saylah did not question whether Julian was mistaken about the Irishman's passion. His description of the painting alone had convinced her. "Surely we would have noticed." Uncomfortably, she remembered that her daughter had stopped confiding in her after the night of Old Grandmother's stroke, and that she had wondered if something was amiss. But something as important as this? She could only pray to the spirits that she had not been so blind. "I know he is unwise, and not the one we would have chosen for our daughter."

"He's more than unwise. He's tortured and would put her through hell. I won't let it happen. You're going to say we can't protect our children from everything, but I *can* protect her from this. He will bring her nothing but pain. What's more, he's far too old for her. We can't let her make this mistake."

"What mistake?'

"Of falling in love with a dangerous man."

Saylah smiled secretly. "I fell in love with a dangerous man."

"What? Who?" Affronted and confused, Julian frowned fiercely.

"You, my love."

He was taken aback. "I'm not dangerous."

"Oh, but you were in those first years. Angry and hurting and full of helpless rage. Does that sound like someone you knew?"

Staring at her aghast, he gradually relaxed and even half-smiled.

"And for you I was a dangerous woman. Wounded, not trusting, lost in the past. But those feelings disappeared as we grew together."

Julian took her into his arms and kissed her, though his thoughts were still whirling. "Are you saying we should not try to stop this?"

"If we try, we might only push her closer to him. Illiann is stubborn, like her father. And Devon—well, you *know* Devon."

"We could forbid her to see him," he murmured with uncertainty.

"That would not be fair to anyone. Kit loves Devon as well, and you need him at the shop."

Julian shook his head. "I feel so helpless. I can't protect her anymore." Or you, my wife, or Kit, he added silently.

"She knows you love her and want what is best for her, but her heart is her own, and that you cannot save her from, just as you could not save yourself.

"The heart speaks louder than common sense, and when it speaks, Julian, we cannot help but listen. Illiann's heart is very strong. It will not fall silent just because you warn her that it might get broken."

Saylah smiled tenderly. "I will speak to her and we will see if perhaps your daughter's heart is ready to listen to other voices. In the meantime, my husband, it is time for you to recognize that Illiann has become a woman. She might not yet be wise, but she is passionate and proud and tender. And though you ache for her, you must trust her. She deserves your faith."

"She deserves much more than that. She saved my life, even at the risk of her own."

"Oh, Julian!" Rising swiftly, his wife put her arms around his neck. "You do not owe her for that. She did it out of love."

"She was weaker, but she protected me."

"It is *because* she was weaker that the men stayed back. Even in their madness, they knew they could not hurt a young girl, especially not two of them. Illiann was sensitive enough to understand that, and brave enough to take the risk of proving it."

Julian ran his fingers through his hair nervously. "There was nothing I could do for her, not then and not now, to take away that nightmare, to make it cease to haunt her. I just hoped that by keeping her from Devon, I could stop another nightmare from coming true."

Chapter 136

Illiann was sitting in the back garden when Saylah found her, staring at the brown grass, stained here and there with melting snow. She looked dejected, and there were purple smudges beneath her eyes. When she heard her mother coming, she looked up anxiously. "Mama! Are you all right?"

"Ilya, I fear that you are too much like me."

"Really?" the girl said eagerly. "Do you think so?"

Saylah sat beside her on the wooden bench that had begun to peal from the cold and rain. "I meant that you torture yourself too much over things you cannot control. You care fiercely, and that leaves you open and exposed to so much suffering. You need not carry the burdens of others; you have enough of your own to bear."

Saylah had never talked like that before, and her daughter wondered if the lilt of regret in her voice came from her fear and doubts about the fire. Regarding her mother in concern, Illiann took her free hand and examined the burned palm. "You need some more ointment. I'll get the healing bag."

"You see? You have just done it again." She sat back so she could look into Illiann's eyes. "Listen to me, *Ladaila*. I do not want you to do what I have done—to try to be stronger than anyone else; to know, when you look at people, where and how and why they ache; to crawl inside their grief because you know no other way to heal them. It is too difficult and it is not necessary. You will always have compassion, and it will guide you, along with your instincts and your giving heart, but you must not let it control you."

"Mama." Illiann did not know what else to say. "I didn't know you regretted your gift that much. I should have, but I didn't. I'm sorry."

Saylah was appalled. What had she done? She never spoke of her private burdens, except to Julian. "I do not wish you to grieve for me, but only to protect yourself. I chose who I wanted to be, long after my people told me who I must be, and I have been happy. You know that.

"Besides, I came to speak of you, not myself," she insisted, "to tell you that your heart is large, and therefore others can reach it and break it too easily. Especially those who are consumed by their own demons."

Illiann sat up straight. Not only had her mother changed the subject, she had turned it in a dangerous direction. Tension coiled in her belly. "What do you mean?" Or who?

"I think perhaps you have guessed. Your father and I have just realized that you care for Devon more than we imagined. And that he cares for you." Her daughter stared at her blankly. "Julian went looking for him last night. Instead, he found the painting."

Illiann knew immediately which one her mother meant. Her pulse slowed and a dull ache throbbed in her chest. "You don't have to worry," she said sharply. "We don't...he isn't...I don't want to see him again. Not ever."

"I see." Illiann's bitterness revealed the depth of her affection. She would not have been so angry if she did not care. "You have quarreled?" Saylah wondered if that could possibly be why Devon was drinking so heavily, and that made her sick to her stomach. If the feelings between them were this strong already, how could Illiann be saved?

Illiann had to think quickly. She could not tell her mother the truth. She had known this conversation would happen someday, but she had not been prepared for it just now, when she was frantically trying to let go of Devon and the things he made her feel. "He frightens me sometimes, and

I don't like how he acts. I think he only cares about himself."
She compressed her lips into a thin line. "He's angry and
bitter, and so stupid it makes me want to shake him to make
him stop. Except I think he *likes* being angry."

Saylah understood. "When I first met your father, he
clung to his fury and would not let it go. Sometimes I thought
he was fighting to preserve it. But his anger was private. It
almost destroyed him, but *only* him. I fear Devon's is deeper
and more dangerous."

"Was Papa angry with Grandmamma then, too?"

"Yes, and with your grandfather and the earth and me
and the future."

"Like Devon."

"In a way, I suppose. Perhaps that is why Devon and
your father get along so well; each understands the wildness
in the other. But I knew from the beginning that eventually
Julian would awaken from his nightmare."

"You showed him how. I know you did. He told me
once." Illiann sighed. "For a while, I thought I could do that
for Devon. I wanted to make him see there are other ways to
live, ways to be happy, or at least contented."

"I fear Devon will never be that. It is not in his
nature." Saylah rubbed the flaking skin off the edges of her
palm. "You do not merely wish to love him, do you? You
wish to save his soul."

Illiann looked away, fighting back tears that fell
anyway. "I wanted to, but not anymore. I can't, that's all."

Holding out her arms, Saylah drew her daughter
close. " I am sorry, *Ladaila*. I should have guessed before.
Perhaps then I could have saved you from this pain."

"No, you couldn't. I wanted him too much, and he
wanted me." She felt her mother tense and realized what she
must be thinking. "Don't worry. He only kissed me twice."

"And that made you sad?"

"Yes. When we were touching, he seemed to forget
his anger and frustration. And *I* forgot everything."

Saylah's mouth went dry, but she hid her distress with an effort. She understood too well the frustrated yearnings of a young girl's body. "Was there no other time when he let go of the bitterness?" she asked cautiously.

Illiann took her time answering. "Yes, when I first stumbled on his room full of paintings. It was a secret, but he let me in." She turned in Saylah's arms. "Oh, Mama! It was so beautiful. *He* was so beautiful. I've never seen anything like it before, or anything like *him*. It was magic. That was when I knew." She grew pensive. "But now he's destroying those paintings one by one, and they were the very best thing about him. I mean, what he *could* be, you know?"

Her cheeks were streaked with tears, and she gazed at her mother pleadingly. She very much needed someone to understand.

"I know. Once you have seen a man's soul, it hurts beyond bearing when he hides it away, as if he expects you to forget what you have seen, to deny the radiance you know is inside him. It was like that with Julian's father. He was in too much pain to pretend anymore, and he closed his eyes and thought *we* could no longer see the light.

"I fear Devon's eyes are tight closed, and he is battling a darkness which he cannot defeat unless he opens them again." She stroked her daughters thick, long hair, rubbing the shining strands between her fingertips. "I hope that he will, but if he does not, you must not stand in his way. He will not know his enemies from his friends. He may not remember; perhaps he will not even care."

Illiann closed her own eyes to fight off a wave of dizziness. Already he had misjudged his friends, already he had forgotten; already he did not care. Why, then, did she long so much to bring him back, to make him see, to free him from the nightmare he did not wish to escape?

Why did she long so much for him to kiss her one more time?

Chapter 137

Parnell opened the boardroom door and stuck his head inside. "Someone to see you," he announced with a glint in his eye. "May I present Simone Ivy, Madame de Marchand."

Mathilde and Simone had discussed it, and decided to use the Comte's name, because the Board would find it more impressive.

"But who—"

Blanshard broke off when Simone entered the room, head high, graceful hands extended, a charming smile lighting her face. She wore her most expensive gown -- cloth of gold trimmed with sixteen rows of pearls — which she had put on only once before, at Mathilde's insistence, when the servant knew she would encounter de Marchand at a salon in Rouen. Simone hated the dress, but Mathilde had insisted once again. Now that Simone faced the four old men ensconced in their richly comfortable retreat, she knew the servant had been right, as usual.

"Good afternoon, gentlemen. It is so kind of you to see me when I have no invitation. Or perhaps I mean appointment. You will forgive me. I am so confused." She fluttered her eyelashes, letting the words roll off her tongue like honey wrapped in her sweetest French accent. She curtsied with great elegance, extending her hands so the men could see the many rings on her fingers and the bracelet on her wrist. She was sure they had already noticed the ruby pendant at her throat and the bejeweled hummingbird aigrette in her curled and shining hair. "You are not angry with me, I hope?"

"Of course not," Frederick Johnson assured her, fairly certain he was speaking for the others. "Is there something we can do for you?"

Parnell watched from the doorway, smiling whimsically. When he first spoke to Simone, she had been intelligent and concise, certainly not the defenseless and empty-headed female she was portraying now. He did not know why she had revealed her true self to him, but he was glad. It made the old men look all the more ridiculous, eyeing her like a piece of rare and tasty caviar, fairly salivating at the thought of kissing her long white throat.

"Oh, I am so glad, because I need your help. I am sure I do not know what to do." She nodded at Parnell, who set an ornate chest on the table and spilled out the contents.

Even *he* gasped at the pile of tangled jewels that sparkled against the rich mahogany. He had only caught a glimpse when she opened the lid to convince him to allow her to see the Board.

"You see, I have so many, and they are very worrisome. They are also very heavy." She stretched out her hand and turned it so the diamonds and sapphires caught the light. "See how they weigh down my hand. And this," she flicked the pendant casually, "it rubs against my skin and leaves a mark. Look, on my chest, just there." She leaned across the table so her breasts were just visible above her bodice, and lifted the large ruby and pearl ornament to reveal the soft white skin beneath. There was no mark, but the board members did not notice.

"I wish to be rid of them." She stopped and grinned so the dimples appeared in her barely flushed cheeks. "Oh! But not to sell them. That would be foolish, *non*? Money is so common, do you not agree? I would not have you think that I am common *or* foolish."

'Far from it,' Parnell thought with admiration, wondering where on earth she was heading. He suspected the others had not even noticed she had called them all common.

"We'd never do that," Blanshard declared.

"Never!" the other three agreed in unison.

"Now tell us, my dear, what you would have us do."

"*Et voila*! That is easy, is it not? I wish to leave them here where they are safe and I need not worry every minute that they will be stolen. I would no longer have to wear these uncomfortable monstrosities, and my poor hands and throat could have *un petite* rest. I should be very grateful."

"I think we can be of service," Douglas said. "We *are* a bank you know."

"*Oui*. That is why I have come. Oh, but—" She frowned, and her eyes filled with sadness. "I do not know if I can part with them after all."

"Of course you can!" Stephen cried, unwilling, for even a moment, to relinquish the idea of all that wealth lying glittering in the vault.

"Yes, but my father, he told me I must never waste them, that I must use them to help others." She leaned forward again. "He suggested that perhaps my wearing them alone would ease the pain of those who must look at ugliness every day, but I think he was being silly, do you not agree? No, I weary of the responsibility of having them, but I must not let them pine away uselessly in some dark vault."

Stephen narrowed his eyes. Was she reading his mind? He sincerely hoped not, since the jewels on the table were not the only ones he had been admiring.

"My father always said it is good to help the poor, and I have tried so hard to be good." She tapped her foot, chewing on her lower lip. Noticing that the board members were also frowning, she turned to Parnell. "Is there not some use to which my gems can be put while they are here? I will have to leave them for many years, I am afraid."

All at once, Parnell understood. Simone *Ivy*, but no one had noticed that with the other, grander name attached. Could this astonishing woman possibly be Julian Ivy's mother? Now that he looked closer, he could see a strong resemblance. His admiration for her increased tenfold. "I've had a thought." He spoke to her, not the Board. "Suppose we were to promise that your jewelry will become surety for a loan we wish to make?" He wanted to applaud her doubtful expression and wide, innocent eyes.

"I am not certain…this loan of which you speak, it would be for a good cause?"

"It would very much help some workers who are, at present, in dire straights."

"And they are poor? I must know if they are poor. My father says—"

"Just a minute!" Blanshard rose abruptly, pounding his clenched fist on the table. "I am the Chairman of the Board, and you *must* speak to *me*. Mr. Parnell is not authorized to make such a suggestion. It is a foolish one, and one we can not possibly consider."

The others blinked in confusion. A few days earlier, the chairman had been looking for any way he could find to stand surety for Arthur Hart's loan. Yet he had just let his pride cheat him out of a solution so simple, so amenable to everyone, that he might have planned it himself.

"Oh, but *Monsieur* Blanshard! That would break my heart. Do you mean that you do not wish to help the poor?"

She stamped her foot and Parnell had to bend down and wipe a piece of smut from his boot to keep from laughing out loud.

"I do not believe it. Every man wants to be generous and good." Simone stared pensively at the pile of finery, to which she added her rings, bracelet and pendant. "But perhaps I have been impertinent. My father used to tell me always that I was, but I did not believe him. There, you see, if I had, I might not have ruined your lovely plan. Please say you will forgive me, or I shall be very sad and have to take my little nest of jewelry to some other bank in some other city. That would be very arduous for me, *non*? But if I have insulted you, I do not see how else to make amends."

"Well, now, it's not that serious, to be sure." Blanshard assumed his most beneficent expression.

The Johnsons and Douglas exhaled jointly.

"Perhaps, after all, we can work something out, Madame de Marchand. It's true that we have an application for a loan from a man who might benefit from your generosity, but if we agree, you must not speak of it to anyone."

"*Non*! Never, Monsieur. And you will never mention where this surety you speak of came from. That way we will each have the other's secret to keep and all will be well, and my father will be able to rest in peace, and I to sleep again without this terrible line of worry across my brow. That would be lovely, would it not?"

"It would," Blanshard agreed. "Lovely."

Tea was brought in and terms discussed and papers signed as the chairman sat back watching in amusement. Like Parnell, he admired the Frenchwoman's skill and considerable charm. Like Parnell, he had not believed for a minute in her naiveté. He had played along, because he enjoyed a good game now and then, and because the bank would clearly benefit from this transaction. Besides, he had enjoyed Madame de Marchand's performance; it had been worthy of Blanshard himself in better days.

He put his feet up on the table and puffed on his cigar with pleasure. All in all, he thought, it had been a good day's work.

Chapter 138

Kit and Illiann were in their rooms doing schoolwork when the Ivy's doorbell rang that evening. Saylah went to the door, and was astonished to find Agatha and Laura Hart on the porch. She had never met Arthur's wife, and would not have known her, except for the faint hint of Laura in her lips and the shape of her cheekbones.

"Who is it?" Julian came up behind his wife and stopped in surprise. He had been about to reproach her for opening the door when they did not know who was on the other side. The Ivys never used to worry about the arrival of strangers, but things had changed in the past few weeks. He was relieved to see it was only his daughter's friend. "Laura?"

"This is my mother," she said flatly. "She needs to speak to you. Mother, this is Mr. and Mrs. Ivy, the ones who have been so kind to me. They made me feel I had a second home here."

Saylah and Julian were taken aback by her tone. It did not sound at all like the girl they knew. They exchanged a glance and then stepped back. "It is lovely to meet you, Mrs. Hart. Please come in. I will ask Su-ling to bring some tea. Laura, if you like, you can take a cup up to Illiann. I believe she has been missing you."

"No thank you," the girl said grimly. "I'll stay here."

"As you like, of course." Saylah was baffled. It was all very strange and off-putting.

Su-ling appeared, and her mistress asked for tea and digestive biscuits.

"This way." Julian ushered their guest into the parlor while trying to catch Laura's eye, but she kept her head averted, which in itself was very strange.

Agatha Hart stood in the middle of the floor, very stiff and proper in her cardinal red suit and cream blouse. The epaulettes and military buttons on the blouse only made her look more severe. The skirt was narrower than usual, and it seemed to restrict her movement. Her brown hair was pinned carefully atop her head, and she wore a hat with a tiny cardinal in a nest of feathers and tulle. Laura never took her eyes off the woman, who, in turn, never once looked at Laura.

"My husband could not come. He had some business in town," she said, after everyone was seated.

"It doesn't matter," Julian said as warmly as he could. Mrs. Hart did not particularly inspire warmth, and her daughter's chilly glare did not improve the situation. "I hope things are going well for him. Ask him to drop by the shop and let me know."

"I will n—"

"Mother!" The single word was a reprimand. There was no other way to describe it.

Agatha felt ill. She was certain her corset was too tight, and she was wearing her best kid boots, which rubbed blisters on her feet. She smiled bleakly at Julian, who was so perplexed that he hardly knew where to look.

"Is there some particular reason you need to see us?" Saylah asked, hoping to encourage the woman to speak. Laura's behavior was so extraordinary that a sense of foreboding crept over her. It was becoming too familiar. "May we help you in some way?"

Taking a deep breath, which only served to tell her that her stays were indeed too tight, Agatha decided to forge ahead. She could not believe she was actually here in this house, facing a half-breed. Her hair was caught in a loose braid that swung down her back, and she wore a simple forest green wrapper without frills or flowers or ruffles to minimize the tedium. Her feet, appallingly, were bare. She folded her legs beneath her and tucked her skirt over her feet. Agatha had never seen anything like it.

Laura was glad Saylah looked so casual and comfortable; it made the contrast to her mother sharper. That was important to her tonight. She felt almost as ill as she had when she returned home from the ironworks. Her hands were clammy, her forehead damp and her stomach churned, but she had insisted on coming.

"I just wanted to inform you," Agatha stumbled over the word. "To tell you, that is, that I'm sorry for your recent troubles."

"That is kind of you. Others have said the same, and it makes it easier for us to know we have friends." Saylah wondered what made her say it. Mrs. Hart was quite obviously not their friend, but Saylah sensed a darkness in the woman which aroused her compassion. When Su-ling placed the tea tray on the table, it remained there, untouched.

Laura frowned. She was sure this was not what her father had meant his was when he told his wife to apologize.

"I'm sure your children are quite safe now, and your home. I'm certain the villain who endangered them will not be back. Positive, really." She tried to sound sympathetic, but the words came out like the taste of rusty filings on her tongue — harsh and metallic.

Laura choked on her tea. She was incredulous at her mother's obstinate refusal to take any blame upon herself. The girl had to think of a way to *make* it happen.

Saylah and Julian could avoid it no longer; they turned to stare at each other, eyes wide with disbelief. Why was this woman here, where she so obviously did not wish to be? Whatever Mrs. Hart's reasons, they did not believe she had come to reassure them.

"I do not see how you can know that for certain," Saylah said. She wished Agatha *could* explain who had been trying to intimidate the family. She wished it were that easy.

"As you must know, things are still unsettled with the workers." Julian decided it was time to intervene. "As long as Robert Barrett feels threatened, I'm afraid—"

"It has nothing to do with Robert Barrett!" Agatha blurted out, then covered her mouth with her hand. For the first time, she looked uncertain.

The Ivys sat back in astonishment. Mrs. Hart sounded very angry. Saylah's foreboding became a certainty.

"I—" Agatha tried to speak, but her throat was suddenly raw. "It was I—" She coughed. It was too humiliating. She could not bear it.

"Mr. Smith was working for you? Is that what you are trying to say?" That would explain Laura's reticence and her anger, and even her absence form Illiann's life, but it was too horrible to contemplate.

"I'm afraid that is the case." Agatha took refuge in her rigidly familiar mask of propriety. "That is what I came to say."

Laura let out a sigh of relief, but the feeling didn't last long.

Julian exploded from the sofa and stood a few feet away from Agatha, clenching and unclenching his fists. "You threatened my son? Had him followed? You destroyed some of my wife's most precious possessions?"

"Julian," Saylah said quietly but firmly. She knew he was barely keeping himself from striking the woman; she had seen this kind of anger in him before, long ago. "Please."

Her husband took a step back, but continued to seethe.

Agatha actually leaned away from him, and even Laura was afraid of what he might do. She had not considered how the Ivys would react to her mother's confession.

Swinging her bare feet to the floor, Saylah moved in front of Julian, her compelling green eyes fixed on Mrs. Hart. "Why?" Her voice was so soft it was barely audible, yet her bewildered question rang louder than Julian's rage. "I do not understand why."

Even Agatha was caught off guard. Her hostess was not angry or judgmental or disdainful. She was hurt, and the pain was both visible and palpable. Agatha could feel it just as surely as she could her own, and that made her forget, for an instant, about her pride. "Because I was afraid. Your husband…." She looked over Saylah's shoulder. "Mr. Ivy, you're obviously a fearless man, a determined man, a man with a voice to which others listen. My husband admires such men unduly. He has a conscience, you see, and that has always troubled me. In *this* world, good men are a weakness. Good men do not triumph, because they care too much, and that makes them defenseless against men like Robert Barrett. And women like me."

She licked her lips, which had gone dry. "Or so I thought. But you have proven me wrong, haven't you? I can see you are both kind and sensitive and caring. You wouldn't think I'd recognize such qualities, but I do. It helps me to avoid them. I used to think that was the wisest course. Now I see that I was wrong."

There was nothing they could say, so Julian and Saylah remained silent.

"If this is a war, then you are the victors. I've lost my integrity, my pride and my security to you, but that is not the worst. I have lost Laura to your daughter, and to you, Mrs. Ivy, because you offered her warmth when I did not know how to give it, comfort when I could not provide, and love without condition. And my husband I have lost to you, Mr. Ivy, to your idealism and virtue. I wanted to destroy those things or at least frighten you back to your ranch in the wilderness where you could not hurt my family or me. It was stupid and cruel, and though I can't replace what you've lost, I can promise that I know when I've been vanquished. I am surrendering. The war is over."

No one interrupted her. "I was mistaken about everything, it seems, and have been for years. I learned to value success over virtue and manipulation over kindness."

A heavy silence fell. No one seemed able to break its spell.

Finally, Saylah spoke. "Would you change those things if you could, now that you know?"

Agatha looked over at her daughter, tears in her eyes. "If I could, but I fear it is too late."

Saylah followed her gaze. "I do not know if I can forgive you; I do not know if I am that generous." She took Julian's hand, lacing her fingers with his, feeling in the meeting of their skin that his fury had retreated, though it would never disappear altogether. They would both heal; they had each other. Mrs. Hart had no one but herself. "But I will hope, for your sake, that there is still time for you to make amends to your husband and daughter. That is another kind of war. I cannot say whether you will win it, but I do know you will always regret it if you do not even try."

She turned away, and Julian took her in his arms.

Noiselessly, Laura and Agatha left the way they had come. There was nothing else for them to do.

Chapter 139

Old Grandmother waited, watching with her keen black eyes. She had hoped every day that Saylah would come, had lingered often at the crescent of beach where she sat weaving and singing her mysterious song. Today, at last, she had been rewarded. Now that the danger she had smelled in the wind for months had passed, her friend had returned to the beach where she could reach out and hold the sea close to her heart.

The old woman understood. As a child she had wandered freely, and every place had been her home. Now her feet were stiff and she could not walk far, nor did she wish to. This was all she needed—the smell of fir and cedar, the stillness, the sea on the sand, polishing the stones in a hushed whisper. The gentle waves took the small stones and left the large, smoothing them until they reflected sunlight, until hands and feet slid over them, caressing their cool sleekness as Saylah did now.

"You are troubled," the old woman murmured when her friend settled beside her. She sat at her loom, weaving silver hairs into the fabric that gleamed beneath her gnarled hands. The scent of fir and spruce enfolded her, along with the sound of the lapping water. "Tell me," she said.

"Since I was sixteen summers I have written down the legends of our People. Those stories were my connection to my youth, to the People, and the words of all the generations before me. They were nearly destroyed by an enemy of my husband, and I thought them gone forever." She waved her frown away as she added, "But Illiann saved many of them. She was making them more permanent and had them all along. But thinking I had lost them, even for an hour, made me realize how very precious they are. All the lengends and stories of our People are."

Old Grandmother nodded. "It is so. Saylah, my child, the stories and legends do not end. They were not born with you, but long before your parents' parents were conceived, and they will not die with you. They were born of the People and the history and the spirits, and they will go on as long as the spirit of the People burns. You will tell them again and, for it seems that is your yearning as well as your destiny.

"And if your words are dimmed by mist or time, if they are crossed out and made unreadable, even if they are touched again by flame, they will go on. Because they live in here." She leaned over to touch Saylah's head. "And in here." She placed her hand on Saylah's heart. "In all of us."

Smiling, Saylah whispered, "Yes."

The old woman turned, her black eyes bright with challenge. She cleared her throat, choosing her words as carefully as she would tiptoe over a rocky beach, trying to avoid fragments of shells and sharp stones. "From the moment of your birth, you have been set apart, made special, and in some ways, very much alone. Even when you went to live with the Whites, you remained illusive and wise and unlike all the others, because of the voices of your spirit."

When Saylah began to object, the old woman shook her head. "I have not yet finished. I know you often found this separateness a burden, and the Peoples' faith a curse, but I think you are too used to being special, much as you might wish it were not so. I wonder, do you have the strength to be ordinary, no one of consequence, simply human and nothing more? No matter how much you regret the powers with which you were born, they are a part of you, and it will not be easy for She Who Was Once Blessed to live without the reverence and adoration of others."

The crash of the waves grew louder, more imperative in Saylah's head. She felt as if she might be drowning.

Old Grandmother did not pause in the motion of the living loom. "Can you believe that we want you among us, not above us? All we ask of you is your silver voice. As long as you have that, you can tell our stories and preserve them. Perhaps it is time that you learn to accept the help of others in this task. It would comfort the People to help you build upon your house of stories, to absorb those you have already restored. Here the sea will nourish you as you sit on the sand with the drums all around you."

Saylah stared at her hands, not yet healed from the burns. It seemed she must learn this lesson time and again, and time and again forget it. She had been trying to set the world to rights all by herself, and she had never been meant to do such a thing. Yet it was difficult and painful to admit she was an ordinary woman. Old Grandmother was right; she had cherished her magic and the awe it inspired. She had been afraid that without these things, she was not worthy of her family's love, though Julian had told her often she was wrong.

"What is important, *Ladaila* is the people you love, not the words you have written. Words can be rewritten, but the people are unique and will not come again. We here in the village can be, wish to be, your refuge, because we share with you the sense of having lost something precious beyond words -- our place, our home and our heritage. Like you, we are grieving for something irretrievable.

"Perhaps it is time for you to *live*, not relive old dreams and a half-remembered life. Perhaps now you can begin, unbound by memories."

Saylah shook her head, eyes full of tears. "I do not know how."

"You will learn, as you have learned so many other lessons in your life. For in the months to come, we will make you new. This alone I can promise, and it will come to be.

"You have many stories, and here the sea will nourish you as you sit on the beach with your People around you."

Unaware that she was moving, Saylah nodded.

"Perhaps it would be easier to wrap yourself in silence, though it is poor protection from cold and wind and rain, and most of all, from time, which moves beyond you no matter how you try to hold it back? Will you take the easy way?"

"No," Saylah whispered. "I could never do that." A cold wind skittered across the sand, and she shivered at the sudden chill.

"You are welcome here, Samaya. You have always been so."

Shivering at the sound of the familiar name on human lips at last, Saylah looked out over the water, and saw that the sun had burned its way through a bank of clouds to make a trail of gold upon the undulating sea. Had she found her final name on this peaceful curve of shell-scattered sand? "Samaya." She said it once, softly, to feel its whisper against her tongue, and knew that it was real, that it was hers, that she had been waiting for this moment all her life.

She rose and waded out, oblivious of her sodden skirts, and filled her cupped hands with water touched by sparks of cool fire. She waded back, hands dripping, to sprinkle the water on Old Grandmother's bent head. "It is the only gift I have still to give–the light upon the water."

Accepting the gift in silence, the old woman fell silent and allowed the breeze to answer for her. Then she said quietly, " I have for you a single gift, as well, friend of my heart. Since the moment I first dreamed of you, I have woven this cloth, fashioned from the glow of sun and moon upon the streams and rivers, ponds and lakes, and finally, the boundless sea. Now it is nearly complete, and I shall make of it a Robe of Light, and you shall put it about your shoulders and discover that, within its folds, you are sheltered from the darkness and the rain and the sting of your lost memories."

Saylah was speechless, for she had admired the fabric, had felt the power and mystery as it became real. She knew without being told that there was no other like it, and that Old Grandmother had touched a part of her that had lain silent since the night her mother died and she left her native village, releasing her at last–by drawing her close—from the threads with which her People bound her.

Chapter 140

Robert Barrett tapped his walking stick on the frozen ground, peering into the shadows at the far edge of his property. He saw an irregular shape leaning against the high fence and decided it must be Smith. The shape moved, tilting awkwardly from side to side, and he knew he was right. He met the man halfway.

"What is it now?" He did not even try to hide his irritation.

Smith flinched, which only made Barrett angrier. He hated cowards.

"Heard an upsettin' rumor today."

Barrett waited.

Unsettled by the silence, Smith hurried to fill it. "They're sayin' the bank's gonna give Hart the money, and if they do you're gonna take it, abandon the Works, maybe even leave town."

"Are they?" He could not have looked more unconcerned.

"Well? Is it true? I need to know." Smith's voice was hoarse from arguing with the rumormongers who'd been disturbing his sleep the past few nights.

Barrett raised one eyebrow skeptically, though the other man could not see it. "Do you, now? And why is that?"

"'Cause of all I've done to help ya hold on. Why'd ya give up and run away now?"

That was too much. Barrett drew in a sharp breath. "I do not require your help to 'hold on', as you say. I have merely decided that I've gotten all I can from this city. The struggle has become wearisome, and I have grown bored. Especially with you and your constant whining. Besides which, you would do well to remember that I do not give up, ever, and I most certainly do not run away. Any man who says so is a damned fool."

Smith listened but did not really hear. He was beside himself with worry; he knew no one else would hire him in his present condition. Lately, the tide in the city seemed to be turning against his boss, and those who hated Barrett, hated Smith more for doing his dirty work. He did not intend to be abandoned to the rage of those he had persecuted in the past. "Ya can't do it, is all. 'Less you give me enough money to keep me for a good, long while. See, Mr. Barrett, I know things ya wouldn't want ever'body to find out. Hunt you down and hang you, if they did. Don't want that, do ya?"

Barrett was incredulous that a small, worthless man like Smith would dare to threaten him. "I'm not afraid of you. You're little more than a ruffian. I gave you the only importance you've ever had, and you threw it back in my face."

Smith knew he could not let his happen. He'd worked too hard, kept his hands in the muck so Barrett could keep his expensive gloves immaculate. He raised his crutch, pointing it at the other man's chest and leaving himself off balance. "I'm not stupid, you know. I could bring you down. You'd better think about it."

Lips compressed in rage kept tightly under control, Barrett snapped, "That won't be necessary. I've thought about you once too often, and I won't waste another moment." With quiet deliberation, he raised his walking stick and brought it down across Smith's head. With not a little satisfaction, he heard one little gasp of horror and the snap of the man's skull cracking. Smith crumpled to the ground.

Barrett glanced about idly and saw that no one was anywhere near. He would come back later with a wagon and drag the body into the marsh. Everyone hated the man; when they found him, no one would bother much with how he had died.

He leaned down, close to where he could see a dark pool forming in the frozen grass. "You really are rather appallingly stupid." He turned sharply on his heel and strolled away, swinging his walking stick rhythmically from side to side.

Chapter 141

The print shop was humming with activity as Devon folded and stacked the latest issue of *The Voice*, Casey ran advertisement flyers on the main press, Julian set type and a new apprentice worked the press. The place had begun to feel lifeless and stuffy without Devon's, but that afternoon the atmosphere was lighter. Devon was favoring them with an Irish drinking song.

He had finally returned to work, bathed, trimmed and in clean clothes. Though he was still somewhat shaky on his feet, the color was returning to his face, and he'd managed to eat a large breakfast for the first time in a week.

Saylah had been by his house twice in the last couple of days to feed him tea and herbs and biscuits with honey – the only thing he'd been able to stomach. She had not mentioned his drinking, though the empty bottles told their own story. Instead she explained that Julian had gone looking for him and found him unwell. Her husband had asked her to see if she could help.

Devon took heart from this. Surely if Julian suspected the truth about that day at the factory, the last thing he would have done was send his wife to offer comfort. Illiann must have kept his secret. But then, he had known she would, even though he did not deserve her silence. Still, it had taken time for him to work up the nerve to face his partner again. He had taken a risk by stumbling out of bed early, cleaning himself up and returning to the shop, but he had grown weary of his own company. He missed Julian more than he'd expected, but was not certain he could pretend nothing was different between them.

His partner and Casey had greeted him warmly, which only added to his guilt. Though Julian was alive and apparently unharmed, if somewhat thoughtful and distracted, Devon's insides were twisted with nerves. Ellen was right. He refused to allow himself to be happy.

That was another thing. He missed her—too much. True, she was annoying and self-righteous, and he had been determined to send her away, but in the end, she had made the choice. He was intensely aware of the void where her caring used to be. He had pushed her away before, but always she had come back. Except this time he had pushed too hard.

Devon wanted to weep, so he sang.

The shop door flew open, setting the bell dancing wildly. "Mr. Ivy! Julian! I've got it. The bank okayed the loan." Arthur Hart was panting and his face was red from exertion. A trickle of sweat ran down the side of his nose, but he did not care. "I can't imagine what made them change their minds. They were very dour when I first went in, but today they were all smiles and congratulations. I had to tell you first. None of this would have happened without you."

Julian was dumbfounded. "That's…wonderful. Really."

"I don't believe it," Devon exclaimed.

"Neither did I, but it's true." Hart waved a sheaf of papers, nearly losing his grip more than once. "I'll make an announcement at the Works tomorrow." He grinned and began to dance a jig.

Casey went to embrace him warmly. "Congratulations! I know ye've waited a long time."

"Yes, congratulations. I never thought it would happen," Julian added.

Hart stopped dancing. "As I said, it wouldn't have without you." All at once he looked awkward. He lowered his voice. "Could we perhaps speak in private?"

Reluctantly, Julian led the way to his office and closed the door. He suspected he knew what Arthur wanted to say, and it made him uncomfortable. Both men continued to stand.

"Julian, I can't tell you how sorry I am about what my wife has done. I can never make it up to you, but please know that I had no part in it. I would have stopped her if I could. I simply didn't realize—"

"There's no need for all this." Julian was still reeling from the confrontation with Mrs. Hart; he was finding it difficult to accept that anyone, besides a villain like Barrett, could behave so recklessly and spitefully. But he was sure of one thing; it had not been her husband's fault. "I'm serious, Arthur. I can't exactly say that I'm glad to know the truth, but at least now we can stop wondering who and why. At least now we can stop being afraid."

Hart looked deflated and a little desperate. "I can personally assure you that nothing like it will ever happen again, even if I have to lock her up. Naturally, I'll pay for the damage, though Laura told me you can never get what your wife lost back again. I can't imagine what that must feel like, but it makes me ill to think of it. I'm so sorry. All you've done is help me, and it seems all I've done is endanger you. If there's any way I can make it up to you—" He broke off. "There is one thing that might help, if only a little. They're saying Smith has disappeared. They think he left town. I hope it's true."

"So do I." Julian's sigh was heartfelt. He tried not to think of Saylah and her sorrow, because he didn't want Arthur to see his disquiet.

The other man sensed something was wrong, and deci9ded it was time to go. "I really must find Laura. I haven't told her yet."

As they left the office, he raised the papers he had been holding in his now clammy fist. They slid to the floor, making an uneven path for him to follow. He shrugged. "At least this will make my life easier."

"Will it?" Devon was grim. He had long since stopped singing. "Mayhap you're forgettin' something. All the money in the world'll do you no good unless Barrett agrees to sell. The bank may've decided to curb him, but that'll make him furious, and he can no' strike them, so he'll strike at you."

A pall fell over the little group. Devon was probably right.

He did not mention that there was one way to make certain the man never hurt anyone again, and that he himself meant to see to it. Even if he got himself hanged for his trouble.

Chapter 142

"Something is bothering Saylah," Simone announced to the back of Mathilde's bent head.

The servant was seated at a table laid with silver and china and crystal set off by a plump roast chicken, curried potatoes, baby peas and a decanter full of fine burgundy. She was absorbed in appreciating everything to its fullest, although Simone had done her best to spoil the succulent meal. Keeping her head firmly averted, Mathilde took another bite of moist breast meat, followed by a healthy swallow of wine.

"Are you not aware that I am speaking to you on a matter of import?"

"Couldn't help but be, could I? Haven't stopped palaverin' since you got back from the bank the other day. Worryin' about this, worryin' about that, drivin' us both mad, and to top it off, starvin' yourself to a shadow. Whyn't you go for a walk? Air'll do you good. Give me some peace for a change," she added under her breath.

"I am surprised at you. Were you not the one who insisted I become involved in my son's life, in the concerns of his family? Or am I mistaken?"

"Wish you were. Alas, s'all my fault." She risked a peek at her mistress, who had not touched a single platter, and had refused even a cup of wine. "Wouldn't be surprised if you topple right over, weak from hunger."

"I have more important things on my mind than food. I am very worried about Julian's wife."

"Seems more cheerful to me, the last few days. Lighter or something."

"Yes, but now her sorrow is of a different kind. Something has changed. Perhaps her burden has become too heavy."

Obstinately, Mathilde took a forkful of potatoes and swallowed it too fast. She started to choke, but caught herself before she fell off the chair. No point in giving her mistress something else to worry about. "You goin' to carry the sorrow *for* her? Seems like a waste of time, both of you bein' disturbed at the same time." She had chosen the word 'disturbed' intentionally, and took a drink of wine to congratulate herself.

"Might as well, I s'pose. Been carryin' the rest of their problems on your shoulders. Didn't think you could fit any more on there, but then, you always manage to surprise me." She yawned, mouth open wide. She had not gotten much sleep in the past two nights; Simone had kept her awake. She'd never thought she'd miss her tiny room back in Rouen, but she longed for it fiercely at the moment. Her mistress had only followed her there once; here Mathilde could not escape her.

Simone was perfectly serious, and the servant was not being at all helpful, which was unlike her. Leaning over Mathilde's shoulder, she tapped her finger on the nearly empty glass of wine. "Is something wrong? You do not seem to be listening."

"*Not* listenin'. Hearin' you just the same. Curse of my life. Gone on a crusade, that's what. Goin' to starve to death, but not goin' to take me with you." She speared another piece of chicken and popped it in her mouth.

"I only want to help." Her mistress actually sounded hurt.

Mathilde gave up. "Know that, don't I, Madame? Can't do everything yourself, is all I'm sayin'." She backed her chair away from the table with obvious reluctance.

"I think perhaps this is something I *can* do. You see, the look in Saylah's eyes—I know it. Just before I left Jamie, I used to see it in my mirror."

Finally, she had caught Mathilde's attention. "Frightened, you think?"

"More like wounded. I think this time it is she who needs to be healed, and I do not believe Julian or Illiann or Kit know how."

"Do *you*?"

Simone rose, rubbing her arms, though the room was warm. "I know how I have too often dealt with my own sorrow. I ran."

"Think she'll leave?" The servant became unusually dejected.

"I do not know her well enough to guess what she will do. I only know that Jules' heart is once again in danger."

"Maybe our boy knows more than you about politics and such, but a grievin' woman — well, that's your specialty, isn't it?"

"I was hoping I had left all that behind."

Looking up with a lopsided grin, the servant said, "Family's family. Not goin' to change any time soon. Might as well accept it. Boredom's not to be your lot."

"You are right, Mathilde, as always. And I suppose I would not wish it otherwise."

Chapter 143

Devon made his way to the Barrett mansion after dark. This time he did not plan to hide in the bushes or go sneaking around the back. He climbed the impressive steps to the front door and used the doorknocker to express his frustration, knocking it against the base until he caught his finger there and cursed. He had just reached up to start again when the door swung open soundlessly and young Will stood blinking up at him.

The boy was flushed and glanced anxiously over his shoulder twice. He knew Devon was not welcome there, but he was unwilling to send Kit's friend away. He felt in need of a friend himself. His parents had been fighting all week, and he feared that this time, violence was the only thing that would stop them.

From where he stood, Devon could hear raised voices coming from the sitting room directly off the foyer. He was surprised when Will grabbed his hand and pulled him inside, shutting the door as quietly as possible. He motioned for Devon to follow him to the stairwell, from where they could just see Diana and Robert Barrett through the sitting room door. Will had obviously been hiding there for some time. There were biscuit crumbs and crumpled paper and two damp hand prints on the banister.

Devon crouched out of sight. He sensed Will did not want to be alone, and decided it would not hurt to listen for a little. He might learn something useful. Besides, the longer he waited, the tighter his rage and resolution coiled, and the feeling reassured him. He turned his attention to the angry voices in the other room.

~ * ~

"…at what's happening all around us. Victoria used to be a pleasant city, but since you came, especially lately, children have been injured, families threatened, and now a house burned. You don't care who you hurt, do you?"

"I didn't do those things. I told you that."

"No, if I remember, you said, 'How can you believe I would do something like that?' A question, you see, Robert. If you've taught me nothing else, you've taught me that every question has more than one answer. You didn't defend yourself at all."

"You're my wife. I shouldn't have to." His face was dark with anger, his mouth turned down in an ugly scowl.

Sighing, Diana waved his surliness away. "One has to *earn* trust, and the only thing you know how to earn is money and enmity. I don't want you spinning your poison from here anymore."

Barrett was not capable of giving up or in. "I did *not* have Christopher Ivy followed; I did *not* threaten that family; I did *not* try to have the Ivy house burned down. What good would it do me if I did?" He hated having to defend himself; it was beneath him. She really should know better.

Scrutinizing her husband with new interest, Diana said, "That's what I could never understand." She shrugged. "Perhaps you didn't after all, but that doesn't change anything. Think of the many other acts of cruelty, larceny and intimidation you have perpetrated. How many people have you cheated? Possible even murdered? I know Smith has done whatever you asked. What if I found proof?"

Barrett's expression did not change, but all at once his palms were sweaty. Had Diana somehow discovered what he'd done with Smith? Surely not. He'd been careful. Perhaps she was only guessing. He felt lightheaded and had to force himself to concentrate on what she was saying.

"I know there are other transgressions we'll never discover, but don't think for a moment that because they remain in shadow, I won't know they exist." She tapped her finger on her chin. "Perhaps I should ask Devon Fitzgerald. Do you think he'll tell what he knows about the crimes you committed in Ireland?" She regarded him intently. "You must have hurt him pretty badly if he still hates you so much."

"I did what I had to do. I won't apologize for that."

"I doubt if it would take much to convince Fitzgerald to expose you for the fraud and murderer you are."

Barrett blanched. There was that word again. And her oddly piercing gaze that asked a silent question. "He won't say anything. He'll save his own pride first."

"Not when he realizes that everyone in this city, including my father and the Board of Directors, are tired of you playing tyrant. They agree with Devon about that, which gives him more power than you. Did you ever think of that?" She smiled. "I don't suppose you did."

Barrett was beginning to feel desperate. "Please, Diana, stop this. What can I do to convince you that I'm not the man you describe?"

His wife pondered the question for a long while. "I suppose you could accept Hart's offer to buy you out, but refuse to take the money, since you've cheated him out of more than he could ever even guess at. Or at the very least, take the money and leave the man in peace."

"I can't," he snapped. "You know I can't."

"Precisely. I just wanted to see what you'd say. At least you didn't lie about it. It doesn't really matter anyway; I want you out of here as soon as this business at the Works is settled. You can stay in the east wing in the meantime, and you'll have nothing to do with my son or me. Oh, and, when you're gone, I'll tell my friends you abandoned me, that you put your money beneath your arm and ran, because you were afraid of what the workers would do, and Julian Ivy. That in the end, you were nothing more than a coward. And you won't be here to deny it."

He stared at her in horrified admiration. He remembered now what had first attracted him to the widow Diana Blanshard, aside from her money. She was sharp and unrelenting, a formidable adversary who would never allow herself to be taken advantage of. Unfortunately, he had forgotten that in the few years they had been together. And unlike unfortunates like Fitzgerald, she had the social standing and wealth to back her up. He felt sick with fury and desire. He wanted her more now than he ever had, because she had defied him. Perhaps she had even won. She had not accused him outright of getting rid of Smith, but the threat hovered between them like a portent. Still, he could not afford to appear weak. "What do you plan to do with your 'freedom' once you imagine I've gone?"

Diana's face softened, shocking him much more than her vindictive attack.

"Do you know what bothers me the most? That you made Will a stranger in his own house. You made me a widow again, even though you're still alive. I've been a wife twice, but there's one thing I have never been. Though it's nearly too late, I intend to learn how to become a mother to my son."

~ * ~

Crouching uncomfortably in the stairwell, Devon attempted to detach Will's clawing fingers from his arm. The boy was profoundly upset, as much by the fierceness of the voices as he was by what they said. He looked frightened and hopeful and despairing all at once, and his inability to hide those things tugged at Devon's heart. He realized that Robert Barrett's fate mattered a great deal more to this young boy than it did to Devon himself. He did not know why he hadn't thought of that before.

Perhaps because he had not been thinking of others before. *You don't even care about justice, do you? Unless it's*

558

for yourself. He thought he had silenced Ellen's voice. He should have known better. *I never thought I'd see you cowering, hiding in the shadows.* Just as he was now, concealed with a boy who had no way to protect himself, except to listen in on other people's anger. *I used to think you were brave, because you wouldn't back down, but you're not.*

Ellen was right, and so was Diana; he and Barrett were nothing more than cowards, one hiding behind his money, the other behind his hatred. Arthur Hart was the brave one, standing up to his partner, refusing to give in, refusing to abandon hope. Of all of them he was the one who cared most for the workers. He and Julian.

Even Ellen was braver than Devon. Not only had she stood up for her father, but she'd also faced Devon squarely and told him truths he did not wish to hear. *Don't touch me. You're dangerous. You don't care who you hurt.* She could have lied or kept silent, but that had never occurred to her, any more than it had occurred to her to leave her father to the mob that meant to kill him. And what had *he* done? Sneered at her and sent her away. *You aren't listening. You don't trust me. Why can't you do that, just once?*

He had no answer. All he had was a young boy shivering beside him because he did not know what his future would be. Will was truly defenseless; Devon had only believed he was. *'Tis what I've always done: stand back and let people I care about die because I don't know how to save them.*

Barrett's fault, he'd told himself over and over. He'd made himself believe it. *Ruining Barrett won't make you stop hurting. I think you might even know that.*

Was he really any better than the man he claimed had ruined his life? Barrett had wealth, position and power. Devon, it seemed, had nothing. He had thrown it all away. *That's not true. Look around. You know all about capturing beauty with paint.*

It was one last gift from Ellen. He wondered if he was strong enough or wise enough to accept it.

Chapter 144

Saylah dreamed again of the water and the loon and the enticing name Samaya in the wind. She awoke full of expectation laced with a bittersweet ache of sadness. She smiled quietly, tears in her eyes.

She turned to find Julian awake and watching. He had recognized that there was something different about her when she returned from her last visit to Old Grandmother. He knew her well enough to guess that, in escaping from her anxiety and dread over the past few months, she had moved farther away from him. He could not regret that she was happier, but he was terrified of what it meant. Yet he had not asked a single question. She understood what that effort had cost him.

"You have chosen," he said. "I can see it on your face."

His hand lay on the bed between them, reaching for her, yet not reaching. He believed there was nothing to hold onto that was not already beyond his grasp.

"There is no choice to make, my husband." She sat up, confused by the power of her dream, the echo of Samaya in her ears and the look of despair on Julian's face. "I have only learned my new name after many years of searching, waiting, wondering. My dream is no longer a mystery, but a promise."

"Yes, of a new life. Isn't that what a new name means? A new beginning. A sloughing away of what's old and stale and fading?"

Saylah reached for his hand, but he withdrew it. "It is not a denial of the past. You should know I do not wish for such a thing. It simply means that I have begun to understand my place and my time and my worth."

Years ago, in the first month they had known each other, she had spoken of that place, and her voice came back to him now, as clear and confident as it had been then. *I have told you before that the best part of me is Salish, told you also that you did not wish to know this. Yet I cannot wish it otherwise. The Salish songs and prayers run in my head and the beat of their drums fill my ears at night. To forget those things, to hear them no more, would be to die. I am not yet ready to die. I have chosen to survive.*

Julian looked away. "I know with the Salish you find happiness and tranquility. I knew you'd have to return someday."

She moved toward him, but again, he moved away. Resolutely, she backed him against the headboard and put her hands on his shoulders. "Listen to me," she said softly, but with an intensity that stopped his struggle to escape her. "You are right. For a long time, I thought I would have to decide between two worlds—yours or the Salish. For a long time, I thought I could not survive in this city, where there was no justice, and apparently no kindness or forgiving."

Julian shifted uncomfortably, but Saylah did not release him. "I was wrong. You brought integrity, kindness and forgiveness back to life. You fought for what was right and won, without violence, with patience and passion and a sense of what was fair. You asked questions others were afraid to ask.

"And there will be more victories to come, but this first is the most important, because it will give others courage. They will turn to you, and you will help them, because you have found *your* place and *your* strength."

"Are you saying the People need you in the same way you believe I'm needed here?"

"It is *I* who need *them*. Like you, I have found a purpose, one that will preserve the traditions of my people. I do not do this because I must, but because I want to. I am lonely for the singing of waters and the voice of the breeze, the sound of drums rising like thunder to the sky."

She turned, curling herself against his body, head in the hollow of his shoulder, hand on his heart. "Sometimes the truth is simple and beautiful and healing. That is what my dream taught me, along with my new name."

He was losing the battle, and the knowledge was a dull, constant ache in his chest. "I don't want to lose you."

"You will never lose me. I *am* you. Part of me lives and breathes only through you, but sometimes it is not enough."

Julian knew it was true. He would not have been happy if he had stayed on the ranch and forsaken this new life. "You'll come back?"

"I cannot help but do so. To stay away forever would be to remain incomplete—just as I am now without the knowledge of what my life would have been if I were not born Tanu."

He could not argue with so plain a truth. "I know the Salish can give you a kind of freedom you never had with us. You've been a mother all your life, in one way or another." He took her face in his hands and ran his thumb along her cheek. "Go, my wife, and make yourself a childhood."

Chapter 145

The sound of pebbles hitting the window roused Illiann from the paper she was writing for school. Miss Reynolds had given the girls the topic—HOW THE CITY OF VICTORIA IS MOVING TOWARD THE FUTURE. She had written it that way on the board, all in capitals, and Illiann had instinctively glanced at Laura to roll her eyes. But Laura had her head down, as she always did these days.

Another barrage of pebbles struck, making Illiann sit up eagerly. "Maybe that's Laura now," she said out loud. Disentangling herself from a sheaf of paper, she pushed the typewriter back and hurried to the window.

Laura was not trying to get her attention. It was Devon. The smile forming on her face stiffened with the rest of her body. He waved at her, pointing to the back of the house, but she did not respond. She couldn't. She had not expected to see him, and was shocked by the hollow feeling in her stomach and the harshness of her breath. Somehow she had to make him go.

Just then he raised his hands, arms spread wide—in confusion? In annoyance? In surrender?—turned and loped away, ducking behind the bushes of honeysuckle, then the dogwood and maple trees. So no one from the house could see him, Illiann realized. What did he want? Why had he dared? How could he take the risk of coming here after what had passed between them?

She waited for a long time, staring at the break in the bushes where he'd disappeared until her breathing calmed and the questions in her head stopped spinning. Finally, drawn by a curiosity more powerful than caution, she slipped downstairs and through the ruined sunroom. She had some trouble opening the newly built and bolted back door Julian had installed after the fire, but she was determined and forced the bolt aside after several attempts.

Once outside, she stopped to make certain Devon was really gone. Her palms were damp with sweat, and her chest ached when she crept toward the spot where he had stood. At last she saw something leaning against the gardening bench below her window. It was wrapped in coarse brown paper, but she knew at once it was a painting. Kneeling beside it, she reached out, hands trembling. She thought he had burned them all. Before she tore the wrapping paper, she took the note he had attached and opened it.

My Dearest Illiann,

I want you to have this gift to prove I didn't destroy it, and because you once said you loved it. I want you to know I care about you very much. I see now you were right about so many things.

I'm sorry, my dear. So very, very sorry for everything. Though I know 'tis not enough.

Love,

Devon

P.S. I ~~was~~ am wrong.

She read it several times, but was not quite certain whether to believe it. A spark of anger burned in her throat, because she knew how easy betrayal was for Devon. Still, this did not sound like betrayal. "Stop it, Illiann," she said to herself. "You can't believe him. It isn't safe or wise."

As if of their own accord, her hands reached for the parcel once again. She could not resist. Tearing the wrapping down from the top, she gasped at the painting of vibrant meadow and distant mountain, of stream and a wall made of stone in the foreground. The vivid washes of color blended sky to grass to fern-covered bank, yet each was distinct from the other. Illiann felt, as she had when she first saw it, that she could walk through the meadow and climb the stone wall with the gurgling of the stream in her ears.

Breathless, she sat back and read the note again. Though she hesitated, she was beginning to believe Devon was sincere. Because he had not burned every painting, every piece of his artistic soul, as she had feared. Because he'd remembered how she felt about this painting, and had risked it being shown to the world by giving it to her. Because he could not have chosen a finer or more touching gift. Because he had apologized and admitted he was wrong: something she never expected. And most important of all, she realized only in that instant because, finally, he had stopped pretending she was someone else and called her by her true name.

Chapter 146

Later that morning, Saylah was seated on the floor, bare feet crossed in front of her, singing the words and cadence that had haunted her since dawn. A noise from the end of the oak bedstead made her look up to find her daughter watching.

"It's been a long time since you sang an Indian prayer. It's beautiful." Illiann's eyes were damp; they shimmered from green to brown as she moved closer. "You've been dreaming again, haven't you, Mama?" The girl knew because, last night, she had dreamed her own dream, and though it had escaped her, she had heard once more the warning of the Indian drums. When she awoke, she understood at last. She was losing her mother.

She crouched down to touch the sacred stones spread out on the rug, picking up the most beautiful—dark green on the bottom, with a piece of fern caught inside a clear, rippled surface that transformed it into an island pond.

To be so close to Saylah, suspecting what she did, was harder than anything she had ever done. Harder, even, than turning her back on Devon. And now she was not sure she could keep it turned. She had planned what to say, but the words were sharp and painful in her throat. "I dreamed of such a pond," she murmured. "And a voice begging me to come."

"Old Grandmother," Saylah whispered. Her cheeks were flushed.

"I know you've often heard her too. I know you feel the need to answer." She said it simply, as if every morning she followed the voices in her dreams, as if her body were not covered with chills from head to toe. As if she and her mother often talked of parting.

"I know what you are asking without words, and the answer is yes. I am going to join her for a time. I know too that this is not easy for you, and yet I ask for your good wishes. I shall carry them with me in my healing bag so they are always near."

Illiann fought back tears, and Saylah was overwhelmed by a wave of mourning for the girl's sake, for the loss of her childhood and her mother both at once. It would not be forever, but when one was fifteen that was hard to understand. She looked at the stone in her daughter's cupped palm. "That one is the most precious. It is the one that started me on the journey to your father."

Illiann rubbed the smooth surface, trying to feel the texture of the fern, but it was too deeply buried. She sighed. "Papa did what he thought was right, even though it was dangerous." She pressed the stone to her cheek. "You too, Mama. You must do what you think is right. At least for you there isn't any danger."

"Long ago I told you there is danger," Saylah reminded her daughter, "but it is of another kind."

Illiann did not wish to consider the different kinds of danger. She set the green stone among the others, running her fingertips over them in a light caress. "I will miss you." She frowned. "It won't ever be the same between us, will it?"

Saylah took her daughter's chin in her hand. "Not the same, my Illiann, but better."

Illiann buried her head in her mother's lap and wept.

Chapter 147

"It's done! He took the offer!" Arthur Hart lifted his daughter off her feet and spun her in a circle.

Laura could hardly believe it. All morning, she had studiously avoided imagining what was happening at her father's meeting with Barrett. "You're free?"

"*We're* free. Finally." He could not begin to contain his excitement.

"I'm so proud of you, Papa."

"Thank you, my dear. Your faith in me means a great deal." He took her shoulders and regarded her solemnly. "Even though you haven't said so, I know you've been worried about how we're going to make the payments on the loan until the Works gets back on its feet." He released her with a bemused smile. "And really, it was the most extraordinary thing, but when I asked about it, the Board of Directors sort of waved me off, as if it were an inconsequential matter. Not even worried about the surety I never produced. I didn't like to ask too many questions, fearing they might change their minds, but I did think it important at least to mention my concerns." He scratched his head. "Try though I might, however, I couldn't make them fret. I did my best, you understand, but I suppose I shall simply have to accept it. I have no other recourse."

Laura smiled half way, and looked beyond him to the misted light through the lace under curtains. "Are you going to tell Mama?"

Arthur's smiled disappeared. Hands buried in his pockets, he fought the dull pain that curled inside him every time he thought of Agatha. "I suppose I must. She has a right to know her future won't be crumbling to dust any time soon." He wished she could have believed it without feeling compelled to take the matter into her own hands. He wished she had had just a little faith. He was surprised that it still hurt so much. He had thought himself numb and had welcomed the lack of feeling.

"Don't worry, Papa. We'll be all right." Laura kissed his cheek.

"You're being very good about this."

Laura shook her head. "Not to her. I've tried to be kind, but it's so hard."

"You're trying," her father replied. "That's what matters. Your anger might even fade in time."

His daughter looked doubtful.

"If you find it in your heart to speak softly to her now and then, that will be enough for now. What I don't want is for you to try to take care of her as she should rightfully have been taking care of you all these years. You're older than you should be already." He gazed at her steadily.

"The only thing that's kept you young the past few months is your friendship with Illiann. Don't let your mother spoil that as well. Don't you think it's been long enough?"

Shaking her head back and forth, back and forth, Laura whispered, "I don't know if *ever* will be long enough."

Chapter 148

Kit caught Illiann coming out of their parent's bedroom. Several times recently he had caught his sister staring off into space. He could not guess what she was thinking, and it bothered him. Not that he'd always known exactly what was in her mind; she *was* a girl after all. But she had been unusually quiet, and he felt she might not hear him if he spoke to her or asked a question. And he had an important question to ask.

Though the light was dim in the hallway, he could see that her eyes were red and puffy. She was trying to sneak away, but wasn't doing a very good job. On the ranch, she had moved silently, gracefully, barely disturbing the air around her. She must have grown rusty in the city. Kit shook his head in disappointment. Poor Illiann. He himself had only gotten better at skulking without being noticed. Which reminded him of Will. He had not seen his friend in a long time. Perhaps now that Smith had disappeared, he would be allowed to go out again, unencumbered. His heart raced at the idea.

But his sister was getting away. He followed her to her bedroom door. "What're you doing?"

Illiann jumped. She had been lost in her thoughts and had not heard him approach. That would never have happened before they came to the city. Anyway, she could not talk about what she was doing, which was grieving. "Nothing. Go away."

Her brother put his hands on his hips and scowled. "I'm *talking* to you."

Illiann was startled by his anger. "What's the matter?"

"That's what *I* want to know. Something's happening to Mama, isn't it?"

Retreating into her room, his sister tried to think of an answer that would satisfy him, but she couldn't. "She's dreaming again, that's all."

"So?"

Her brother was persistent, and she knew how hard it was to distract him when he got like this. He felt left out, and she couldn't blame him, but neither could she enlighten him. She didn't want to be the one to break his heart. That was their parents' job.

"You were just in there. I saw you. What happened?"

"We talked. It doesn't matter."

The boy refused to be deterred. "What about?"

Illiann sighed. "About the sea and the wind and smooth round stones," she said obscurely.

"And about the Indians?"

She was surprised he had guessed that much. He had never felt the pull of the Salish culture as she had, had probably never guessed how profoundly Saylah felt about her past. But she had to tell him something. "We talked about the First Salmon ceremony, and the dances at festivals, and how Mama learned to heal from her People."

"*We're* her people!" Kit declared. "Why doesn't she know that?"

"Oh, Kit! She does. You know she does. But we're different from the Salish who raised her. You and Papa and I are still the most important people in her life. You have to believe that."

"Why should I?"

Illiann wanted to cry in sympathy with her brother's angry confusion. "Because it's true."

"But how do you *know*?"

His sister had no idea how to answer. She couldn't explain an instinctive certainty, an emotional tie which, while strong and binding, was nevertheless invisible. Kit was a photographer. He didn't understand what he couldn't see. "I just do. I know our mother. I don't know how to make you understand; you just have to trust her, and me." It was woefully inadequate, and she knew it. "You always have before."

"Before," he said ominously, "things were different. Our father didn't hide from his mother; Mama didn't cry over little bits of paper; you didn't sneak out to see Devon, and our family didn't creep around behind closed doors keeping their secrets. Everything's changed, hasn't it?"

She could hardly deny it. But how did her little brother know about Devon? She had to force the question to the back of her mind. Illiann spread her hands in a gesture of defeat.

"Yeah," he said. "That's what I thought."

Helplessly, Illiann watched him disappear into the shadows, which seemed to swallow him so completely that she wondered if he might be lost.

Chapter 149

Through the fog that shrouded the shoreline, Illiann could hear the muted thunder of the ocean. Balancing herself with her arms straight out at her sides, she walked the stone wall above the cliff. She was lonely and bewildered, and hoped that visiting the spot where she and Laura used to meet would make her feel better. But it didn't.

"Illiann? Is that you?"

She raised her head, tilting it like a curious bird, and peered into the fog. "Laura?" Jumping off the wall to the well-worn path beside it, she retraced her steps and collided with her friend. The breath was knocked out of them, and they bent over, gasping.

When she could speak, Illiann took Laura's shoulders. "I'm so sorry."

"Don't be silly. I'm the one who came to apologize. You don't have anything to be sorry *for*." Laura was glad that the mist obscured her expression. She was almost ready to look her friend in the face, but not quite.

"About your mother," Illiann explained. "Mama says you're upset, and I just wanted to tell you I'm sorry. I mean, if you stayed away this long because you thought…." She trailed off, having no idea what she intended to say. She was just talking to fill the protracted silence between them.

"That's absurd." Laura sounded irritated, but secretly, she was relieved. "I just felt so bad. I'm so sorry, Illiann. I know what my mother did is unforgivable, and I couldn't even look at you, because I felt so guilty."

Illiann was honestly confused. "The thing is, your *mother* did it, not you. Why should you feel guilty?"

Grasping her friend's hand, Laura slid down until they both sat at the base of the wall. "If your mother had done it, wouldn't *you* feel bad?"

Illiann considered, imagining what such a betrayal would feel like. Saylah conspiring to hurt so many people so much? Even though it was not real, the thought made her feel ill. "I'd want to hide in my room until everyone forgot."

"Which is exactly what I did until today. But when I found out about Papa's loan, I knew I had to come. To apologize and to thank you."

"For what?"

"We wouldn't have gotten it without your father's help. Everyone knows that." Laura regarded her friend in silence. "Don't *you*?"

Illiann was at a loss. "Papa didn't do anything about getting the bank to give your father the money. He wanted to, but he didn't know how."

"Really?" Laura bit her lip and tried to think. "Huh." She twirled the end of her braid between her fingers. "So if it wasn't your father, I wonder what made old Blanshard change his mind?"

"I don't know. I'm not sure I even care. Just as long as it *did* happen, and you stop hiding in your room. I've missed you, and so have Mama and Papa. Even Kit, but don't tell him I said so." Illiann paused, then turned to put her hand on her friend's shoulder. "How are you? I mean really?"

Laura hunched over to rest her head on her knees. "I don't know. Mostly, my whole life is like this day." She indicated the fog that billowed around them. "Like I'm wrapped in tulle or something, and nothing's really real. Or maybe I just don't want it to be. Mama's trying to make it up to Papa and me. Sometimes it makes me sick to my stomach because I'm so angry, and sometimes I just feel sorry for her. I don't know what's going to happen, and it's scary. She was always so strong, and it made me mad a lot, but seeing her like this is just plain scary. But you wouldn't understand. Your mother's so…so Saylah."

Illiann understood completely. She had always depended on Saylah's wisdom and serenity, but since the fire, and everything that had happened, uncertainty had overshadowed her mother's strength. She swallowed dryly and finally said the words she had been avoiding. "My mother's sad a lot lately, and now that she knows we're safe," she paused to shore up her crumbling composure, "she's going away."

Laura stared at her, incredulous. "I don't believe it." But she did. She could feel her friend's misery as acutely as she felt her own. "Why didn't you say so before?"

Shivering as the mist settled on her skin in a damp chill, Illiann whispered, "I couldn't. I didn't want to cry." It was too late for that; tears spilled down her cheeks and settled in the hollow of her throat. "I can't at home because I don't want to make her feel bad. She's going to join her People and gather more legends, so I should be happy. But it hurts, and I can see it's hurting Papa too. But I can't be angry with her, can I? That wouldn't be fair."

Laura knew a thing or two about that kind of anguish, though she'd only learned in the past week. "It doesn't matter if it's fair. It's what you feel, and you should *feel* it, not pretend it isn't there. Wouldn't your mother tell you that, even now, if you asked her?"

Though her tears continued to fall, Illiann gave a faint smile. "Yes," she said. "I guess she would."

Chapter 150

Evening had fallen, enveloping the world in mist, softening the harsh edges of the day and whispering enticingly of the night to come, when Kit approached Julian solemnly. If Illiann wouldn't tell him the truth, then his father would have to. "Something's wrong with Mama and you look pretty sad. Lily won't even talk to me. I don't like it."

The boy was trembling, and Julian realized that while Kit had appeared calm lately, he was more shaken than he had let on. He was, suddenly, the helpless child who used to come to his father, asking him to make everything all right.

He knew he had to reassure his son, no matter how wretched he himself felt. He had told Saylah to go; he knew it was something she had to do, but that didn't mean he was happy. It broke his heart that he could not heal her, that she had to turn elsewhere for comfort. But that was not for Kit to know. Quietly and calmly, he explained to Kit about Saylah and the legends, her tie to the Salish and her desire to join them.

Kit was incredulous. "She wants to *leave* us?" He did not pretend to hide his hurt.

Julian drew his son close until he stood between his father's knees and could look directly into his eyes. "No, Kit. She wants to be with us always, except for a while. You see, though she doesn't speak of it, it has been difficult for your mother to move to the city and give up her freedom to roam as she liked, to discover so many people who wanted to harm us. She grew up in a wilderness, and the ranch was not the same kind of freedom, but it was close enough to feed her spirit.

"Now she must re-write some of the stories and gather others, and she needs to stay with the Salish for a while to do that."

"Like a holiday?" Kit asked doubtfully. "But I don't understand. Why does Mama need a holiday from *us*?"

"I know this is hard, but I want you to understand that we aren't the only ones who need her."

"Perhaps I can help?"

Simone stood on the threshold, enwrapped in the hush of breath withheld that seemed always to drift about her. She had heard her grandson's question and his father's answer, and had waited until Julian paused. Her heart fluttered in her chest, and she prayed that this risk would not shatter the fragile concord she had established with her son.

Julian nodded. In that moment, he was grateful for her presence, for the soothing whisper of her skirts and the quiet grace with which she moved. "Come join us."

Simone sat down and took Kit's hands gently. "I do not know your mother well, but I do know she loves every one of you so much that sometimes she cannot contain it. I have seen it on her face, in her lovely eyes, in her manner when any of you enter a room. Kit, *ma petite*, she loves and needs you as much as you love and need her."

"Then why does she have to go away?"

"Do you think it is possible that when you grow up you will want to go away to college, or to study in exotic places as your Uncle Theron does?"

The boy relaxed only enough to answer briefly, "Maybe. But that's different."

Tilting her head as though considering this, Simone regarded her grandson seriously. "Not so very different. Your mother needs to study these legends, to write them down so others can one day hear the voices of her people. They are depending on her. It is not easy for Saylah to make the choice to fulfill that obligation, any more than it will be for you when you decide to leave home."

Kit rubbed his chin between thumb and forefinger, as he had seen his father do. "You think so?" His gaze was earnest.

"I do. And I think you can make it easier for her if you wish to."

He still looked uncertain. "Maybe."

Julian was impressed that Simone had taken the time to find out so much about Saylah, and he was not quite certain what to say.

Just then, Illiann called to him from upstairs, and Kit seemed relieved. "Have to go."

"All right," Julian murmured, "but, Kit? Will you think about it?"

"I'll try," he called over his shoulder as he ran from the room. At the last minute, he turned back. "Goodnight, Grandmamma."

Julian had never heard that name on his children's lips, and the sound of it made his eyes sting. That caught him off guard.

For a moment, mother and son sat in silence, but before it could become awkward, Simone turned. "I know you do not wish to hear what I think, for which I cannot blame you. But nevertheless, I must say it. Let her go, Julian, with your blessing.

"She will come back, just as she promised. She is not me, my son. She carries no burden of guilt, and is neither weak nor afraid. She cannot stay away from you; it is not in her nature. Whatever you think of me, you must see that, you must know it in your heart."

Julian was less shocked by what she said than by the realization that he had unknowingly been comparing the two women for some time, blaming his wife for keeping the wound his mother created always fresh. But Simone was right; they were not the same. Saylah would never desert him. She kept no secrets from him and shared her mysteries freely. She had told him why she was going. In fact, he had guessed it might happen from the moment she met Old Grandmother. Always, she had been honest, and he could not repay that gift by pretending he did not understand.

As for his mother, he knew that just a few days before she would not have dared point out to him a truth which he should have understood without her help. She had not judged him for his blindness, merely tried kindly to open his eyes. And she had been gentle with Kit, tender and sensitive to his doubts and fears, just as she used to be with Julian. Saylah had tried to tell him that, and Mathilde. He'd listened, but he hadn't really heard, or simply hadn't *believed*.

He had refused, in order to stop himself from being hurt again, and had convinced himself that he was being strong. He had been determined not to forgive, and thereby give Simone power over him once more.

He rested his hand on hers, looked into her gray eyes flecked with green, and it came to him that here was no need to forgive her.

He had already done so.

Chapter 151

Saylah sat back on the clifftop with the wind in her hair. Below the waves pounded the gold-tinted rock, marking out yet another ridge into the layers of water battered stone. "You will be busier than ever, my love. And though both Illiann and Kit have worlds and projects of their own, I would like to know there is someone at home for them." She leaned her head into the sound and scent of the sea.

"I've been considering that," Julian said. "*Maman* has been by nearly every day, and both Kit and Illiann adore her *and* Mathilde. Perhaps they could move to the house. I'm sure they'd be more comfortable there than at Nellie Howard's. And we have plenty of room." He turned to his wife. "Would you mind? To my surprise, my mother is very good with the children, and Mathilde amuses them endlessly."

Saylah could tell he had been practicing the speech, and the knowledge made her smile. "It is what I hoped you would say. I have been so pleased at the children have made friends with your mother and Mathilde."

She looked up at him, a shimmer and a sadness in her moss-green eyes, and as always, he could not resist her. Since she had made her choice, she had begun to wear her hair loose, and her doeskin slippers lay beside her so she could run her toes through the thick green grass. She never wore shoes in the house, but went barefoot all the time, though it was still winter and the floors were cold. That freedom and her secret smile had given her an air of mystery, as she'd had when he met her. He caught his breath. She was so beautiful, now that she was going, and he wanted her so much.

"I want you too, always," Saylah whispered. So he leaned through the wind and the ocean-heavy air, and kissed her long and tenderly.

Chapter 152

Everyone had heard the rumors; Barrett was leaving town. Devon was restless and unable to stay still. He had tried to keep occupied by repairing the canvasses he had damaged, but the work had not silenced the sense of foreboding in the back of his mind. In spite of himself, the inspiration that had eluded him for so long burned bright, and he had begun a new painting, unlike anything he had done before. Though he worked on it obsessively, he did not look at the canvas closely. He was nervous and excited and did not want to be disappointed. He wished he could show it to Illiann. He knew she would tell him the truth. But he had not heard from her since he left her the note and the gift. He tried not to think about that, but failed miserably.

After the night when he overheard the argument between Barrett and his wife, Devon had sworn he would not return to the mansion. There was no reason except to torture himself. But he didn't quite believe it. He no longer craved justice or revenge, but something more intangible. When he realized the last daub of color he had smeared on his palette was too dry for the brush to lift, he knew he could not help himself. Covering his new painting with damp cheesecloth, he closed the door of his sanctum, grabbed his overcoat and hat and went out into the night.

He made his way automatically, finding a spot beneath the trees halfway up the drive where he hovered, watching the front door, not knowing what he was waiting for. As his eyes adjusted to the dark, he noticed several trunks stacked on the porch. Too many bags for a business trip, even an extended one. So it was true. Barrett was going to leave a richer man by far than when he came, and he would not have to pay the debt he owed to those he had wronged.

Devon knew then he should not have come. He wondered what Illiann would say if she knew he was here. The old weakness had invaded his limbs, though she would have called it strength. He no longer wondered who was right. Then he saw the silhouette of Diana Barrett in the doorway. Young Will stood beside her.

The crunch of wheels over pebbles distracted him, and he turned to see a hansom cab roll up. He realized Barrett had been on the porch all along, hidden in the shadows. The man shuffled about uncertainly, something Devon had never seen him do, then reached out to his wife, who extended her hand politely. Barrett stared at it, tried to get closer, perhaps even to give her a kiss, but she stepped back ever so slightly.

"Diana, I just want…." He trailed off, another thing Devon had never seen before. "Won't you even wish me well?"

"I wish you peace, but you don't wish it for yourself, so I fear you will never find it. That saddens me, Robert. So all I can do is bid you goodbye."

Devon could not move, and soon it would be too late. He was, after all, the worst kind of coward, but, again, Illiann would have called him brave for his restraint.

It seemed to take forever for the coachman to load the bags, but Barrett stood in the drive until the last second, looking back at Diana and her son. They raised their hands in farewell, but it was a stilted gesture. Finally, Barrett turned away, and just before he stepped into the cab, he straightened, raising his head and throwing his shoulders back. He seemed to have decided he would not go in defeat.

Devon thought of lunging for the man, but his body seemed to be frozen. He watched in silence as the cab rolled down the drive in the direction of the harbor.

Chapter 153

Kit never dreamed, but that night his sleep was invaded by the scent of pine and the soft tickle of a feather across his cheek. Brow furrowed, he woke to find his mother sitting on the bed watching him. Her expression was so tender, her eyes so full of love that he was embarrassed, and he squirmed under her unfaltering gaze. She put her cool hand on his forehead.

"Do not worry yourself, my son. I did not wish to frighten you. But I have missed you, and I want to talk with you for a while."

He was wary, regarding her suspiciously through narrowed eyes. He did not know what to expect from her anymore.

Saylah sensed his mood and sat patiently, humming one of his favorite tunes. Kit could not fight the contentment that came over him at the touch of her hand, which was always magic, and the sound of her voice, pitched low because it was the middle of the night. He felt certain she would wait forever if he wanted her to, and he smiled.

"I have made a surprise," she whispered. "Get your robe and I will show you."

Her son did not hesitate, but followed her as, finger to her lips, she made a show of creeping soundlessly past the rooms where the others slept, then down the stairs. At the bottom, she took his hand, and though he was too old for such gestures in the daytime, he found he did not mind in the middle of the night.

"So, we have arrived," Saylah said as she opened the swinging kitchen door.

Kit stopped on the threshold, staring in awe. He had expected the gloom of the low-burning fire, banked for the night, the chill of the deserted room, the immaculate countertops of which Su-ling was so proud. Instead, the fire burned high and merrily, warming the room with a golden light. The countertops were strewn with canisters of flour and salt and sugar and cinnamon, and a tray of stuffed buns, clearly just out of the oven, sat in the middle of the table. It was set with a cloth, patterned napkins, knives and butter, and a pot of hot chocolate steamed beside two large mugs.

Saylah stood beside him, hand on his shoulder, looking around as if she had never seen such a sight before. "This must be our secret, Kit, or Illiann and your father will be jealous."

He grinned up at her. "They won't. You're making that up." Then he grew solemn. "But if you want, I won't tell. I like secrets anyway." He had also forgotten that a few days before, he had hated secrets, because no one ever told him any.

His mother pulled out a chair and he saw that she had put one of her woven cushions on it, the fern design he liked so much. Saylah made much of settling him comfortably and pouring him a mug of hot chocolate, and of choosing the fattest bun to put on his plate. He watched, transfixed, as she moved gracefully about, her loose hair brushing his shoulder now and then.

Finally, she pulled out her own chair and sat buttering the second fattest bun. Kit had noticed that often adults made treats of buns and cakes and candies, set two places at the table, and then did not eat anything. It made him feel uncomfortable, but his mother understood; she did not like to eat alone either.

Saylah took a bite from the warm bun, catching with her tongue the sticky string of cinnamon and honey that unwound from the bread. "Now," she said, "tell me, have you seen your friend Will lately?"

Kit launched into a description of the last time they had worked together in the darkroom, and how Will had helped with the fixing and drying of the prints. He sighed and pressed together with his fingertip the last few sweet crumbs. "But that was too long ago. I miss him, Mama."

Saylah leaned toward him conspiratorially. "That is another reason I have brought you here tonight. To celebrate your newfound freedom. I believe it is safe now for you to go to school and the shop and the park on your own, just as you used to do, though I want you to promise to be careful. I would consider it a special favor if you would take Lord Byron with you, but that is your choice. And you must invite Will for dinner tomorrow."

The boy kicked back his chair and flung his arms around her. "Thank you, Mama."

"It is not me you should thank, but your father, and I suspect, your grandmamma."

"What do you mean?"

She put her arm around his waist. "I will tell you, but it is a very important secret. You must never tell another soul, not even Will, and especially not your Papa. Do you promise?"

He nodded eagerly.

"Well then, I think—I do not know for certain, but I think—that somehow your grandmamma convinced the Board of Directors at the bank to give Mr. Hart the loan he wanted. And once that was settled, the danger passed. Mr. Barrett has gone."

Kit wrinkled his forehead in thought. "But if you don't know for sure—"

"Ah, my son, you have forgotten. Sometimes I know things I cannot know, mysterious things, wonderful things."

"You mean like magic?"

"It is a sort of magic, yes. But remember, I have only confided in you. You must protect our secret very carefully."

He smiled in delight and gratitude. Somehow his mother had made him feel they were the only two people left in the world. They sat together on the hearth, with the firelight on their faces, and she told him stories about other kinds of magic. He was captivated, luxuriating in her warmth and attention.

When he began to feel drowsy, Saylah knew it at once, and she guided him back up the stairs while he struggled to keep his eyes open. When he had crawled into bed, she drew the covers up to his chin and leaned down to kiss him.

"Remember, my son, it will always be like this between us. Nothing can change that, ever."

Before Saylah could whisper 'goodnight', he was asleep.

Chapter 154

Illiann ran her fingertips over the note in her pocket as if she could read it by touch. She did not have to see the words; she knew them backward and forward.

Dear Illiann,

I haven't heard from you, but am hoping you haven't given up on me altogether. I know you think I didn't listen when you talked, but you're wrong, me darlin'. I heard every word straight into me heart. I want to redeem meself for the pain I caused you and your father and others. If you believe me at all— and even if you don't—I'm askin' you to meet me one more time. I'm trying very hard not to be angry, and that's because of you. Please come. I will not hurt you. Not ever again.

Love,

Devon

"Don't promise me something you're not sure you can do," she muttered as she paused outside the print shop. He was supposed to be waiting inside. In the beginning she was not certain she would respond to his message, let alone meet him. Except she had his first attempt, and the painting hanging in her room. Even her mother had been moved by it, and her father had hugged her and smiled while she paced, trying to decide. Illiann felt compelled to read the neatly-written note again and again, until Devon's obvious sincerity wore her down. So here she was, coat buttoned against the bitter cold, muffler wrapped tightly around her neck, trying to stay on course as gusts of wind buffeted her from side to side. The sky overhead was gray-blue, drifted with a veil of clouds that dimmed its true color.

Hands buried in her pockets, Illiann waited for a glimpse of Devon. Except for Casey, who had the Fairhaven press in pieces on the floor, the shop appeared empty and eerily silent. Heart racing, feeling numbed by the cold and her own trepidation, she stayed where she was, irresolute yet expectant—anxious yet hopeful and eager.

Looking over his shoulder, Casey could not help but grin. "Why are ye after hidin' back there? What are you afraid of?"

Devon, tall and imposing in his finest blue shirt and black trousers, was incensed, though he hovered in Julian's office, where he could not be seen from the street. "I'm no' afraid—" He swallowed the rest of the sentence. "Now that's a lie. I was after bein' afraid she would no' come. I was afraid I'd no' see her again."

"Well, I'm thinkin', with her standin' out in the cold, and you hidin' back there, you'll not accomplish anything, me boyo."

In spite of his pride, Devon managed to laugh. "Right you are. 'Twould be a shame, that."

Casey nodded wisely as his friend sprinted past.

Devon unlocked the door and motioned for Illiann to come inside. She hesitated a moment longer, then met him on the threshold. He quickly secured the door behind her.

"You came," he said unnecessarily, at the same time she asked, "Are you afraid I'll run away?"

That brought Devon up short. "Don't be daft."

They faced each other warily. Illiann could see that he had changed. his eyes sparkled with a new light, one she had not seen before, but one more dangerous than the other, because it moved her. It heated her skin like a lamp held too close to her face. Though the warmth raced from her lips to places inside where she'd never felt it before. How could that be? He wasn't even speaking.

She was acutely aware of how close he stood, of the tension in his body. His arm was still extended toward the latch behind her, and when he drew it forward, his hand brushed her sleeve. Even through her heavy coat she felt the slight touch, and it made her shiver as the biting wind had not.

Devon shook himself awake. They could not stand there forever, held apart by inches and air. "Your father said it was all right if we met here." He turned and led the way into the shop.

"Where is he?" She followed him to her father's empty office.

Devon turned to face her with the cluttered desk between them, though she could feel his regret at the physical distance. "He went to do some errands. Said he'd no' want to hover. But he would no' leave us alone, either. 'Tis why Casey's here."

Illiann glanced at Casey, who was ostentatiously busy with the press he was repairing. He kept his back turned and tried his best to pretend the other two were not there. It was kind of him, she thought, to give them as much privacy as he could. "But I don't understand. Why would Papa agree to let me see you at all? He was so upset when he saw the painting you did of my dance." She felt like she was in the sea up to her waist, treading water until the next wave crashed around her, forcing her to move.

Devon recognized the waiting in her eyes. "Aye, well, things've changed since then." He reached across the desk to tilt her chin with his fingertips. "So many, many things, Illiann." He wondered if she knew how she smiled when he said her name. That smile sent a lick of flame through his body that threatened to defeat him before he began. He wondered if she knew that too. Sucking in a huge breath, Devon prayed it would douse the flame.

"I've apologized twice now," he said, "and I'm doin' it again, though I know it'll never be enough. I can't undo what I did before, but I can start over, my lovely, my dear." Sliding his fingertips along her jaw, he traced the line of her cheekbone slowly, enticingly.

Illiann leaned toward him without being aware of it. The light touch of his fingers was more alluring than a long, hot, fierce kiss would have been. She looked into his face and wanted to feel his scratchy beard against her cheek, the tickle of his mustache on her lips, and the strength of his arms holding her close. She was ashamed and moved out of his reach.

"There are things I have to tell you," he said, feeling the chill of her absence. "Important things. I need you...no, that isn't right...I *want* you to listen."

He was so serious. It was not like him.

"Please, Illiann. I'm askin'."

He had taken the first step, and the second, and now the third. The least she could do was listen.

"Knowin' you has changed me, lass. I've no' met anyone stronger or more courageous than you. And none near so lovely."

Illiann sighed. Was he lying again? "Wait," she cried.

"Please let me say this," Devon insisted, "or you'll never know. I admire you because you tell the truth and don't play about or pretend. You're passionate and perceptive. You made me think, though I was no' wantin' to. Made me want to be better. No' many people have the power to do that."

His praise made her uncomfortable, though it also thrilled her.

"Once Barrett left the city, I found without him to hate, my life was odd and empty. Except for the memory of you. 'Twas that kept me goin'. I painted you over and over, and you were always with me, even though I thought I'd lost you."

"I know." Even in the midst of her astonishment at the reality of her grandmother, the shock over Agatha Hart's betrayal, the hurt at her mother's loss and impending departure, Devon had always hovered somewhere just out of sight. She had known he was beyond her reach, but that did not make her wish to reach him any less.

He took a step closer. Her eyes were soft and damp and her smile so tender it hurt him. A wave of affection washed over him, different from what he'd felt before—not only of his body, but of his mind and heart.

"You were right about me bein' afraid to care about Ireland. Afraid to go home. But I'm no' fearin' it anymore. 'Tis what you wanted, is it no'? For me to face my past instead of runnin' from it?" He took a deep breath. "So I'm goin' back."

Illiann went cold, though she had been perspiring under her coat a moment earlier. "Oh, I see…." She felt so ill that she became dizzy and her hands shook. "Of course…that's what I wanted. I…always hoped you would." Despite her determination tears filled her eyes.

"Don't be weepin' now, lass. I can't imagine goin' without you. I want you to come wi' me." He did not touch her, though he wanted to with all he was.

Shaking her head in confusion, Illiann frowned. Her heart began to pound so hard she had to struggle to breathe. "You want—" she stumbled over the words. "I couldn't. I can't. I'm too young. Besides, my mother's leaving. I need to stay at home."

"I know," Devon said, unable to suppress his smile. "That's why I'll be after waitin' for you."

"Waiting?" she asked skeptically.

"Aye, for as long as it takes. It'll be years, and I'll be stayin' right here in Victoria, courtin' you all that time, so you won't be after changin' your mind."

"Courting me?" She was stunned and overcome with tingling excitement both at once.

"Just so, *mo chride*. That is, if you'll have me. I wasn't after wantin' your father to tell you we'd talked. I asked him to wait. I wanted to be the one."

"You *are* the one," she murmured, before she could stop herself.

Illiann thought he would laugh or grin or say something ridiculous. Instead he reached across the desk and leaned forward to kiss her.

She met his lips willingly, her own opening as he brushed them lightly with his tongue, then harder, then traced her jaw with kisses until her reached the shell of her ear. "I've found a new home after all," he said into it.

The word 'home', the tender tone of his voice, pierced her deeply and brought tears brimming to her eyes, but she fought to keep them back.

"It came to me, by and by, that the worst thing I'd done in my whole life was to give Barrett the power to keep me away from the place I love most on this earth. You're right; his leavin' no' stopped the pain, but sometimes, for hours in a row, paintin' does, because I'm creatin' something instead of destroyin', and it scares me half to death."

Chills ran up Illiann's arms. She could feel his excitement and impatience, and for the first time, those things did not frighten her. What frightened her was the beguiling gleam in his dark eyes, his tentative smile, the energy he exuded. She was fascinated by his long red lashes, his flushed and freckled face, his lips surrounded by the curling hair of his red beard. She had forgotten how attractive he was. How was that possible? He spoke, and she knew it only because her gaze was fixed on his parted lips, which began to move.

She wanted nothing more than to be back in his studio with his paintings all around them, and the incandescence in his smoky eyes calling.

He must have read her thoughts, because the composure that had been keeping him apart from her, safely on the far side of the desk, deserted him. He leaned forward, ever so slightly, and their gazes locked. They stared at each other, yearning and lost. The tension was palpable, and the thread that connected them strong, though if either had pulled back just then, it would have snapped. If either moved forward, it would draw tight, binding them in the web of their own desire. So they stepped beyond the desk and moved toward one another.

The moment was far more perilous than when they'd fought and tried to hurt each other. It was full of promise and unspoken invitation. They had forgotten how that felt. Eventually, the tension was too great to bear, and Devon brushed his lips over hers, then kissed her. She kissed him back leisurely, her lips warm and soft, just long enough to leave them both breathless. They parted, but did not go far. All they could hear was the hushed sound of their own heartbeats.

Devon guessed she would not be the one to pull away. Straightening with a pain that tore through him and left him raw, he closed his eyes and took a step back. "We can't do this, Illiann." Again that irresistible smile. "Not yet," he added in a whisper. "I promised Julian I'd never hurt you again."

"But you can't promise a thing like that," she whispered back. "You don't know what will happen in the future. No one does."

"I know I'll try, and not only because of the promise. But because I love you."

She parted her lips but no sound came—only the memory of the Salish drums. Not until that instant did she realize what she should have known all along. "I love you too."

They smiled broadly at each other, even knowing they could not know what was to come. Because they had made each other a promise.

"That's why I brought you a gift." A canvas covered in cheesecloth was propped against the desk. "The other you discovered on your own, but this one I want you to see with me here to watch your face."

He glanced over her shoulder to see that Casey was very busy keeping to himself. More gently than he had ever touched her before, he cupped her face in the palms of his hands. "I thank you, Illiann Ivy, for bein' unafraid of who you are."

Slowly, with infinite tenderness, he brushed his lips across hers in the whisper of a caress. She could hear his soft breathing and the beat of his heart in the sudden stillness, and the ache inside, the need, the pleasure grew deeper, but she didn't say a word.

Devon took a deep breath, tracing her eyebrows, her lips, her forehead with his fingertips. He put his hands lightly on her shoulders; she put her hands lightly on his, holding them apart as he leaned down to kiss her. Their lips met softly, warmly, and they dropped their hands until they met palm to palm and their fingers intertwined. They moved closer, their bodies still not touching, but so close there was only a breath between them. Teasing a single lock of her hair that had come loose around his finger, he smiled and turned to present her with the painting.

This time he had done a self-portrait. It was rough around the edges, the colors swirling and blending into one another, the brush strokes strong and glowing. Illiann could feel the energy in the image, the inspiration that had driven him to paint it. The portrait was animated, captivating, compelling. Just like Devon himself.

She looked more closely and caught a glimpse of something in his eyes. Her own face, golden skin and large brown eyes partially covered by her long, black hair. It reminded her of something, but she could not remember what. Then it came to her. The portrait of himself and Deirdre that had been turned to the wall. Devon's face reflected in the mirror had disappeared into Deirdre's. They had been fused. One did not exist without the other.

In this portrait, Illiann was separate, herself, yet part of him still, because of what he saw outside himself.

She smiled at what she understood at last was still to come, and waited for the joy and the pressure in her chest to allow her to take a breath, and the pulse of her blood to begin again.

Chapter 155

"Whew!" Will sank back against the trunk of the cedar around which his tree house was built. "I didn't think we'd ever get to come here again. But we're safe now. My stepfather's gone." He could not hide his relief.

"But why would he leave? He's richer than anyone now. Devon said he could run the whole city if he wanted to."

Will frowned. "I don't think he could. I guess a lot of people hate him as much as I do. Maybe they don't want him to run the city. And anyway, that's not why he went." He paused for dramatic affect. "My mother sent him away."

Kit nodded wisely. "Because of what he did to us."

Will considered thoughtfully. "Partly. But it was more than that. I guess she wasn't as happy as I thought. So it's really because of my mother that we're safe now."

Saylah had said it was because of Kit's father and grandmamma. He hit the heel of his hand against his head to try and shake the muddle clear.

"My mama's changed, Kit. I think I like it." Will was caught up in his own thoughts, and did not realize his friend was unusually quiet. "The thing is, I won't be able to spend as much time with you anymore. Since my stepfather's gone, I have to take care of her." The tenderness in his voice was unmistakable.

"You do? But why? Isn't *she* supposed to take care of *you*?"

"Doesn't matter. She needs me. She's forlorn, even though she says she's not. And I know what that feels like. I don't want her to be lonely like I was."

"She left you alone and ignored you for a long time. Why do you have to change for her?" He was not being cruel; he was only trying to understand. It was important, and not just to Will.

His friend shrugged. "Sure she ignored me. But that was before."

For some reason, Kit felt ashamed of his doubts. "My mother's leaving us," he blurted out.

Will stared at him, wide-eyed. "Are you sure?" It was a stupid question, but the only one he could think of.

"Of course I'm sure."

"I thought she was happy, and she's sure not lonely, like my mother. So why is she doing it?"

It was the exact question Kit had been trying to answer for himself. "She says she wants to live with the Indians for a while and write down their stories."

"But you don't believe her?" Will was confused and didn't know how to comfort his friend, though he wanted to. Desperately.

"I do, but...I don't know. I just don't understand."

"Are you mad at her? You sound mad."

"Papa and Grandmamma say I shouldn't be, but sometimes I can't help it." Sunk in gloom, he tried to concentrate on the magic night Saylah had given him, but instead of making him smile, it made him want to cry.

Brow furrowed, Will pondered his friend's miserable fate and his own inadequacy. Surely there was someone who could make Kit feel better. "Hey!" he said, "Why don't you ask your sister?"

Kit's frown only deepened. "I don't want to talk to Illiann."

Will was startled by his friend's vehemence. He thought Illiann had been wonderful helping them with their injuries, not lecturing them about being foolish, as his mother would have done, and not betraying them to her parents. If he had a sister, he would want her to be just like Kit's. "Why not?"

Kit thrust out his jaw stubbornly. "Because she's keeping secrets."

Will was even more confused. "But so are you." Unless he'd finally told his parents the whole truth abut the afternoon in Chinatown.

Shifting uncomfortably, the other boy shook his head. "But not from her." He thought about the things his mother had told him. "Well, at least not many."

"You would have, though, that day, if she'd let you."

Kit glared and said nothing.

"Well, *would* you have told her about Baldhead if she hadn't made you?"

"No, I guess not."

"Then maybe *you* need to make *her*," Will suggested practically.

"She thinks I'm too dumb to notice how different she's acting. Or she doesn't trust me, 'cause I'm only a kid." He had trusted Illiann with everything, and now she was shutting him out.

"Grown-ups do strange things, you know. They always have secrets."

Kit refused to be mollified. "She's not a grown-up. She's my *sister*."

Staring at his feet for inspiration, Will found only pine needles and dust and flecks of mud. Kit had an answer for everything, and he seemed determined to be sullen. "I don't know," he said. "Maybe you should twist her arm behind her back and *make* her tell."

The other boy looked at him in alarm. "I don't want to hurt her. She's already sad. I think that's what the secret's about."

Scratching his head with two fingers, Will exhaled impatiently. "I don't get it. You want to be sad *with* her?"

Kit stared at his friend, unblinking. "That sounds pretty dumb, doesn't it?"

At that point, Will decided it would be wiser not to answer.

Kit rested his head on his bent knees. "Maybe I'll let her have her secret all alone." He made it sound like a magnanimous gesture, a gift of kindness from the bottom of his young, compassionate heart.

"Yeah," Will said. "Okay then." He was infinitely relieved that the thorny problem had been settled.

Chapter 156

Saylah stood beside the bed, running her fingers over her sacred stones: the fern preserved in water, the white feather in shiny black, the pink streaked with gray (*I have many sacred stones*, she had told Julian when she found it on a day they forgot their troubles and learned to be happy together, *but none found in the midst of laughter*). There were many others, and she touched each one reverently.

She was surprised that she should feel the same fine-spun thread of connection she had felt with Simone when she first ran her fingers over the parchment pages of her diary. A thread of shared pain and a blurred but vital memory. Julian's half-brother Theron, only five at the time, had asked anxiously if it was all right for him to handle the book which had been hidden away in a chest for so many years, if he had been right to share the secret with her. Saylah had replied, *Now someone else will know it is safe, someone who values it as much as you do. Simone would like that, I think. To know that someone still smells her scent with pleasure, wonders about her, touches her things with reverence. I would like to know, if I had left my home and my family behind, that they took out my treasures sometimes and touched them and remembered me. It would make me happy, even if I were far way.*

The memory was so vibrant it might have been yesterday, but it had been many years ago, before she understood her feelings for Julian or what having a family would mean to her. Saylah was leaving the stones in the house on Crescent Street, not because she no longer needed them, but because she thought, or perhaps hoped, her family might.

She picked up the green stone with the fern caught at its heart. It felt lighter than she remembered, as if time had worn away some of the burdens she had carried when she found it. This one was special: *It started me on the journey that led me to your father*, she had told Illiann. The journey that had taught her wisdom and forgiveness and loss, and, finally, joy. A lump rose in her throat and her vision blurred with unshed tears. Kissing the cool surface lightly, she placed the stone in the center of her husband's pillow.

Years earlier, before she became a woman, she had left another stone for the friend and brother of her childhood. He had been little more than a boy, though he had lived the hell of many men. But for him, the stone had been a sign that their parting was forever.

To Julian this was a vow, a promise that she would return.

The night before, long after they should have been asleep, Saylah and her husband laid awake in each other's arms.

"Are you sure this will heal you?" Julian had murmured, so softly that the words had nearly been lost in the linen pillowcase.

I have always gone to the woods and the water to find my peace, she had told him years before. *Does it always help?* he had asked. Her answer had been soft but firm. *For some kinds of sorrow there is no relief. You know that, Julian Ivy, as well and as deeply as I do.* She knew he was remembering that moment, though she could not say how she knew it. "I am certain that my sadness and the weight inside me will be lifted, for the sea cannot help but wash away such infinitesimal feelings. I am certain that the songs of prayer and celebration will return to me."

There had been other songs, which had lost their melodies in the demands and disappointments of her People. In an instant, she was back in the blustery day of cold and unforgiving wind when Julian had demanded that she let him make her happy. *I do not deserve happiness,* she had told him, *because I am not enough. I have never been enough.* He had stared at her, incredulous. *Did you think you were a god with the power to ease all suffering? I do not need a shaman who makes miracles. All I need—no, all I want—is that you be Saylah and that you love me.* She had tried to resist, because, more than anything, she had feared what he made her feel; he had stripped her of her defenses by stripping himself of his own. *I am Saylah*, she had told him at last, putting her hand in his. *And I love you.*

"I don't know if I can do this," he said.

"You are, and always have been, stronger than you think. It is part of why I love you. It is why I will never go far or forever from your arms. Once, you made me see that I was a woman, a human, not a queen, and that it was enough for you. For both of us. You have made me happy, Julian, and for all my life before you, that was the one thing I could never be. If I have made you happy too, if you believe in me, in us, then you will find the strength to let me go. But not just now."

He kissed her so hard and so long that both were shaking when he raised his head, and then, slowly, lingeringly, they made love. When they curled into each other, spent, he undid her long black braid and slid his fingers through the shimmering strands, lit by the light of a single candle. They lay silent and unmoving as he combed out her hair until it fell around them, dark and gleaming, like a soft cloak to protect them from the night, and even more, the coming light of morning.

~ * ~

"Kit! Open the door."

The boy sat on his bed, feet straight out in front of him, arms crossed over his chest. Even the sound of his father's plaintive voice did not budge him.

There was a long, tense silence, and then Julian said firmly, "If you don't open it at once, I'll break the lock, Christopher. It won't ever work again. I won't have it repaired. I know you're upset, but you will not disobey me like this. Do you hear?"

Kit chewed his lip nervously. He had thought if he locked them out, they would go away, leaving him to his private grief. But his father was more determined than the boy realized. Even today of all days, that tone in his voice had the power to make Kit tremble. He slid off the bed and shuffled over to the door, just as the knob began to shake again. He tried to turn the lock but could not make his fingers work. He fumbled with it several times. "Wait!" he called when he heard Julian curse under his breath.

Opening the door just far enough to peer out, the boy glanced up and down the hall. "Is she with you? Are you trying to trick me?" He did not want to see his mother.

"I don't make it a practice to trick my children, as you well know." Julian squeezed around the door, closing it behind him. Saylah had tried to speak to their son several times, but he kept the door locked against her. As far as Julian knew, the boy had never locked his door before. He had refused even to acknowledge that his mother was in the hall. Julian did not need to see the devastated look in Saylah's eyes to know he had to try to get through to the boy any way he could.

In spite of himself, the pallor of his son's face touched him. Kit's eyes seemed over-large in his face, and his lip was torn where he had obviously been biting it repeatedly. He understood exactly how Kit felt.

He went to the oak rocker and sat down, motioning for his son to follow. Reluctantly, Kit stood beside him. Julian touched the boy's shoulder gently. "I know you're hurting, son, but I want you to listen to me. It's more important than you can understand just now." He paused. "Many years ago, my mother went away. It was very sudden, and she went in secret and didn't tell me why she was going, at least, not in a way I understood."

"It's not the same!"

"No, in many ways it's not. Your mother has explained. I have explained. She is not creeping away in the night, leaving us bewildered and abandoned.

Kit shook his head, but Julian ignored him.

"I refused to say goodbye to my mother, and I realize now that I never ceased to regret it, even to this day. Her leaving was a betrayal in a way your mother's could never be, and yet I wish I could take back that moment when she tried to kiss me and I turned away."

"But it *is* a betrayal! We're not enough for her! She doesn't love us at all."

Julian's eyes were dry, but he blinked rapidly, as if they were full. "You know that's not true. Saylah loves you so much that this…what you're doing today is tearing her apart. You don't know that yet, because you haven't looked into her eyes or felt her arms around you. If you had, you wouldn't be able to hide from her." He paused. "Or perhaps you want to hurt her, but I can see what hurting her has done to you."

Kit kept his gaze stubbornly lowered.

Shaking his head, Julian lifted his son's chin with one finger. "Besides, she'll only be gone for a while. It's not as if it'll be forever."

Raising his head sharply, the boy blurted out, "Is that what *your* mother told *you*? Because she was gone for *twenty-five years*. That's *more* than forever."

Julian was taken aback by his son's vehemence. He had not realized how much Kit understood about Simone's disappearance. "I promise you, Kit, Saylah will return soon, just as *she* promised. Don't let her go without telling her you love her. That would break your own heart as well as hers. I know, because I once did the same. And I'm asking you, begging you not to repeat my mistake."

The boy's eyes were damp, but he fought to keep his expression blank.

"I want it to end here," his father whispered. "For so long, this family has been living my father's dreams and nightmares. Even Edward Ashton," he added to himself. "I want you to be strong enough to wish your mother well. Let's not keep living and re-living our parents' lives. Let's make lives of our own, Kit. Please."

~ * ~

Saylah knocked on her son's door one last time, but he did not answer. She gripped the knob in stiff fingers, feeling again the resistance of the lock. She leaned against the smooth wood, but it might as well have been full of splinters that scratched her cheek and made it bleed. "Kit," she whispered, "please. Let me say goodbye."

Silence.

She kissed her fingertips and pressed them to the door, pretending it was his forehead. "My son, I will miss you. Perhaps you will not believe me, but it is true. I love you. Perhaps you will not believe that either, but someday you will know. This I promise." She waited a moment longer, but the stillness became oppressive and she turned away.

The others were waiting at the open front door. As Saylah approached, healing bag over one shoulder and a satchel over the other, they moved instinctively onto the porch. Because it was safer? Brighter, in the first light of dawn, than the hall full of lingering shadows?

Saylah picked up a parcel and joined them, embracing Simone, embracing her with one arm arms. "Having you here with my family is a blessing I can never repay. I know you will take care of Julian and Illiann and Kit while I am gone. I know you will love them."

Simone, dressed elegantly in lilac silk, touched Saylah's cheek. "Though they might not have accepted it yet," she whispered, "they know in their hearts that this is a beginning, not the ending that my own dark flight became." She coughed, struggling with an affection so intense and unexpected that it took her voice.

Noticing this, Mathilde interrupted. "Goin' to keep us standin' out here in the cold all day? Dawn's the time when ghosts creep about in the shadows. Don't care about myself, of course, just the girl. Wouldn't want her to remember the day you went off as they day she got consumption."

Impulsively, Saylah hugged the servant tightly. Then she turned, parcel in hand, to her daughter.

Illiann was not weeping, but the tracks of recent tears shimmered on her cheeks. She was trying to be brave, and it slowed the rhythm of Saylah's heart. With great care, she placed the package in her daughter's arms. "You are a woman now, and I have re-made this for you. I have walked many dreams in this lifetime, and, of late, you have walked one beside me. Take this gift and learn now to weave your own dreams, and to walk them proudly and without fear."

Feverishly, Illiann undid the string and unfolded the paper from around the heavy object it concealed. She noticed the edge of a doeskin scallop and gasped in disbelief. "Mama!" she cried, "your cape!"

"Yours now, my daughter. I have altered it to fit you."

Illiann shook it out in wonder, afraid to see the charred edges and smoke stains from the fire, but Saylah had trimmed the edges away and smoothed them, making them look like new, then bleached the gray patches until they blended with the rest. "I can't…" the girl stuttered, "I don't know what to say. It isn't right. This belongs to you." She was not aware that her tears were flowing freely once again.

"It *is* right. It is yours now. That is the wish of my heart." Saylah did not know how she managed to speak around the lump in her throat, especially when Julian sensed her distress and slid his arm around her protectively. Perhaps she was making a mistake after all. He shook his head mutely, and she bowed hers until her forehead touched her daughter's. "Think of me sometimes when you wear it, but remember, the winter will not last forever. In the spring you will be warm again, and you will find your way. I am proud of you, Illiann."

The girl gripped the cloak tightly. "I love you, Mama," she whispered, and then she followed the others inside.

Now only Julian and Saylah remained.

She locked her hands behind his head, and he locked his behind hers, holding on as if to let go would be to fall. They looked into each other's eyes and Saylah had to fight to catch her breath. "I do not think I can do it. I am not strong enough." She could smell him, feel his warmth, his breath, his heartbeat.

Julian's grasp tightened when he realized that, for perhaps the first time since he'd met her, he was stronger than she. "Do you think I'd let you stay when I know how much you want this? When I know that if you don't go, it's because you are afraid?"

His wife did not deny it.

"I'll be here when you come back. You know that, Saylah."

They gazed into each other's familiar faces, their eyes damp with tears, their lips parted in a soundless caress. They looked hungrily, greedily, as if for the first time—or the last.

"Whoever I am, wherever I go, and whatever I am called, I love you. Always."

Julian held her a moment longer, then kissed her fiercely. "Go," he whispered, and turned away.

~ * ~

When she reached the sidewalk, heavy with sorrow, Saylah looked back at the house one last time. Kit's window was on the second floor and her gaze was drawn there inexorably. She froze when she realized he was standing there watching, and that over his shoulder, there was a flash of shimmering lilac.

The boy seemed torn, his face a mask of despair and regret and sorrow. Finally, he opened his mouth to speak words she could not hear, and then reached up to press his palm hard against the glass. Saylah closed her eyes in a prayer of gratitude and raised her own hand as if pushing against an invisible pane that bridged the distance between them.

Her son had said goodbye in the only way he knew how, and she blew him a kiss and smiled through the mist upon her eyes. He did not want her to go, but, like Julian and Illiann, he would be waiting when she returned.

Saylah glanced down, and when she looked up, Kit had gone. She took a deep, ragged breath, and, summoning all her strength and all the spirits and the blessings of her life, she continued on her way.

EPILOGUE

She stood on the beach where the canoe waited, filling her lungs with the smoke of a hundred spirits to give her strength on the trip across the ocean that would carry her home.

Naked, her clothes in the sand at her feet, she felt cool dawn caress her skin, and lifted the Robe of Light toward the sky—toward Raven, who had banished the darkness—and enfolded herself in its inimitable radiance.

She stood alone, yet not alone, surrounded by the people who had walked the beach before her and those who were not yet, but were to come.

She stood with the drifting clouds above and the pebbled sand below, with the singing waters calling and the wind urging her on, and pushed the boat into the sea, murmuring one last prayer to the fading moon, whose face was pitted with age and wisdom.

Head tilted toward the sky, the water whispering promises at her feet, She Who Is Blessed, who had grown into Tanu, who had taken the name Saylah when she turned toward womanhood, gave herself up to the faint, hypnotic rhythm of the drums, and became, at last,

Samaya.

Balancing herself in the canoe, she took up the paddle, felt the pull of the waves and the glow of the rising sun. In that moment, newly born,

she smiled

and wept

and felt a freedom running.

ABOUT KATHRYN LYNN DAVIS

Kathryn Lynn Davis was born with what the ancient Celts called "the fatal gift of the imagination: a crown of stars and a stinging sword." She had no choice but to become a writer. Since Scotland is the home of her heart, and she loves history (having a Masters in the subject), it was inevitable that she should write historical novels, most of which are set in Scotland. An award winning, New York Times best-seller, she has published nine historical novels and two historical novellas.

Kathryn has a BA in English and history from the University of California, Riverside, where she graduated Magna Cum Laude, Phi Beta Kappa. She also received her MA in history there.

Toward the end of the 20th century, she gave up writing out of frustration. Only when she discovered Indie publishing did she return to her love of writing with great enthusiasm. She has re-published part of her backlist as e-books: Child of Awe, and the Too Deep For Tears Trilogy: Too Deep for Tears, All We Hold Dear, and Somewhere Lies the Moon.

She has also released two novellas, A Tear for Memory and Highland Awakening, both prequels to her Too Deep Trilogy.

In December 2015 she re-released a revised version of Sing To Me Of Dreams. She's currently working on other backlist titles as well as new projects. She's so excited by all this activity, and all the new friends--both authors and readers--that she's made on Facebook.

Follow Kathryn Davis on Facebook:

https://www.facebook.com/kathrynlynndavis.

MORE BY KATHRYN LYNN DAVIS

Sing To Me Of Dreams

One woman's journey of discovery…through all the mysteries of the human heart.

As a child, Saylah held the magic and wisdom of her Salish Indian people. But when tragedy ravages the Salish, she must leave them for the world of the Ivys – an English/Scottish family whose traditions are as strange to her as her spirit world is to them. The Ivys have come to fertile British Columbia in search of paradise, but the secrets and mysteries surrounding them are overwhelming – until Saylah comes to help them understand the darkness holding them back.

Frustrated Julian Ivy, in whom sophistication and fury entwine, is drawn to Saylah's healing strength and disquieting beauty. Through sorrow and elation, the two discover the fullness of love…but no one can resolve for her the contradictions of her birthright. Following the songs of her heritage, she will finally make the most wrenching choice of all…

Child of Awe

From the moment of her birth, Muriella Calder is heiress to a great fortune many Highland clans desire to make their own. Touched by The Sight, she struggles to understand herself, while fighting those who threaten her world: the violent clans who relish war; her cunning guardian, Archibald Campbell, the powerful Earl of Argyll—callously ambitious, and bound by loyalty to the Crown; John Campbell, the Earl's second son—a strong, experienced warrior on the battlefield—who cannot begin to understand the mysterious woman he is forced to wed; and Elizabeth Campbell Maclean, a gentle woman whose heart is forfeit in a treaty with a man her father hates.

Completely captivating, Child of Awe carries the reader from the wild beauty of mist-shrouded glens to the horrors of war, from the hatred of ancient feuds to the wonder of new love: enchanting us, heart and soul, with the seamless skill of a genuine storyteller.

A Tear for Memory

How can a seer paint 'Truth' when she's lived a life of lies? Will she allow a man who has twice deceived her to open her heart to the truth?

In the Highlands of Glen Affric, years after The Forty-Five—the Jacobite rising led by Bonnie Prince Charlie—Celia Rose lives happily in Faeries' Haven, where the lies that protect her from the past keep the magic and the faeries away. She finds her only magic when she paints, and "sees" things she cannot possibly know.

When a stranger comes on a mysterious errand, he threatens those who want to keep her safe at home. Little by little, he shows her new colors, new worlds and, most compelling—new passions. But he also brings danger, for he, too, lives a lie and is not what he seems. Still, danger comes in many forms, and the truth he offers leaves Celia with a difficult choice: to believe in those who loved and raised her; or trust this man, and learn the dark secret that could both destroy her innocence and forge in her a woman's heart.

Highland Awakening

Can the transforming power of magic help two people on a perilous journey create a miracle—even when one of them doesn't believe?

Since she lost her brother and nearly her father, Esmé Rose fears the world beyond her family and her garden. But one year when winter clings overlong, a dream begins to haunt her, forcing her to take a journey and face a challenge more difficult than she could ever imagine.

Magnus MacLeod is a skilled healer, always curious to know more. He, too, is called by a dream he doesn't quite believe in, despite its physical effects on him. He and Esmé travel a treacherous road that takes them to a magical place. There they must put aside their feelings for one another—and their difference in beliefs—long enough to make a miracle.

Too Deep For Tears Trilogy

"Kathryn Lynn Davis is a master storyteller. Too Deep for Tears is beautifully written, emotionally charged, and unforgettable. Immersed in her richly crafted 19th century world, you won't want to leave—one of my all time favorite reads."

--Lucinda Brant, New York Times bestselling author of Salt Bride.

Too Deep for Tears

Late 1800s: Three sisters. Three corners of the British Empire. Three lives intertwined… forever.

As he travels the British Empire, diplomat Charles Kittridge leaves behind three daughters: Ailsa in the Scottish Highlands; Li-an in Peking, China; and Genevra in Delhi, India. Bound by threads they neither see nor understand, the three sisters are haunted by their absent father--each in her own way. Creative and intuitive, often lost and without hope, they come together through their dreams in times of fear and need. Those dreams grow vivid, changing as these extraordinary women learn the lessons the Empire has to teach. And the all-important lessons within their own hearts. No matter the courage and passion, betrayal and loss they experience, their dreams never leave them.

In the end, they believe Charles Kittridge has the power to heal them. But the truth is far more complicated than any of them understand.

All We Hold Dear

All We Hold Dear is Book II in the Too Deep for Tears Trilogy. Full of suspense and haunting emotion, it follows Mairi, Ailsa and Alanna—three generations of Highland women--who must call on all their strength and the wisdom of the ancient Celtic gods, when strangers come to Glen Affric. The intruders bring greed, conflict and treachery, pitting brother against brother, father against son, husband against wife. Yet among them is a new love for Alanna. More mysteriously, and without intention, they reignite Ailsa's old and precious memories… In the epic struggle of man against man, and man against nature, who will suffer and who will thrive?

Somewhere Lies the Moon.

Four generations of Scottish Highland women live in Glen Affric. Their stories intersect through Ena Rose—barely past childhood, not yet a woman—who faces choices she cannot understand, and a love that may never fulfill her dreams. Ailsa Rose is content in her familiar home, until she finally recognizes the turmoil she has refused to see, the pain she knows not how to heal. She calls out across the world to her half sisters: Wan Lian, struggling to outlive the shadows of her past in a small country town in France; and Genevra, back in India, searching for her future among the multi-colored patterns engraved in her soul. Together again in their Glen Affric sanctuary, they learn that they are strong enough to face any challenge…as long as they hold on to one another.

ABOUT DUNCURRA

Duncurra is a small independent publishing company. We highly value the heart and soul, energy, time, and talent that our authors pour into their stories. Unlike many independent publishers, we help authors build their readership by investing significantly in marketing platforms to complement the author's own promotional efforts.

We are particularly proud of our YouTube presence and ever increasing subscribership there, which is unique to the publishing industry.

Whether you are a reader, an established author, or an aspiring author, we have a lot to offer. We take the reader experience to a new level, connecting authors and readers in unprecedented ways.

Visit our website at www.duncurra.com.

To stay up to date on all Duncurra releases, sales, giveaways, and more. Sign up for our newsletter here: https://tinyletter.com/duncurra

Experience the difference.

Experience Duncurra!

OTHER DUNCURRA TITLES

Award Winning, Bestselling Author
Lily Baldwin
Highland Outlaw Series

Jack: A Scottish Outlaw

Although they come from different worlds, Jack and Isabella are more alike than they first realize. They both crave freedom from war and despair, but in a world where kings reign and birth dictates one's station, *freedom is not won, it is stolen*.

Quinn: A Scottish Outlaw

He is an outlaw...And the only man she can trust.

Lady Catarina has been accused of a horrific crime and is forced to run or face a fate worse than death.

But she is not alone.

Thief and Scottish rebel, Quinn MacVie, is at her side. With a price on her head, they must disappear into the wilds of the Scottish Highlands where the only thing greater than the danger following at their heels is the desire burning in their hearts.

Rory: A Scottish Outlaw

Lady Alexandria MacKenzie is one of Abbot Matthew's network of rebels, fighting for Scottish independence. When her father dies, leaving their clan without a laird, she asks the abbot for aid in finding a husband. He sends her a selection of three noblemen from which to choose. Accompanying them is secret agent and reputed rake, Rory MacVie, who must assist Alexandria with a perilous mission for Scotland. But the abbot makes one point very clear--Rory is not a potential suitor.

This is a passionate story of honor, rebellion, and forbidden love.

Alec: A Scottish Outlaw

Two broken hearts unite, becoming one love that will last forever.

Sold from one ruthless master to another, Joanie is a servant who has lived her whole life in fear.

The first time Alec sees Joanie is in his dreams. He has a vision of a young woman standing on a bridge alone, bleeding, and broken hearted. He must rescue her, and when he does he soon realizes she holds the power to rescue him right back.

Join Alec and Joanie on a journey of healing, passion, and hope, where their love and strength forge a new destiny for themselves and for Scotland.

Award Winning, Bestselling Author
Ceci Giltenan
Fated Hearts Series

Highland Revenge

Does he hate her clan enough to visit his vengeance on her? Or will he listen to her secret and his own heart's yearning?

Hatred lives and breathes between medieval clans who often don't remember why feuds began in the shadowed past.

But Eoin MacKay remembers.

Can he forget his stubborn hatred long enough to listen to the secret she has kept for so long? And once he knows the truth, can he show her she is not alone and forsaken? In the end, is he strong enough to fight the combined hostilities and age-old grudges that demand he give her up?

Highland Echoes

Love echoes.

Grace Breive is strong and independent because she has to be. She has a wee daughter to care for and, having lost her parents and husband, has no one else on whom she can rely. Driven from the only home she has ever known, she travels to Castle Sutherland to find a grandmother she never knew she had.

As Laird Sutherland's heir, Bram Sutherland understands his obligation to enter into a political marriage for the good of the clan, but he is captivated by the beautiful and resilient young mother.

Will Bram and Grace follow the dictates of their hearts, or will echoes from the past force them apart?

Highland Angels

Anna MacKay fears the MacLeods. Andrew MacLeod fears love.

Anna, angry with her brother, took a walk to cool her temper. She had no intention of venturing so close to MacLeod territory—until she saw a wee lad fall through the ice.

Andrew becomes enraged when it appears the MacKay lass has abducted his son, his last precious connection to the wife he lost—until he learns the truth. Anna risked her life to save his beloved child.

Now there is a chance to end the generations old hate and fear between their clans.

Fate connects them. The desire for peace binds them. Will a rival tear them apart?

Duncurra Series
Highland Solution

Laird Niall MacIan needs Lady Katherine Ruthven's dowry to relieve his clan's crushing debt, but he has no intention of giving her his heart in the bargain.

Lady Katherine must forfeit everything in exchange for a husband who does not want to be married and believes all women to be self-centered and deceitful. Can the lovely and gentle Katherine mend his heart and build a life with him or will he allow the treachery of others to destroy them?

Highland Courage

Her parents want a betrothal, but Mairead MacKenzie can't get married without revealing her secret and no man will wed her once he knows.

Secrets always have a way of revealing themselves. With Tadhg's unconditional love, can Mairead find the courage she needs to handle the consequences when they do?

Highland Intrigue

Lady Gillian MacLennan's clan needs a leader, but the last person on earth she wants as their laird is Fingal Maclan.

In spite of the challenge, Fingal is confident he can rebuild her clan, ease her heartache, and win her affection. However, just as love awakens, the power struggle takes a deadly turn. Can he protect her from the unknown long enough to uncover the plot against them? Or will all be lost, destroying the happiness they seek in each other's arms?

Duncurra Legacy Series

Highland Redemption

Tomas's life changed forever when at the age of seven he was adopted by Laird and Lady Maclan ending the abuse he'd suffered at Ambrose Ruthven's hand.

Now, nineteen years later, he runs headlong into his past. Laird Ruthven's daughter is not what Tomas expected. Vida Ruthven is sweet, smart, and utterly irresistible.

Tomas must choose between being the savior or taking the ultimate revenge.

The Pocket Watch Chronicles

A mysterious old lady and an extraordinary pocket watch offer those chosen an opportunity to travel through time in each of these stories.

The Pocket Watch

When Maggie Mitchell is transported to the thirteenth century Highlands, will Laird Logan Carr help mend her broken heart or put it in more danger than before?

Maggie finds herself in the thirteenth-century Scottish Highlands with a handsome warrior who clearly despises her. Her tender soul is caught between her own desire and the disaster she could cause for others. Will she find a way to resolve the trouble and return home within the allotted sixty days? Or will someone worthy earn her heart forever?

The Midwife

Can a twenty-first century independent woman find her true destiny in thirteenth-century Scotland?

Elizabeth Quinn, a disillusioned obstetrician, is transported to the thirteenth century. She switched souls with Elsie as the old woman said she would, but other things don't go quite as expected. Perhaps most unexpected was falling in love.

Once Found

Elsie thought she had found love.

The handsome young minstrel awoke her desire and his music fed her soul. But just as love was blossoming, the inconceivable happened—Elsie awoke more than seven hundred years in the future, in the body of Dr. Elizabeth Quinn.

Gabriel Soldani thought he had found love several times, only to have it slip from his grasp. In medical school, he had fallen hard for Elizabeth Quinn, but their careers led them in different directions. When their paths cross again, he hopes they've been given another chance.

There's only one problem…the woman he's never forgotten doesn't remember him.

Once love is found…and then lost…can it be found again?

The Christmas Present

Faced with an empty nest, and heartbroken, Anita Lewis is given the chance to experience Christmas in another time with the help of a mysterious old woman and a pocket watch.

The gift she receives is priceless as she rediscovers the magic of Christmas in the past.

The Choice

The Choice contains 2, brand-new, full-length novels, each with a different HEA.

Sixty days in another life, another time…it's tempting. Now the decision to accept the pocket watch is yours. What choice will you make?

Sara Wells is in Venice, preparing to leave on a fourteen day cruise to Greece, when Gertrude offers her the pocket watch.

Will she take it? You choose.

Once you've read one, you can go back and make the other choice.

One choice, two souls, two different happy endings.

B.J. Scott

Talisman of Light

Will changing the Past destroy their future?

Intent on setting a wrong to right, Alex Innes flies to Scotland to return an Ancient Talisman to its rightful resting place. But his plane crashes and he finds himself in twelfth century Scotland, where winter holds the country in its icy grip and only one maiden can set it free. Ciara Dunmore offers her life to appease the winter hag on the Imbolc Festival, but Alex has different plans for the beguiling lass who has captured his heart. Will changing the past destroy their future?

Forever and Beyond

Katherine MacDonald trades her luxury Manhattan apartment, high paying job, and abusive fiancé for what she believes is a rundown estate, deep in the Scottish Highlands, unaware that her future, and perhaps her very life, depends on secrets deeply rooted in the past.

When she discovers a ring with a sentimental inscription and a journal written by one of her ancestors within the ancient croft, she suddenly finds herself in fourteenth century Scotland where she comes face to face with Ayden MacAndrews, a braw Highlander who has haunted her dreams since she was a child.

Will Katherine and Ayden be able to right an ancient wrong? Will their love stand the test of time?

Stephanie Joyce Cole

Compass North

Can you ever run away from your own life?

Reeling from the shock of a suddenly shattered marriage, Meredith flees as far from her home in Florida as she can get without a passport: to Alaska.

After a freak accident leaves her presumed dead, she stumbles into a new identity and a new life in a quirky small town. Her friendship with a fiery and temperamental artist and her growing worry for her elderly, cranky landlady pull at the fabric of her carefully guarded secret. When a romance with a local fisherman unexpectedly blossoms, Meredith struggles to find a way to meld her past and present so that she can move into the future she craves. But someone is looking for her, someone who will threaten Meredith's dream of a reinvented life.

James Donbar

Pacificus

What happens when a group of the world's wealthiest people desire a haven for themselves and their assets?

Pacificus is built one hundred miles off the coast of Ecuador. This manmade island is governed solely by a set of principles and relies on the common sense of its inhabitants instead of laws.

What could go wrong?

For Gaspar Delgado, the island's administrator, nothing. He need only find the balance between the privileged indulgence of its residents and order.

However, Conrad Silverstein, a smug self-serving newspaper editor, is certain something sinister lurks under the high-minded values supposedly espoused by Pacificans and sends reporter, Alicia Jones, to find out what it is.

Will this utopia be threatened by those willing to exploit liberty at any expense?

Ford Murphy

Taking the Town

Lissadown, Ireland

A ruthless, violent criminal gang has held the small midlands town in its grip for too long.

Innocents have been maimed, raped, killed.

Law enforcement is paralyzed.

Finn Lane has had enough. A newcomer to Lissadown and an expert MMA fighter, Finn can't be intimidated. Keeping his head down and minding his own business is not an option. The gang may think they own the town and everyone in it but those days are coming to an end.

He will have vengeance…

M.J. Platt

Somewhere Montana

Can Callum "Mac" Maclain make Sage Burnett believe in his love for her and
save her from her stalker?

Escaping from a stalker, Sage Burnett crashes her plane on a mountain, part of the ranch owned by the man who rejected her eight years ago. She still loves him and prays he isn't around because she dreads facing him to only have him reject her again.

Callum "Mac" MacLain, the ranch owner, a Marine home on medical leave rescues her from the mountain. He persuades her to stay until she heals. He realizes he is still in love with her. Can he save her from her stalker and convince her his love is real?

Jennifer Siddoway

Dealing with the Devil

Wynnona Hendricks has some shocking surprises in store. Struggling to figure out her comatose mother's secret, Wynn gets more than she bargained for, and ends up caught between the realms of Heaven, Hell, and Earth, fighting for her life.

Family and friends are stunned by her bizarre behavior; the only one who believes in her is Caleb, an angel who chose to spare her life. But by saving her, he may have started a war between the factions, throwing the Mortal Realm into mayhem. Wynn discovers new allies, new enemies—including her own human weakness—and new powers as she fights to protect her family from being ripped apart.

The Devil's Due

After tragedy strikes the Hendricks family, Wynn leaves for college, hoping the Demon Lords follow her. She is reunited with Caleb after his fall from grace. Now, they no longer have to hide their feelings for one another. Together, they prepare for Wynn's three remaining trials and encounter another demon who has infiltrated the Mortal Realm.

Charlene is strong and beautiful, with complete control of her demonic powers – everything Wynn hopes to achieve one day. She learns that to defeat Aidan once and for all will come at a terrible price, taking her away from the ones that she loves most. The Demon Lords aren't holding back, but they're not the only ones who are conspiring against her. Maya is on the war path and blames Wynn for Caleb's decision to leave.

With the help of some unlikely allies, can Wynn defeat the Demon Lords and finally make Aidan pay?

Coming Fall 2017 – Down in Flames